THE
RED SEA

ALSO BY EDWARD W. ROBERTSON

THE CYCLE OF ARAWN

The White Tree
The Great Rift
The Black Star

THE CYCLE OF GALAND

The Red Sea

THE BREAKERS SERIES

Breakers
Melt Down
Knifepoint
Reapers
Cut Off
Captives
Relapse
Blackout

REBEL STARS

Rebel
Outlaw
Traitor

THE
RED SEA

THE CYCLE OF GALAND, BOOK 1

EDWARD W. ROBERTSON

Copyright © 2015 Edward W. Robertson

All rights reserved.

Cover illustration by Miguel Coimbra.
Additional work by Stephanie Mooney.
Maps by Jared Blando.

ISBN: 1512291870
ISBN-13: 978-1512291872

To Glen Cook and the Black Company.

Mallon, Gask, and other lands.

The Plagued Islands.

EDWARD W. ROBERTSON

1

Riddi gazed up the mountain, and the mountain gazed back.

The sun was high but the air was colder than midnight in the Dreaming Peaks. The trees were hard, bitter things. Sheathed in harsh, scratchy bark. Sprouting thin, sharp needles. Dribbling sap so sticky it was impossible to wash it from your hands. As if they wanted you to be as miserable as they were. The birds in the boughs cawed like they were cursing her. The mountain itself was full of gravel slopes, cracked black rock, and forests of the hateful trees. It didn't want her to be there.

The feeling was mutual.

She hiked her pack up her shoulder and moved on. Stones clacked under her feet. Three days ago, Docco had left to scout for a better route through the crags ahead. He'd been gone twice as long as he'd promised. She kept her ears open for the tweet of his whistle, but she no longer did so with any sense of hope. They had left the islands with six people. Three thousand miles later, she was the last.

She pressed harder, sweating despite the chill. With every step, the thin wooden box inside her coat brushed her stomach, reminding her why she was here. The sun slid west. To the north, the mountains were a fortress wall. They were close, though. Maybe no more than another day or two of hard walking.

And a few days after that, she would find the sorcerer.

Past the next ridge, a steep-sided valley had been scooped from the mountainside. Western crags painted the valley with shadows, but Riddi had at least an hour of sunlight left. Low shrubs studded the descent. They smelled stale, dusty. She'd been wearing boots since her unexpectedly early arrival on the mainland, but after years of sandals, they still felt large and awkward.

The slope steepened. She switchbacked down it, pebbles trickling away in tiny avalanches. Halfway to the valley floor, her path ended before a short cliff. She swore. She didn't have time to backtrack. The descent was already taking longer than she'd expected. The sun was now screened by the trees on the western heights. Another few minutes, and it would be gone completely.

She moved closer to the cliff. It was only seven or eight feet high. If she lowered herself from its lip, she'd only have to drop a few feet to the slope below. Riddi stepped up to the edge, moving her pack from her shoulder.

Her right foot slipped. She threw out her hands. Her bag flew over the edge. A sharp crack popped from the stone beneath her feet. It gave way. And she went with it.

She hit the rocks piled at the bottom of the cliff, breath rushing from her lungs. The unsteady scree slid forward, sweeping her away, pummeling her body. Dust spumed into the air. She flung out her limbs to arrest the slide.

Pain exploded in her head. A flash of light—then darkness.

A rushing noise, in and out. The sound of surf? But not surf. Not breathing. A roar in her ears. The roar of pain.

She moved to sit up. The pain spiked so badly she whited out. When the rush receded from her head, she breathed carefully, assessing. Her whole body hurt, but it was the pain in her legs that made her scream. Lying on her back, she rolled her neck forward. White feathers poked through the rips in her coat. Below that, white shards of bone poked through the tears in her trousers.

She passed out again.

Wan yellow light stretched across the valley. She'd only been out a few minutes. Her leg was broken. Bone speared through the skin. Blood soaking the leg of her pants. She shifted; pain lanced through her other leg, too. This was also broken. A wave of heat, then a wave of nausea, then a wave of pain. She lay among the rocks until these feelings receded, then reached into her coat and withdrew a pouch on a string. The egg of a shark, the cured leather was smooth and smelled of the sea.

She withdrew a pale green succulent studded with red bumps. The hern plant was so bitter she gagged, but she forced herself to swallow. Within a minute, the pain eased.

She was still bleeding. If she didn't stop it, her mission would end here. Careful not to jostle her legs, Riddi eased into a sitting position. Dust and rock chips fell from her coat. She got a knife from her belt and cut the leg of her trousers away from her bloody shin. Seeing the mess, she went faint. As bad as she'd feared. But the hern was fuzzing her mind, helping her to bind the wound without dropping into shock.

The sun was set, the bowl of the valley falling into twilight. Frozen winds hissed over the rocks. Her exposed leg felt strangely warm. It was her own fault. She should have made camp, tackled the valley in the morning, looked for the safe route rather than jumping down the ledge. She'd pressed herself too hard. And failed her father.

She'd failed the others, too. Jerr and Lassa, dead in the shipwreck. Vollo, murdered by bandits on the trek from the sandy southern coast where they'd made landfall. Su, drowned in the river they had forded south of the mountains. And Docco, who had disappeared two days ago. They'd left home knowing some of them might not return to the islands. But so long as one of them made it, no death would be in vain.

She had to move on.

Lying on her back, she laughed senselessly. The hern was making her loopy. Any more, and she might forget her wounds and try to walk, or simply lie on her back giggling until she froze to death in this hateful place.

Yet her laughter wasn't entirely drug-induced. The question in her mind—How do you climb a mountain with two broken legs?—sounded so much like one of her father's philosophical questions. For a pirate and a frequent drunk, he could be a thoughtful man.

The thought of him gave her the answer. You *didn't* climb a mountain with two broken legs. First, you healed them.

Riddi sat up again, taking deep breaths, trying to clear her head. She didn't have the power within herself to heal the damage. But the shells could. Using them, though, meant that she wouldn't make it home.

Was he worth it? The man beyond the mountains? Or had this mission been a march toward suicide? For a moment, although she'd never met him, she hated him.

Above, a star glimmered from the deep blue sky. She had to find the pack. She rolled on her stomach and pushed herself up for a look, trying not to scream at the pain penetrating the fog of hern. Her pack was thirty feet uphill, half buried in loose rocks. Getting to it would hurt worse than anything she'd ever felt.

Was there another way? She could shred the other leg of her pants. Tie the strips into a rope. Tie this to her boot and fling it at the pack until she was able to snag a strap with the boot's toe and drag the whole thing to her. But this was a fantasy. It would take too much time and too much strength. There was only one way out of this.

Pain shrieking in her skull, she dragged her broken body up

the hill.

By the time she reached the pack, the pain was so bad she no longer knew where she was or what she had intended to do with whatever was inside the bag. She opened it, staring dumbly.

The idea returned. She was about to save herself. And guarantee she'd die within another two weeks.

She set the box on the flattest rock she could find and opened the lid. The smell of brine wafted from it, along with a faint tang of ocean rot, but she was used to that. Four shells lay within. In the gloom, they were no more than indistinct lemon-sized lumps. She had the feeling she would need all four.

Riddi closed her eyes. Reached within. She found the shadows inside her and those in the shells. Dark, viscous fluid streamed from the box and into her legs. When the shadows touched her skin, they were even colder than the mountain air.

Her legs began to itch. Then to burn. Tears slid down her cheeks. With an agonizing tickle, the broken bone slipped beneath her skin. Her leg straightened. The pain faded, replaced by numbness. The stream of nether shifted to her other leg. This too itched, burned, numbed.

When it finished, there was nothing left but empty shells. She dumped these in the rocks, then tossed the box aside. It would only be dead weight.

She stood. Her legs held. She laughed softly, the only noise besides the shifting of the wind. She picked up her pack and walked carefully down the scree. Though her right leg was bare, completely exposed, it still felt warm. Once she reached flat ground, she sat and got out her fire kit and struck sparks onto the waxy length of a candlefruit.

The flame caught. She held it over her leg. The skin was marred with black streaks as vivid as paint.

Her heart caught in her throat. She had less time than she thought. There was no time to rest. Not until she found the man beyond the mountains.

With the moon peeking from the eastern ridges, she hitched up her pack and trudged across the valley floor.

One step after another. Nothing but the rocks before her and her feet beneath her. She didn't look up. The mountains had lasted longer than she'd expected. If she crossed one more ridge, thinking it was the final, only to see another before her, she thought she might sit down and not get up again.

The ground sloped down, then up. She'd wrapped her exposed leg in a blanket, but she still couldn't feel the cold on it. She checked it often to make sure her flesh wasn't freezing. The air was starting to do funny things. Usually, it was still deadly cold, but sometimes she walked into a streamer of wind that was so much warmer it reminded her of home.

She had been forcing herself not to think of the islands. In time, though, knowing she would never see them again, she let herself get lost in them. The beat of the sun and the caress of the shade. The gem-like hues of the sea in the shallows. The dolphins that swam beyond the breakers and the whales that cruised much further from shore where the water was a deep and brilliant blue. The way the purple sands of Sworl Beach changed their design every time she visited.

She had lost these things, but she could save them for the others. Or would it be better if she failed? They couldn't undo what had been done, but if they repented, the gods might still show them mercy.

The ground beneath her grew level. A cold wind struck her face, but was soon washed away by a warmer one. It carried the smell of fresh water. She frowned and lifted her eyes.

Miles away, mountains encircled a vast plain, the slopes lush and green. Below, mist rose from three lakes, each one far larger than any bay in the Plagued Islands. On the south shore of the nearest lake, a city claimed the land up to the hills. Twists of

smoke rose from chimneys.
 She had arrived.

EDWARD W. ROBERTSON

2

Gallador Rift was the hub of Gaskan trade, but it possessed one small flaw: the gigantic mountain range cutting it off from the Middle Kingdoms to the south. Historically, Gallador's merchants had three options for dealing with this impasse. First, they could detour two hundred miles to the east, take the pass at Riverway, and then swing southwest toward the bustling cities of the kingdoms' interior. Very safe, but very slow.

Second, the traders could drive their wagons west to the coast, which was exactly as far away as the Riverway, and sail south to Allingham. This was the fastest but also the most expensive option. Third, they could challenge the West Dundens directly—though in addition to the snow that only vacated the passes for a month in late summer, the routes were also snarled with the corpses of those who'd challenged the mountains and failed.

None of these options were what you'd call "good." So Dante had decided to give Gallador a gift. A way to repay its people for their aid in Narashtovik's war for independence years earlier. He would bore a hole straight through the mountains, giving the Galladese merchants a fourth option that was the fastest, cheapest, and safest of all.

Like all good deeds, however, it was turning out to be a royal pain in the ass.

First, a subset of the TAGVOG, the lakelands' governing body of trade, had questioned whether the tunnel would expose them to bandits, raiders, or invasion. Once Dante convinced them how easy it would be to destroy the tunnel if need be, the argument shifted to the passage's placement. This was a strategic matter (they needed a defensible, practical location) as well as political (the entrance couldn't be too near nor too far from the holdings of the TAGVOG's major members).

As discussion raged, Dante had grown so frustrated he'd been on the verge of calling off the whole thing. Blays saved the endeavor by asking him how *he* would handle it if someone were proposing a new route into Narashtovik, the city where Dante ruled. Would he give them leave to stick it wherever they pleased? Or would he fuss and fidget over every tiny detail?

Unfair, for Blays to know him that well.

For the sake of his sanity, while the TAGVOG argued on, Dante trekked across the mountains to the agreed-upon site of the exit and started tunneling north toward Gallador. The work would take weeks. Surely the merchants would have made a decision by the time he neared the lakes.

Now, though, he was no more than three days away from completion. And as he worked away on the tunnel, converting the stone into mud and sluicing it away, the TAGVOG still hadn't chosen exactly where to place the tunnel mouth. If they didn't decide soon, he would.

He shunted his mind away from that line of reasoning. Other than the politicking, the job was surprisingly pleasant. He was the only one between Pocket Cove and the Wodun Mountains capable of shifting solid rock in this way, which was rewarding in its own right. And the tunnel's solitude was a welcome break from his endless responsibilities administering the Sealed Citadel of Narashtovik.

Once, he'd been hungry for that role. And, admittedly, the power and prestige that came with it. But he'd been overseeing the city for several years now. While he knew his work was important—among other things, he had freed the city (along with Gallador and others) from the Gaskan Empire—there were times when he wished he had no status at all, and was able to pursue his study of the nether in peace.

Near the blank wall of the tunnel's end, his torchstone was fading. He picked the white marble up from the smooth floor and blew it out. He could have worked in darkness, but darkness was creepy. Especially when you had a mile of mountain looming over your head. He called forth the nether and shaped it into a tame, pale light.

He glanced down the tunnel. Assured there were no horrors sneaking up on him, he turned back to the blank stone wall and delved into it with his mind, finding the nether within it, the ancient death that seemed to lurk within all things. The stone flowed away, the wall retracting, bringing the tunnel another five feet closer to the squabbling, bureaucratic, but mostly charming merchants of Gallador. Dante paused to reach further into the rock, making sure there were no cracks or faults exposed by his efforts.

"Sir?" a voice spoke in his ear. It was Stedden, the monk he'd brought with him to oversee communications and scheduling. At the moment, the man was miles away in Wending, Gallador's capital.

Dante spoke into the loon affixed to his ear like a bit of jewelry. "Yes, Stedden?"

"There's someone here to see you, sir."

"Is that someone a mole?"

"A mole?"

"You know," Dante said. "Small. Furry. Freakish nose. Likes to burrow."

"Ah, no, sir. She appears to be human."

"Then she's going to be a disappointed human, as I am currently a mile underground."

"I'm aware of that," Stedden said. "But she has a message for you. She says it's from…"

"Yes, Stedden?"

"Well, sir, she claims it's from your father."

"Then she's lying."

"She says she's from the Plagued Islands. That your father's name is Larsin."

Dante's spine stiffened. "Put her on the loon. Let me speak to her."

"That's the other thing, sir. She's fallen unconscious. I tried to heal her, but there's something stopping me."

Dante scowled at the wall. He was far from drained of nether. If he left now, it would cost him hundreds of yards of work. Yet he needed the strength to help this woman. Not because it was the good thing to do.

But to find out why she was trying to deceive him—and which of his enemies she might be working with.

"I'll be back as soon as I can," he said into the loon. "Thank you for informing me."

He turned and jogged down the tunnel, his pale light floating in front of him. He had to run close to three miles before reaching the nearest side tunnel out to the mountains overlooking the lakes. His horse awaited, tethered in the shade. He rode down the switchbacks, descending through terraced slopes thick with tea bushes. The outskirts of most cities tended to be slums, but Wending's upper slopes were fancy suburbs: the sprawling lawns, orchards, and manors of the city's wealthy traders. Swooping roofs capped three-story buildings. Outside many, a forty-foot pole jutted from the center of a ring of cleared dirt. Personal churches, harkening back to the days Galladese wagons would gather to barter under poles like these set along the roads. Outsiders often considered this blasphemous, but in Gallador, trade was god.

He took the main boulevard through the city. Below, the massive blue lake glittered in the sun. He reached the docks, which smelled of fresh clams and not-so-fresh fish, stabled his horse, and found the ferryman waiting for his arrival. The man rowed him to the pocket-sized island where Lolligan made his home. A salt miner and tea vendor, Lolligan had been rich well before the wars. After the assistance he'd provided during the conflicts, he'd become one of the region's preeminent businessmen.

This came with a cost, though: Dante now expected the man to put him up whenever he was in town.

The ferryman docked at the island's private pier. Dante thanked him and hopped out. As he crossed the lawn toward the manor, Stedden emerged from the ground floor and dashed toward him in a flurry of black robes.

"She's still alive," the monk announced. He was a bit chubby and had a habit of staring through you, like he couldn't wait to get back to monk-work. "Still unconscious, though. And I'm not sure she'll wake up without your help."

"Show me to her."

Stedden led him inside and down a hallway to the ground-floor guest rooms. There, a woman lay in bed, dressed in a heavy coat and patchwork trousers. The woman was a few years younger than Dante and her skin was a medium brown not often seen this far north. She didn't look sweaty or feverish, but there was a faint cast to her, like a reflection in a bubbly pane of glass. A cloying smell of burned cinnamon hung in the air.

Yet for all that was strange about her, he was struck by an uncanny sense of familiarity. Like he'd met her before.

Dante reached for her wrist. Rock dust clung to the hairs of his arm. Her pulse was fluttery, weak. Her breathing was shallow. Dante pushed up his left sleeve, drew an antler-handled knife, and nicked the back of his arm. The nether flocked to the dribbles of blood, feeding hungrily. He reached out to the nether inside the woman.

And was stung as sharply as a bee. He took a step back, wincing and shaking his head. He turned on Stedden. "You idiot. She's netherburned."

The man hunched his shoulders. "I'm sorry. I've never seen a nether burn before."

"I know it's difficult to gather firsthand experiences of everything in the world. That's why they invented 'studying.' Aren't you a monk of Arawn?"

"I'm sorry," the man repeated, more softly this time.

Dante let out a long breath and leaned over the woman. "We can't heal her. Touching her with the nether will only make it worse. Give her water, if you can."

"You're sure of this?"

"Check in with Nak. He treated me for it once. But I'm afraid this is one of those annoying injuries where the only treatment is time."

Dante opened her coat and made a quick assessment for other wounds that could be treated through mundane means. Other than a few small scabs on her palms and knuckles, she looked perfectly fine—until he got to her shins. There, her brown skin was striped with finger-sized lines as black as the inside of the mountain tunnel.

"For future reference, that's what a nether burn looks like." He pulled a sheet up to cover the woman's shoulders and turned to Stedden. "Tell me everything she told you."

Apparently, the woman had been staggering down the southern foothills toward the city. Found by a small-scale tea farmer, she'd spoken Dante's name in an accent the farmer had never heard before, refusing to say anything else. Concerned for her well-being, the farmer had escorted her via ferry to Lolligan's. There, she'd spoken to Stedden, giving the same details the monk had relayed to Dante.

Dante plunked down in a chair. "I suppose she said nothing

of the message itself."

"No." Stedden moved to a desk at the front of the room. "However, she seemed to understand she might not make it to your arrival. She made me swear to Arawn that I wouldn't open it. And then she gave me this."

He picked up a wooden rod and brought it to Dante. Roughly ten inches long and two in diameter, it was a piece of polished wood, bright brown and warm orange-reds. It appeared to be seamless, but it was light enough it had to be hollow. After a great deal of fooling around, Dante discovered it twisted open in the middle. It carried a rolled-up sheet of paper inside it.

He skimmed its contents. "I'll be in my quarters. If she wakes, or shows any change in her condition, come to me at once."

Stedden bobbed his head and sat down beside the foreign woman's bed. Dante exited and climbed the stairs to the much larger and nicer room Lolligan had assigned to him. He locked the door, sat on his bed, and unrolled the paper. It was a single sheet, covered on both sides. It was written in Mallish. Had his father been able to write? He couldn't remember. He could hardly remember the man's face.

He read the note in full. He let the page rest on his leg, remembering, then read it anew time, lingering on each line. He dropped the note on the bed and went to the window. Light shimmered on the lake. He didn't see it. Instead, he saw the grassy fields of a village outside Bressel.

He felt something in the room with him. A presence. The hair stood on his arms and neck. Dante gathered the nether in his hands and turned toward the door. Across the room, a blond man stood before him, a sword hanging from each hip.

"Lyle's balls," Dante said, dispersing the shadows. The bolt on the door was still firmly locked. "You walked through the wall, didn't you?"

Blays shrugged. "Like you wouldn't if *you* could?"

"What if I'd had someone in here?"

The other man folded his arms. "Like who?"

"Like, say, a woman?"

"Then I would have had a heart attack and died. Sparing you and your imaginary companion the embarrassment."

"Let's return to the antiquated practice of knocking, shall we? Unless you'd prefer that I enter *your* room by blasting the wall down."

"That would be rude. It's Lolligan's wall, not mine." Blays rocked on his heels. "So. Is it true?"

Dante eyed him. "What have you heard?"

"They say a strange woman staggered out of the mountains. And that she's here on behalf of your father. Shocking."

"I know. I haven't seen him in nearly twenty years."

"That, and I always assumed you were hatched, not born."

"I think it's real." He nodded at the note on the bed. "No one else would know some of those details."

Blays gestured to it. "Can I?"

"I'm surprised you asked first."

"It's much easier to ask for permission knowing you can always sneak in later." He picked up the page, eyes tracking the words. When they'd met as teenagers, Blays hadn't been able to read at all. The fact he was now literate in both Mallish and Gaskan struck Dante as nothing short of proof of the existence of the gods. Blays finished reading, lowered the note, and raised his eyebrows at Dante. "He knew your mom. He knew *you*. The events he mentions, they're like you remember them?"

"It was a long time ago. But yes."

"Right. So when do we leave?"

Dante laughed. "We're not going anywhere."

"But you just said this is your dad."

"And?"

"And he's sick and dying. You're one of the only people in the world who could help him."

Dante sat on the cushions of the window seat. "He's the one

who decided to leave. I've done perfectly well without him. Why mess with a good thing?"

"We're only issued one father per existence," Blays said. "Most humans, when given the chance to see a parent they thought was long dead, would leap at the chance."

"He left me. Alone. That was *his* choice. This may be difficult for you to understand, but after that, I've had no desire to ever see him again."

"You're right. I don't understand. I'd give anything to see my dad one last time."

Dante watched him a moment. "Really? You'd give up Minn? Trade your relationship with her for one last chat with your dad?"

Blays batted at the air. "I didn't mean it like that."

"How about our friendship, then?"

"I'd give *you* up for a good ham sandwich."

Dante rose to collect the note. "If you won't take this seriously, then I won't, either."

"All right, point conceded. It wouldn't make any sense to trade a meaningful relationship for a few more minutes of an old one."

"So we've established that you wouldn't give up anything. That there are, in fact, real limits to what you'd sacrifice. The only thing left to do is find out exactly how little you *would* give up."

Blays glared from beneath his blond eyebrows. "Clearly more than you."

Dante crumpled the note and pocketed it. "People like to pretend there's nothing more important than family. That they'd sacrifice anything for it. But parents abandon their children every day. Kids forsake their parents. Brothers betray each other. There's nothing sacred about blood."

"Family isn't sacred, it's an ideal. We all have to break our ideals sometime. But having them gives us something to live up to." He leaned against the wall, arms crossed. "If you won't go, mind if I do?"

"You absolutely will not."

"I'm not up to much here. I may as well go make myself useful."

"Don't you dare try to threaten me with this." Dante's voice was soft, concealing its quaver. "This is my family. My decision."

"Maybe it's none of my business. But I've known you long enough to know that, in a situation like this, you'd rather reject it out of hand than give it real consideration."

"I've made enough mistakes to be able to live with one more."

"Just think about it, all right?"

"Why do you care so much?"

"I'm not saying you have to go make nice with him. You can go heal him up, then rub it in his face that you're such a raging success."

Dante frowned. "What exactly would that gain me?"

"If you're that sure you don't care, then stay here. But if you've got any uncertainty at all, and you don't see him, you could regret it forever."

"I'll think about it. But I make no promises."

"That's all I ask." Blays pushed off from the wall. He moved to the door and unlocked the bolt. "If you decide you're going, you know I'll go with you."

He walked outside, using the door this time. Dante sat on the bed, removed the wadded-up note from his pocket, and smoothed it against his leg.

An hour later, he left his room and found Lolligan in his study. The room overlooked the lake and was cozy with bric-a-brac gathered over a lifetime of travel. The salt merchant was approaching seventy years of age, but his white goatee remained neatly trimmed, and he showed no signs of slowing down, be it in his business or the speed at which he walked between meetings.

Seeing Dante, he smiled and rose from a plush chair. "Back from work already? I didn't expect to see you until this evening."

"The tunnel entrance," Dante said. "Has the TAGVOG decided where it will go? Or are they still having a contest to see who can waste the most of my time?"

The old man's smile fell. Unlike many businessmen, he seemed primarily motivated by the desire to explore what was possible and to forge connections between people. Unnaturally good-natured, he now looked hurt.

"I understand your frustration," Lolligan said. "You're giving us a boon and we're so busy squabbling about where to unwrap it that it sounds like we don't care what's inside. But I promise you, everyone in the Association knows what this will mean for the lakes."

"Two days from now, I'll finish the tunnel. If your people haven't decided where they want it by then, I'll make that decision for them."

The old man frowned lightly, then rediscovered his smile. "We discuss things too much, I'll agree, but that's only because words are free. I'll let them know we've indulged ourselves long enough."

Dante left to check in on the woman, but she was still unconscious. There was a stillness to her body that he didn't like at all. Stedden informed him that she hadn't so much as shifted position during the hour-plus since Dante had first seen her. He stood over her for some time, but nothing explained why he felt like he'd seen her before.

At first light, he hiked back to the tunnels. Inside, he pushed the passage's end closer and closer to Wending, shifting the nether within the rock until he felt a tingle in his veins. He slept right there in the tunnel, curled in his blankets. When he next awoke, he had no idea how long he'd been out, but it was long enough to have recovered. He returned to the stone, melting it away down the passage, leaving the way forward as smooth as the surface of a pond.

Via loon, a message came in from Lolligan. The Association had made its decision. Dante extracted himself from the tunnels and hustled back to Wending. They had selected a spot in a small hollow outside the city, presumably so that if bandits or soldiers from the Middle Kingdom ever tried to use the tunnels to invade, it would be a simple matter to assault them from the ridges above. Dante cut his arm, fed his blood to the nether, and opened a hole in the side of the hollow.

Within a day, he connected this leg of the tunnel to the one he'd driven up from the south. He emerged from the tunnel tired and dusty. Along the ridges of the hollow, dozens of faces appeared. The merchants of the TAGVOG lifted their arms and cheered his name.

This marked the beginning of a two-day celebration of feasting, drinking, and drunken promises of greater feasts to come. Of all the festivals Dante had been invited to, he thought he liked Gallador's the best. The lakes held so many different varieties of fish, crabs, and mollusks that he doubted he'd ever be able to sample them all.

The first day of the event was held at Lolligan's. It was fun, but a little stuffy. The second day, they convened on the city docks, which took on the air of a proper holiday, complete with food stalls, wandering entertainers, and children tearing about the streets without looking where they were going. Tables were dragged to the docks and loaded with seafood of all kinds, accompanied by the tea and spiced rum the lakes were famous for.

As the sun drooped toward the western peaks, the people began a slow migration to the tables. Once the seats were filled, Lolligan rose from his seat beside Dante and rang a silver bell. Two hundred faces turned his way.

"Tonight, we celebrate the essence of trade: a connection built between two people. It's there, in our new pathway to the Middle Kingdom." He gestured in the direction of the tunnel's mouth, two miles to the southwest. "But it's also right here beside me, in the form of the man who made it possible. Years ago, Dante Galand came here as a young man with a crazy idea: that his lands, and ours, could be free. That they *should* be free.

"At the time, backing him against the Gaskan Empire felt like madness. In time, though, that decision has repaid our investment of trust many times over. Tonight, we celebrate our dear allies in Narashtovik!" Cheers erupted from across the tables. Lolligan let them fade, then winked at the revelers. "And you know what? Let's celebrate ourselves, too. For having the wisdom to set us down this path in the first place!"

This drew even more shouts and upraised glasses. Blays smiled at Lolligan and took a long drink. Gazing across the happy, rum-flushed faces, Dante felt at odds with himself. He'd given them something of great value. In the process, he'd strengthened the bonds between the lakelands and Narashtovik. He should have felt satisfied. Proud. Accomplished.

Yet the arrival of the netherburned woman had stolen that from him. He never thought about his father because he never had to. After the memories contained in the letter, though, he no longer knew if the past was buried as deeply as he'd thought.

He tried and succeeded to drink his way to good cheer. Late that night, he went to bed intending to spend a day or two longer in Wending to recover from the work—not to mention the celebrations—and then return to Narashtovik. He'd been away for weeks and was looking forward to going home.

Someone shook him awake. The room was dark, chilly from the breeze off the lake. His head swam with drink.

"Stedden?" he croaked. "What the hell's the matter with you?"

"It's the stranger, sir." The monk drew back, staring down at him with a face as serious as a cat's. "She's awake."

Dante jumped out of bed. Dressed only in his sleeping robe, he followed Stedden downstairs. Three candles barely lit the woman's small room. She was lying in bed, but her eyes were wide open. The room smelled like meat kept sealed for too long. Dante moved beside the bed. The woman's eyes snapped to his.

"You are him?" Her voice was raspy, weak, accented in a way Dante had never encountered. He leaned closer. She grabbed the collar of his robe. "You are Dante?"

"I am. Who are you?"

"He will soon die. You must go see him."

Dante drew back. "He doesn't deserve it."

"Perhaps not. But you do."

"You don't even—" He cut himself short. She had begun to shake, limbs jerking, teeth clacking. Her eyes rolled back. Her back arched like a drawn bow. A dark blot moved up her cheek. He tried to swat it away, but it was within the skin, staining it pure black.

The stain reached her right eye, painting it out. A second tendril crept up her left cheek. He watched, helpless, as it moved into her left eye and filled it with blackness.

Her body relaxed, pooling on the bed like cool oil. He felt for her pulse and found none.

"What's happening?" Stedden whispered. "Has she..?"

Dante whirled on him. "Did she say anything? Before you came to me?"

"Only that her name was Riddi. I ran for you as soon as her eyes opened. Did I do wrong?"

"No." He unclenched his fist. "There was nothing more to do for her. Thank you for coming to get me."

A part of him wished to study the body, to see if he could learn more about the nethereal burns that had taken her life, but at the moment, he had no stomach for it. He exited the room and headed upstairs. Rather than returning to his room, he went into Blays'. The man was snoring loudly, tangled in his sheets. Dante pulled up a chair and sat, thinking.

He wouldn't have been surprised if Blays had gone on snoring for another six hours, but hardly fifteen minutes had passed before the man's breathing hitched. Blays stretched, yawned, and opened his eyes. He saw Dante and shrieked.

"Not much fun, is it?" Dante said.

Blays scowled, his face puffy from sleep and drink. "What are you doing here? Besides being so creepy that poison centipedes think you've gone too far?"

"Did you mean what you said? About going with me to the islands?"

"Yeah. Of course." He slumped forward, rubbing the corners of his eyes with the tips of his forefingers. "Has something happened with the stranger?"

"I've decided to go. As soon as we can. I'll just have to make a few arrangements first."

"Er, well. That probably won't be necessary."

"Yes, why would we need to prepare? We're only traveling thousands of miles to a set of islands I'd never heard of until two days ago. I'm sure all we need to do is buy a few meat pies and bring an extra pair of socks."

Blays looked sheepish. "I mean I've already spoken to Olivander and Nak. They're fine with you taking the time away from Narashtovik."

"There will still be food. Travel. Logistics."

"Yeah, Lolligan's helped me out with that. All good to go."

Dante's jaw dropped. "You said it was my decision!"

"And I haven't as much as spoken to you about it since then, have I? I simply wanted everything to be prepared so we could move as fast as possible."

"You might have at least consulted me."

"This is what I'm here for. To lend a hand. Make rough business a little more bearable." Blays rested against the headboard. "Besides, you were spending all day out climbing around mountains and tunnels. It got boring back here."

Dante got up and moved to the window. It would be dawn

soon and the fishermen were already paddling out to check their nets. He knew their lives weren't as simple and placid as it appeared, yet sometimes he envied them for knowing where each morning would take them.

"Do you think I'm making the right choice?"

Blays yawned loudly. "What time is it? Minus five in the morning? Right now, I wouldn't know whether it's the right choice to fry an egg or scramble it."

Dante stared into the darkness a moment longer, then turned and kicked the bed. "Come on then. If you've already got everything prepared, there's no sense wasting time."

"Next time, I'm going to rent us some of those horses that refuse to wake up until noon."

Dante closed the door and jogged down the stairs. Blays may have wrangled the logistics, but there were two tasks left before they set out.

Examine the woman who had brought him the news—and then bury her.

3

Blays stood in the ship's prow, hair tousled by the wind of the voyage. The sea was gray and the spray hissing over the railings was as cold as winter rain, but he was grinning like he'd just been promoted to Chief Ale-Quaffer.

"Reminds you of the good old days, doesn't it?" he said over the smack of the waves and the creak of the boards.

Dante tightened his grip on the rails. "Which days were those, exactly?"

"Before all these dratted responsibilities. When all we had to do was roam. Us against the world."

"You mean like when we were being hunted in the streets of Bressel. Or in Whetton, when they dragged you off to be hanged for murder. Those good old days?"

"All right, maybe they weren't so good. Maybe they were just old." Blays wiped spray from his forehead. "Even so, they were fun, in their way."

Dante grunted, turning to port to watch the city of Allingham fade into the mists of the horizon. It had been his first visit to the jewel of the Middle Kingdoms, but they'd hardly spent eight hours there before boarding the *Thornwind* and shoving off. They would sail south for a day, then turn east and pass through the

Slanted Straits on their way to Bressel, capital of Mallon, to arrive in another three or four days. After the *Thornwind* made port, Dante hoped to hire Captain Collins to take them south to the Plagued Islands. Failing that, they'd look elsewhere. Bressel remained the largest port he'd ever seen, and after leaving a note of credit with Lolligan, Dante was practically carrying enough silver to buy his own vessel if he had to.

There were many varieties of sea captain. Collins turned out to be of the highly unctuous variety, more of a hotelier than a naval commander. Or perhaps he only behaved that way when he had two lords paying lodging on a pair of cabins. Whatever the case, whenever he passed by, he asked Dante whether he could be of service.

The fifth or sixth time the captain came by, he hardly slowed down. "In need of anything more, m'lord?"

Dante stood from his bench, bracing himself on a nearby railing. "Yes, in fact. Passage to the Plagued Islands."

Collins threw back his head and laughed. "Gladly! And while I'm at it, shall I deliver you to the back side of the moon?"

"I'm afraid I'm serious. Can you help us?"

The captain went dead sober. "The Plagued Islands are not on our schedule."

"I'd be happy to pay you for the detour."

"I will not sail into death for any fee."

"Then do you know anyone greedy or stupid enough to do so in your stead?"

"I will see if I can think up a few names," Collins said. "Though I think it would be best for you if my memory failed me."

The man bobbed his head and strolled off. Dante watched him go. During the ride from Wending to Allingham, he'd spoken to Nak about the Plagued Islands, lacking any information about their destination except its name. However, as with all exotic, faraway locations, the stories and rumors were less than credible. It was possible that the people lived on the slopes of living volcanoes—he'd seen much stranger arrangements, like the tree cities of Spiren—but Dante highly doubted the islands were actually so warm that you never needed clothes. Winter came everywhere.

As for the meaning of the islands' name, he'd gotten nowhere. Some claimed that no one who ever visited them ever came back. This was nonsense on the face of it: if so, then no one would know anything about the place. Others claimed that it was so rife with poxes that the *lucky* ones left the islands with melted faces. This was surely exaggerated, but even if it held a kernel of truth, Dante was unconcerned. There were very few diseases he couldn't treat or cure outright. Besides, the autopsy he'd conducted on Riddi hadn't turned up any buboes, sores, cancers, or rots. If she'd carried any sicknesses from the islands, they were no more than a nuisance.

From the way Captain Collins spoke, however, Dante was beginning to doubt his ability to heal would convince many sailors to take the risk of the voyage. Then again, all it took was one captain looking for a score.

Early on the second day of their voyage, the *Thornwind* sailed directly toward a mountain. Dante watched in consternation as the peaks grew nearer and nearer. Just as he began to suspect Collins had gone mad, the ship hove to port, entering the strait that separated the mainland from a chain of rocky islands. Blays was back in the prow, gazing at the peaks in solitude.

As Dante approached him, he understood where they were: the Carlon Islands. He turned to go.

"Don't." Blays didn't remove his eyes from the mountains. "It's all right."

Dante stayed where he was. "What is?"

"I know why you did it. To save those who could be saved. It had to be done."

For a moment, Dante was back in the courtyard of the

Citadel, where he and Lira had been all that stood between their people and the conquering armies of the Gaskan Empire. It had smelled like guts and smoke; in their red uniforms, the enemy soldiers had looked like a rushing tide of blood. Lira was out in front, striking down the sorcerer who'd been about to kill Dante. In perverse payment for saving his life, Dante cracked apart the earth itself, dropping her — and the king's army — to their deaths.

She had been from the Carlons. She had also been Blays' first love. After the Chainbreakers' War, it had taken three years before Dante saw Blays again, and even longer before their friendship resumed. Seven years after her death, Blays hadn't said anything about forgiving him. Nor had Dante expected it.

"Maybe there was no other choice," Dante said. "Even so, I'm sorry."

"Me too. But I imagine she was happy to die in such service. You know how she was."

"When she fell, she actually smiled. Did I ever tell you that?"

Blays chuckled, glancing his way. "Are you serious? She was an odd one, wasn't she?"

"I suppose that's why she fit right in."

Other than the sighting of a lone pirate vessel, which the *Thornwind* outran handily, the rest of the trip was quiet. Soon, they came within sight of Bressel. It was the first major city Dante had spent time in, and remained the archetype he compared all others to. Shacks and slums on the outsides. Incomplete walls. Muddy streets, few of them cobbled, all of which stunk of dung. Church spires, including the Odeleon, said to be over five hundred feet high.

And the docks. Larger than most cities, these encrusted the estuary where the Chanset River flowed out into the sea. The *Thornwind* maneuvered into the river and soon made berth.

Collins strode up and down the deck, delivering orders loudly but calmly. Dante packed up the book he'd been reading and shouldered his bags. As he debarked, Collins pulled him aside.

The bearded captain passed him a small square of paper. "I can't promise they're here. But if anyone is willing to help you, it will be these men."

Dante blinked at the paper. It contained two whole names. "Thank you for going to such lengths."

The man bowed, spreading one palm before him. Dante crossed the gangplank over the brackish-smelling waters. Blays followed behind him, smiling at the bustle of the longshoremen, sailors, fishermen, and vendors. There were even a few neeling within the crowds—short, pale, hairless creatures with a fishy cast to their faces. Dante hadn't seen one since leaving Bressel a decade earlier.

"So," Blays said. "Pub?"

"New ship first," Dante said. "*Then* pub."

"Counterpoint: by pubbing first, we'll be more enthusiastic about finding a new ship. Not to mention more charming toward its quartermaster."

"Our list is only two names long. The pubs will be our morale booster if those fall through."

Blays narrowed his eyes, then nodded once. "Wise. Extremely wise. First name on the list?"

This was one Captain Davids of the *Lurcher*. After asking around, and discovering his Mallish was still fine despite years of neglect, Dante was directed to a pier a short ways upstream. On finding the *Lurcher*, he was met by a quartermaster named Lorrie, a man whose ruddy face was wreathed in red whiskers.

"We're looking for passage to the Plagued Islands," Dante said. "You came recommended by way of Captain Benn Collins."

Lorrie gave him a long, level look. "We won't be headed that way. Perhaps if it were summer."

"Summer's only a few weeks off," Dante said. "How long would we need to wait?"

"I wasn't finished. Perhaps it if were summer. And the whirlpool were down. And my men were starving and in need of immediate coin. And if I was promised nine virgins of—"

Blays exhaled loudly. "We get the point. You're not man enough to take us there."

Lorrie smiled, red whiskers twitching. "If you're trying to goad me, you'll have to find far worse slander than that."

"Your mother is a tramp?"

Dante held out his scrap of paper. "We were told the *Yasmina* might make the trip. Do you know where it might be?"

"Yes," Lorrie said. "In pieces at the bottom of the Red Sea, off the coast of your precious islands."

"I see. So do you know anyone who would be willing to take us there?"

"Well, under normal circumstances, and assuming there was a bit of silver coming my way for it, I'd send you to Captain Twill. Of the *Sword of the South*."

"But what are the abnormal circumstances stopping you from doing so?"

"Those being that, last I heard, Twill was about to die of illness."

"Let me guess," Blays muttered. "Picked up on a trip to the Plagued Islands?"

The man scratched his neck. "Can't say I got close enough to her to find out."

"Is she here now?" Dante said.

"Like I said: silver."

Dante fished into a pouch and removed three Galladese coins, careful not to let the others clink.

Lorrie hefted them in his palm, frowning deeply at them. "Where are these from?"

"The color of money doesn't care whose face is stamped on it."

"Agreed." He pocketed the coins and stood, rolling his neck with a series of cracks. "And for this much, I'll introduce you myself."

The hefty man ambled down the dock and into the mucky

thoroughfare fronting it. Boards were laid in the mud, but these trails were dominated by men bearing handcarts and wagons piled with crates and casks. After years spent among the Gaskans, who favored long coats and fur hats, the Mallish jackets looked flimsy, more decorative than functional.

After a brief jaunt, Lorrie turned off the thoroughfare and onto a pier. So far, every dock had been jammed with merchant vessels, but this one berthed a single ship. If the wallowing carracks they'd seen previously had been broadswords, the *Sword of the South* was a rapier: sleek and slim, with a short foremast and a taller mainmast. Its decks were empty and it rode high in the water.

Lorrie stopped before it and cupped his hand to his mouth. "Hoy!"

After a moment of silence, he repeated himself, more loudly. A scuzzy-looking young man popped up from the deck.

"Mr. Naran, if you please," Lorrie said.

The young man eyed them, mouth half open, then disappeared once more. After a minute, another man appeared, brown-skinned and green-eyed, wearing an orange-trimmed white jacket, the sleeves of which appeared to be connected to its vest using laces.

"Is that you, Lorrie?" He spoke with an upper-class Mallish accent, but this was accompanied by a second accent Dante had never heard before. "Looking to finally join a *real* crew?"

Lorrie gawked. "You have a real crew on this ship? I'm sorry, there must be some mistake. Y'see, I was looking for the *Sword of the South*."

Naran removed a pick from his breast pocket and scraped between his teeth, which were remarkably well-preserved for a sailor. "Mind getting to the point? Some of us have work to do."

"This is Dante," Lorrie said. "And this is..." He gestured at Blays, then shrugged. "Someone who didn't pay me enough to remember their name." He flicked his hand in a salute and turned to go.

"What, that's it?" Blays said.

"I said I'd introduce you, not arrange you to be married." Lorrie strolled away in the direction of the *Lurcher*.

Naran folded his hands behind his back and gazed at them from behind the railings. "Did you have something you wanted? Or did you just come here for a look at my handsome face?"

"We heard Captain Twill is unwell," Dante said. "I'm a healer."

The man's mouth tightened to a thin line. "Thank you. Not interested."

"Mr. Lorrie made it sound as though your captain's condition is very serious."

"And that is precisely why she is in no need of whatever toad ichor you've come to peddle."

Dante raised his eyebrows. "You will want to let me see her."

"And how do you expect to be compensated for your services?"

"I need passage to the Plagued Islands. Therefore, my ability to reach my destination depends on my ability to heal your captain."

Naran regarded him for a long moment, then sighed. "Permission to board."

Dante bowed his head and climbed the portable staircase set beside the boat. As he crossed onto the deck, he caught a whiff of something floral and spicy. Naran was wearing some kind of perfume. Possibly that was the custom in his land, but Dante feared he might be using it to deal with the scent of death.

The man led them to a cabin in the aftercastle. "Wait here."

He opened the door, a bell jingling from the handle. The interior was too dark to make out. As he closed the door behind him, the room exhaled a whiff of something fetid.

After two minutes of silence, Naran reopened the door and nodded them inside. The cabin was spacious, as far as ship's cabins went, meaning that it was merely cramped rather than claustrophobic. A bed took up the left wall. Within it, a woman lay propped up by pillows, her features barely visible in the thin sunlight sneaking past the curtained windows. Her blond hair was sun-bleached to the point of whiteness, and though her youngish face was heavily tanned, this couldn't hide her drawn, wan skin.

She might have been quite attractive if not for the oozing sores pocking her face. Despite these, she met Dante's gaze head on. Her eyes were a pale, washed-out blue common to the Collen Basin.

"Mr. Naran tells me you consider yourself a healer."

Dante shrugged. "I imagine the hundreds of people I've saved would agree."

"I'm impressed," she said. "And of those hundreds, how many did you cure of the Weeping End?"

"Never heard of it. Fortunately, a complete unfamiliarity with my enemies has never stopped me from defeating them." He moved nearer to the bed. The fetid smell intensified. Dante breathed through his mouth, doing his best not to display his distaste. "Where did you pick this up? The Plagued Islands?"

"The Golden Isles. That's the only place the Weeping End is found."

"Do you know what caused you to be afflicted with it?"

"I thought *you* were supposed to be the physician."

"Humor me. No pun intended."

Twill continued to stare at him. "They say it comes from contact with the snorriba. A kind of snake favored here for its skin. This trip, we took some aboard. Rubbing your hands with tint leaves is supposed to ward off the sickness, but it didn't help me."

Dante nodded vaguely. In Narashtovik, he'd established an institution known as the carneterium to study the causes of death, but the roots of sickness remained elusive. Some diseases seemed contagious, but others didn't appear capable of passing to others. Everywhere he traveled had competing theories as to how these illnesses came to be. Dirt and filth was a common one. In Mallon, where they believed in the purity of the ether, impurities were pegged as the cause. These could come in the form of rotten food, vices (particularly sex, or the consumption or smoking of various herbs), even blasphemous thoughts. Removing the impurities could be achieved through leeches, emetics, sweating, enemas, or anything else that expunged liquid from the body. No matter which land you went to, traveling physicians sold a panoply of oils, pastes, incenses, and ichors.

As for Dante, he wasn't certain what he believed. Nether was drawn to blood and death, so there were times he suspected an imbalance of shadows could cause sickness. But foul air seemed to be the most common factor: that's why there were so many diseases in swampy, warmer places. Or in houses with too many people and too few windows. This suggested that when no nethereal treatment was available, a cure might involve fresh air and isolation.

Exploring these matters could be the secondary focus of his voyage. That way, no matter what happened with his so-called father, Dante would return with something valuable.

"Well, no matter the cause, I have a cure," he said. "This will only take a minute."

He drew his knife and scratched the back of his left arm. Blood welled in the nick, shadows flocking to it like dumb moths. On the other side of the bed, Naran gasped.

"Nethermancer!" He rushed for the door, grabbing the handle. "All hands! All—"

Steel whispered on leather. In a blink, Blays drew both swords, putting one to Naran's outstretched wrist and the other to his neck.

"A suggestion," Blays said. "Shut up."

The cords of Naran's neck tensed and flexed like rigging in a gale. "You came to kill us? Why?"

"I'm sure this looks very bad. What with certain people's swords pressed to certain other people's jugulars. But I promise you, we mean you no harm."

In the gloom of the cabin, Naran's eyes were as white as little moons. "Who are you people?"

Dante let his hands dangle at his sides. "I'm as you say: a nethermancer. And I will make your captain whole—if you'll allow it."

"That's not my decision to make. Captain Twill?"

The woman tried to speak, but her throat caught. She swallowed, baring her teeth. "The Weeping End is a death sentence. Slow and nasty. If this bastard means to kill me fast, that sounds like a blessing."

Naran removed his hand from the door. Blays put his swords away. Dante exhaled, then moved his vision to the shadows inside the woman's frame.

Her body was being broken. Wrongness whirled within it, tearing her apart from her spine to her skin. Dante drew streams of darkness from all corners of the room. It settled on Twill's skin, sinking into it like the water left on the sand from a retreating wave, penetrating to the deepest sources of that wrongness.

She gasped, sitting up in bed. Naran started forward, then stopped himself. Twill closed her eyes. Her entire body trembled. Dante paid her no mind, smoothing out the ulcers within her, then sending the nether through her veins to cleanse her blood. The sickness was deeply rooted. He could leave no trace behind. Scouring her clean took many minutes. His hold on the nether grew less fine.

Finished with her insides, he moved to her outsides. The sores on her face sealed. Scabs formed, then dropped to the sheets, revealing smooth, unbroken skin. Beside him, Blays looked completely nonchalant. Naran looked ready to jump out the porthole. Twill's eyes remained closed.

Dante reeled in the direction of the nearest chair and sat. Twill's eyes sprung open. She sat up cautiously, turning her hands palm up, then palm down. She opened the dresser beside her bed and withdrew a mirror. Without being asked, Naran raked the curtains back from the windows, spilling sunlight into the cabin.

Twill held the mirror to her face. She laughed, touching her smooth skin. "Is this some kind of trap?"

"What do you mean?" Dante said.

"The ethermancers refused to see me. So are you here to taint me with nether? Prove I'm as debased as they say?"

"Healing the unwell is about the only thing they've ever given back to this city. Why would the priests turn away a sick person?"

"Because she's from a place that deserves no saving."

"Collen Basin?" He gestured toward her eyes. "Why?"

"It's the seat of Arawn's sedition. Worshipping the wrong god leaves our souls impure. And opens our bodies to sickness." She swung her legs out of bed and planted her stockinged feet on the floor, looking surprised by how easily she was able to stand. "What's the deal? You talk like a local, but you're as ignorant as a child."

"I grew up here. But I left Mallon many years ago."

"Be happy about that, shadowslinger. If you hadn't gotten out..." She mimed wrapping a noose around her neck and pulling it tight; she popped up on her toes, sticking her tongue from the corner of her mouth. "Naran told me you want to go to the Plagued Islands. That's why you healed me?"

"I thought it would be a little easier than stealing your ship and enslaving your crew."

"Well, I'm certainly grateful to have skipped out on death. But we have a problem: my gratitude won't do anything to feed and pay that crew."

"Don't worry about payment." Blays smacked Dante on the

shoulder. "This guy's got more money than a pub on Falmac's Eve."

Twill smirked, then sobered. "Whatever you're offering, I'm sure I'd make more by turning you into the priests."

"The only thing you'd earn doing that," Dante said, "is an abrupt booting through death's door."

She laughed and threw open the windows. A cool wind swept through the cabin, carrying the smell of fresh water. "No worries, Mr. Dante. I can still feel a heart beating down in me somewhere. I'll take you to the islands. But I'll need a few days. My crew's out drinking—I choose to pretend they're mourning my fate—and my holds are empty. I won't travel to the Plagued Islands without a full belly of iron."

"Fine by me. We could use a few days in the city ourselves."

"Be careful out there. If they know what you are? They'll kill you."

Years ago, Mallon had been his home. He'd been looking forward to revisiting it, to learning what had changed and what had stayed the same. But after Twill's revelation that netherusers were now enemies of the state—an affront to Taim, first god of the Celeset—Dante spent as little time on the streets as possible.

Most of his time was spent in libraries and monasteries, seeking anything they had on the culture and history of the Plagued Islands. There wasn't much to find. When he stumbled on something useful, he made the monks a donation in exchange for their making a copy of it, or more rarely, to purchase the book outright. The gods of the Celeset were the same in Mallon as in Gask: Taim, Carvahal, Lia, Mennok, and so on. Dante was able to navigate the monasteries with minimal gaffes.

As he made his rounds, however, the single difference between the two nations grew more and more glaring: here, there was no Arawn. The god of death—and of nether.

He allowed himself a very small amount of chatter with the monks. Some were completely apolitical, either from devotion to their gods or exasperation with the games of the court. Others, however, couldn't get enough of it, either because they had designs on entering the political arena, or because gossiping about lords, ladies, and the clergy was the only fun they were allowed to have.

So they thought nothing of Dante's interest in the subject. He picked up the gist very quickly. After Samarand's failed war to revive Arawn's worship in Mallon—the same war that had brought Dante from Mallon to Narashtovik—anti-Arawn sentiment flourished. Arawn's believers revealed by the war had been driven out or killed. His worship was outlawed once more. And anything related to him, such as the wielding of nether, was outlawed as well.

Six or seven years ago, when Dante had been closer to Mallon, this oppression of Arawn's people would have infuriated him. Now? It only made him sad. When he at last departed on the *Sword of the South*, he turned his back to Mallon, happy to leave it to rot.

Two hours later and the city had vanished completely; the only land in sight was Sentinel Mountain, behind and to starboard. Dante retired to his cabin. Due to the smallness of the ship, he had to share the room with Blays, and was not looking forward to the snoring. Out of sight of the crew, he used his loon to contact Nak. A member of the Council of Narashtovik, Nak acted as their de facto secretary, coordinating communications through their small (and extremely secret) network of loons.

"So you're off," Nak said. "Any idea when you'll be back?"

Dante gripped the edge of the bunk as they hit a swell. "Tuesday? Certainly no later than Thursday."

"I'm not trying to schedule a dinner date. I am merely looking for a rough estimate."

"If the winds do what they're supposed to—and winds are

proverbial for their steadiness and predictability—Captain Twill thinks it will take a week to get there and two weeks to get back to Bressel. So depending on how long things take at the island, I'd think we'll be back in Narashtovik in six weeks. Eight at the utmost."

"Just in time for summer! I bet you can't wait."

Summer. When the heat and humidity lay on the city like a drunk husband. Dante closed down the connection and opened one of his books, hoping to take his mind off his most hated time of year. Now and then he ventured out for fresh air and a glance at Captain Twill, who he hoped to speak to regarding the Plagued Islands, but she was busy seeing to the needs of the ship until that evening.

The night was chilly and blustery, but possibly in response to her recent time spent trapped indoors, Twill met him atop the aftercastle. She stood with her shoulders thrown back, her hair kept from blowing in her face by a number of braids and ties.

"I want to thank you again for making this journey," Dante said. "There's only one problem: I have no idea what our destination is like."

"If you don't know squat about the islands, what makes you so keen to get there?"

"Family business."

She looked him up and down. "You don't look like an islander."

"That's because I'm from one of those families that enjoys living as far away from each other as possible." He pulled his cloak tighter around his chest. "So what are they like? The people there?"

"I couldn't say. I've never met them."

"I'm sorry, there must be some mistake. I was under the impression you were Captain Twill, veteran traveler of the Plagued Islands."

"The *Sword of the South* has been making this trip since before I was a swabbie. The inhabited islands have designated trading bays. They call 'em swappers. You drop anchor and sooner or later somebody comes down to the beach. We use telegraphy—flags, in our case—to explain what we've got and what we want. Once we've agreed on a price, we row out to a little island off the shore and drop off the goods. The locals come out, make their inspection, and if everything's on the up and up, they take our stuff and leave theirs in its place. Then we pick it up and go on our way. System's smoother than a greased otter."

"What if they take your goods and run off?"

"Then our boat never comes back. I've heard of the occasional theft, but most towns value a good trade partner more than a one-time score."

"I can see that working," Dante said. "What manner of goods do you get in return?"

"Spices. Flowers. Herbs. Stuff that smells good, tastes good, or makes you feel good."

"And is it really that dangerous there?"

"Everyone else seems to think so. Which means my crew thinks so. Which means that if I, a skeptic, were to get in breathing range of the locals, I'd turn around to find my ship has left without me."

Dante scratched the side of his jaw. "So how will they react to when Blays and I expect a ride home?"

"Don't worry." Twill smiled. "We'll just tow you behind the boat."

"You don't believe the islands are diseased, then?"

"They have their share, same as anywhere else. Including one I've never seen elsewhere: the Black Creep. If that one gets you, you won't even know it until a week or two later. A week after *that*, you can hardly stand. After that?" She hummed a Mallish funeral dirge.

"Do you know the cure? Or how you contract it?"

"Wouldn't have any idea. Like I said, the men would mutiny

if we tried to spend any time on shore. Anyway, the Plagued Islands might not be as bad as they say—but the name had to come from somewhere, yeah?"

The next day, clouds scudded in and out of the skies. Dante read more, mostly in his cabin; he found he got seasick when he could see the horizon rolling around in his peripheral vision.

As the afternoon drew on, Blays swung the door open, letting in a rush of sunlight and salt air. "Some day, I'll stop being surprised that you'd rather jam your nose in a book than look at the new world unfolding around you. But it isn't this day."

Dante didn't look up from his book. "What am I missing? Let me guess: it's big, flat, and blue."

"There are also birds."

"I'm trying to learn about what we're getting ourselves into. There's virtually no information about the Plagued Islands out there. It's almost as bad as Weslee."

Blays stayed in the entrance, keeping one hand on the door to keep it from whacking him. "I've got a surefire way to learn about the islands: by going to them."

"They weren't always this isolated. Hundreds of years ago, they were on the route between Mallon and the continent to the south."

"A place so important you don't even know its name." He wiped his nose on his collar. "What made you decide to do this after all?"

Dante shook his head slowly. "Idiocy, I suspect. Along with a large helping of spite."

"Ah, spite. The only force capable of giving love a run for its money."

"I thought about what you said. The few parts that were useful, anyway. And I found myself upset."

"Sorry about that. I only wanted you to give it some serious thought."

"I wasn't upset at you. I mean, no more than usual. I was upset at him. For leaving me alone. Maybe he had a good reason—or maybe he's just an asshole. I decided I needed to find out which. While there's still time."

"So it doesn't even matter what the answer is so long as we find one. That should make things easier." He jerked his head at the doorway. "I'll be outside. I've never been south of Bressel before."

Dante closed the book and followed Blays out of the cabin. The sea was slate gray. Just as it looked from the south shores of Mallon. As the days went on, however, the sea's hue shifted from gray to gray-blue, and then to navy. Every morning, the air felt a little warmer. As he ran low on reading material, he spent more and more time outside the cabin, but there wasn't much to see besides gulls and petrels whose wingspans were wider than a man was tall.

None of the books he read laid out the islands' history in full, but bit by bit, he pieced together a tenuous approximation. Many centuries in the past, there had been a fair amount of trade between Mallon, the Plagued Islands, and the lands further south. About six or seven hundred years ago, however, a series of wars had broken out between the islands' clans. At the same time, a terrible sickness had emerged.

These two events had killed trade for decades. Over time, though, it resumed—only to be brought to a sudden halt roughly four centuries ago, when another conflict had engulfed the island. No specifics were mentioned, but hundreds of Mallish had perished in the fighting and the ensuing plague. Ever since, sickness had ravaged the land, limiting contact to the few souls brave or greedy enough to tempt disaster.

He fell asleep compiling his notes. A knock woke him sometime later. Blays threw open the door. It felt as though he'd been asleep for no more than two hours, meaning it should be early afternoon, but the light from outside was dull and gray.

"I think," Blays said, "you're going to want to see this."

Dante was tired enough that he wouldn't have cared if a pod of dolphins were fluke-waltzing on the surface of the water, but the earnestness in Blays' voice drew him from his bunk. Outside, most of the sky was clear and blue. Yet it was as dim as twilight.

Ahead and to starboard, a pillar of clouds connected the sea to the sky, wider at the top than the base. Behind it, the sun was a dull coin. A dense mist hung around and above the miles-high pillar. At its base, the ocean wasn't flat—rather, it was concave, the horizon dented like a ball dropped in the middle of a taut sheet.

Twill appeared atop the aftercastle, leaning her arms on the rail. "So is that all it takes to extract you from your cabin?"

Dante drifted toward the starboard edge. "What is it?"

"It's the Mill."

"*Arawn's* Mill?"

"That's what they say. I've never met the big man to ask in person."

He gawked across the waters. "Can we get any closer?"

Twill snorted, walking down the castle stairs. "Sure. If you've decided you want to go to hell instead. We're already closer than anyone else dares to get."

"What is it?"

"Whirlpool. Miles across. Biggest one I've ever heard of."

He pointed at the sky. "Is it causing the spout? Or is the spout causing it?"

"Again," she said, joining him at the rail, "although Arawn is surely aware of my curiosity, he's never seen fit to give me the answers."

She watched for a minute, then strode away, yelling orders. As they drew closer, the winds worsened, buffeting the sails. Sailors kept busy in the rigging, trimming the canvas to every shift in direction. The sky grew darker yet.

Blays strolled up to the railing, grinning vacantly. "I've never seen so much nether in the air. It's like someone dumped a flock of crows in a thresher." He glanced at Dante. "What?"

"I still can't believe you learned how to use it."

"Sorry to have encroached on your hallowed ground. I'll remind you the only reason I learned to wield it was so I could try to escape from you."

At the time, Blays' departure from Narashtovik had wounded him to the core. Now, Dante found himself laughing about it. "It's very strange that tragedy can become comedy through the simple addition of time."

"I think that only happens when you've endured something together. Go through it alone, and it may always feel sad."

"I could buy that."

"Having someone else around also helps you know you're still sane." Blays stared at the grim spout towering over the ocean. "A benefit that is coming in very handy right now."

They passed the Mill from miles away. The waters were so dark they were almost black, churning in a vortex, fighting and foaming. Mist soaked them, followed by a pelting rain. The sails luffed madly. Waves bashed the hull, spitting foam over the deck. Dante took a chair outside the cabin and plunked down. There was no way he was going to hide indoors when there was a chance to learn something about the whirlpool.

The skies lightened. The winds calmed. The whorl of water and the pillar of storm fell behind them. If anything, though, they skimmed along faster than ever. After a few minutes convincing himself this was so, Dante found Twill atop the aftercastle overseeing the helmsman.

"You're right," she confirmed. "We are going faster. That's the whole point of sailing around the Mill. We caught the Current. We'll be at the islands within a day."

There was no further excitement between then and nightfall. Dante went to bed early. He woke before dawn. The cabin was humid, sweaty. When he went outside, it was hardly any less stifling. The only thing keeping it tolerable was the constant wind.

The sun rose on an azure sea. They weren't traveling as zippily as the day before, but the *Sword of the South* was still making better time than at any point prior to the Mill. A few white clouds adorned the sky like strips of lace. The sun was punishing, driving Dante into whatever shade he could find.

"Land ho!"

High in the rigging, a sailor pointed dead ahead. Dante moved to the prow. Ahead, a dim blue shape lay on the horizon. With the ship still streaking forward in the Current, the shape quickly resolved into a green island of jagged, knife-like heights and wave-battered coasts.

Twill dispensed commands, prompting another round of sail-trimming. White birds soared with hardly a flap of their wings. The waters were now a bright sapphire blue. Those surrounding the island were pale, but no less gem-like. Low black cliffs skirted the shores. Above them grew the lushest, greenest forest Dante had ever seen.

They sailed past the northernmost point, diverting to the east side of the island. A small bay swung inward, ringed by vivid purple sands. Animals shrieked from the trees, their calls so strange and piercing he couldn't tell if they were birds or creatures. He saw no sign of inhabitation at all, but given the crush of the jungle, thousands of people could be living inside it and you'd never know.

The ship swung around another outcrop of rock, revealing the island was much bigger than at first blush. The letter delivered to Dante by the dead woman had instructed him to come to something called the Bay of Peace. He, of course, had no idea where this was, but Captain Twill strode up and down the deck giving orders as naturally as if she were directing a carriage driver to her home.

They veered past a long arm of black rock gleaming with pools of water, its fringes shifting with birds and crabs. The *Sword of the South* hove around it and entered a calm bay sheltered from the northern currents. Tiny islands spangled the waters, low and level enough to serve as swappers. Dead ahead, a small river fed into the bay. The shores had been cleared of trees and were crowded with a mix of stone and wooden buildings. Despite the heat of the day, columns of smoke rose from the settlement.

"Here you are," Twill said, grinning crookedly. "The Bay of Peace."

Half the sails were down. As the ship coasted inland, slowing in advance of the reef protecting the inner bay, men tossed lead weights over the side, measuring the depths with lengths of cord. Dante kept his eyes on the settlement.

As they passed the first of the little islands, yellow flickered from the shore. Dante craned forward. Figures dashed between the houses. The smoke, it wasn't coming from cook fires. The town was burning.

4

Twill stared at the blooming flame, spine straightening. "Mr. Fredricks! Come about. We're getting out of here."

Hollers and screams filtered from the shore. The ship lurched, heaving around. Dante ran toward the captain. "What are we doing?"

She barely looked his way. "That appears to be a war. I'm removing ourselves from it."

"Do you intend to find somewhere else to land?"

"Assuming the entire island isn't on fire."

"Good enough." He moved back, giving her space to conduct her business.

As the ship turned, avoiding a black rock spiking from the waves, Blays thumped up beside him. "Where exactly are we going?"

"Away," Dante said.

"There's a problem with that: those people over there appear to be getting killed."

"We haven't yet stepped foot on this place and you already want to start meddling? How would we even know who to help?"

"Easy rule of thumb: you help the side whose village is being burned. In all the wars we've seen, have you ever known the village-burners to be on the right side of justice?"

Across the bay, a shirtless man stumbled onto the shore, clutching a staff or spear. A figure stalked after him, dressed in chain mail, sword gleaming in the harsh noon light. He battered the spearman to the ground and drove his blade into the man's body.

"No," Dante said. "I haven't."

He jogged across the deck toward Twill, who was deep in argument with Mr. Naran. "Captain, we need to go ashore."

She scowled his way. "First rule of successful trading: never, ever get involved in local affairs."

"These people are about to be slaughtered. It may be very easy to get a corpse to agree to your price, but you'll find it rather more difficult for him to pay you."

"I won't feed my men to a war they have nothing to do with."

"You don't have to," Dante said. "Give us a longboat. We'll do the rest."

Twill gritted her teeth, then gave the command. A minute later, her crew had lowered a longboat to the water. Blays scampered down the rope ladder to the boat, Dante on his heels. They paddled toward an empty beach just south of the town, soaring over the bay's placid waters, which shallowed rapidly, turning an outrageous aquamarine.

Dante watched the shore, but between the smoke, buildings, and jungle, there was no way to get a clear view of what was happening. "Should I assume you have no plan whatsoever?"

"I thought I'd charge at them waving my sword around and whooping like a barbarian. Or were you looking for something more subtle?"

"Given the circumstances, I suppose that's as good as we can get. But make sure you don't hurt anyone who doesn't deserve it."

Blays glanced over his shoulder. "If we're going by your generous standards, I don't think I have anything to worry about."

The longboat made landfall, sand grinding its hull. The beach was forty feet deep, fringed by ground-hugging grass. Beyond that, tall trees grew in profusion, their trunks naked of leaves, giant fronds sprouting from their crowns. Dante hopped out of the boat and sprinted for the cover of the trees. As he ran, he pulled his knife, slicing a shallow cut into his skin. Nether surged forward. Beside him, Blays drew both swords.

Inside the treeline, they paused to assess what lay ahead. Two hundred yards up the sand, three men ran toward a wooden building, stilts elevating it a few feet above the grass. The men charged up its steps. While two of them ducked inside the front door, the third turned and fired a bow up the beach at five men carrying swords and piecemeal metal armor. The archer loosed a second round, staggering one of the pursuers, then ran inside the house and slammed the rickety door.

The four remaining armored men continued toward the house. One carried a flaming brand.

Blays rushed forward. Dante swore under his breath and ran after him. As the man with the brand touched the flames to the door, Dante splayed out his hand. A bolt of shadows streaked through the sweltering air.

It took the soldier in the side of the neck. His head snapped to the side. He crumpled, half smothering the brand. The three survivors looked around in shock. One rolled the body aside and picked up the torch. Another reached into his pocket, and withdrew a round, apple-sized black object.

Dante was now less than two hundred feet away; with little cover besides the unadorned trunks, the soldiers spotted him, pointing and jabbering. White smoke curled from the door. As the brand-bearer scampered from the flames, Dante loosed another spike of nether. It arced toward the man like the idea of a bird.

An instant before it struck the foe in the chest, it burst into a shower of black sparks, winking away to nothing.

Dante inhaled sharply. "Stay close. They've got a sorcerer."

Blays grunted. "As if bows weren't bad enough. Is it too much to ask people to fight fair?"

Dante shaped the nether and slung forward a third bolt. The soldiers were backing away from the burning building, hands held out before them. As the third bolt neared, one of them jerked a hand across his body. Darkness speared toward the bolt, deflecting it to the side. The three soldiers turned and ran.

The door and roof of the house crackled and burned. A rain barrel rested at the side of the building. Dante veered toward it. "Give me a hand!"

"No time!" Blays tromped up the steps, skipped to the side of the flames, and crashed his sword into the wall. Rather than hardwood, this was made of a thin, knobby-jointed plant like the bamboo that grew on the slopes of Gallador. The sword crashed through several sticks and lodged fast. Blays twisted it side to side, cracking a hole in the wall.

He stepped aside for fresh air, waving at the smoke. As he did so, an arrow whisked through the air where he'd just stood.

He ducked to the side, pressing his back to the building. "Knock it off! I'm trying to help!"

The barrel was a quarter full of stagnant water. As Dante attempted to lift it, it sloshed forward, unbalancing itself. He danced away and water hissed into the patchy grass. Above him, a window covering rolled up with a clatter of sticks. The archer stared him down from behind a nocked arrow.

"They're gone!" Dante gestured broadly, making a shooing motion. "You have to get out!"

The man licked his lips, nostrils flaring at the smoke wafting past the window. His green eyes stood out from his heavily tanned face. He withdrew into the darkness.

Dismayed shouts rang out from further up the beach. Dante couldn't understand a word of it, but panic sounded the same in every language. He dashed away from the house. His sword slapped against his hip, but with no desire to draw any more attention than necessary, he left it sheathed.

Blays vaulted off the steps, stumbled, and caught up. His face was drenched in sweat and streaked gray with ash. Wood splintered behind them. The archer burst through the wall of the house, coughing into the collar of his simple shirt. He glanced at the dead soldier on the burning porch, then at Dante.

Stilted houses flashed by on either side. The soil was a purplish clay that clung to Dante's boots. After passing through irregular rows of houses, a plaza stretched before them. Once upon a time, it had been cobbled, but now it showed more gaps than stones. At its north end, a man with a long, curved sword advanced on a line of spearmen. He wore a visored steel helmet, with greaves and vambraces around his shins and forearms. He was outnumbered six to one, but as he moved forward, the spearmen stepped back.

Blays jerked his chin at the helmeted man. "Keep him off me?"

Before Dante could respond, Blays bolted to the southeast side of the plaza, where a trio of swordsmen were shouting at a woman clutching a black box to her chest. With no desire to charge his target across open ground, Dante loped toward the houses at the edge of the plaza.

The helmeted man gestured fluidly. Hammers of shadows struck the guts of the two nearest spearmen. They bent double, flying backward. One of the survivors cocked back his spear and hurled it toward the nethermancer. The helmeted man skipped to the side, flicking his sword at the incoming spear and batting it aside.

The man was already drawing more nether. It flowed to him greedily, hungry to be used. Best to take him out in one stroke. Ideally, one he'd never see coming. Dante moved into the shadow of a weathered stone building. As the man lashed out with his sword, lopping off the head of an outthrust spear, Dante delved into the nether in the clay beneath the sorcerer's feet. Softening it. Preparing to swallow him in it—and then turn it to stone.

The man halted. Without turning, he pushed both palms toward Dante. Dante yanked his mind from the clay, but before he could refocus his attention, a wave of nether hammered into the side of the building. With a deafening rumble, the upper story gave way.

In his time, Dante had used the nether to solve any number of impossible problems. Not once, however, had he deployed it to stop a house from falling on him. There was no time to run. As the stones tumbled down around him, he softened the ground beneath him to muck and plunged beneath the surface.

Mud flowed into his nose. He held his breath tight and returned the ground around him to solid earth. Blocks bashed the surface above him. Encased in hard clay, unable to move, he tried not to panic, forcing himself not to breathe. Within moments, the thuds and vibrations ceased. Once again he softened the earth, then hardened it beneath his feet, pushing himself upward. With a slurp, the top of his head crested the surface. His eyes cleared. His crown bumped against unyielding stone. To prevent himself from inhaling, he blew muck out his nose, then twisted his head to the side, freeing his mouth.

He stayed put, catching his breath, letting his body adjust to the idea that he was no longer buried alive. Shakily, he wiped viscous clay from his eyes and nose. Light glowed from small gaps in the rubble. He appeared to have half a building on top of him. He heard nothing from the plaza. At first he imagined the stone was muffling the fighting—or perhaps that everyone had turned to gawk in wonder—but then he heard a bird caw from nearby. The skirmish had ended.

And he had a bad feeling about who remained in the plaza.

Last he'd seen Blays, the blond man had been charging after the soldiers accosting the woman. If the helmeted man came for him, he'd be defenseless. Dante needed to sink back into the clay and "swim" out the other side of the house.

Outside, footsteps crunched toward him. Dante went still.

"Dante?" Blays called. "Come on, Dante. I know your head's hard enough to survive a few tons of rock!"

"I'm here," Dante said. Sand gritted his mouth. He spat. "Don't touch anything. It's not stable. What's going on out there?"

"They ran off."

Stone flowed away from Dante's head. Once he had room to straighten his neck, he went to work on the rocks in front of him, drawing them away as smoothly as water.

"Ran off?" he said. "Weren't they kicking our asses?"

"Thoroughly. But they came here for something besides imprinting their sandals on our backsides. Once they got what they came for, they cleared out."

A shaft of daylight appeared before him. "What were they after?"

"Not sure. Turns out I've never been here before. You all right in there?"

Dante finished the cramped tunnel and wormed his way out on his hands and knees. His shirt and trousers were caked with pounds of purple clay.

Seeing him, Blays burst out laughing. "You look like you lost a fight with a vineyard."

"Did you see where he went? The sorcerer?"

"Lost track of him."

Dante stood, knocking grit and clay from his clothes. "He'd just buried me alive. And you thought it was a good idea to take your eyes off him?"

"It's surprisingly easy when you're running in the opposite direction."

"Now that makes a lot more—"

He cut himself short. Across the plaza, a man stalked toward them bearing a stone-tipped spear. He wore knee-length trousers and what appeared to be a sleeveless undershirt; on one foot, he wore a complicated sandal, but he'd lost the other in the fighting. He barked something unintelligible.

"Do you speak Mallish?" Dante said in that tongue. "Gaskan?"

The man repeated himself, pointing at Blays' swords, then the ground. When they didn't move, he lifted his spear, drawing back his elbow.

Blays frowned. "Listen, friend, these swords were just deployed in the protection of your people. Considering that…"

Two men and two women jogged into the square, three armed with spears, one with a bow. One of the men called behind him. The reinforcements flanked the lone man, weapons trained on Blays.

"I think," Dante said, "you should put down your swords."

"The problem with the act of disarming yourself is it's typically followed by getting stabbed."

More armed townsfolk filtered into the plaza, dividing themselves between the commotion around Dante and Blays, and in looking to the bodies scattering the grounds.

"If you don't put them down, there's going to be an incident," Dante said. "And if there's an incident, we're going to have to kill all these people and flee to the boat."

The spearman yelled again, a vein throbbing in his forehead. Blays sighed and crouched, lowering his swords to the half-cobbled ground. The warrior leveled his spear and advanced toward the blades.

To their right, a young woman ran into the square. She carried a curved sword and wore bone bracers studded with steel. Her eyes locked on the two foreigners. "Dante. Is which of you?"

Dante blinked. Her Mallish was accented and slow, but wholly intelligible. "That would be me. And who are you?"

The woman turned on the others, speaking rapidly, jabbing a finger at them. The language was foreign, but every now and then, a familiar-sounding word leaped forth like a salmon from a mountain stream. Several of the warriors jogged off, faces sober with purpose.

She turned back to Dante. Like everyone they'd seen on the island, her skin was light brown. Her eyes were the same hard blue as the sea. "You came on a boat. This boat brought iron?"

Dante nodded. "It turned about when it saw the fighting. But I'm sure you can flag it down."

The woman spoke to the spearman who'd made Blays lay down his arms. The man argued a moment, then held up a hand in surrender, glowered at the cobbles, and trotted off.

"You were just attacked," Blays said. "And your first concern is the shiny stuff our boat brought?"

"The attackers, they have steel. Without it, we can't defend ourselves." She glanced at the slopes above the city. "You will come with me."

"Where to?" Dante said.

The woman met his eyes. "To see your father."

Despite the heat, goosebumps stirred on his arms. "Soon enough. First, I will tend to your wounded."

"That is not why you are here."

"My father brought me here to heal his sickness, didn't he? If he's lasted for weeks already, I'm sure he'll survive another few hours. Let me see to those who might not make it that long."

She touched her right elbow with her left hand. The gesture had the crispness of a salute. "My name is Winden. To help? You will follow."

Winden strode west from the plaza. The land sloped uphill, carrying them past more of the bamboo-ish houses. Some of these were perched atop thigh-high foundations of black stone. Most of the streets were unpaved. The few that were cobbled were as gappy as the plaza. The sun was relentless, but a steady offshore wind dried most of Dante's sweat.

Flakes of ash fluttered in the wind. Townsfolk jogged toward shore with rods braced over their shoulders, a bucket of water hanging from each end. They all glanced at Dante and Blays, but no one said a word. The men and women both wore sleeveless shirts. The men wore short trousers. The women dressed in skirts, with one side hanging below the knee, the other side rising to mid-thigh.

"It's funny," Blays said, staring after one of them. "I've always heard people from climates like this stroll around with everything out to the wind. But these people are as modest as people who *have* to wear clothes."

"Try not to sound *too* disappointed about it."

The road leveled out. Houses and shops surrounded a large square, the center of which held a large building of black and purple stone. Carved columns held up overhangs. At the structure's base, a row of weathered, somber statues gazed out to sea. As Dante watched, a man cocked a metal-headed mallet and slammed it into the side of a statue. With a painful crack, it split in half, tumbling to the clay.

"He's supposed to be doing that, is he?" Blays said.

"The stone," Winden said. "We will need it to rebuild."

She climbed the steps. Arched, doorless entries led to a cool foyer. Four men and two women lay on mats on the stone floor. A woman and a man tended to them, dressing their wounds with redolent poultices, the scent unfamiliar to Dante's nose. Winden spoke to the couple, who eyed Dante, then showed him to a man with a deep gut wound. The foul smell it produced promised he wouldn't live out the week.

The cut on Dante's arm had scabbed, but he'd suffered a few scrapes from the destruction of the house. He used the blood from these to feed the nether and sent the shadows to work. Within moments, the man's wound sealed, leaving nothing but a bright pink line.

As Dante worked on the others, someone called Winden outside. By the time Dante finished treating the wounded, his hands were a little shaky, but after his work on the tunnel in Gallador, he knew his limits very well. He hadn't reached them yet.

"Have you delayed seeing him for long enough?" Blays said. "Or would you like to stop for a beer on the way?"

"I was helping the injured. Good enough? Or is your compassion all for show?"

"I meant a celebratory beer. For your good deeds."

Winden walked back inside and rejoined them. "Your captain. She says that they will go. That they will be back in two weeks. That you will meet them here at the bay then, or they will move on again."

"They're leaving?" Blays glanced toward the building's entrance, which was elevated enough to have a view all the way down to the bay. "Was that part of the plan?"

Dante shrugged. "We don't know how long we'll be here. We can't expect them to stay." He turned to Winden. "We're ready to see him."

"Then we walk." She led them around the back of the building and into the jungle.

There, people rested in a hot springs, easing their muscles after the exertion of the raid. Steam wafted from the waters. The bathers glanced at Winden, then rested their gazes on Dante and Blays.

The path bent to the right. Within a few feet, vines and shrubs grew so densely that someone had had to hack them back, tunneling their way up the hill. Winden drew a long, square-headed knife, chopping at the stray twigs that had already begun to encroach on the trail.

Since making landfall, Dante had been too busy killing strangers and stopping other strangers from dying to let Nak know they'd arrived. As they marched on, Dante touched his brooch to activate his loon.

He felt nothing. Heard nothing. He tried a second time, then a third. He switched the device to allow him to speak to his friend

Mourn instead, but this failed as well. As did every other connection he attempted. Keeping one eye on the clay trail, he sank into the bone that comprised the loon's main functionality. The nether that fueled it was gone.

"My loon," he murmured to Blays. "It's gone dead."

Blays cocked his head. "Gone dead? What, have you been using it too much?"

"I haven't been using it at all."

"Well, you have to use it *sometimes*. Otherwise it'll use itself while you're asleep."

Dante stared, then scowled. "You're disgusting. And this is serious. Is yours working?"

Blays gazed into the distance, muttering to himself as he tested the loon. He shook his head. "Nothing. Has this ever happened before?"

"The only time they go dead is when you use them too long, without allowing their nether to replenish. It's possible we're too far away from the loons they're paired with. The distance could have depleted the nether. Broken them."

"In other words, we're completely on our own here."

Dante stared up at the woman's back. "Looks like."

They climbed on. The trail rolled up and down but did more ascending than descending. Within twenty minutes, the air was notably cooler, though still as warm as an early summer day in Narashtovik. And far more humid. Dante sweated nonstop. Birds hooted and squawked. Insects buzzed everywhere. Dante was soon slapping himself whenever he felt the faintest tickle.

"Who were they?" Blays said. "The people who attacked your town?"

Winden's jaw tightened. "People of the High Tower. Tauren, as we call them. Raiders from the south coast."

"They had swords. Chain mail. Where'd they get it?"

"Raiding. Trade. Wouldn't know."

"Does this happen often?"

She drew a leathery canteen, eyeing him. "It didn't used to. Now it does."

Patches of the trail were staggered like high steps, requiring them to scrabble up the slick clay. After a few minutes, a rhythmic noise began ahead, booming, hissing, and repeating. It sounded like surf, but they were currently a few hundred feet high and at least a mile inland.

Ahead, the sun brightened. Winden came to a stop. Stepping up beside her, Dante squinted against the glare, then gasped, shuffling back from the edge of a cliff. Hundreds of feet below, waves sluiced through a gap, white-headed and roaring. Sixty feet away, the land resumed. The ravine was spanned by a web of ropes.

Blays laughed in disbelief. "I'm to believe a sick old man crossed this?"

"Of course he didn't," Winden said. "Are *we* sick or old? No? Then we will cross. It's much faster."

A set of steps had been hacked into the cliff's edge, leading down to a platform in the rock three feet wide by six across. On it, Winden reached into a wide sack spiked to the wall of the platform and grabbed a carved wooden hook. A thong dangled from a hole drilled through its handle. She tied the cord around her wrist, then secured the hook over the topmost rope and stepped onto the lowermost. As she walked forward, she used her free hand to grab the vertical ropes connecting the upper and lower ones.

Dante observed her methods, then descended to the dug-out platform, took a hook from the bag, and edged out onto the ropes. These swayed beneath his feet, but he adjusted quickly. Far below, the sea crashed and boomed. Dante didn't mind. The crossing took his mind off the destination.

By the time he stepped foot on the solid ground of the other side, Blays hadn't budged. Dante grinned, enjoying the rare opportunity to be the first to have braved something ludicrous.

"Come on!" he called, hands cupped to his mouth. "Or would you rather wait alone in the jungle?"

As if to punctuate this, an animal roared from inland. Blays grimaced, got out a hook, and crossed over.

Safely on the other side, Blays glowered at Winden. "Tell me there's a reason you have him stashed in the forbidden heights."

"It helps the sickness. Not much further."

They walked on. The woods were as thick as before the rope crossing, but where previously the land had rolled up and down, it now progressed in a series of rises and plateaus, as if it had been sculpted into steps by a giant.

As Dante grew winded, they topped another plateau. The ground ahead was clear, a pocket of sunny grass within the shaded forest. A square stone building rested in the clearing. It was smaller than the one in town where he'd healed the people wounded in the raid, but given its remoteness, its presence felt greater, like a hidden temple. They crossed to it. A cool breeze stirred the grass.

"Wait." Winden climbed the three steps to the doorway and entered.

"You ready for this?" Blays said.

"I don't see how I could be." Dante wiped sweat from his brow. "But I'm here."

The woman walked back onto the stoop and nodded. Heart pounding, Dante walked up the steps. The front half was one large room. Though slits were cut in the walls to allow a cross breeze, it was as dim as twilight; after the glare of the tropical sun, he could hardly see a thing.

At the far wall, a figure stirred from a pallet, gingerly propping himself upright. As Dante's eyes adjusted, he gazed on the face of his father.

5

The man was older than he remembered, yet younger than Dante had imagined—late forties, wrinkled around the eyes and mouth, black hair streaked with gray, his beard the white of dirty snow. His face was drawn. A blanket wrapped his shoulders, obscuring his form.

A wave of heat rolled over Dante's body. He had virtually no memories of the man left, and the few he did possess were vague. He supposed, at first, he'd been trying to forget. Better that than to dwell on them, to be constantly reminded that his father had sailed off to the Golden Islands, orphaning Dante to the care of a monk in a sleepy village.

After a few years, however, Dante no longer had to make any effort to leave those memories behind. By the time he found his copy of the *Cycle of Arawn*, and began his journey into the ways of the nether, where he'd come from had become irrelevant. Like clearing your throat before you speak. Or the memory of a dream fading as quickly as you woke up.

The emotions Dante felt on seeing Larsin again were as just as hard to catch on to.

The man's eyes were blue, and though the rest of him was tired and weak, these still bore the shine of life. His voice was a whisper: "You came."

Dante drifted closer to the pallet. "You caught me at a good time."

"I didn't think you would. And I wouldn't have blamed you." His gaze moved to Winden, then Blays. "Where are the others? Those who sought you?"

"Only one of them made it to me. A young woman. She died after delivering your message."

The sick man winced, eyes crinkling. "Sorry to hear that."

Dante stopped beside the low bed. "I hope it was worth it."

He felt for the shadows. After healing the people in the town, his hold on the nether was tenuous, but he wasn't exhausted yet. He should be able to stabilize the man at least. If the work proved difficult, he could finish it tomorrow.

Dante stretched out his hand. "Do you know where your illness came from? Bad air? Old meat? Did you share clothes with someone who was sick?"

"None of the above." The bearded man chuckled, then coughed, his suntanned face paling. "Went somewhere I wasn't supposed to. Like I always do."

"What do you mean?"

"The Stained Cliffs," Winden said. "They're cursed."

"And the act of visiting them causes you to fall ill."

"That's the lore."

Dante maintained a neutral expression. "Know what, it isn't important. Neither are your symptoms. All that matters is that something is wrong and I will make it right."

He closed his eyes and followed the shadows into the man's body. Treating him in this way, it was easy to pretend that the man before him was simply one more in the long line of people Dante had mended. Not to suggest that he was any kind of saint. He had hurt as many as he'd healed. Putting people back together was a type of penance. A way to remind himself that, although effective at it, the nether wasn't made to destroy.

It obeyed its user's wishes. For good or for ill.

He had been causing and healing injuries for a decade. Finding the wrongness inside Larsin was no more difficult than lacing up his boots: it existed in spots across his organs and limbs, dark and opaque. These spots looked and felt like nether—but when Dante tried to move them, they refused to budge.

And when he sent the nether to cleanse them out, he could find no purchase.

Frowning, he withdrew, observed the spots from afar, and tried again. Again, he couldn't so much as make them wobble. They were as slippery as a wet fish, as intangible as sophistry.

He had seen these stains before—inside Riddi, the woman who'd been netherburned. He'd taken them as an odd symptom of the burns. However, attempting to treat a netherburn with more nether actively made the condition worse. In Larsin's case, Dante was unable to do anything at all, for good or for ill. After ten minutes of mental strain, his grasp on the shadows was as clumsy as a dead limb.

He stepped back from the pallet, wiping sweat from his brow. "It's no use. I can't help him."

He turned and walked out of the doorway into the blinding afternoon sun. Speech drifted from the house. Footsteps rustled. Blays joined him in the grass.

"Er," Blays said. "So that's it?"

"I can't help him. It's almost like he's netherburned. Whatever's wrong with him, the shadows can't touch it. I can't believe we came all this way."

"But he's not netherburned, is he?"

"I don't think so. It's odd, though. Riddi had similar symptoms. I assumed the netherburn was what killed her, but maybe it was masking something even deadlier."

"If this is that unfamiliar to you, maybe you're missing something. You can't give up this fast."

Dante untucked his shirt, flapping its hem to dry his sweat. "I tried everything I know. Whatever this is, it's beyond me."

"How odd." Blays folded his arms. "I don't think you've *ever* admitted something's beyond your power. Why are you so quick to give up on this?"

Dante was spared having to respond by Winden, who emerged into the clearing, the steady wind ruffling her brown hair. Around them, bugs were singing, but her face had gone as stolid as a tombstone.

"You can't help him."

Dante shook his head. "I can try again tomorrow. After I've rested. But I'm afraid it won't do any good."

Her eyes dimmed. "This outcome will be disappointing to many."

"Why? Who is he to you? The people he sent to Gask, why did they give up their lives for his?"

"Years ago, when he first came here, he brought the trade back, too. Iron tools and steel blades. For that, he was made part of the family of Kandak. Later, he helped drive off the Tauren, too. He was good to us." Winden tugged the bracer up her left forearm. "But he was no good to you."

Dante snorted. "Are you always this blunt?"

"Do you find it better to hide from truths?"

"The truth is he was neither good nor bad to me. He couldn't be either, because he wasn't there. So guess why I came here?"

"To learn why he left."

He smiled ruefully. "Wrong. I came here to make him well. To show him what I had become without him—and to rub it in his nose."

Winden laughed. "But you couldn't. Good haid."

"Haid?"

"One of our words. It is like..." She gestured as if reeling in string. "When mean feelings are thwarted. You should be happy for the chance to be corrected by your failure. But it only makes you feel worse."

Dante creased his brow. "That's a big concept for a small word."

"Regret, it has many forms. It's important to know the differences." Winden nodded back at the black building. "We stay here tonight. And you will try again in the morning."

Dante had little desire to stay. He had no interest in the explanations or apologies he expected Larsin to start making, especially if it became clear Dante couldn't help him and he was on his deathbed. But between the fighting, the hiking, and the expenditure of all the nether he could safely command, he was exhausted.

Thankfully, Larsin was, too, and slept through the afternoon. Winden passed the remainder of the day beneath a thatched shelter in the trees, grinding roots on a stone table. Dante wandered around the woods examining the insects. There were your typical ants and spiders and such, but most of the species were new to him. Some of the creatures were very slightly new—a perriwen beetle that was iridescent blue rather than matte black—but others had no analog to anything he'd seen, such as the thumb-sized red insect that walked on six tiny snapping claws.

Blays had a rare bout of good sense and left him alone. The sun set, alighting the clouds with red, pink, and orange. Back at the house, Winden fed them a mealy paste. It was spiced with a substance that tasted like the distilled sweetness of fruits, but an underlying brackishness permeated the mush.

As soon as Dante finished, he went to sleep on a pallet in the back room. He slept fitfully, woken twice by Blays and Winden murmuring in the adjoining room. Probably discussing whether he could heal Larsin.

He woke with the dawn. Winden helped Larsin outside to tend to the obligations of nature. After a meal of the leftover paste, Dante returned to the main room and kneeled beside the ailing man's bed.

"Taking another go at me?" Larsin rasped.

Dante nodded. After the night's sleep, the shadows flowed without resistance. He attacked the black stains inside the man from every angle he could think of. Lost in the work, he gave no thought to the individual he happened to be working on.

By mid-morning, with his command slipping, Dante let out a long breath, stood, and walked to the front stoop to sit in the shade.

Winden followed him. "You found nothing."

"I tried everything. Whatever's afflicting him, the nether's no use. What exactly does your lore say about how the disease is contracted?"

"That it comes through visiting the Stained Cliffs. The ground there, it's tainted. When storms stir it, you can get sick."

"Is it contagious?"

She looked down, thinking. "Sometimes it takes people who haven't been near the cliffs, but I think that's when winds and rain flushes the tainted ground into the air or streams. I've never seen anyone tending to the sick fall ill as well."

"And do you know of any potential cures? Even anything to treat the symptoms?"

"There is another option." Winden stared down the mountain slopes to where the sky met the sea. "A plant. It is known to sometimes reverse the wasting sickness."

Dante gawked at her. "Let me get this straight. There *is* a cure. Right here on the island. But instead of going and getting it yourselves, you thought it was a *better* idea to send a team of people on a journey of over two thousand miles—a journey that cost them their lives—to fetch me. And as it turns out, I'm completely useless."

"The cure? It kills the one who takes it as often as it works. Also, getting to it is very dangerous. Can cost more lives than it saves." Winden met his stare. "As for the idea to find you. It wasn't mine. It was his. Make of this what you will."

"No need. I'll ask him myself."

He went back inside. On the pallet, Larsin's eyes were closed, but as Dante approached, he blinked them open, smiling sadly. "It didn't work, did it?"

"I can't help you."

The older man nodded, sinking back into his blankets. "Thanks for trying. It was a big ask."

Dante stood over him. "Do you have anything to say to me?"

"Could I say anything that mattered?"

"I doubt it."

"I don't expect your forgiveness," Larsin said. "I just wanted to see you one last time."

"Selfish to the end."

"I wonder how far the apple has fallen."

"I'm here, aren't I?"

Larsin grimaced, working his way up to his elbows. "I left you with a friend. Someone I trusted. Didn't mean to stay gone—just to fill my pockets with enough silver to see you never went hungry. But life takes its own turns. When I got here, I found I couldn't leave."

"Oh, I've heard. Winden says you're a man of high influence on this island. I'm sure you found it very difficult to give up the first prestige you'd ever found in life."

"You asking why I left you only to help them instead?"

"I *wonder* why I should care."

"You shouldn't. I made my choice to help these people fight for what was theirs. I knew what it would cost me."

Dante ran a hand over his stubble. "What was happening here that these people couldn't handle themselves?"

"The Tauren. Twenty years ago, they were on the verge of enslaving the entire island. Nasty people—they leave their newborns on the slopes for three days to see if they're strong enough to deserve life. Imagine how they treat their enemies." Tired out by so much talk, Larsin rested his head on his blankets. "I convinced the captain of our ship to reopen trade. We brought these people the steel to fight back. Forced the Tauren all the way back to their tower."

"But they're here again. Did they resume their attacks once you grew sick?"

His father shook his head. "The raids started up again two years ago. I discovered our old alliances had decayed too far. I might have been able to revive them, but the sickness stole my strength away. And the Tauren grow stronger by the day."

Dante nodded. When the man said nothing more, he walked outside. Blays stood outside the entrance.

"How much did you hear?" Dante said.

"None. And your insinuation is shocking."

"I can't help him. But Winden says there's something that might help. A plant. Sounds like it will involve travel and personal risk."

"Hmm."

"Hmm what?"

"'Hmm' as in 'I have no opinion what you should do, so consider this grunt my acknowledgement that I was listening.'"

Dante raised a brow. "You're not going to tell me exactly what I should do? I thought that was the basis of our entire friendship."

"You came here," Blays said. "That was the goal."

"Without you spouting moral imperatives at my every decision, I'm like a ship without a rudder." He pinched the bridge of his nose. "Thirteen days until the *Sword of the South* carries us away. I suppose we might as well try to do some good." He glanced back at the temple. "Besides, I have no intention of sticking around here with him."

Winden was nowhere in sight, but a rapping noise pinpointed her spot in the jungle. Dante found her smashing roots with an iron-banded stick.

"This plant of yours," he said. "Let's go find it."

She wiped her hands on a rag, expression the brightest it had been all day. "To town. We will need supplies."

She jogged to the temple, returning a minute later and heading down the pathway toward the bay.

Blays glanced back up the trail. "Who looks after him when you're not here?"

"There are others in Kandak. The town. One will go if asked."

"Who is he to you, anyway?" Dante said.

An unreadable emotion crossed her face and swiftly disappeared. "When I was very young, he saved my life."

"From what?" Blays said. "The raiders?"

"Yes."

She didn't seem inclined to explain further. Dante walked into a cobweb and batted at his own face. "This plant of yours. What makes it so treacherous to get?"

"It only grows near the Tauren's tower. To get there, we will need to cross the Dreaming Peaks. We will have to bring shells for the Dreamers."

"Naturally," Blays muttered.

Her smile was faint, but compared to her normal flintiness, it gleamed like the seas below. "Your land. Does it make sense to outsiders?"

"Certainly," Dante said. "If only because people have heard of it beforehand. There's virtually nothing known in Mallon about the Plagued Islands, but long ago, trade between them wasn't uncommon. What changed?"

Her smile vanished. "Mallon got greedy."

"That would be historically consistent."

"Do you know of the swappers?"

"The islets where you trade goods."

"That was always how we made our deals. Hundreds of years ago, after decades of trading with them, Mallish merchants asked to see our island for themselves. We let them in. We showed them. They left. When they came back? It was with a great fleet."

"They were mapping the place," Blays said. "Checking out what was worth stealing."

Winden swung her heavy-bladed knife through a thorny twig that had grown across the trail in the last day. "And where our defenses lay. They arrived. Invaded. Attacked us with steel. Their treachery, it wasn't enough. We burned their ships. Trapped them on our shores. The fighting, this took months. At the end, every last Mallish man was killed. After? They called the islands 'Plagued.' And trade came to an end."

"We should compare notes. One time, they tried to hang me."

Dante stepped over an oily puddle. "Considering the bad blood, you speak Mallish very well."

"That's your father's work. He came from Mallon. He brought others with him and he knew there would be more. He thought teaching us their language would make them respect us."

"Did it work?"

She thought. "No. But it has made it easier to see through their lies."

At the rope bridge, Blays crossed without complaint. Other than a few mud holes and slick spots, the remainder of the descent was no trouble, and they soon overlooked Kandak. At first, Dante thought the fires were still burning, but this turned out to be nothing more than the steam of the hot springs right outside town.

From above, he saw several black stone structures all but reclaimed by the jungle, hidden within the crush of foliage. Within the city proper, others were placed with no rhyme or reason, even though they were obviously expensive, and should have been clustered in wealthy neighborhoods, or centers of prayer or business. In fact, something about Kandak reminded him of the city of Narashtovik prior to its renaissance: a shadow of itself, a monument to an age of glory long gone.

As they neared the settlement, two men with spears materialized from the brush. Recognizing Winden, they relaxed, settling their spears on their shoulders and launching into what proved to be a lengthy conversation.

"This is driving me crazy," Blays said. "I swear I recognize some of those words."

"Mallish, right? From the traders." Dante flicked a fly off his forearm. "Bet that would make it much easier to learn. Want to try?"

"Gods, no! Learning Gaskan was torture enough. Besides, if I learned to speak Taurish, then you'd expect me to learn how to *write* it."

The sentries padded off on foot. Dante realized he hadn't seen a single horse or beast of burden since coming to the island.

Winden continued forward, looking preoccupied. "We have a problem. We don't have enough shells."

"Then I have some very good news," Blays said. "It turns out you live on an ocean."

"Shaden shells. The raiders, that's what they came for. We'll need them to pass through the Dreaming Peaks."

Dante cocked his head. "These are currency?"

"To dream, they eat a certain plant. The plant is poison. The antidote is the shaden."

"And these are difficult to obtain?"

"Very."

"Here's an idea," Blays said. "We get a boat. Then use this ocean of yours to sail around the peaks to wherever the hell the plant *we* need grows."

Winden favored him with a sour look. "The Current would destroy us. And it's too strong to paddle back against. Even if the boats made it down, we'd have to travel overland to return."

"So how do we get these shaden of yours?"

"This matter? Leave it to me."

In Kandak, men drew wagons down the streets, the beds heavy with lengths of the knobby, bamboo-like wood. Stone-headed hammers clonked against wood—women were bashing down burned timbers from houses damaged in the raid while men loaded the rubble into wheelbarrows and carted it away. The air smelled like baked shellfish, roasted fruit, and the root paste they'd eaten at the temple. On their way to the shore, they passed several people carrying baskets of food to those cleaning up the mess.

Soft waves rolled up the sand. The bay was even busier than the cleanup. While men hauled in nets of fish, clams, and mussels, women sanded down wide-bodied canoes. A crew of men struggled with an iron anchor, wrestling it into a waiting canoe that looked far too small to need such a weight. Presumably, it was to stand against the Currents.

Nearby, a thatched roof was suspended between four tall posts, providing shade for sailors and fishers who needed a break. Winden brought them beneath it. "Here. Stay."

She walked down the sand without another word. Blays watched her go. "She's lucky I'm housebroken."

They plunked down on a bench of red hardwood. The townsfolk glanced at them, then went back to their work. A man scraping the bones of some large mammal looked their way repeatedly. Like many of the men, his head was shaved. He was in his mid-twenties and he had a mean scar on his throat. After some vigorous carving and sanding, he rinsed his hands in the surf, then padded into the shade of the thatch.

"Mallon?" His accent was much thicker than Winden's.

"Sort of," Blays said.

The man frowned. "Sort of?"

"By birth," Dante said. "Not by choice."

"You're here. Why?"

Dante glanced down the shore, but there was no sign of Winden. "We're going on a journey. We need shaden."

The man's face brightened. "Shaden? I have shaden."

"Larsin Galand," Blays said. "Do you know him?"

"Yes. A great man."

"Yeah, but I hear his son is a lackwit, unable to lace his own boots. Anyway, we're here to help Mr. Galand. Any shaden you can spare us would be of great assistance."

The man shook his head. "No gift. Will trade." He tapped the scabbard on Blays' right hip. "Steel?"

Blays drew the straight-bladed sword, turning it side to side. "This was my father's. I wouldn't trade it for all the shaden in the sea."

"Ah." He pointed at Dante's sheath. "Yours? Also from your father?"

Blays burst out laughing. Dante couldn't help smiling. "My father's still asking favors of *me*. But I can't trade my sword, either. I find myself needing it too often."

"So the swords are a no," Blays said. "Fortunately, I brought some travel-sized models as well." He tugged up the leg of his trouser and produced a knife with a nine-inch blade. He held it out to the young man. "How many shaden is this worth to you?"

The man took the blade and flicked its edge. After some fiddling and prodding, he held the knife to his ear, gazing out to sea.

"Its song is..." He waggled his hand side to side. "For this. two shaden."

Blays gave Dante a look, which Dante quickly sorted from the catalogue of Blays Looks. This one was skeptical, but not overly so, with a softness to the eyes indicating mild enthusiasm, and a crook of the mouth showing self-aware amusement. If Dante was interpreting it correctly, Blays thought the man was trying to take advantage of them, but not in a spectacularly outrageous way. Furthermore, Blays seemed to be indicating that even if they *did* get screwed, it wouldn't be a big deal. Presumably because it was only a knife.

Of course, they could have had this exchange in Gaskan and their ostensible trade partner would have been none the wiser. But that would have made them look shifty.

"Two?" Blays said. "I can't part with *this* knife for less than Four."

"Not four. This knife, it doesn't sing. It..." The man gestured, searching for a word, then he began to hum.

"It doesn't hum! It sings like a soprano in the Odeleon of Bressel. Four."

He sighed through his nose. "Three. No more."

Blays crossed his arms, brows bent, then nodded. "I can't believe I'm agreeing to this robbery. Fine. Three it is."

The man hesitated, then nodded. "Get shaden. Wait."

He loped off. Dante watched him go. "We're sure that was a good deal?"

"He agreed. So probably not. But it's only a knife."

"And you probably have nineteen more of them on the left side of your body alone."

Blays shifted on the bench. "Let's just say you wouldn't want to hug me."

Within two minutes, the man with the scarred throat returned bearing a small sack made of pale leather. He loosened the drawstring and withdrew a black shell. It spiraled tightly, small spikes sticking from its curls.

"Shaden," the man said. "Very good."

Blays took it and made a show of inspecting it, hefting it in his palm, then stepping into the sun and holding it up to the light. "Bit small, don't you think?"

"No. Very good."

He showed them the other two. They smelled very faintly of old rot. They seemed to be intact. Dante took one down to the water, approached a woman tending a net, and after a brief, gesture-filled talk, confirmed it was a shaden. He returned to Blays and the scarred man and they exchanged goods. The man smiled, bowed, and walked off, jabbing his new knife at the air.

He'd hardly been gone five minutes when a young woman joined them in the shade. Sun-blond strands streaked her light brown hair, which was braided in tight plaits and tied behind her head.

"Shaden?" she said.

Blays rose with a smile. "We're happy to trade. What've you got and what would you like?"

Over the course of a lengthy haggling session, she convinced Dante to part with his belt (which had a large silver buckle and steel studs) in exchange for two shells. The bartering drew a small crowd, several of whom were also looking to swap. By the time Winden walked up the sand toward them, they had collected thirteen shaden.

She eyeballed the lingering townsfolk. "What is going on here?"

"We're making your life easier." Blays lifted the two pale sacks of shaden, jingling them. "Thirteen shells."

"You got shaden?" She grabbed one of the sacks and plucked out a shell. She lifted it and stared into its hollow mouth. "How?"

"This isn't our first time in foreign lands. We know how to get around."

"You fools. These shells. They're worthless."

"But they're shaden," Dante said. "I made sure of it."

She tossed the shell at his chest. "These are shaden shells. The Dreamers, they need the *meat*."

Blays' mouth fell open. "I don't mean to alarm you. But it appears you live amongst a society of thieves."

Dante glared at the townsfolk, who'd begun retreating rapidly. "We traded for these. You have to get our goods back. I traded my belt."

"And my third-favorite knife!"

"This is not possible," Winden said.

"But they cheated us," Dante said. "Look, they're right over there."

She shook her head sharply. "This is not cheating. This is tonen. The Sweet Lie."

"The Sweet Lie?" Blays said.

"The lie that tastes better than truth. You swallowed it. So you are to blame for what comes after."

"Well, that's rude. No wonder no one likes to come visit you all."

"In your land, you always tell the truth?"

"Sure. Except to our magistrates, tax collectors, and in-laws. But when it comes to trading—particularly with people who are trying to help us—there's a certain expectation of *not* skinning each other alive."

"The truth is whatever tastes best," she said. "If you prefer a lie, it would be cruel to give you something bitter. This is how it is done."

Dante muttered a curse. "You might have told us that."

"I told you to wait. Not to trade."

"At the very least, you have to admit it's confusing to refer to shaden as 'shells' when it's what's inside the shells that matters."

"Everyone knows what is meant by this." She sighed in annoyance. "I have more left to do. Try not to get skinned again."

She stalked away. Dante gave Blays a look.

"Like this is *my* fault?" Blays dropped back to the bench. "You were so eager to deal I'm surprised you didn't trade them one of your balls."

"I think they got those anyway."

Blays gazed out at the people hauling nets, launching boats, and slicing up mussels. "They may be filthy, thieving liars. But they sure are hard workers."

"Don't observe their honest labor directly, your mind will be overcome by its strangeness." The waves washed the shore. A breeze blew past them, ruffling the ragged leaves of the roof. "You know, I'd like to be angry about this. But it's just too damn nice out."

It was close to an hour before Winden returned. She bore two bags on her shoulders and an impatient look on her face. "We leave."

Blays stood, planting his hands on the small of his back and stretching backwards. "You'll be happy to know we were perfect guard dogs in your absence. I may have even bit a kid."

"You are terrible at this. The essence of a good lie is that other people want to believe it."

As she made to go, an older man approached her and spoke briefly. Winden looked annoyed, but that seemed to be her resting state. The man scampered down to the shore, rummaged through a bag, and returned with a bone flute. He put it to his mouth, eyes downcast, and began to play.

The tune was mournful. Yearning. Winden nodded toward the road they'd taken in and walked away from the beach. As Dante fell in behind her, the flutist was joined by a second, then a third.

"What are they doing?" Blays whispered.

"The song of going," Winden said. "It is always played before a journey. So if you die, the gods will know you were loved."

"Well that's nice."

"It's tonen. Another lie."

She didn't slow down until they'd hiked out of town. The canopy enfolded the path, dousing them in welcomed shade. After a few hundred yards, she took a fork in the trail, heading west of the slopes where Dante's father lay in the temple.

He found he felt very little for the man. It had simply been too long. Dante had assumed he'd died long ago. Perhaps that had been tonen—a sweet lie, better to believe than the unknown truth—but it meant Dante had also made his peace long ago. And while he believed Larsin had wanted in part to see Dante one last time before dying, Dante thought his father had primarily summoned him to the island because he believed Dante was the only one capable of curing him of his sickness.

Even so, Dante was happy enough to try to find the plant that might help him. Not for Larsin's sake. But for that of the people in Kandak. They deserved the chance to live free of the Tauren raiders. Since learning to use the nether, Dante had hurt countless people with it. But he'd also used it to free far, far more of them. If he could mend whatever was wrong with Larsin, and allow him to help his adoptive people to fight back, then Dante would leave the island with no regrets.

They spoke little. The trail degraded quickly, with some portions so washed-out and steep they had to detour through the shrubs. It was so warm that Dante had been toying with the idea of cutting his trousers off at the knee, but after struggling through a patch of oozing orange thorns, he was glad he'd left his clothes intact.

After one such detour, they stopped on the path to drink and catch their breath. Dante got a rag from his pack and wiped off the worst of his sweat. "How far is the march to the Dreamers?"

"Three days," Winden said. "If we can keep up this pace."

"And from there?"

"Two days more. Don't worry. We'll be back before your boat."

"You said the trip's dangerous," Blays said. "Anything we should watch out for?"

She tucked her hair behind her ear. "Snakes. Spiders. Floods. Quicksand. Cotters. The Tauren. Poisonous thorns—"

"I thought you were supposed to lie to me in situations like this. Maybe it would be faster to list the things that *won't* try to kill us."

Winden considered this. "Me."

She moved on. Within minutes, the ground leveled out. Worn black stones jutted from the ground. Most were all but hidden in ivy, moss, and brambles, but the visible portions were straight, squared off. The walls of buildings. The path led through the middle of the ruins, but Winden diverted around them into the jungle.

"What was this place?" Dante said.

"Destroyed by the Mallish during the old wars." Winden made a sweeping gesture above her brow. "It should be left in peace."

Even the birds seemed to agree, going quiet as the three of them skirted around what remained of the city. It took ten minutes to bypass it. A minute after they'd gone by the last building, the ruins faded behind them, lost to the jungle.

"These plants of yours," Blays said. "What do they look like?"

Winden paused to pluck burrs from the straps of her sandals. "We won't see them here."

"Yes, and if you won't tell me what to look for, *I* won't notice them even if they start growing out of my nose."

"Molbry. A red flower. Small, with two petals like the ears of a rabbit. Grows in the shade of the waterfalls on the southeast side of the island."

"Wonderful." Blays stooped low, examining the foliage alongside the crooked trail through the clay. "So all we need to do is find a flower shaped like a foxhound. Then it can do the hunting for us."

Late that afternoon, rain pattered the leaves of the canopy. Within a minute, the sprinkle transformed into a deluge. Dante strung a tarp between the branches and crouched beneath it. The storm blew itself out within twenty minutes, but it left the ground sticky and sodden. Dante's boots soaked through. He doubted they'd make three more miles before the overcast skies darkened toward night.

At day's end, they made camp beneath a tree that was twice as wide as it was tall. Its leaves grew in such greedy profusion that the ground around its trunk was almost dry. They ate another meal of root paste. With the hour no later than seven o'clock, Winden dug into her bag, removing several finger-shaped bulbs covered in rough skin. With a series of quick flicks, she peeled the skin away, then used her flint to light two bulbs. They burned with a soft, steady light and the smell of camphor. With the candlefruit providing light, they spent two hours gathering and preparing san root, then slept.

The rain returned in the night. In the morning, the air was damp and cool, warming within minutes from the rising sun. As Dante walked downhill from camp, a small golden-furred creature flung itself through the branches. Its limbs were long and loopy and its eyes bulged like melons. Rather than paws, it had hands—on its back legs as well as its front. As it dangled from a branch by its tail, shelling a nut with its front teeth, Dante finally understood how far away he was from everything he knew.

Throughout the morning, the terrain continued to rise, until streams of mist rolled through the trees, condensing and falling like fat, inconstant raindrops. Late that morning, they ascended from the mist and found themselves at the edge of a cliff overlooking a shallow, tree-choked valley miles and miles long. Scores of rocky plateaus jutted up from the sea of vegetation.

Winden moved to a squat tree. Two ropes, one fat and one thin, stretched from the cliffs to the branches of a tree a hundred yards away. Winden pulled in the lighter rope hand over hand. A length of wood emerged from the branches of the lower tree, straps dangling from its underside. Beyond the connecting tree, another length of rope carried on for hundreds of feet, forming the second link in a chain that appeared to span the entire valley.

"Oh no," Blays said. "This is going to be even worse than the bridge, isn't it?"

"The Broken Valley," Winden said. "Full of cliffs. Falls. Ravines. You can spend days hacking your way across its floor. Or you can spend an hour soaring over its roof."

"Is there an option to nap in its bed?"

"Sure. When you land after the rope breaks."

She reeled in the length of wood, which looked distressingly like handlebars, and tied a sturdy strap around her left elbow and wrist. Gripping the handles in each hand, she moved to the edge of the cliff and stepped off.

She whisked along the rope, hair streaming behind her. Dante laughed out loud. Blays looked pale. After her swift initial descent, the rope line leveled out and she slowed, coasting. She made landfall on a wooden platform, brushed herself off, then hauled on the rope, returning the handlebar to the upper cliff.

From the trees at the edge of the drop, a family of the small golden creatures emerged, oversized eyes blinking, dangling from the branches by their tails and hands.

"Great," Blays muttered. "And now we have an audience."

"What's the big deal?" Dante said. "Normally, you collect death-defying experiences like a child collects bugs."

"Then heights are the equivalent of those bugs who eat shit." The handlebars arrived, rocking side to side. Blays grabbed for them and tied the strap around his left arm using the most secure knot they'd ever learned at sea. He shuffled up to the cliff's edge, scowling so hard it looked like his face might break free of its moorings with a rubbery clap. "If I die, I want you to bag up whatever's left of me and bring it to Minn. I know she hasn't had enough of me yet."

"Would you like me to reanimate you, too?"

Blays closed his eyes and hopped into the void. The rope tensed under his weight. He swooshed along it, slowing as it grew horizontal. At the platform, Winden steadied his landing. He unstrapped and heaved on the rope, returning the handlebars to Dante. Dante tied the strap around his arm, took a deep breath, and let himself fall from the cliff.

His stomach surged into his throat. His eyes watered; the wind rushed past him so fast he couldn't breathe. But it streaked through his hair, too, and his heart beat like the hooves of a galloping deer. Too soon, he found his feet skidding across the platform.

Fortunately for his inner thrill-seeker, this was only one leg in a trip of dozens. It wasn't until his fourth ride that he found the poise to take proper stock of his surroundings. The trees supporting the ropes grew from high islands of rock separated from each other by channels of empty space. These channels ran at least fifty feet deep. Within their heavy shade, Dante glimpsed green vines, trickling streams, and jagged rocks. The trees bearing the ropes added another twenty to fifty feet of distance to the bottom.

They advanced platform by platform. Between having to make three individual crossings per plateau, including the time spent returning the handlebars and strapping in, their overall progress was somewhere around walking speed. Even so, this was infinitely faster than trying to navigate the channels.

Winden crossed to the next platform. Blays followed, then hauled on the rope, returning the handlebars to Dante. Dante tied himself to them and swung off the little island of rock.

With a bow-like twang, the rope snapped. Dante's guts lurched as he plunged downward. Beneath him, branches rose to meet him like a field of spears.

6

He sliced downward through the warm air. Years ago, chasing arcane secrets around the tree-city of Corl, he'd fallen from a much higher elevation than this. He'd saved himself by softening the earth and plunging into it like water. Here, though, he plummeted toward dozens of branches. He was about to be gored and thrashed. His only hope rested in staying lucid enough during the aftermath to heal himself before he bled to death.

Something hissed through the air. A vine appeared from nowhere, stringing across his upper chest. He jolted, slowing. The vine snapped and he resumed his fall. He hadn't traveled five more feet before he was arrested again, this time by three vines which tangled around his shoulders and waist. Dante dangled there a moment, reassuring himself this wasn't some perverse trick, then grabbed hold of the vines, tied one around the rope he'd used to replace his stolen belt, and climbed up the others to the thick branch they were hanging from.

Over on the platform, Blays gaped. Winden leaned against the trunk of the tree, bracing herself as if overcome by Dante's near death. Dante scooted along the branch toward the trunk, then climbed down to the ground.

Blays rushed over to him, grabbing his shoulders. "Those

vines came for you like you owed them money! How did you do that?"

"I didn't do anything." Dante nodded at Winden. "She did."

Blays cocked his head. "Winden. And I thought you were only here for your sunny disposition."

She moved toward the edge of the rock and stared at the next platform two hundred feet away. "The rope. It's broken. We have to figure out how to cross."

"That won't be a problem," Dante said. "You know what is, though? You being able to do something I've never even heard of before, then trying to act like nothing happened."

"I'm not responsible for your ignorance. How do we get down?"

"My plan was to use my awe-inspiring powers. But that would be pretty dumb of me if you're capable of growing a vine between this tree and the next one."

She thrust her jaw forward. "Everything that you can do, have you told me of it? High Priest Galand?"

"I'm starting to think I should. We're out here in the wild. Our survival might depend on knowing what we're all capable of doing. So I'll start. I'm a skilled nethermancer. I can harm and heal. Create light and darkness. I can reshape dirt and rock. I can see through the eyes of the dead. And if we ever find ourselves really, really bored, I can make a troupe of dead rats stand up and dance."

Blays lifted his hand. "I can disappear. Walk through stone walls, too. Impressive, I know, but I must warn you: I'm already married."

"I am a Harvester," Winden said. "And you have just seen what I can do."

"Grow things? Then why not start with that molbry flower we're after?"

"I can only grow what is already there." She gestured toward the next island. "I can't simply string a vine between here and there. I wouldn't trust it to hold us. But we can use one to climb down, and another to come up."

She tipped back her head. A few feet above their heads, a vine detached from the high branches, nosing forward like a snake. It lowered itself to the ground and slithered over the side of the cliff.

Dante kneeled on the rocky edge and watched the vine disappear into the shrubs clinging to the almost vertical slopes. "Are there many of you?"

"Very few. So my people will appreciate it if you would not get me killed."

Blays nodded, got a look on his face, and burst into laughter. "Hang on a second. I think she just said something funny."

Once she'd extended the vine to the bottom of the defile, Winden led the way down. The face of the rock wasn't completely vertical, and though it would have been highly dangerous to descend without their makeshift rope, there were enough holds for her to pick her way down.

"Have you ever heard of anything like that?" Blays said. "These Harvesters?"

Dante shook his head. "Never. But it makes a certain amount of sense. The nether resides in all living things. What she's doing isn't so different from when I make a body regrow from its wounds."

"Oh boy. You're going to spend the rest of the trip trying to figure this out, aren't you?"

"The thought had crossed my mind."

Winden called from below. Dante made his way down. The bottom of the ravine was so densely filled with shrubs, thorns, and dead branches that he gave up any thoughts of trying to cross the entire valley from below. At the next island, Winden crawled another vine up to its top. They ascended to its surface, spent a very long time inspecting the rope there, and continued on their way.

By early afternoon, they stood on the far side of the valley, having suffered no further mishaps. More heights rose ahead. That meant climbing, but after his experience with the rope, Dante was happy with any method of travel that kept his feet in contact with the ground.

"What if you had died in the fall?" Winden said as they hiked up what appeared to be a game trail. "What would have happened to you?"

"I imagine," Dante said, "I would have gotten very bloated. And very discolored. And then been devoured by insects until I was nothing but bones and hair."

"Not your body. Your spirit. Your god, Arawn—he is a god of death. He must be hungry for your soul."

He shook his head vehemently. "That's nothing but Mallish propaganda. An attempt to discredit him. We all die in time. Why would Arawn be in some special hurry?"

"Do not get him started on this," Blays said. "Not unless you want a nine-hour sermon on all the ways Mallon has distorted the holy message of the guy who gave us pestilence, famine, and beheadings."

"I don't give sermons. And it's not about clearing Arawn's reputation. It's about letting people worship as they please without fear of getting strung up for it."

"This hike," Winden said. "It's long. And it's boring. So I don't care if it takes nine hours to explain. I want to know where Arawn sends you when you die."

Dante glanced up at the sky. It was hard to see through the leaves, but it was dimming as gray clouds mounted against the peaks ahead.

"A hill under the stars," he said. "Where you join him in the hereafter."

"This is a reward? What about those who did wrong? Bad people?"

"They go there, too."

"That can't be. This must be a trick. A lie."

Dante ran his forearm across his brow, which had grown grimy during the tree crossings. "To accomplish what?"

"To deal justice to those who deserve it."

"Not having visited the place, I couldn't say. But if he's looking to trick us, you'd think he could come up with something more enticing than a hill beneath the stars."

"I died once," Blays said. "It was nice. Scenic. No fancy hills or stars, though."

Dante swatted at a fly. "Is that what happens when you die, Winden? You're brought forth to be judged?"

She nodded, glancing down as a small pink lizard scampered off a rock and into the brush. "Brought to Kaval to tell the story of your life. But there is a problem. Living can only be done by hurting others. So all are guilty."

Blays made a face. "Some kind of universal exemption seems in order, then."

"There is a loophole. Kaval lives in his world, not ours. How is he to know what's true about our lives and what isn't? When you face him, you tell him tonen, the Sweet Lie. That you were not so bad. That you deserve mercy. If the lie is convincing enough, he will spare you. Send you to sail through the Worldsea."

"And what happens if you're judged to be a jerk?"

"Then you are chained to the Rock. Where your ancestors are gathered to watch your shame as you are torn apart by the birds and the crabs for 180 years. Then you are made whole again, to witness the tearing apart of your descendants."

"That sounds…extreme."

"This is why we practice tonen all our lives."

To match the mood in the air, rain began to sprinkle the canopy. Dante lowered his head and tried to ignore the percussive droplets on his crown. "Your language. Will you teach it to me?"

"Why?" Winden said. "You leave here in twelve days."

"Which means that for the next twelve days, you're our only way to communicate. With people who appear to be professional liars. If we're separated, or you get hurt, we could find ourselves in deep trouble."

"Our language is for ourselves. Outsiders have no claim to it." She was quiet for a moment. "Why are you here?"

"You know that. To save my father."

"You barely saw him. You ask no questions about him. It's obvious you care nothing for him."

"You're right. I came here because I would have regretted it if I didn't. If he had been all I'd found here, I doubt if I'd be hunting flowers with you now."

"What else did you find?"

"People who, despite their fondness for scamming strangers, seem peaceful. Who deserve to live free of the threat of constant violence. If I can help give that to them, then I'll leave here happy I came."

She pressed her lips together. "I'll teach you. But if someone asks, it wasn't me. You will lie."

She started at once. The language was called Taurish, named for the raiders, who were said to be the island's first inhabitants. Over the years, Dante had tackled several foreign languages, but soon found Taurish to be the easiest he'd encountered. Structurally, its only major difference from Mallish was that it tended to place the subject of the sentence at the very beginning, or even to isolate that subject as a chopped-up sentence of it own, which explained Winden's occasionally curious Mallish grammar.

Besides that, though, Taurish was very intuitive. Learning a conversational vocabulary was going to take far more time than he had, but by the time they made camp that night, he was already able to form simple sentences.

In the morning, they resumed the march. A single mountain loomed ahead, abutted by a lower shoulder that Winden confirmed was the Dreaming Peaks. Within an hour, the jungle thinned to a tree-studded veldt. A few hundred yards to their east, the land fell away in a series of sheer cliffs. A mile below, the sea shimmered and tossed. When the wind was right, Dante could hear the surf booming.

Streams trickled through the grass. Soon, there were no trees at all. Small pools of water blistered the rocks, steaming and churning, the vapors smelling of bad eggs. The banks of the pools were encrusted with blue, red, and yellow crystals.

Ahead, the eastern edge of the land bulged up into spires of naked rock. A trail was worn through the grass, leading straight to the pass between the spires and the mountain to their right. Cresting it, they looked down on the ruins of a city.

"Can't imagine why they abandoned *this* place," Blays said. "The location is so convenient."

"It's not abandoned." Winden withdrew a small bone flute from her pouch. She blew three quick notes. They seemed to linger on the air longer than they should.

After a minute, a man appeared at the fringe of the ruins. He carried a tall staff and wore a purple robe the exact shade as the ever-present clay; it must have been dyed with it. He stopped ten feet from them and spoke a few words that Dante couldn't catch.

Winden replied. After a brief conversation, she took off her pack, kneeled, and withdrew a shiny black box. The man lifted the lid and withdrew a shaden, water dripping from its black shell. He put it back in the box and tucked the box under his arm, then gestured down the path.

"We proceed," Winden said. "Don't speak to anyone. No matter what they say or do."

The man in the purple robe led the way. Winden continued to speak to him. Dante hardly understood any of it, but heard one word repeated: Tauren.

Crumbled walls rose to the sides of the street. Five minutes later, Dante hadn't seen a single soul. He didn't smell wood smoke or any of the general miasma associated with permanent human habitation. A white crow perched on a crumbling wall, raucously criticizing them as they passed. To the right, a solitary woman tended rows of orange flowers.

From their left, the spires of rock veered closer, channeling the ruins into a narrow canyon. The way ahead was blocked by a high wall in better repair than anything they'd seen so far. The path led straight to an entry in its side. There, the man in purple swept aside a shaggy-haired pelt hanging over the doorway, leading them into a cavernous chamber with twenty-foot ceilings.

Bodies stretched from wall to wall.

They lay on thin pallets, eyes closed. The nearest of them, a middle-aged woman, was breathing evenly, yet even with the rise and fall of her chest, she looked more like she was dead than asleep. There were perhaps forty of the sleeping people in all, dressed as simply as the fishermen in Kandak. Candlefruit glowed on black stone pedestals. Despite the height of the ceiling, the room felt close, smelling faintly of sweat and something floral, along with the pungent odor of the burning fruit. Down the way, another man in a purple robe trimmed a sleeping man's unruly beard with a pair of silver scissors.

Something jabbed Dante in the side. He whirled on Blays, then grabbed his rope belt to restrain his fist from flying into Blays' face. Winden walked down the middle of the room and Dante hurried after. The man in purple carried the box of live shaden off to a side room. Winden continued forward. Ahead, daylight peeped around a hide draped over the exit.

As Dante neared it, a woman sat bolt upright on her pallet. Her eyes blazed from the pallid sheen of her face, locking on his.

"De tregen!" she yelled. Tears streamed down her cheeks. She lunged at Dante, hands outstretched like claws, but her legs gave out and she spilled to the floor, jaw hitting with a crack.

Dante moved to help her. Winden grabbed his upper arm. Across the room, the man with the scissors stood, gathered the folds of his robe, and swished toward them. He took the woman by the shoulder and poured a viscous fluid down her throat. Winden hauled Dante outside.

"What are the monks doing in there?" he said.

She walked down the grass-dotted clay. "What they have to."

"Really? Because it looks like they're keeping them unconscious."

"Those people? They're the luckiest ones on the island."

"Here's my question," Blays said. "Why'd we have to use shells to bribe our way through? The way those guys are snoozing, we could have cartwheeled through here and they'd never have known."

She glanced around them, but they were alone again. "I don't know why I'm telling you this. Where we go when we die. Do you remember what I said?"

"Despite trying very hard not to."

"The Dreamers. When they eat the flower, they sink deeper than sleep. To the brink of death. Once they are there, they fight to rescue those who Kaval damned to be torn by the birds and the crabs."

"They're saving souls?" Blays said. "How does Kaval feel about their efforts to defy his will?"

Winden shrugged. "The Dreamers, most spend their lives here. Some die without saving a single one of the damned. Even Kaval respects their dedication. For us? There is no higher calling than to free those who have been burdened. That is why we bring the shells. Shaden treats the poison they take in order to enter the Dream. They do our holiest work. It is our duty to support them."

A cold wind ran down from the peak. Dante tugged up his collar. "What was the old woman saying? 'He forgives'?"

"Kaval must have freed one of the damned. A rare event."

"Do they ever visit the dead? Speak to them?"

"So they say." She stepped around a length of masonry that had fallen across the unpaved road. "For what the Dreamers do, the Tauren leave them alone. But the monk I spoke to said the raiders have been more active than ever. We'll have to be far more careful from now on."

The land before them widened out. To their right, a stream cut down from the cloud-swept mountain, gashing a frothy, white channel eastward, then spilling over the cliffs. A wooden bridge spanned the roiling waters. Within minutes of crossing it, they were back in the wilderness, with no sign the island had ever contained anything else.

As they descended the southern face of the Dreaming Peaks, Dante got a clear look at the way ahead. The island, as far as he could make out—and Winden confirmed this—was essentially two land masses, bridged by the peaks. The southern lobe was roughly circular, with jungle on its higher east side, savannah on the lower central regions where the Tauren held sway, and a scrubby desert on its west.

The molbry flowers grew in the lower elevations of the southeast jungle. Particularly around a formation called the Bloodfalls, which Dante dearly hoped was just a historical name. Winden set a relentless pace, breaking from the jungle wherever possible to strike out across the grassy middle of the southlands. When questioned, she seemed less worried about them missing their return trip on the *Sword of the South* and more concerned that Larsin Galand wouldn't survive to see their return.

To try to save two days, she intended to stop in to see the Shigur, who lived on the way to the Bloodfalls and might have the molbry flowers on hand. On the way, she continued to teach Dante the Taurish language. Once, they saw white smoke pluming from the coast where the Tauren held a village under siege. After that, Dante used the nether to kill a handful of jungle rodents (rats with long, powerful back legs like jackrabbits), then used the shadows to revive them, bonding his eyes to theirs. He sent them loping ahead to scout for Tauren warriors. A part of him wanted to recruit some of the four-handed, golden-furred tree creatures—Winden claimed they were a species of monkey—but he couldn't bring himself to hurt them.

On the second day, his undead scouts spied three men in the jungle carrying bows and spears. Long bone daggers hung from their hips, curved like scythes, serrated on one edge. When he described these to Winden, she identified them as coming from sawteeth, a species of shark that swam around with their mouths always open. Along with these, the warriors wore dark hoods. Winden said they were wandren, people attached to no particular clan or settlement who roamed the island as traders. In desperate times, they often turned criminal or sold their services to raiders. Wary of being betrayed to the Tauren, Winden cut a wide berth around them.

The morning of the third day, as their jungle trek continued, they came before a matted wall of branches and thorns eight feet high. Red-striped hornets as big as Dante's thumb lumbered between the flowers growing from the kudzu. They diverted around it. Dante sent his rat scouts bounding ahead. Five minutes later, he still hadn't found a gap in the growth, but for some reason, Winden was smiling.

"What are you so happy about?" Dante said. "The fortress of thorns in our way? Or the kitten-sized wasps guarding it?"

She gestured at the brambles. "This wall. Does it look natural to you?"

"Not especially. But neither does the island's perpetual summer. Or those golden monkeys that keep following us around."

"This is new. It must have been put here by the Shigur."

Blays examined the wall. "Well, their tactical error was making these plants out of wood. That blade of yours should be through it in a minute."

"You think they'll be eager to trade with us after we've torn down their defenses?"

"If they get mad, remind them their wall will regrow on its own."

"Grow a vine over it," Dante said. "We don't have time to spend all day hunting for a gate."

After a moment's thought, she did just that. Ten minutes later, the three of them stood on the other side of the wall, picking burrs and thorns from each other's clothing and hair. The forest inside the wall was significantly thinner than the jungle outside it. Almost every one of the trees bore fruit of some kind, few of which Dante recognized.

"If you see someone," Winden said. "Stop. Let yourself be known."

She'd no sooner said this than a young man appeared a hundred yards ahead. He froze, gaped at them, then turned and ran.

Winden halted. "We wait here."

A great number of birds flitted around the trees, snapping up any bug that attempted to land on the fruit. Blays left his blades sheathed, hands folded over his stomach. Dante pulled the nether closer. Where the young man had run off, five warriors emerged, approaching them. They were armed with spears, at least two of which bore metal tips. Two of the soldiers were men and three were women, but they all wore the same purple-trimmed yellow tunics. After a conversation Dante could almost but not quite follow, the warriors escorted them to a trail through the trees.

After a few hundred yards, the fruit trees fell away. Lone trees stood isolated from each other among patches of manicured grass. These trees were graceful, trunks rising like the necks of swans. They were bent downward at the tips, each one burdened by an enormous seed pod. Long, narrow ovals, the smallest were three feet in length, with some upwards of twenty. The largest were supported by scaffolds erected around them.

Blays nudged his shoulder. "Do those look like bananas to you?"

"Oh yeah," Dante said. "Especially the part where they're as long as a house."

"Those aren't bananas," Winden said. "Look."

She pointed to the left. Beneath an open-walled thatched roof, four people swarmed around the shell of a nut that was thirty feet long if it was an inch. It had been split in half along the seam. Two workers scrubbed dark brown fiber from the outside of the shell while two others scraped the interior.

Dante craned his neck. "Is that a *boat*? Like you have in Kandak?"

Winden smiled faintly. "Shigur. Boat-Growers. The ships they make are seamless. Hard as rock but as light as bamboo. Finest on the island."

"They grow boats. On trees."

"Wait until you see their houses."

Just as Dante began to glimpse them—they were round and onion-roofed, and though they were asymmetrical, that only made them look more solid—a woman moved to intercept them, accompanied by four more armed locals. She wore a leaf-like green cape that tapered to a point. As she neared, Dante saw it *was* a leaf, clasped around the neck by a thin curling vine like a pea plant.

Winden offered a greeting, which Dante understood, then said a lot of words he didn't. There was much gesturing, particularly to the southwest. The direction of the Tauren.

"We have bad news," Winden said. "This woman is a Harvester. They have no molbry flowers and know of none between here and the falls."

Dante folded his arms. "I suppose it would be too much to hope to catch a break at some point."

"Also, they were attacked. By the Tauren. Some died. Others maimed."

"All right," Blays said. "That's slightly more tragic than not being able to find a flower."

Winden glanced at Dante sidelong. "Would you help them?"

"Why?" Dante said. "Not to say I won't. But is there some reason you want me to do this?"

"The Tauren. If they keep pressing, we won't be able to fight them by ourselves. We'll need every ally we can get."

The woman wearing the leaf-cape gazed at him steadily. Dante inclined his head to Winden. "Tell her I'll do anything I can."

The two women spoke briefly. The woman in the cape gestured Dante on, leading them into town past the round houses, which appeared to have been grown from the ground. In different circumstances, he might have marveled at this, but he was too busy being led into one of the black stone buildings that speckled the entire island. Inside, three people lay on pallets. Each was in the fetal position, right arms clenched to their chest. Their wrists terminated in wads of bloody bandages.

Dante unwrapped the rags from the wrist of an unconscious man. The blood was rusty, at least a day old, and the rags clung to the dried fluid. "Why did they do this?"

Winden conversed with the other woman. "They couldn't pay what the Tauren wanted. The Tauren said, if you won't use your hands to work, then we'll take those instead."

"Lovely people," Blays said. "You ought to invite them for a swim in the Current."

Dante cut his arm and fed the nether. He couldn't regrow their hands, but he could smooth over the wounds. Fight off the infections. He did so, then washed his hands and stepped out into the courtyard behind the building, joined by Blays, Winden, the caped woman, and her warriors.

"She thanks you," Winden said. "She says you must be very powerful."

"That sounds like flattery," Blays said.

"She wants your help."

"*Definitely* flattery."

Dante glanced at the other women. "Help with what? Do they have more wounded?"

Winden shook her head. "Two months ago. The Tauren came. When the Shigur couldn't pay their demands, the Tauren took four children. As ransom."

Dante drew back his head. "I see where this is going. No way."

Blays squinted at him. "As in, no way are we going to help these people recover their kidnapped children?"

"Where are they being held? At the tower?"

"Correct," Winden said.

"Which is how far from here?"

"Forty miles. But not much is forested. Two days of walking."

Dante held up a palm. "Which means four days round trip. Plus whatever time it takes to free them. That's too long. We'll miss our boat."

"So we won't walk," Blays said. "We'll run."

"Using the horses that don't exist here?"

"Using our legs. Which you will refresh with the nether. Allowing us to be there in no more than a day."

"And on arrival, my supply of shadows will be as exhausted as our legs."

Blays sighed raggedly. "Remember that year I spent learning to shadowalk so I could hide from you? Well, my plan here—and let me know if I need to slow down—is to use those same abilities to infiltrate the tower and get those kids back."

"And you'll get them outside how, exactly? Give them a quick shadowalking lesson? And then we carry them back here for forty miles? And *then* go look for the molbries, and hope we find them right away, and also that nothing else delays us on our return to Kandak, or that my dad doesn't die in the extra days we're gone?"

The Harvester and her people were staring at him. Dante lowered his voice before continuing. "We came here to help my father. He may be useless to me, but to the people in Kandak, he's a savior. You want to help the Shigur? Fine. But you can only do so by sacrificing the Kandeans."

Blays rubbed his jaw, which was beginning to sport a blond beard. "I hate it when you use logic."

"Do you even want to help these people? Or do you just want to argue with me so you can tell yourself you tried?"

"Some of both. And quit knowing me so well."

Dante smiled. "Don't worry, I'll be the monster for you. Winden, please tell them we're sorry, but we can't help. My father's too sick. If we don't get back to him, he'll die."

Winden stared at him, an unreadable emotion flickering in her eyes. She turned to the other Harvester and spoke in Taurish, her voice heavy with regret. The woman replied sharply.

Winden raised a brow. "She says you must help them. That the Tauren's demands are too high for them to meet."

"We've already faced them," Dante said. "And fared no better than the Shigur have."

She translated more. "They will pay you. Whatever it takes."

"It's not a matter of payment. We don't have the time or the strength to help them."

Winden passed this along. While she was mid-sentence, the Harvester snapped back at her. Their voices rose; within seconds, they were yelling over the top of one another. The Harvester jabbed a finger into Winden's chest and pointed to the south, then spat at Dante's feet.

Winden's jaw bulged. "We are to leave. Now."

She continued to glare into the other Harvester's eyes. Dante touched her on the shoulder and walked southward away from the stone building. The Harvester and her soldiers followed a few paces behind them. Winden was breathing hard, but she kept her tongue. The path led to a gate through the wall of brambles. The gate's edges blossomed with tiny flowers of all sizes. If their mood had been better, it might have been beautiful. The Harvester and her people watched them walk away.

"Sorry if we offended them," Dante said once they were out of earshot. "It was certainly not our intent to make you any enemies on this trip."

Winden rolled her eyes. "You have nothing to worry about. Their Harvester, she's ridiculous. Full of herself. Did you see her cape?"

Blays glanced behind them. "The big leafy thing? Is that fancy?"

"Do you see me wearing one? Flaunting it for all to see? Acting like I am some blessed spirit that fell out of a tree to make your lives better?"

"Not exactly," Dante said. "But if anything, you should be dressed in whatever the mischievous spirits wear."

She gave him a look, then chuckled, expression softening. "The Boat-Growers, they're famed for their harvests. They must look the part. Much as you arrived in your finery."

Beyond the Boat-Growers' living wall, the forest was untamed. Rough footsteps marred the mud. Wary of raiders, Dante removed the dead rats from his pouch—he'd hidden them away while climbing the wall—and sent them out to range ahead. They would alert him of their own accord if they saw any people, but when his path ahead was clear enough to not require his attention, he delved into the rats' sight, eyes sharp for the rabbit-eared red flowers that continued to elude them.

Twilight neared. Since crossing to the south lobe of the island, ants had been a problem at night, and Winden spent the last of the daylight locating and growing a patch of peppery-smelling leaves which she shredded around the camp. No ants infiltrated their blankets, but Dante's undead rats repeatedly alerted him awake. No matter how hard he strained his eyes into the darkness, he saw nothing but the shifting of leaves in the wind.

In the morning, they veered deeper into the jungle. On the first ridge they crested, Winden pointed ahead. A mile away, the land rose, more gently than a cliff but far steeper than a hill. A scarlet line ran down the center, as though a god had cleaved it like a peach.

They had reached the Bloodfalls.

7

Blays stared at the red line cascading down the bluff. "Tell me that's not actually blood."

"It looks like it to me," Winden said. "But you can taste it and find out."

"That sounds more like Dante's thing."

"What is it?" Dante said. "And is its presence why the molbries only grow here?"

"Probably, yes." Winden moved on, swerving around something that looked like a plant but smelled like a rotting carcass. "As to your first question. Our people tell a story. Long ago, a woman named Dre lived above the Bloodfalls. She was a gardener of mushrooms. Each type she grew did something different. Some made you strong. Others helped old men remember their vigor. Others helped those with failing vision to see. She was born with a disease that made her limbs weak, so she also grew one to prevent further withering of her muscles. Her mushrooms took a long time to grow, but she made enough to trade for everything she needed.

"There was also a Harvester named Martin. He heard of Dre and traveled here to see her mushrooms for himself. And discovered they were even more wonderful than he imagined. In awe of her skill, he fell in love with Dre. He offered to help her Harvest more. To sell across the island. To become rich.

"Dre resisted. But Martin wouldn't leave the falls. He asked her over and over. Telling her how many more people she could help heal. At last, she agreed. He set to work, harvesting her crops to grow ten times as many. Then a hundred. And one day, Dre woke to find her legs wouldn't move.

"By growing so many, Martin had caused the mushrooms to lose their spirit. Dre's medicine no longer worked. She tried to regrow it, but before she could do so, the wasting illness reached her heart. It crumbled to shards and she died in her fields. Ever since, the blood of her cracked heart has stained the falls."

"Are any of her mushrooms still here?" Dante said.

"Many mushrooms grow around the falls. But Dre was the one who made them special. Without her, their powers have been lost."

Dante nodded. Much in the way that a dream was only interesting to the one who'd had it, a region's fairy tales were rarely of interest to outsiders. A few minutes later, water burbled ahead. Red water glimmered through the trees. As they neared, the vegetation thinned. Instead, the shores of the Bloodfalls were crowded with mushrooms. Some rose knee-high, the caps big enough to function as end tables. Up close, the water looked no less like blood, swirling scarlet and opaque. It smelled earthy and metallic.

Winden pointed to the ill-defined border between the mushrooms and the plants. "The molbries usually grow there. We'll follow the stream. Don't drink it."

"Thanks for the warning," Blays said. "What about those jagged rocks? Should I avoid consuming those, too?"

"By all means, feast. Then I won't have to listen to you any longer."

Dante smirked. They walked up the shore, scanning for molbries. After a quarter mile, they reached the first of the many waterfalls cascading down from the heights. Red water tumbled forty feet and crashed into a pool of unknowable depth. The banks of the pool were smooth red stone, though Dante couldn't say whether this was the cause or the effect of the water's tint.

Vines and ivy hung over the brow of the cliff like an urchin in need of a haircut. After a sweep of the area revealed no molbry flowers, Winden extended the overhanging plants downward and ascended to the plateau above. They worked their way upstream, coming to another waterfall and corresponding pool. Mist swirled in the air. It smelled of fresh water and the damp, freshly cut rock of the stoneworkers' district in Narashtovik.

This level didn't have any of the flowers, either. Neither did the third or the fourth. Hours later, they were six plateaus up. It was nearly noon, and with no trees around the creek, the sun's rays beat down on Dante's face and neck like fists of heat. The only reprieve came from the mist whipped up near each waterfall.

"Hey!" Blays called. Without Dante noticing, he'd crossed the stream to the far bank and was now waving his hands above his head. "I have flowers! Flowers that think they're rabbits!"

At a wide spot in the stream, red rock broke the surface in natural stepping-stones. Dante made the first few steps, then slipped, plunging knee-deep. He slogged the rest of the way across, dripping over the toadstools and the slimy yellow fungus that sat on the shore like scoops of cold jelly.

At the fringe of the leafy plants, Blays stood triumphant over a waist-high bush. Small red flowers hung from its branches, two long petals drooping from their top edge.

"Molbries," Winden confirmed. Dante reached out to pluck one and she slapped his hand. "Stop that. You'll kill them."

He frowned. "They need to be living to work? Then I'm afraid we've made a huge mistake, as we've left our patient on the opposite side of the island."

"They need to be kept fresh. This is why we have no dried

supplies in Kandak. But I have methods to preserve them." She unrolled a leather sleeve filled with numerous knives and snippers.

"That looks like a set of thieves' tools," Blays observed. "But, you know. For gardening."

She gave him a look, then trimmed off several branches. She got out a narrow black box similar to the one she'd carried the shaden in. The bottom was layered with dried-out sea sponges. She soaked these with water from the stream, sticking the stems of the molbry cuttings into the now-pliable sponges. She sealed the box's lid with a wooden click and repeated the process with a second box.

When this one was filled and sealed, she handed it to Dante. "Carry this. If something happens to me, give them sun and water daily. If they die, you'll still have a few days to get them back to your father."

He repacked his bag so the tall box would stay upright while he walked. They rinsed off in the red water—Winden assured them it was safe to touch the skin—then began their descent from the heights.

"After this, he's going to literally owe you his life," Blays said. "Think of the ways you'll be able to hold *that* over his head."

"The possibilities are staggering. I might even come away with an apology."

Blays laughed. "I won't pretend like this will make up for years of abandonment. But I do think that, once we're back home, you'll be happy you came here."

Dante grunted, unwilling to agree out loud even though he suspected Blays was right. He did feel a certain thrill at having traipsed across such a strange and wonderful land. After weeks in the tunnels at Gallador, the sun and the sights were a joy.

Finding the molbries was quite an achievement, too. Seeing what the Tauren had done to the Boat-Growers had cemented his conviction that it was important to help his father stand against them.

On top of that, he was starting to have ideas about opening trade between Narashtovik and Kandak. Successfully completing this mission would earn him a great store of goodwill. The Plagued Islands had much to offer—food, medicine, dyes, the creations of the Boat-Growers. As much as he had strengthened Narashtovik's military and political position, its navy remained anemic. Hence why he had to hire diseased sea captains from disapproved-of corners of the world. If he could open up a line of revenue from the islands, he could use that to build the fleet Narashtovik sorely needed.

As they walked toward the ledge of the third plateau before the bottom, Blays slowed, then stopped. He turned to them, a funny look on his face. "Was this here when we came through the first time?"

Dante moved beside him. At a shaded spot within the prolific fungus not three feet from the edge of the falls, a baby rested on its back, hands balled into fists. Red mist dewed its skin.

Winden gazed down at it. "Tauren."

"Tauren?" Blays said. "How can you tell? The chain mail diaper?"

"Their young. They leave them here for three days. The strong live, to make their people stronger. And the weak don't return to burden them."

"Do *any* return? Doesn't the crying draw predators?"

She laughed dryly. "That is why the Tauren's children haven't cried in hundreds of years."

"Why here?" Dante said.

"To them, the Bloodfalls are a place of courage. The will to fight. They hope their babies will absorb this." She kneeled beside it and slid her left hand under its neck, tipping back its head. With her right hand, she drew a steel knife and put it to the child's throat.

"What are you doing?" Blays said.

"What does it look like? I'm killing this child."

"Do you *need* me to ask why?"

"If it lives? It will join the Tauren. Become our enemy." She looked down on the baby's smooth, pudgy face. "One day, it will kill Kandean children instead."

"Not for fifteen years or more!" Blays grabbed her wrist, pulling the blade away. "By then, you and the Tauren might be friends. For all you know, this kid will grow up to be the one who ends the war between you."

With her unrestrained hand, she pulled a knife from Blays' belt and set it against the infant's throat. "I'll take that chance."

"You're right," Dante said.

"To murder a baby?" Blays honked with laughter. "No wonder you believe all of your people wind up condemned to be eaten by birds and crabs!"

"Her people weren't the ones that started this war. It was the Tauren. They maim and kill adults. Kidnap children. When the people they've wronged do the same to them, you're going to blame them?"

"Is this a trick question?"

"But you shouldn't do this, Winden," Dante said softly. "Even though you're right. Because it will crack you inside. It will weigh you down every day of your life. Even sleep won't be an escape from it."

She clenched her teeth. "If this saves a single one of my people? I'll be able to shoulder the guilt."

"And what happens when you die? And you're brought before Kaval? There's no way to lie nicely about killing a newborn. When you tell him why you did it, do you think he'll spare you?"

Her face twisted with anger, then frustration. She withdrew the knife, flipped it in her hand, and held it out to Blays hilt-first.

"All right then," Blays said. "So where shall we take it? The Boat-Growers?"

Winden lowered her eyes. "They'll know where it came from.

And they will kill it. As will the Kandeans. And even the monks of the Dreaming Peaks. Do you want this child to have any chance to survive? Then we have to leave it here."

Blays stared down at it for a long moment. "I can't believe we're doing this. At least if it survives, it'll be too young to remember to come hunt us down."

Dante moved to the cliff's edge and climbed down the plants Winden had extended across its face. In time, they reached the bottom of the falls. There, they paused to clean themselves up and eat a meal of mashed bananas and jods, a pale green fruit that tasted like sweet eggs. Not exactly Dante's ideal flavor, but Winden insisted they were almost as nutritious as san root.

With the molbries boxed away, they headed back toward the Dreaming Peaks by the most direct route available, with Dante using dead rats to locate game trails through the woods. They made good time through the afternoon, pushing on until last light. Winden thought they might be able to make it back to Kandak in as little as four days.

In the middle of the night, Dante woke with a gasp. One of his rats had just winked out; the severing of the nethereal connection between them had stung Dante like a wasp. He directed his lone remaining rat to the site where the first had disappeared. The turf was torn up as if by hooves.

The next day, they hiked past the Boat-Growers' territory, giving it a berth of a few miles. Whenever they stopped to rest, Dante checked on his molbry cuttings, giving them air and light and water. The flowers looked the same as they had on the bush. Now that they had them, he was much less confident they'd work. Winden had said they often didn't cure the sickness—and that they could cause a toxic reaction instead.

He didn't like the thought of failure. Blays would tell him that he should be proud to have done all that he could, but Dante didn't find that much consolation. Common wisdom held that it was better to have tried and lost than to never have tried at all.

Maybe that worked for most people.

For him, though, he'd always wonder what he could have done to win.

The land sloped up gently. They stuck to the jungle, as much for the shade as for the concealment. As they walked up a dry creek bed, Dante felt a twitch in his head. He shifted his vision to that of the rat's. Grass flew past its face. Hooves thundered behind it. He made it look back just in time to see a tusked mouth gawping like an eel.

Darkness enfolded the rat. Bones crunched. The connection went dead.

Dante staggered down the gully, rubbing his eyes. "That's a new one. Guess what just ate my rat?"

"I'd rather not," Blays said.

"A pig."

"A carnivorous pig? I don't know whether to be hungry or scared."

Winden stopped in her tracks. "It's a pig? You're sure of this?"

"Flat snout. Little tusks. Beady eyes. Bit of a beard right here on the chin."

"We're being hunted."

Blays tilted his head to the side. "By a pig? Do you think we can talk two slices of bread into hunting us as well?"

"This is a jone," Winden said. "Its sense of smell is better than any dog. The Tauren use them to track prey. Can you send another scout?"

Dante nodded vaguely. Another rat might get eaten. Or look suspicious. That ruled out birds, too; to get them light enough to fly in undeath, he had to trim off everything unrelated to flying and seeing. Like legs. And guts. Not exactly sneaky.

Light sparkled on an iridescent blue butterfly flapping along the bank of the creek. Dante knocked it down with a toothpick-sized spear of nether, then reanimated it, sending it flapping clumsily into the canopy.

Through it, he saw nothing but an uninterrupted sea of treetops. As the butterfly neared where he'd lost contact with his rat, he ordered it to descend. It bashed into several branches on its way down, cutting through the canopy and into the shadows below, where he let it hover.

Dante hated using flying bugs to do recon—their vision was shifting and kaleidoscopic, and between that and their erratic flight paths, he often got sick on his shoes. Yet the butterfly's sight was sharp enough to spot a jone loping from the undergrowth, heading in the opposite direction of the Dreaming Peaks. He directed the bug to flap along behind it.

Voices rang out from ahead of the hog. The butterfly cleared a moss-draped tree and gazed down on some fifteen people. The man in the visored steel helmet jerked up his head and stared straight at the butterfly.

8

"You're right," Dante murmured. "We're being hunted. By the Tauren. Including the sorcerer I fought on the beach in Kandak."

"Son of a bitch!" Blays said. "How did they know we're here?"

"Because the Harvester from the Boat-Growers is there, too."

Winden spat a Taurish curse. "We didn't help them get their children. So they turned on us."

"They can't possibly blame us for that," Dante said. "We have nothing to do with any of this."

"Not to punish you. But because this was the only thing they could give the Tauren to get their children back."

"What interest would the Tauren have in us?"

"Do you want to go ask them?" She swept a loose plait back into place behind her head. "You're a rixen. Foreign liar. Unless they cast you out or kill you, they disgrace our ancestors who died fighting off invaders and swindlers."

"Does the entire island see foreigners as some kind of pestilence? Or just the Tauren?"

"Most of us are wary. They're hostile. But it's commonly thought that this is a pose. A way to exert control over people and trade." She sniffed. "Or maybe Vordon simply wants to destroy you for having stood against him."

"That's the nethermancer?" Dante said. "The one I fought in Kandak?"

"Who cares what his name is?" Blays said. "Right now, all I care about is how far away from him we are."

"Less than two miles. They're in no hurry, but they could be on us in fifteen minutes."

"Going to be hard to ambush them. Not when they've got a magic pig that can smell us out when we're close."

Dante laced his fingers together. "I don't think we should try to fight them. Vordon's dangerous. And we have no idea what his companions are capable of."

"Judging by the village-burning, it doesn't sound like he's the negotiating type. What does that leave us with? Fleeing?"

Prompted by that, Dante resumed walking up the dry creek bed. "Winden, if we can beat them to the pass through the Dreaming Peaks, will they follow?"

"It's holy ground," she said. "They won't fight us there. And the Dreamers stopped letting them through the pass two years ago. To get past, they have to take a route through the heights. Much slower."

"Surprised the Tauren haven't taken the peaks for themselves, then."

"That would risk turning the entire island against them."

"They'll know exactly where we're heading," Dante said. "But we can beat them there."

"So we've agreed we're fleeing, then?" Blays frowned at Winden. "When you're singing our ballads, would you leave this part out?"

Dante increased his pace. Concerned that Vordon had recognized the butterfly was a puppet, Dante had sent it out of the man's sight, then severed his link to it. As they advanced up the creek bed, he spotted one of the little green frogs that Winden called dorts. They lived in the trees, soaring between branches with the aid of the webbing between their front and hind legs.

With a small twinge of guilt, Dante slew the frog and returned it as his new set of eyes.

He left it in place until the hunting party neared its position nearly a half hour later. After a look at the Tauren, he sent the frog bounding ahead through the trees, keeping it at least a hundred feet ahead of them, too distant to attract attention. The Tauren didn't appear to be in any hurry, but as the day stretched on, the gap closed to 25 minutes, then twenty. Vordon hadn't called a single break.

"Something's wrong here," Dante said. "We're pushing as hard as we can sustain. Yet they're catching up to us." He narrowed his eyes at Blays. "And it's not because I'm fat."

"You're obviously not fat. Just weak."

He wasn't, but the hours of hiking were starting to wear his legs out. Telling himself that the will usually gave out before the body, he pressed on. After another hour, the Tauren still hadn't stopped for a break. They were now less than a mile behind. Dante got out his knife and drew a small cut on his arm. He drew the shadows to him, then sent them into his muscles, repeating with Winden and Blays.

"I think we should run," he said.

Blays glanced behind them. "I can't believe we're running from pigs."

"It's more about the violent sorcerer wrangling the pigs."

Dante broke into an easy jog. He felt more refreshed than he had since the start of the journey, and despite the gentle rise of the land, with the nether's help, he was able to keep up his pace for nearly two hours before his breath flagged. As they walked on, catching their breath, he left the frog behind them in the trees. It was more than thirty minutes before the pigs at the vanguard of the Tauren force trotted into view. The frog resumed pacing the Tauren from ahead, gliding webbily from branch to branch.

Over the next few miles, their lead shrank until they had to start jogging again. They slowed to a walk, resting, then resumed running. Sunlight rarely penetrated the canopy, but the air was deceptively humid. Dante had sweated through his clothes long ago. The next time their group began to flag, he wiped the exhaustion from their limbs again before they could slow down. By late afternoon, they were roughly five miles ahead of their pursuit, but Vordon still hadn't called for his people to halt.

"They must be using the nether, too," Dante said. "We can't stop until they do."

They ran on. The sun dimmed, then disappeared. To preserve nether, Dante lit the way with his torchstone; when this faded, Winden lit candlefruit, which gave just enough light to see the ground ahead. When they grew tired, Dante flushed the weariness from their muscles yet again. With the sun gone and the air cooler, the Tauren ran, too.

Midnight came, then the small hours. Clouds blotted out the stars. Rain hissed against the leaves. Fearing a flash flood, they clambered out of the stream bed and moved along the banks, slowed by the thicker brush. With the stars gone and no way to tell the passage of time, Dante's mind entered a plodding fugue. There was nothing but the next step and then the one after.

Dawn broke, spying pinkly from behind a tattered sheet of clouds. They were still running. And so were the Tauren.

"This doesn't make sense," Dante blurted. It was now light enough that they no longer needed the candlefruit to see. "They have five times as many people as we do. This Vordon shouldn't be able to sustain that many for so long."

Blays' voice was scratchy from disuse. "Unless he's five times the adept that you are."

"How far are we from the pass?"

"Fifteen miles?" Winden said. "At this pace, little more than two hours."

Dante nodded. He could get them that far, he knew, but his

grip on the shadows was loosening. By the time they reached the Dreaming Peaks, he wouldn't have much left. And while his body felt good enough, considering the circumstances, he hadn't slept in a day. His mind was foggy, prone to mistakes.

Still they ran on.

The land ramped up. The jungle thinned, spitting them into the grasslands high on the sides of the mountain. Dante had to leave the tree frog behind, but he no longer needed it to keep tabs on their pursuers: the Tauren had been gaining for some time, emerging from the trees a few minutes later, visible within the thigh-grass less than a mile away. Two minutes later, a second band of troops appeared from the jungle, twenty strong. They quickly caught up to Vordon's men.

The skies were overcast and the slopes were sodden and muddy from the prior night's rains. In places, the clay was so soft and thick they had to divert laterally across the hillside to find solid ground. Though the Tauren continued to close distance on them, by the time they neared the Dreaming Peaks, it was clear the enemy wouldn't catch them.

"They're still coming," Winden said. "They don't intend to stop at the pass."

Dante grimaced. His boots were so thick with purple clay they felt twice as heavy. "Will the Dreamers help us?"

"You saw them. They aren't warriors. Not in our world."

"We can't keep this up much longer. I need to rest."

"Doesn't look like rest is on their agenda," Blays said. "Think we can lose them?"

Ahead, clouds bruised themselves on the mountains. The grass was patchy, avoiding the steaming pools filled with their multi-colored crystals. The air stank of flatulence.

"Sure," Dante said. "All we have to do is take a stroll off the cliffs."

"We tried running. We can't hide. The only question left is where you want to make our stand."

"It won't be much of one," Dante said. "Right now, I could barely call enough shadows to stop us from getting sunburned. We should have ambushed them yesterday."

"Running was the right plan. We couldn't have known this would happen."

"You sound defeated," Winden said.

"Yes, that would be the defeat talking." Dante trudged on. "I don't hear you coming up with any ideas. At least we have the excuse of being new here."

"These men. If you had nether, do you think you could stand against them?"

"Judging by our confrontation in Kandak, I'm not sure. Thankfully for us, I would have no intention of fighting fairly." His enthusiasm faded like a gust of wind. "But there's no point. We should head to the way through the upper mountains. At least we can keep the enemy away from your Dreamers."

"I can give you the nether." She slung her pack forward and withdrew a black wooden box similar to the ones they were carrying the flowers in. Inside, it bore six shaden. She handed one to Dante. "Can you feel it?"

He weighed the shell in his hand. Its opening was stopped by the mucusy foot of a snail. And he felt something of far greater gravity within the shell.

He gawked down at it. "It's full of shadows!"

"These things have nether in them?" Blays said. "Like kellevurts?"

Dante crinkled his brow. "Grim-slugs?"

"They have them at Pocket Cove. Eat dead stuff. The People of the Pocket told me they consume the nether, too."

Dante sent his mind inside the shell. Darkness bloomed within him, cool and wonderful. "This could be enough. No wonder the Tauren want these so badly. This must be how they've kept up with us." He glanced uphill. "We should do this at the bridge. From there, we can fall back to the ruins."

"Here's another idea," Blays said. "I lure them onto the bridge. And you knock it out."

Dante grinned. For the first time in hours, he felt like he could see a way to the future. Winden ran ahead to pass word to the Dreamers. Foul-smelling steam bubbled from the springs and wafted down the decline. They reached the bridge. The river ran a few feet below, coursing toward the cliffs. Dante delved into the rock at either side of the bridge. It was solid, tough, but that wouldn't make any difference to him.

They stopped at the bridge's north side. Winden ran back from the ruins. Her normally stoic face was fissured with anxiety. "The monks can't move the Dreamers to safety in time. Please. We can't let the Tauren through."

"That aligns with our goal of not dying," Dante said. "Got any tricks to help us out?"

She stared across the rapids. "Not much to work with. But I'll do what I can."

Below them, the Tauren climbed on. The arrival of the second band had swelled their numbers past thirty, and as they neared the bridge, they fanned out in a semicircle. The man in the steel helm stepped onto the edge of the span and tipped up his visor.

"You run." Vordon spoke Mallish; his accent was so faint there were times it sounded like he didn't have one at all. "Does that mean you are guilty?"

"Why are you following us?" Dante called over the gurgle of the waters.

"You came without permission. You attacked me. You will answer."

"Is this the tonen you tell yourself? Victims of your raids are the real murderers?"

Casually, the man drew a longsword, resting its tip on the bridge. "We deal with you now. Or we come to Kandak. And they will answer for your actions instead."

"There's no need for this." Dante moved his consciousness

into the rock around the southern end of the bridge, preparing to yank it away. Within the earth, he felt something warm. He blinked, tracing the warmth west, away from the cliffs. "Surely, we can reach a peaceful agreement."

"My terms, they are clear. Hand yourselves over. Or be stained by what befalls Kandak."

"I need a moment to decide." He lowered his voice and turned to Blays. "New plan. That thing you do. Can you do it through water?"

"Sure," Blays said. "Way easier than walls."

"Don't let them get through. And I'll make sure any survivors can't follow."

"Can do." He swung his pack from his shoulder. "Hang onto this for me?"

"Why?"

"There may be a non-crying baby inside," Blays said. Dante's jaw dropped. Blays looped the pack's straps over Dante's outstretched arm.

On the other bank, Vordon lowered his visor. "Too long. I choose for you."

Nether scythed across the bridge. Dante grunted in surprise, lashing back in kind. The streaking shadows crashed together, exploding in black sparks. Dante fell back a step, hoping to coax the other man forward, but Vordon held position, attacking again. Drawing on the nether condensed in the shaden, Dante deflected it handily.

They matched each other strike for strike. Vordon was technically skilled, as quick and fluid as a snake. After the fourth such exchange, Vordon grinned and flapped his hand at Dante. He stepped off the bridge and gestured to his people. Archers moved onto the foot of the bridge.

"It's like fighting my mirror," Dante said. "He'll knock down anything I throw at them."

Winden stared across the span at the gathering archers. "Fall back."

As they ran off the bridge, she grabbed a molbry cutting from her pack. Once she was off the boards, she jammed the cutting into the dirt. As soon as it touched soil, it expanded like a fire. Bows twanged behind them. The branches of the plant shrouded their heads, casting them into shade. Arrows rapped into the living roof.

Dante blinked. "That's a neat trick."

"And if I have to do it again, I'll be drawing on the shaden, too."

The archers plinked away, trying to find gaps in the cover. Dante flinched at each arrow that knocked into the tightly-woven branches. Across the rushing water, Vordon barked commands in Taurish. Ten soldiers carrying swords and chain mail trotted onto the bridge.

Blays drew his swords. "About time I had some fun."

He stepped onto the bridge and strolled forward. The archers moved to the sides and unleashed a volley past the swordsmen. Blays vanished. Arrows whisked through the space he'd occupied and thunked into the boards. The swordsmen slowed in confusion, putting up their guards.

Dante plunged his focus into the rock, finding the heat and following it upstream. Blays reappeared in the middle of the bridge mid-spin. His lead blade bit through the neck of the closest man to him. His other sword lashed across the hamstring of a second man, felling him. The troops shouted in surprise and closed on him. He winked out again.

Shadows flowed from the shaden to Dante. He sent them flooding deep into the rock, opening a massive channel between the pocket of heat and the rushing waters. A rumble drowned out all else. As Blays reappeared, stabbing a third soldier in the throat, a tsunami of boiling water burst upstream into the small river, swelling it several times over.

Steam clouded the air. Men shrieked. As the water thundered

toward the bridge, Dante backed away from the cover of the molbry. The bridge stones hazed with mist. Men sprinted toward the far end. Blays vanished. The wall of water crashed into the bridge.

Wood groaned. The bridge tore loose from the south bank, pivoting, planks snapping. Clouds of steam washed to all sides, choking and hot. Dante staggered away, wiping his eyes. With a great pop, the northern foot of the bridge yanked free, tumbling away in the flood, headed for the cliffs.

Dante's heart squeezed tight. "Blays!"

Though the initial flood was subsiding, the underground reservoir continued to feed into the stream, obscuring everything in mist. Dante wandered forward, mind numb with horror.

Blays appeared in front of him and patted his cheek. "No time to cry for me. Let's get the hell out of here."

Dante barked a laugh and jogged away from the swollen river. "Didn't get Vordon. He's missing half his people, though."

Winden fell in beside them. "The flood. How did you do that?"

"There are underground pools everywhere. They're what feed the hot springs. Like in Kandak."

Blays sheathed his swords. "If they try to cross, they'll be boiled like human dumplings. Think it'll last?"

"No idea. But it should give us enough time to give them the slip."

They jogged onward into the ruins. By the time they reached the hall where the Dreamers slumbered, Dante had observed no sign of pursuit.

They didn't slow until they reached the Broken Valley. Knowing the Tauren's jone would be unable to follow their scent from plateau to plateau, they got halfway across the valley and descended to the floor. After hacking a hollow from the brambles, they lay down and slept.

~

Two days later, they entered the clearing surrounding the black stone temple. A boy peered from the stoop, then ran to meet Winden. Dante picked out enough of the Taurish words to infer that Larsin still lived.

Inside the temple, a steady cross-breeze blew from one side to the other, but it wasn't enough to carry away the smell of burned cinnamon that marked the advance of the disease. Larsin lay on the pallet. He was unconscious, his face pinched with pain.

Winden called in the boy, then sent him off. He came back with a small bowl of root paste. Winden kneeled, shredded three molbry flowers into the paste, and used a thin stone rod to mash it together. She shook Larsin's shoulder until his eyes blinked open, then methodically fed him the paste. When she was done, she walked out to the stoop and sat.

"That's it?" Dante said.

She didn't look up. "You expected what? A naked dance around the fire?"

"At least a blood ritual of *some* kind. What now?"

"He improves," she said. "Or it makes him worse. We'll know by morning."

She had brought her box of molbry cuttings outside. Dante touched a red flower, the ears of which were starting to droop and wrinkle. "What will you do with the rest of them?"

"Throw them out."

"Seems like a waste. We went through so much for them."

"Plant them if you want. They'll die. They can't survive away from the Bloodfalls."

After a minute of uncomfortable silence, Dante went inside and got his box of cuttings. Thinking the mist blowing in from the sea might remind the cuttings of their home in the falls, he brought them near the edge of the cliffs and planted them into the soil. He was still tamping the dirt around their edges when Blays walked up to him.

"So have they decided on your punishment?" Dante said.

"Punishment?" Blays nudged a cutting with the toe of his boot, testing its hold. It listed to the side and toppled. "For what?"

"For bringing back a baby enemy."

"They should be hailing me. I captured a prisoner of war. One you don't even have to lock up."

"Are they going to care for it?"

"I'm not sure." Blays wandered toward the edges of the cliffs. "If they won't, do you suppose Captain Twill will charge us more for a third passenger?"

Dante shaded his eyes against the sun. "You can't possibly be thinking of taking it back to Pocket Cove."

"Of course not. They'd never go for that. I'd have to bring it to Narashtovik."

"Bad news: henceforth, all babies are banished from the city."

"Winden is not happy with me. You'd think the kid was prophesied to plunge the island into eternal darkness. Oh well. Another three days and we'll never have to see these people again." He lowered himself to the grass. "Think he'll make it? Your dad?"

"There's no telling." Dante righted the cutting Blays had knocked over, planting it more securely. "What if he does?"

"That's a bad thing? If so, I'd like to have the last ten days of my life back."

"But what happens then? Am I supposed to write letters? Come *visit* him?"

"This presumes you saved his life. So if he turns out to be a huge pain, you'd be within your rights to rescind his life." Blays picked up a pebble dislodged by Dante's excavations, cocked his arm, and slung it off the cliff. "You didn't have to come here in the first place. You've already exceeded your filial responsibilities tenfold. If he survives, wherever you go next is your decision."

Blays hung around a minute more, decided he had more important things to do than watch Dante tend a doomed garden, and wandered off. Dante remained there for some time.

That night, it took him a long time to sleep. When he woke, he was still tired, but the sun was already up. Early morning was his favorite time of the island's day: neither hot nor cold, with a calm offshore breeze importing the smell of the sea. He forced himself to get up and walk outside. A person stood in the grass with his back to the temple, obscured by the long shadows cast from the trees on the east side of the clearing. At first he thought it was Blays, but then his father turned and smiled.

9

Larsin walked toward him, stirring the tall grass. "You're awake."

"A reluctant daily habit." Dante stayed where he was. "Are you…well?"

"Aye." The older man grinned. He looked tired but relaxed, like a man waking from a nap after a long day of travel. "I feel like I could run all the way to Kandak. Don't worry, I won't try. Too lazy. But I *feel* like I could."

"I'm glad. That's what we came here for."

"I can't believe you did. After all this time, I think I would have wiped my ass with that letter."

"I might have if not for Blays."

Larsin reached out and put a hand on his shoulder. "While I was sick, I had a lot of time to think. And I'm sorry. I should never have left."

Dante's jaw tightened. "You had time to think during the few weeks you were in bed. But not during the eighteen years prior to that."

"I've thought about it every day since then."

"I'll nominate you for sainthood as soon as I'm home."

Larsin got a good laugh out of that. "You're a tough one,

aren't you? Maybe it means nothing to you. But if that's true, why did you come here in the first place?"

"I don't know." Dante stuck out his hand. "I'm glad you're better."

The older man considered Dante's outstretched hand. "Your trip to the Bloodfalls. Any roughness?"

"I almost died crossing the Broken Valley. Once we started to tangle with the Tauren, I found myself wishing I had."

"You knocked antlers with them? What happened?"

Dante still felt irritated by his father's blitheness, but he found himself relating the story of their trip with something like enthusiasm. Halfway through, they relocated to the shade of the temple porch. Dante explained how the Tauren had chased them for a day without stopping, only to be defeated by his flooding of the bridge.

"I'd heard stories of what you can do," Larsin said softly. "I thought they had to be exaggerated. After hearing this, though, I have to think they were downplaying it. How did you learn to do this?"

"Years of almost getting killed can be very educational."

"When did you learn you had this talent? How did it begin?"

"With a wounded dog," Dante said. "I saw a man heal it. Or maybe it was dead and he only reanimated it. Whatever he did, it was as easy for him as the rest of us breathe. Seeing that power, I knew I had to have it. How can this be so strange to you? You used to perform tricks with the ether yourself."

"Aye, that's all they were," Larsin said. "Parlor tricks. I gave that up a long time ago. How did you wind up all the way in Narashtovik?"

Prompted by a steady flow of inquiries, Dante found himself relating his entire adult life. How he'd found himself in possession of the original copy of *The Cycle of Arawn*, and through it, had learned to harness the nether. How he and Blays had been recruited to travel to Narashtovik to assassinate the former head of the Council of Arawn. How Dante had subsequently found himself named to that council.

This was followed, of course, by a detailed recap of the Chainbreakers' War that had freed the norren tribes, Gallador Rift, and Narashtovik from the Gaskan Empire. And following *that*, Dante related how he'd learned of the impending arrival of Cellen, a concentration of nether capable of changing the face of the world. His pursuit of it had taken him into forbidden lands far stranger than he could have imagined.

When he finished, Larsin gazed at him in bemusement. "Are you screwing with me?"

"Screwing with you?"

"After hearing all that, I'm starting to wonder if I had forgotten I was a god. If I had your power, the Tauren would all be in a mass grave."

"Don't be so sure," Dante said. "Vordon is very skilled. Though perhaps that's just the shaden."

Larsin raised his brows. "You know about them?"

"I exhausted myself trying to escape the Tauren. Winden had to give me a shell to deal with them at the bridge. Are shaden common? The right people would pay a fortune for them."

"They're very rare. Our Harvesters used to use them on sicknesses, injuries, and larger projects. Since the Tauren started their raids, we've had to search for them full-time just to find enough to make quota."

"Years ago, you defeated them once. What do you intend to do now?"

"Talk you into staying a few more months?"

"Can't. I have people who depend on me back home."

Larsin chuckled wryly. "Couldn't hurt to ask. During the last war, we won the day by wrecking their boats. When they sailed into the bay, our Harvesters snarled them with seaweed and dragged them down."

"I thought the Currents were too strong to sail north from

their city."

"They portaged their boats across the Peaks, then took them north down the rivers to the Joladi Coast. Sailed south to Kandak from there. This time, they've changed tactics. They're landing further upshore. We can't patrol all of it. The Tauren have better weapons now, too. That armor. Running around like crabs with swords."

"You could try relocating," Dante said. "It would hardly take twenty people to defend the Dreaming Peaks."

"Our people would sooner see themselves wiped out than to bring war to the Dreamers."

"Do you have more Harvesters? Or is Winden the only one?"

"Two others. But she's our best."

Dante gazed out at the fine blue sea. "When we took on the Gaskan Empire, we didn't do it alone. We formed an alliance. Brought in everyone we could. You need to do the same. Or move to another island."

He smiled thinly. "If only it was that easy."

Dante realized he'd been lost in stories and strategy for over an hour. Feeling duped, he stood from the porch, brushing dust from his pants. "Glad to see the molbry worked. I'm going for a walk."

Larsin looked like he might ask to join him, but Dante jogged down the stairs before he could speak, heading straight into the jungle. He needed to clear his head. He had so few memories of the man. What remained was more impressionistic than specific: that he'd been carefree, hard to rile, a fan of roughhousing and exploring. A great dad for a young boy.

But he'd also been prone to drinking. And disappearing on sudden jaunts and voyages. To the point when, even as a child, Dante hadn't been that surprised to hear he wasn't coming back. Hurt? That went without saying. But Dante had transitioned to his new life with the monk with little difficulty. As if he'd known the day was coming. That it had only been a matter of when.

So while Dante surged with anger at Larsin's verbal missteps, he also found it easy to forget the man *was* his father. From there, he felt no compunction against blathering on as if the man were a harmless but not particularly close friend. That, in turn, made Dante feel as if he were discussing matters the man had no right to hear.

He was still dwelling on these thoughts when steps rustled to his left. Winden made her way toward him. She owned a full wardrobe of somber, thoughtful, judgy looks, but he wasn't sure he'd seen the model she was donning now.

"You've seen him?" she said.

"I have. Remarkable recovery."

"Your help. I want to thank you again. You didn't have to do this."

"Trust me, on the list of most ridiculous ventures I've been party to, this venture is several pages down. I just hope Blays didn't offend you."

"With his tongue? He means nothing by it."

"Not that," Dante said. "I mean by bringing back the Tauren infant."

"He doesn't understand," she said. "But when I dwell on it, I wonder if I would have respected him if he hadn't done something."

"Have you discussed what's to be done about it?"

"He offered to take it home with him. But that can't be done. In Kandak, Stav has pledged to care for it. He's a good man. I think he misses when his grandchildren were young."

"Glad to hear it's worked out. For the record, I'm not one to leave an infant on a slope, either. It's your fault for making such a convincing case."

Winden cracked a smile. "Feel no shame. You both did what you thought right. The stories about you, they're wrong."

He cocked an eyebrow. "What stories are these?"

"When Larsin first heard of you. They said you were a butcher. That you cut a swath through Mallon. You were chased from the country, only to flee to the north, where you killed a woman of great power so you could take her place."

"Let me guess. These stories came from Mallon?"

"Are they true?"

"Do you have a word for sour lies?"

"Lanen," she said.

"And what about a story that contains true facts, but which presents them in the most warped way possible?"

"Rolanen."

"This is getting disturbing."

"You have to give words to things. How else can you know they exist?" Winden regarded him, serious once more. "The stories said you'd do anything to gain more power. That honor meant nothing to you. But the stories were wrong. You came here to do good. You haven't asked for anything in return."

"I can think of one way for you to repay me."

The corner of her mouth twitched. "That being?"

"Teach me to harvest."

"Impossible. This is a thing that takes years."

"And I have two days," Dante said. "I know it's not enough. But if you show me the foundation, I can build on it when I get home."

"I used time as a polite way to tell you no. The truth? The Harvest is for us." She gestured to take in the island. "Not for you."

"You said I came here to do good. If you give me this knowledge, do you fear I'll use it to do wrong?"

"That is not the point."

"Larsin is one of you, isn't he? And I am his son. So then I must be one of you, too."

Winden sputtered with laughter. "This argument is good enough for me. We will go to Kandak."

"What, right now?"

"As you said. You only have two days."

He gestured toward town. She led the way down the path, which was muddy as always; it rained once or twice a day here and nothing ever truly dried out.

"To harvest." Winden's voice was distant, as if talking to herself. "In one way, very easy. Convince the plants to do what they do by themselves. In another way? Very difficult. Plants don't eat the shadows. They eat air. Water. Light."

"But nether can't be turned into any of those things. It strengthens or weakens. Brings you further or closer to death. You can't, say, conjure a house out of it."

"When a ship comes to our shores, it doesn't conjure up the steel it brings us. It's a vessel, nothing more. And so is the nether."

"This sounds like something I'm going to need to see in practice," Dante said.

She smiled. "You're going to be very bad at this."

"What on earth makes you say that? There may not be a more talented nethermancer on the continent."

"That is why you'll be so bad. You know too much. It will be like trying to write a message on parchment without scraping the old words off."

"Well, now you've undone your own prediction. The only force stronger than my opinion of my own abilities is my desire to prove others wrong about me."

She turned away, possibly to try to hide the rolling of her eyes. On the descent to town, she recounted the tale of Yee, the first Harvester. According to their history — which sounded more like myth — Yee had lived alone on the Joladi Coast on the north shore, where the Current was most violent. One day, a storm stripped the trees from the land. At the same time, it drove a boat into the shore. Yee rescued the crew from the sea one by one. The men were starving, but the plants had been blown away and the fish had been killed and swept away. All that remained was a single san root—and Yee herself.

As the sailors made plans to capture her and carve her up, Kaval, incensed that these men were going to eat her after she'd saved their lives, showed her how to grow the one root she had left into many. When she did so, and fed the crew, they fell to their knees, recognizing she was a miracle-worker. Yee and the few Harvesters she taught had been venerated ever since.

On their way toward Kandak, Winden stopped a man walking toward them and spoke hurriedly. He nodded and returned to town. Soon after, Winden left the main path, diverting north down a much fainter trail. Just before the trail led to the beach, the trees stopped. Twenty-foot black columns ringed a bowl-shaped depression a hundred yards across. This space was divided radially. Each slice grew a different color of fruits and flowers: one yellow, one red, one purple, and so on.

"Wait here," Winden said. "We can't be seen practicing. I need to make sure we're alone."

She made a circuit of the overgrown bowl. As she neared the red section, something ruffled within it. She delved into the foliage, reappearing a minute later and continuing along the circle, making her way back to Dante.

He nodded at the profusion of shrubs, flowers, vines, trees, and sprouts. "What is this place?"

"The Basket. It's where we keep everything that will grow here. That way, if something is needed, a Harvester always knows where to find it and make more."

"That is an amazing idea."

She brought him to the light green wedge, where clusters of the bamboo-like shoots grew. "This is what I learned on. What we all train with. Watch the shadows."

She kneeled beside the smallest cluster. He sent his focus into the nether within the shoots. Winden drew a small knife. She owned steel ones, but this one was a sawtooth, attached to a handle of polished red wood. She nicked her palm and squeezed three drops of blood onto the dirt.

Nether flocked to the roots and wicked up the stems. The plants lurched six inches taller. Dante blinked. "Slower."

Again, the shadows came and disappeared, stretching the stems.

"*Way* slower. Pretend I'm a dog, and not a bright one. And that it isn't strange for you to be teaching a witless dog how to do magic."

Patiently, she tried again. It took several more slowed-down attempts before he glimpsed it. It wasn't the nether itself feeding the plants. Rather, as she had said, the shadows were serving as a conduit through which other substances (air? water?) were being borne to the plants. It was like a sped-up cycle of all things: through the death held in the nether, inert matter was brought to a living object, allowing it to thrive.

After observing her a few more times—the plants were now twice as tall as when they'd arrived—Dante cut his arm, dribbled blood onto the soil, and willed the shadows forward. They came, but no matter how forcefully he tried to drive them, or how subtly to coax them, he couldn't get them to bridge the gap.

Doing his best to keep his frustration in check, he pressed on, alternating his attempts with Winden's to hone his technique. She didn't offer much in the way of advice. He wasn't sure if that was because she wasn't used to teaching, or if her methods simply mirrored her stoic, laconic personality.

Part of him had hoped to pick it up on the spot, but he wasn't surprised that he was stymied. Different people seemed to excel at different specialties. Though it had taken some time, he'd taught himself to make the earth move, a skill unknown in Narashtovik. Blays, meanwhile, was virtually useless at using the nether to do anything besides shadowalk, yet despite a serious effort, the technique eluded Dante. In Mallon, many of the court ethermancers dabbled in the nether as well, but Dante couldn't so much as get the ether to stir, and struggled whenever it was used against him.

It didn't make intuitive sense. If you gave a skilled-enough silversmith a hunk of metal, he could do just about anything with it. With the nether and ether, however, it was as if the gods would only grant you so much talent. Perhaps they were afraid of being rivaled by a human—or of what a human might do with such power.

Yet he thought there might be more to it. Most lands only possessed a fraction of the many talents he'd discovered across the world. As far as Dante knew, he and the People of the Pocket were the only ones who could move the earth. He'd never heard of harvesting before arriving on the Plagued Islands. Mallish ethermancers crafted a number of trinkets such as torchstones that could be found nowhere else, and Dante himself had invented loons. There were times when he wondered if the only limits were what you'd been brought up with, and what you could imagine.

Whatever the case, he knew one thing for certain: he was off to an inauspicious start as a Harvester.

Winden's hold on the shadows slipped, but he pressed on. As he fiddled and futzed, she wandered off, returning several minutes later.

"Are you hungry?" she said.

Dante rubbed his eyes. The light through the canopy had the piercing glow of late afternoon sun on the sea. Hours had slipped away from him. Now that his brain had returned, his stomach seized the opportunity to alert him that it was starving.

"Sure." He stood, knocking dirt from his pants. "Got any of that paste kicking around?"

"Why don't we go into town?"

"Isn't there plenty of fruit right here?"

"You work too much. Besides, it's not permitted to take from the Basket." She grabbed his arm. "Come on."

She led them toward the calm surf of the bay. The path meandered through the trees, opening to grass and the beach. A second Basket had been built into the tide pools, housing oceanic plants of every shape and color. Winden walked past it and around a spar of rock reaching down to the water.

Down the shore, white smoke whorled from small fires burning on the sand. Dozens of people milled around, tending to the fires, slicing the rinds of fruits, scaling fish. The smell of grilled meat wafted on the air. It wasn't fish, but it wasn't beef, venison, chicken, or anything else Dante's nose could place. He wondered if it was one of the curiosities they'd seen in the jungle. Rather than their typically drab clothes, today the Kandeans wore wraps and skirts of purple, orange, and green.

"Is it some kind of holiday?" Dante said.

"It certainly looks like it," Winden said evenly. "If I didn't know better, I'd say it was for Larsin—and for you."

He laughed. "Is that why you kept me at the Basket all day? To keep me from finding out about this?"

"I didn't have to work very hard to distract you, did I?"

As he neared the locals, several broke his way, speaking excitedly in Taurish. Grinning, one of the men extended a cocked elbow.

"Link with him," Winden said. "It is our handshake. For someone you want to honor."

Dante clasped elbows with the man, somehow managing to acquit himself with minimal awkwardness. The man blurted something. Dante leaned closer, as if that would help him understand.

"He's thanking me?" Dante said. "For saving Larsin?"

"That is right," Winden said. "And for saving Kandak."

"Thank you," Dante replied in Taurish. "But still much to do."

The man looked surprised to hear Dante speaking the island's language. If he had any misgivings about hearing such words from a foreigner, however, he hid them, bowing and lowering his hand to the earth. He turned away. Dante walked on down the beach. He'd hardly made it ten yards before another group of townsfolk stopped him, offering the same elbow-clasp, and refusing to disperse until, relying heavily on Winden for translation, he relayed the events of their return through the Dreaming Peaks. When Winden finished explaining, the Kandeans questioned her some time longer. From what Dante picked up, they were trying to figure out if any of the details had been embellished. When they finally left, they did so shaking their heads, grinning in disbelief.

The next person to intercept him was Blays. He was gnawing on a rib that may or may not have been pork. "Have you tried the food?"

Dante glanced down the beach. "The attentions of the locals have been occupying my attention. It would appear that we're heroes."

"Well, the fare is incredible. Back home, you're a king, right? Why don't you throw yourself a feast every day?"

"I've been a little busy staving off invasion and treachery. But if I ever go insane, feel free to remind me of the benefits of fiscal irresponsibility."

There were at least two hundred people on the beach, with more trickling in by the minute. People played their carved bone flutes while others accompanied them on handheld drums little thicker than plates. Dancers paired up in two lines, facing each other from just out of arm's length. When one reached out to touch or grab their partner, the partner backpedaled, hands thrust out, face filled with longing and regret.

A middle-aged woman approached bearing skins of the pale, tough leather the people often used for purses and such. These turned out to be filled with a very fruity, very strong wine. This was the best thing Dante could have asked for, as over the next hour, he had to repeat the story of their journey to three more groups of listeners.

As he addressed the receiving line, people dragged furniture and torches down to the tideline. Dante kept an eye on the activity. The seating arrangements used in feasts could provide deep insight into a land's political structure—how many layers of aristocracy did they host; were the gentry or the peasants allowed to participate; was the festival more about celebration and entertainment, or the spectacle of the event.

There in Kandak, they were laying blankets on the sand, with people drifting to them in no obvious order or hierarchy. After Dante concluded his latest retelling of the story, Winden led him and Blays to a blanket, seating herself. Men moved from blanket to blanket handing out seamless wooden cups of wine. Rather than servants, the wine-bearers included some of the warriors Dante had seen battling the Tauren on their arrival to the island. Larsin was among them, too, grinning and clasping elbows. He made his way to their blanket, but remained standing. Annoyed, Dante rose to meet him.

"No need to get up," Larsin said. "I'm just making a toast."

Suppressing a sigh, Dante sat back down. Larsin held up his cup. Speaking in Taurish, he called his people to attention, words booming over the sough of the surf.

"I'm looking at my friends." Winden quietly translated his words. "I'm tasting my wine. Normally, this isn't cause for celebration. It's common. But tonight, it is a miracle. A miracle that I'm cured after being certain I was dead—and that this cure came from my son."

He gestured to Dante, then Blays. Still translating, Winden said, "They ask for nothing, but have given me everything. Tonight, then, let us give them the most valuable gift we can: our thanks, our gratitude, and our loyalty."

Larsin lifted his cup, sloshing wine on the sand, and drained it. The people whooped and clapped. Being feted always made Dante feel awkward, but it was hard not to be charmed by the genuineness of the Kandeans.

Larsin waited for the applause to die down. Soon, all that

could be heard was the whisper of the surf. He lowered his gaze. "Few days pass without clouds. Today is no different. An hour ago, I was informed that the Tauren have taken the Dreaming Peaks."

Outraged calls rang out across the beach, followed by babble. Larsin let this take its course, then lifted his hands for silence. "Aye, you hate it. You know what that means? It means the Tauren have made one hell of a mistake. They've profaned the only sacred place left on this island. And they'll die for it. My life has been given back to me just in time for me to spend it driving the Tauren back to their tower."

He stalked down the sand, a smile fighting its way past the sternness of his expression. "Kicking the Tauren's asses in half can wait until later. Tonight, we celebrate. As two of the bravest warriors I've ever seen join our family in Kandak. No more rixen—Dante Galand and Blays Buckler are now rixaka."

There was a moment of silence—hard to tell, but Dante thought it was shocked—and then a new wave of cheers. Winden's throat worked, but she said nothing.

"Mind translating your translation?" Blays said.

"Rixen are foreign liars," she replied. "Rixaka are foreign family. The highest honor. No rixen has been named rixaka since Larsin himself." She gestured up the beach. On the grass near the edge of the jungle, a hastily erected hut stood propped up on short stilts. "That house. It's yours now. Whenever you come back, you can stay there. And when you are away, anyone who looks at it will remember that you are a part of us." She met their eyes in turn. "This gift, it's not given lightly."

Dante looked up to Larsin. In Taurish, he said, "Thank you."

Larsin shook his head. "Thank *you*."

The older man turned back to address the crowds. This time, his words were met with a wave of laughter; every eye on the beach turned toward Dante and Blays.

"There is a second declaration," Winden said. "As rixaka, you are also eligible to be married."

"I'm not," Blays said. "I already have a wife."

"In our lands, yes," Dante said. "But not here."

Blays snorted. "You should be the one seizing the opportunity, Mr. Eternal Bachelor." He glanced toward the hut. "Though if you do wind up married, I'm going to have to demand a separate house."

Larsin wrapped up his speech. This was followed immediately by servings of barbecued red meat that Winden claimed was from the brisket of something called a fodder, and grilled fish whose flesh was even redder. Every blanket was given a heaping bowl of san paste and a tray of tiny bowls containing various chutneys and pastes. The onions, chilies, and spices within them should have been overpowering, but they were so well-balanced Dante suspected they'd been developed by Harvesters, which Winden confirmed.

After the meal concluded, people wandered up to their blanket in a steady stream, welcoming them to Kandak. The well-wishers didn't slow down until the sun was long set and the night's breeze had gone quiet. Larsin went off to speak with some of his warriors. With Blays off fetching more wine, and Winden making her way to the privy, an old man approached the blanket and sat across from Dante.

"Larsin says you are rixaka," he said in accented Mallish. He had a curly white beard, a bald scalp, and eyes so pale blue they nearly looked blind. "Before I agree with him, I say you play Woten."

"Truth-lie?" Dante said.

The man nodded slowly. On the blanket, he laid out a set of bone dice inscribed with Taurish numerals, setting two wooden cups beside them. "Woten, it is vital. Its gamble is not for money. It is for truths. If you win a round? You ask me anything. And I must answer."

"What happens if you lie?"

"Those who lie are damned. They are..." He gestured, searching for the word. "Marked. *Stained*. Kaval sees this. Knows you're guilty."

"This sounds like a strange game," Dante said. "Who would want to play it?"

"Enemies who wish peace talks. Two families whose young wish to wed. When you think a man has stolen from you. All disputes solved through Woten."

"Next question. Why do you wish to play this with *me*?"

The old man smirked. "To get answer? You must play."

"Tell me the rules."

The old man's name was Stav; he was the one who'd promised to look after the infant Blays had rescued. The basics of Woten were similar to many games involving dice and cups: both players rolled their dice, keeping the results hidden from each other beneath the cup. This meant bluffing was an integral part of the game. Whoever won each round was allowed to ask one question of the loser.

But there were three wrinkles. First, you didn't announce your results out loud—you wrote them on a scrap of paper, only comparing them after both players had written down a number. Without knowing in advance what number you needed to beat, bluffing was complicated by how likely you thought your *opponent* was to have bluffed, which depended partly on how desperate they were to receive—or avoid giving—answers.

The second wrinkle was this: if you suspected your opponent was bluffing, you could call them on it. But if you were wrong, then you had to answer a second question as well.

The game had to last at least seven rounds. After that, if you won a round, you could choose to end the match rather than asking a question. This made it sound like a game of Woten might finish in just two or three minutes, but Stav said that many games were played with advisors who (depending on the arrangement) could help you decide when to bluff, whether your opponent was bluffing, what questions to ask, and so on. These discussions could make a single game endure for hours.

The third and final wrinkle: though the dice had six sides, they weren't numbered one through six. Some showed special numbers as high as thirty, meaning that with five dice, your results could sound preposterously high.

Overall, the game was simple. But Dante could see that the psychology behind it was fiendish.

They gathered their dice in their cups, shook them, and slammed them to the ground. Dante's added up to 23. A good score overall, but it would be beaten easily if Stav had any special numbers. Even so, he thought it was strong enough. Using a bit of charcoal, he wrote 23 on a scrap of a pale leaf that felt exactly like paper. When they revealed their scores, Stav had thirteen.

Stav examined Dante's face. "You have 23?"

"Correct."

"I think," Stav said after a short hesitation, "you bluff."

Dante lifted his cup, revealing he'd been telling the truth. "I win. Twice over. First question: why do you want to play this game with me?"

"To learn why you have come here."

"What, nobody told you?"

The old man smiled thinly. "They did. Next round."

Dante swore at his foolishness; he'd had several cups of fruit-wine and had blurted his second question without thinking. This round, Dante got lucky with one of the special dice, picking up a 49. He wrote as much on his leaf. Stav had fourteen. As per the rules, they read their scores out loud, watching each other's faces.

Stav folded his arms. "I accept."

"Good for you." Dante swept the cup away from his dice. "I win again. So you have heard I came here to cure my father, but you don't you believe it. Why not?"

"Two reasons. For Kaval, I answer both. First: I doubt because I doubt all outsiders. Second: I doubt because I heard you are bad."

"What exactly did you hear about me?"

Stav made a cutting gesture. "You earned one question. You have asked it."

"I thought you might want to answer that one out of the kindness of your heart."

The old man straightened his spine, mustering his considerable gravitas. "Roll."

Dante came out with a twelve. Maintaining his best gambling face, on his paper, he wrote a 21. When they made their reveals, Stav showed a six.

"You bluff," the old man said.

"Hang on," Dante said. "Surely *you're* bluffing."

"That is so. And you?"

"Yes. No questions this round, then?"

"None."

As they rolled their next, a man and a woman drifted up, observing in silence. Dante tallied his score (an even twenty) and wrote it on his leaf.

"Eighty-seven," Stav said.

"Eighty-seven. As in eighty. Plus seven." Dante stared him down. It was an outrageous number that relied on maxing out nearly all his dice except the smallest ones. "You're bluffing."

He showed his dice. "Wrong. Two questions. Why *did* you come to the island?"

"It's just as they say," Dante said. "To cure Larsin."

"What does he matter to you?"

"He doesn't. I came here because that would mean I'm a better man than he is." He gazed over the milling crowds seated around their blankets and laughing in the torchlight. "But the trip was worth it in its own right."

Stav won the next three rounds in a row, asking Dante

whether he'd had any contact with the Tauren prior to his arrival in Kandak (no), if he had any enemies in Kandak (also no), and whether the Mallish had any role in his presence here (again, no).

Dante won the next round with a lucky roll that Stav mistakenly called as a bluff. "Does my father actually care about me? Or did he only summon me here because he knew I was his only chance?"

The old man quirked a brow. "Larsin, he searched for you for years. Long before he came sick. Never stopped."

"Why did he come here to begin with?"

"To trade metal. Iron. Earn you a fortune. First war with Tauren, this delayed him. By the time he finished, you disappeared."

Dante took the next round via bluff. "Now that my father's well, do you think you can defeat the Tauren again?"

Stav bared his teeth and turned to stare out at the dark waters of the bay. "I doubt. They have more weapons. Armor. Shaden."

"Second question. If Blays and I stayed, would it make a difference?"

"Hard to say. If anyone can kill Vordon? It is you."

After that, Stav took round after round. After the fourth one—he asked if Dante thought Winden was pretty, which Dante was obliged to confirm—Dante finally won, and declared the match over. Stav gathered his things.

"Find what you came here for?" Dante said.

"Yes." The old man bowed his head. "Welcome to the family."

He ambled away. None of the others had come back to the blanket, so Dante wandered north, away from the torches, seizing the chance to think.

In time, a young man found him, pressed a cup of wine into his hand, and asked if he and Blays would show them how to fight with swords. This drew a significant crowd and resulted in multiple additional cups of wine. There was much laughing and the scraping of knuckles (though at least they'd had the sense to switch to bamboo practice swords).

Dante glanced up and noticed the moon had advanced a remarkable distance across the sky. Most of the torches had been snuffed, leaving the beach dim. Blays was having trouble walking. Dante helped him to their hut, then returned to the beach to try to clear his head. The sands were all but deserted. Recognizing Larsin's silhouette, Dante made way toward the taller man, only stumbling once.

Larsin turned. "Still awake?"

"My mother," Dante blurted. "What was she like?"

His father eyed him. "You're drunk."

"So what?"

Larsin chuckled softly. "Fair question. I suppose you deserve to be. And to know this. Your mother was…very beautiful."

"I mean what was she *like*?"

"Witty. Her tongue was as sharp as broken glass. That was what I liked best—the way she made me laugh. She made everything brighter. She could have charged money to listen to her describe a twelve-hour sleep." As he spoke, his voice lightened with recalled memory. "She loved to learn. To read. Sometimes, I think this was mostly so she'd have more ways to prove others wrong. But she loved it for its own sake, too. She was always hungry. I couldn't always keep up with her. I thought when we had you, that might finally slow her down enough for me to keep pace."

He found a small smile. "After her death, I nearly joined her. So she could make me laugh again. But I knew I couldn't leave you alone in the world. What an idiot I was: I wound up doing that anyway."

Dante took a shuddering breath and gazed toward the entrance of the bay. In two more days, the *Sword of the South* would arrive.

The next time he turned around, Larsin was gone. Dante made his way to the hut and climbed the fresh-cut stairs. Blays snored inside. Between the wash of the surf and the perfect air, it was the most restful sleep Dante had ever had.

The sun woke him too early. Yet somehow, Blays was already up and gone. With a headache and a dry mouth, Dante headed uphill to the town well. When he got back to the hut, Blays was there, puffy-eyed and sweaty.

"I think we should stay," Dante said.

Blays wiped his brow. "Don't tell me you're actually going to take them up on the wife thing."

"We'll ask Captain Twill to come back again in a few weeks. Then we'll conduct a few raids of our own. Arm these people. I can make them loons so they can coordinate with the Boat-Growers or anyone else Larsin can rally. And we'll do our best to knock out Vordon."

"What triggered this about-face?"

"We have the power to help these people. If we don't, the next time we come back here, they may be nothing more than a memory."

"And you're sure that would be a bad thing?"

"You'd leave them to be overrun by the Tauren?" Dante said. "I'm shocked. Actually shocked. I would have expected *you'd* be trying to convince *me* to stay."

"Yesterday, I was thinking about it." Blays slapped his palm against the wall of the hut. "But our circumstances are muddier than they seem. There's something you need to see."

He led Dante to a grassy path into the jungle, refusing to answer any questions. After a short hike, running water splashed from ahead. A small, two-part waterfall coursed into a misty pool. Around its banks, rabbit-eared molbry flowers peeped from the shadows.

"They were growing here all along," Blays said. "Still want to help these people?"

10

Dante moved toward the flowers in a daze. "How did you find these?"

"Last night, a woman came to speak to me, terrified. Once she'd calmed down, she said that since we'd been named rixaka, she had something to show me. And she brought me here."

Dante's hands curled into fists. "Find Larsin. And Winden."

Back in town, they located Winden within minutes. It took significantly longer to round up Larsin, blinking and bleary. Dante marched them through the jungle. Winden fell silent at once, but Larsin kept up a breezy, amiably confused stream of questions right up to the moment they gazed on the red flowers surrounding the waterfall.

"The cure for your sickness was right here all along," Dante said. "Why, then, did you send us across the entire island to find it?"

Larsin gawked. "Molbries? *Here?* But they only grow at the Bloodfalls!"

"Horseshit! They grow wherever they please, don't they?" He turned on Winden. "That's what you were doing at the Basket yesterday, wasn't it? You weren't looking for people who might see us. You were destroying the molbries you grow there. So I wouldn't see them."

She couldn't seem to meet his eyes. "The Basket. There were no molbries there."

"This is a misunderstanding," Larsin said. "We didn't know these were here. If we had, there would have been no reason to send you so far."

Dante rubbed his hand down his mouth. "Unless the trip had some other purpose. Such as exposing us to the crimes of the Tauren. You chose the Bloodfalls because that's where they leave out their newborns. You knew if we saw that, it might be enough to convince us to help you fight them."

"That's absurd. If I wanted your help, I wouldn't send you on some two-tailed fox hunt. I would simply ask for it. There must be something in this waterfall similar to the Bloodfalls. We'll ask whoever owns this land—and then ask why they didn't tell me about it when I was at death's door."

"Why would they withhold the cure from you?"

"I can't say. Maybe they'd have us surrender to the Tauren. Maybe this is an old grudge. Gods know I've made my share of enemies."

Winden strode between them. "*No more!*"

Larsin's eyes shifted. "Winden, what do—"

"I said no more." She pointed at Dante and Blays, then stuck her finger in Larsin's face. "These two, they have done everything we asked. Risked their lives for you. Faced the Tauren in battle. Healed our people. All of this, they have done with honor. We can't lie to them any longer."

Larsin's hand clenched near his belt. "What are you saying?"

"Dante. You're right. After you couldn't heal Larsin with nether, the only cure was the molbries. Those could have been found right here. But they also might have killed Larsin, taking away our only chance to stand against the Tauren."

"So in case that happened," Larsin said, "we needed you to see what they're really like. In the hopes you'd take up the torch."

Dante exhaled through his nose. "Is this why you made us rixaka? To try to make us feel attached to this place?"

"And this is why Stav came to you to play Woten," Winden said. "To learn if you wanted me, and if so, for your wife or your toy."

"That's why you're telling me this now? To avoid having to be my consort?"

"No! I tell you because you have to leave on your boat. If you stay? You will get sick."

"Sick?" Blays said. "You mean with the plague?"

"It afflicts everyone who stays here longer than a few weeks. This is why you must go now."

"But if it affects everyone, there must be a cure."

"It doesn't always work. I won't let you take that risk."

Dante turned on Larsin. "You cared nothing about exposing me to all of these dangers. Why shouldn't I kill you?"

Jaw bulging, Larsin stepped forward. "Because it's exactly what *you* would have done."

"You don't know anything about me!"

"I *have* been searching for you for years. I've heard the stories they tell about you. When the knives are out, there's nothing you won't do to win. You'll lie. Cheat. Let friends die. Because the alternative is far worse. My people are on the brink of destruction! Just as you've always done for yours, I will do anything to save them."

"Then gods help them." Dante stepped back down the path.

"Wait," Larsin called. "The woman who brought you my note. Riddi. She believed in this just as much as I did—and she was your half-sister."

Dante met his eyes. "Your daughter died for nothing."

He walked away from the falls. Behind him, Larsin said something and Winden raised her voice against him.

"I'm sorry," Blays said. "I can't help feeling like this is my fault."

"That would be because it is."

"I would place *some* of the blame on that dad of yours."

"None of this matters anymore. The *Sword of the South* will be here tomorrow. We'll get on it, and we'll go home."

Blays tromped through the grass beside him. "You know he's wrong, don't you? We've made a lot of tough choices along the way. We've had to find answers to impossible questions. But we've never done anything like what he's done to you."

Dante nodded, but he wasn't at all sure that was so. Maybe they only believed it because the only ones who knew better were long dead, voiceless, powerless to speak the truth.

The next morning, they sat in the shade of their hut, waiting for the ship to arrive in the mouth of the harbor. Dante yawned steadily. Wary of betrayal—if Larsin had sacrificed his daughter to his cause, he might be angry enough to try to capture or punish them—Dante had convinced Blays to hide overnight in the jungle. There, the birds, bugs, and constant rustling of the leaves had woken them a thousand times apiece. It had been the smart move, though. They could sleep on the boat.

By the hut, he kept one eye on the town. No one got too near. Around ten o'clock, white sails shined from the bay.

Dante stood, slinging his pack over his shoulder. "About time."

He padded to the shore. A small canoe waited in the dry sand above the waves. They'd take it to the little island in the bay, where the *Sword of the South* would pick them up via longboat. Dante wasn't sure if Captain Twill intended to quarantine them after that, but after the events of the last two weeks, spending some time sequestered in a cabin would feel like a vacation.

"Hey." Winden jogged toward them, carrying a satchel. "Before you go."

Dante grabbed the canoe and dragged it toward the surf. "Don't want to hear it."

"I know my apologies are worthless. I brought you something that isn't."

"Right now, the only bribe I'm interested in is a Larsin-sized coffin."

"If you get sick. And it's not something you can heal yourself? These will help you." She passed him a narrow black box.

It sloshed and smelled like the sea. "Shaden?"

"Eat them. And then come back here as fast as you can."

He held the box back out for her. "Please. I've had enough of your games."

She stepped closer, face barely a foot from his. "No game. No lie. Stab me in the mouth if you don't think it speaks truth."

"I won't do that." He took the box and tucked it under his arm. "But I don't know if I can trust you, either."

"I hope you never have to see me again."

He turned halfway toward her, nodded, and put his things into the canoe. Blays hopped in. Dante gave the boat a running shove, then rolled in over the side. They took up paddles and made way to the tiny rocky island, landing on a smooth apron scraped clean of mussels and barnacles.

Mr. Naran awaited them. "Survived the stay, did you? How was paradise?"

"Hell," Blays said. "Tell me you've got rum?"

"You insult me by asking." He held the longboat steady while they climbed aboard, then deftly jumped in behind them. "As for your stay being hellacious, please tell me you didn't offend our most reliable trade partner *too* badly."

Dante scratched his neck. He hadn't shaved since reaching the Plagued Islands and was looking forward to a visit with the ship's barber. "Don't worry. The way things are going here, it won't be long before they're all dead anyway."

Naran tucked down the corners of his mouth. "I am trying not to imagine the kind of person who could make enemies of the Kandeans."

The longboat splashed toward the *Sword of the South*, which rode higher in the water than the last time Dante had seen it. They climbed aboard and the crew bustled to haul in the longboat and weigh anchor.

On the deck, Twill clung to a rope, her blond hair fluttering around her face. "You're alive. And the village isn't burning. Good news, yes? Yet you look like you just stepped in a fresh pile."

"That would be an adequate description of our stay," Dante said. "I trust your travels went better?"

"Much silver, minor trouble. My definition of a good trip. How's your health?"

"Better than my mood."

Her eyes moved down his form. "Three days confined to quarters. For the safety of my men. You're a hell of a physician, but the islands carry illness beyond any magic."

The ship lurched. Dante staggered, grabbing for a nearby rope. "If that's what it takes to get us out of here, I'll spend the entire voyage stowed in a cask."

"While I encourage you to accept his generous offer," Blays said, "I'll accept a cabin."

They were installed in the same cabin they'd shared on the trip south. The ship entered the rough waters beyond the bay, listing as it hove east to fight free of the tremendous Current driven by the swirling Mill. Between the detour and the lack of friendly seas, Dante understood why the return trip would take twice as long as their initial passage.

He requested and was supplied with a blank book and a quill. While Blays sipped rum, lounged in his bunk, and did considerable napping, Dante wrote down his experiences on the island, describing the people as well as the numerous plants and animals they'd seen. Despite Larsin's shameless attempt to drag them into a war, Dante thought there might yet be room for trade with the people there.

And now that things had settled down, the shaden struck him as the most interesting discovery of all. They carried nether in them. A handheld reservoir of it. It was difficult to overestimate the value of such a thing, particularly in wartime, where a skilled sorcerer could singlehandedly fight off a platoon or tear down a wall. A leader who could bring shaden to the field would have an advantage over anyone he faced.

When he wasn't writing, Dante spent all three days of the quarantine studying the shells. All living things carried the shadows inside them, but the snails' tissue was packed to the figurative gills. Blays had said they were reminiscent of the kellevurts used in training by the People of the Pocket. In his excitement, Dante tried to loon Nak to research the kellevurts in advance of Dante's return, only to be reminded that the loons had broken.

"This is just great," Dante said. "Shaden may be my biggest discovery since the Black Star, but mine may well be dead before we're in sight of a library."

"No library?" Blays said. "Are you blind? Or just being dense?"

"Oh, we do have one? Is it in the bilge? Or the poop deck?"

"This boat makes its trade in this region. You're basically sailing on a floating library full of fleshy, walking books."

"Oh. Right."

"And here's the best part. Unlike your monks and scribes, who like to leave their cloisters about as much as I like being in them, the people on this boat may actually have experience with shaden."

Dante clapped his notebook shut and stood. "How did I ever forget about your ongoing commitment to education?"

He went to Captain Twill first. When questioned, she shrugged. "Don't know anything about shaden."

"They seem to be the Tauren's motivation for the raids. Like the one you delivered us into. That's never piqued your interest?"

"Those things are a big deal on the island. To everyone else, they're just snails."

"Have you ever seen them outside the Plagued Islands?"

"Nope." She glanced across the deck. "I'm really not your man for this. Ask Naran. He seems to enjoy being bored by nature."

Dante thanked her and found Mr. Naran doing paperwork in his cabin. He didn't look pleased to be interrupted.

"The captain said you might be able to help me," Dante said. "I have some questions about shaden."

Naran set down his quill. "And I have complaints about my workload. So make it fast."

"Do they exist outside the islands?"

"Not that I've seen. Though the west coast of Gask has something not entirely dissimilar."

"Kellevurts?"

Naran nodded. "But this is like the difference between a seagull and an albatross. Similar at a distance, but the shaden are far, far grander."

Dante made quick notes in his book. "Any idea why they're confined to the island?"

"If I would hazard to guess? Because it's an *island*."

He didn't write that down. "The locals value them highly. Do you know why they don't farm them?"

"They don't grow in the shallows. Nor the quiet places. Only where the Current is hard and strong. This makes them hard to locate and dangerous to collect."

After a few more questions, Dante exited onto the deck, gazing in the direction of Arawn's Mill. The funnel of clouds was far too distant to see, yet after speaking to Naran, he was certain the Mill's nether-saturated Current was feeding the shells. If true, this meant that even if he could induce shaden to grow in Narashtovik, they would be useless. No different from the diverse snails already populating the northern city's bay.

Even so, he continued to question the crew, jotting down their responses and making comparisons. He started work on a map, too, augmenting it with whatever information he could pry from the sailors. Eight days into the voyage, with six remaining, a storm hit. Even if the crew hadn't been too busy tending to the ship, Dante was unable to pursue his studies due to a violent bout of seasickness. His heavings were so wretched that Blays stuffed cotton in his ears, then left the cabin to assist on the deck. Within hours, the waves were battering the ship so hard Blays was compelled to return to the cabin despite the odor.

The next day, the storm had calmed, but Dante's stomach hadn't. That evening, undressing for bed, he froze. A chill ran down his spine. His stomach and ribs were streaked red.

He doused the cabin's lantern. After Blays was snoring, Dante nicked his arm and sent the nether within himself. Small black spots were suspended in his viscera. When he attempted to touch them, the shadows slid right off.

He sat back on his bunk, limbs quivering. It felt like the same affliction that had nearly killed Larsin. They'd treated his father's illness with molbry flowers, yet Winden had only provided Dante with shaden. And instructions to come back and see her in the event he fell ill. Why? Because the molbries wouldn't have survived the trip? Or had they not been a cure at all? Had they been nothing more than a way to get Dante and Blays to trek across the island?

He took deep breaths until he calmed down, then tried again to heal himself. Again, the nether found no purchase.

He didn't know how suspicious to be of Winden. The shaden she'd given him might be some kind of final trick or poison. Besides, he didn't know if his affliction was lethal. Except for plagues, many diseases had an alternate cure, one that often functioned better than anything a physician could give you: time.

It took him a long time to get to sleep. In the morning, he felt hollow, weak. The streaks on his gut had darkened to a wine-like maroon. He knew they'd soon be black. Blays was already out of the cabin. Dante reached under his bunk and got out his pack containing the box of shells. It was sodden and briny. Damp from the storm, no doubt—but when he opened the bag, the lid of the box fell out. A rotting, marine stench came with it. The box had been knocked open during the jostling of the storm.

Given the smell, he didn't have to inspect the shaden to know they were dead.

He found his thinnest knife and sawed the snails loose from their shells, hoping to find a piece that had avoided the rot. Typically, the shaden's flesh was an even gray; what he dug from his shells was pale, mottled with green and black. He got a bowl, filled it with water, and washed off the least diseased-looking sections. Even after rinsing, they looked awful. He trimmed off the grossest parts, and then, after considering his options, tipped back his head and swallowed the snail whole.

Even without chewing, the taste was intensely bitter. And familiar. He'd had it before. In Winden's paste made from san root.

In the midst of trying to figure out what this meant, his stomach churned on itself like a vat of melted cheese. He barely made it to the tin pot he used for seasickness in time to catch the violent ejecta.

He did his best with the other two shaden, but couldn't keep them down, either. He was flinging the last sour bits out the window when the door opened.

"It smells like a fish's bunghole in here," Blays said, fanning the door. "Hey, are you all right?"

Dante lowered himself to his bunk. "I'm sick. Same as Larsin."

"Did you take the shaden? Like Winden said?"

"The box broke in the storm. They were no good. Hence why the smell is even worse than yesterday."

Blays closed the door. "You're sure you've got it?"

Dante lifted his shirt to show the darkening streaks. "I've tried to fix it. I can't."

"I'd tell you that it's no big deal—that Larsin was sick for weeks and weeks—but I have the feeling they made sure he wasn't getting too bad."

"That's very comforting. Makes me feel even better than when I was heaving up rotten snails a minute ago."

"I thought you would appreciate my unflinching realism." Blays made a fist, tapping it repeatedly against the door frame in thought. "Come on. We're going to see Captain Twill."

Feeling queasy and lightheaded, Dante tucked the empty shells in the box for later study, then rousted himself. Captain Twill was in her quarters and allowed them in.

She took one look at Dante and her face went as hard as the Dreaming Peaks. "Get back to your room. Right now."

"We have a decent idea what this is," Dante said. "I was summoned to the islands to help someone who had it. It didn't seem to be contagious."

"So you went to the *Plagued* Islands to treat someone with this disease. Which you then contracted. And you're telling me it's *not* contagious?"

"It's more of a…condition. And they know how to cure it."

"Which means we have to head back," Blays said. "Right now."

The captain sat behind her desk, propped her boots on it, and crossed her arms. "Can't."

Blays moved directly across from her. "I'm sorry, did I make it sound as though that was a request?"

"What's your plan, tough guy? Take me hostage? Force the entire crew to heave about?"

"Oh, I don't have a plan. Do you think that makes me *less* dangerous?"

A knife appeared in her hand as if summoned from the ether. Blays twitched but didn't draw a sword. Twill bounced the knife across her knuckles, then disappeared it.

"I'd turn back if I could," Twill said. "I owe you my life. Besides, I have the feeling you'd be good men to have owing me a favor in return." She winked at them, then went somber. "But we don't have the supplies. We've had to ration what we've got just to make it to Bressel. If we turned around now, could we make it back to the island? Maybe. But we wouldn't have enough to get back. And if we took on supplies there, my entire ship could get sick."

"And if something happens to Dante," Blays said, "an entire kingdom could crack apart."

"How's that? Who's he on a mission for?"

"Himself."

Her gaze shot to Dante. "You're a *king*? And what kind of monarch has to hire a smuggler to ferry him around rather than the royal fleet? Where do you rule, South Armpit?"

"Narashtovik," Dante said. "Northern Gask."

Twill laughed out loud. "You're *that* Dante?"

"And I need your help."

"Well, I don't care if you're the king of the Celeset. I'm not putting my crew to that kind of risk."

"Yeah, I was afraid you'd say that." Blays sat on the edge of her desk. "So here's my next offer. Take us back to the island. We'll figure out how to cure this thing. And when we do, we'll share the secret with you—allowing you to trade with the islands with impunity."

"Making me very, very rich. Now you're speaking my language." She wore a large silver ring on her right hand, and as she thought this through, she twisted it back and forth. "Can't do it. Out here, the only thing keeping us alive is each other. I have to bring my men in to port. Give the ones that want to leave the chance to do so. We'll resupply. Then we can go back."

"You're unbelievable. He saves your life, and when you have the chance to return the favor, you're worried about facing a few grumbles from your crew?"

"Do you really think he's the first sick man to come back from the islands? We'll take him to the ethermancers."

Dante laughed. "The same ones that were so eager to help you when you were ill?"

"They turned me away because I'm from the Collen Basin. You look as Mallish as King Charles. They'll be happy to take your money."

"And you really think they can help me?"

"They won't be able to cure you. But they'll be able to push it back. Give you enough time for the trip back to the islands."

"Sounds iffy," Blays said. "What do you think?"

Dante shrugged. "It's either that, or we keelhaul her and take her boat."

"I have always wanted a boat."

Twill rolled her eyes. "I'm right here, you know."

"You're right," Dante said. "I can't ask your men to sacrifice themselves for me. But please. When we get to Bressel, restock as quickly as you can."

She stood. "I'll start making preparations."

Dante returned to his cabin. Belowdecks, men scurried around, rearranging cargo with muffled thumps. Dante drew on the nether, sending it back into his body; if the ethermancers could treat the illness, surely he could, too. At least slow it down. Yet after an hour of the closest focus he could muster, he still hadn't found a way to touch the dark spots inside him. Would the ethermancers prove useless? Or was there something specific to the ether that allowed it to treat the sicknesses of the Plagued Islands?

He sat up in bed. *The Cycle of Arawn* spoke of Arawn's Mill. Initially, the mill had ground ether, the substance of the firmament and of purity, but after it had fallen and cracked, it ground nether instead—the substance of life and death, of renewal and decay. He didn't think the whirlpool was the same Arawn's Mill spoken of in the stories—the *Cycle* said Arawn had placed his mill in the sky, not the sea—but what if there was some connection? What if the nether drawn to the islands by the Currents had been corrupted, somehow? And could only be negated by its predecessor, the ether?

He spent the rest of the day reading the *Cycle*, but found nothing that seemed relevant. He woke to the smell of burned cinnamon. Heart pounding, he pulled up his shirt. The streaks had advanced to his ribs. Some had gone purple.

The day after that, they were black.

The captain sent him tea of all kinds, gathered in her manifold travels. Most were bitter or brackish. Dutifully, he drank them down. They made no difference. His body beat with a dull pain that grew more strident by the hour. Skittish shadows swam on the edge of his vision. Sometimes they seemed to take the shape of faces, but when he tried to look at them squarely, they dissolved into amorphous limbs.

One morning, he found himself too weak to walk on his own. Blays helped him totter around the deck to take in the air. Dante shivered uncontrollably. The shadows ringing his sight were no longer skittish. They seemed to be attending him. Waiting. Eager.

The ship pitched down the back of a wave, jostling Dante from his feet. Blays grabbed his arm and pulled him upright.

"If something happens," Dante said. "Ask the Council to continue to look after the norren. At a distance, or the norren will rebuff them. You know how they are."

"I won't be telling them anything." Blays relaxed his grip on Dante's upper arm. "Except that their leader starts making funeral plans whenever he gets the sniffles."

"It's their decision as to who will succeed me. I wish to be buried next to Cally. And tell them one last thing: that you are always welcome in Narashtovik."

Blays blinked at the sea, then scowled. "We'll be in Bressel in two days. A week after that, we'll be back in the Plagued Islands. And everything will be fine."

The pain running down his spine told him otherwise, but he didn't try to contradict Blays. You couldn't soften the blow any more than you could reach up and reverse the course of the sun.

With Blays' help, he made his way back to their cabin and rolled himself into his bunk. Blays muttered something about tea and left. The ship rocked on the waves, its timbers creaking. The shadows at the edge of his vision pulsed closer and closer. The pain pulsed with them. The window was open to the sea air, but the only thing he could smell was charred cinnamon.

Bit by bit, the cabin grew dark. Was it dusk already? Then how was a shaft of sunlight shining through the window?

The shadows filled him, and he saw nothing.

He felt no pain. No pleasure, either, but the absence of his former agony felt so good he never wanted to leave it. It smelled like dust and damp straw. No cinnamon. It was dark, but the shapes in his eyes weren't moving like the shadows had. A beam of starlight glimmered through the window, painting a silvery rectangle on the opposite wall.

His heart crumpled on itself, then expanded with joy. Arawn's hill beneath the stars. He had passed to the other side. No more sickness. No more pain. No more struggle. Dizzy with wonder, he rolled onto his side and managed to stand. Shuffling his feet, he moved to the window, eyes watering as he prepared to look on Arawn.

Below him, a city slumbered in the darkness.

He wasn't on the hill beneath the stars. He wasn't on the Sword of the South, either—he was inside a jail cell.

11

He stared out in disbelief. Iron bars blocked off the window. Fifty feet below, three-story row houses crammed the streets. Torches flapped in the larger intersections. Shouts and drunken laughter echoed off tenement walls. Dante pressed his face to the bars. They smelled like drying blood. The moon wasn't up and he couldn't make out much more than the silhouettes of buildings.

Then the bells began to ring. Glass. Piercing. The Odeleon. He was back in Bressel.

As the last bell chimed, the door squealed open. Dante turned, reaching for his sword. This was gone. The nether, however, was always at hand. He bit the inside of his lip until he tasted blood to feed the shadows.

"I wouldn't do that." The man in the door was dressed in the gray robes of a priest of Taim. In his middle thirties, he was tall, with deep-set eyes and the cheekbones of a cadaver. A ball of gleaming white ether shined in his palm.

Dante let the nether retreat to the corners of the room. "Who are you?"

"Your questions will be answered depending on how cooperative you are in answering mine."

"What have I done to deserve arrest?"

"Arrest?" The tall man moved into the room. Two monks filed in behind him, one male and one female, along with a fourth man armed with a sword and a long knife. "This is quarantine. For the safety of the kingdom. Refusing to aid my inquiry will be considered a threat to the crown."

"I am happy to assist you however I can."

"And I am happy to hear that." He snapped his fingers. One of the monks produced a square wooden board, unfolding two hinged runners from its underside. He set the board on the ground. The head monk nodded at Dante, who sat across from it. His questioner kneeled before the board, sitting on his feet. From his robes, he withdrew a quill, an inkwell, a sheet of vellum, and a bottle of blotting sand. "What is the nature of your relationship to the *Sword of the South*?"

Dante rubbed grit from the corners of his eyes. The man's accent was neutral, neither aristocratic nor plebeian. He was clearly a monk, but wore none of the necklaces or bracelets the Mallish priests used to denote their primary god and their station within that sect.

Highly unusual. In Mallon, where the followers of eleven different gods jockeyed for the favor and respect of the court, going about your business without the signifiers of who you stood for and how important you were was akin to showing up to a battle without your sword and armor. Either this man had no interest in playing their games, or he was so highly positioned he'd already won.

"Commercial," Dante answered.

"And what was your destination?"

Dante glanced between the monk's silent entourage. "Wouldn't these questions be more appropriate for the ship's captain?"

The man made a note. "The captain is not your concern. I am."

"We were going to the Plagued Islands."

"For what purpose?"

"I was visiting family."

The monk looked up from his writing. "You are Mallish."

It wasn't a question. "I was born thirty miles from Bressel. My father, however, preferred to leave a place before his footprints could overlap themselves. In time, his travels took him to the Plagued Islands, which he wound up favoring more than me."

"Then why return now?"

"He was sick. He wanted to see me again. In case it was his last chance."

The monk stared. The irises of his eyes were such a dark gray that it appeared his pupils had swallowed them whole. "Were you able to see him?"

"When I arrived, it looked like he might not make it. He made a full recovery before I left."

"We found these in your belongings." He produced a small bag and methodically clinked the three empty shaden shells on the stone floor. "Why?"

"Because you searched my things?"

"You have one more chance to answer."

Dante suppressed a sigh. "I was given them in case of sickness."

"Are you aware of any other properties they might possess?"

"I was told to eat them. I don't think they're a cure, though, because they told me to come back right away." He raised his eyebrows. "Were you the one who helped me? If so, I owe you my life."

"You were unable to treat yourself?"

"How would I have done that?"

"When I entered, you drew on the nether."

"I've taught myself a few small things," Dante said. "But I wouldn't know where to begin to cure a disease."

The man picked up one of the shells, tracing his fingernail along its whorls. "Are you aware that the use of nether is forbidden here?"

"That's why I left. I live in the Middle Kingdoms now. I had no intention of stepping foot in your city. We were supposed to resupply, then head straight back to the islands."

"Your very presence is profane. An insult to Taim. That's why you left Mallon. Why you intended to confine yourself to your ship. Yet you came to Bressel despite your knowledge that you're not welcome here. Do you think you should be excused because you tried to keep yourself only *mildly* blasphemous before our father?"

"It was a matter of survival," Dante said. "I believed that if I showed the proper humility, Father Taim would show mercy."

The man scratched out another note, keeping his eyes locked on Dante's. "Why would he show mercy to someone who disobeyed his commands? You chose to learn the nether. It should come as no surprise that this sin has cost you your life."

He rose with a whisper of cloth. The male monk folded away the small table. The female monk opened the door and they filed outside. The door closed with a bang. On the other side, a bolt rammed into place.

Dante put his ear to the door. Footsteps rustled down the hall. The cadaverous man had come to him mere minutes after he'd awakened. Were they watching him? The cell appeared empty—it contained no more than a pail and a pile of straw for sleeping—but the monk was an ethermancer. Dante bit his lip again and relaxed his eyes, scanning the cell for any trace of ether.

Finding no sign of surveillance, he sent the shadows within himself. The darkness that had been spreading across his body had been reduced to specks. As Captain Twill had predicted, they hadn't cured him. They'd merely reset the sickness' course.

He moved to the window. Where was he being held? Not the palace; he saw no walls beneath him. Couldn't see the Chanset River, either, yet the ringing of the Odeleon had come from the east. The cathedral was on the west bank of the river, which placed him even further west. In a high tower. That left one option: they were holding him in Chenney Hall. This was no debtor's prison or common jail. You only saw the inside of the Chenney if you had personally offended the court—or the gods.

He knew where he was. And that he was in trouble. If he was careful, and waited till the middle of the night, he'd probably be able to open a hole through the wall and sneak downstairs.

But if they'd taken him, he had no doubt they'd taken Blays, and probably Captain Twill as well. He had no idea how long he'd been out. If Blays knew where he was being held, and Dante fled the Chenney, they'd have little hope of finding each other.

There was one thing he knew for sure: Blays wouldn't leave him behind.

Softly, he began to sing out the window, an old drinking tune they'd learned years earlier while hiding from fanatics in the pubs of Whetton. He'd barely made it through the second chorus when he felt a ripple in the darkness.

A shadow deepened on the eastern wall. Blays resolved from it. He was unarmed and his face sported a number of fresh bruises. "If you're done napping, I'd suggest we flee."

"What's going on?" Dante said. "What happened to your face?"

Blays touched his cheek. "Oh, that? I was a bit tortured."

"A *bit*? Like a hanged man is a bit short of breath? Why?"

"It sounded like they were convinced I was up to no good. Thus if I gave them the truth straight away, they'd think I was lying. Meaning whatever I'd have to tell them next *would* be lies. And if they went on to compare those lies to whatever they were getting out of you and Twill, well, next thing you know, we're all liars waving to each other from the rack."

"So your plan was to lie, get tortured, and then spill the truth."

Blays brushed dust from his shoulder. "I'm here, aren't I?"

"I suppose there's no arguing with results. Where's Twill? What happened?"

"You passed out. Didn't look good. As soon as we made port, Twill shoved you into a carriage and we took you to the Odeleon. The monks had barely started work on you when another monk came in and started asking questions about the Plagued Islands. Twill tried to bluff him, but he wasn't having any of it. Dragged the both of us off."

"On what charge?"

"Going to the islands. Which is apparently illegal without a charter from King Charles himself."

"This monk, what did he look like?"

"Tall. Dead. And dressed like he'd crawled out of a pauper's grave. His name was Gladdic."

"He was just in here," Dante said. "He knew about the shaden. He was trying to find out if *I* knew about them."

Blays walked to the window and eyed what lay below them. "He was trying to unravel the same blanket with me. Think that's what this is really about? Seizing the snail trade? Should we ride out to warn everyone whose lettuce is at risk of infestation?"

"That could well be what they're after. In battle, a single live shell could be worth ten soldiers. But this could be a religious thing. Gladdic thinks the nether's an abomination. He saw me draw it. He might be afraid I was going to the island to secure an arsenal of shaden."

"No way. They want them for themselves. Bet you anything that Mallon's been arming the Tauren. Using them to gather the shaden without risking their own soldiers on the island."

Goosebumps ran down Dante's arms. "Lyle's balls, you're right. We have to get out of here. Do you know where they're keeping Twill?"

Blays' eyebrows raised. "We're going back to get you cured, right? Don't tell me your scorn of the Mallish means you want to get wrapped up in their skullduggery."

"Hardly. When I see Winden, we'll let her know what's happening here, but I have about as much interest in getting involved in Mallish colonialism as I do in naked fence-hurdling."

"One problem. When they took us away from the Odeleon, they put us in separate carriages. Twill's took a different direction. I have no idea where she is."

"Gladdic will know."

"Right, and assuming you can take him, do you really think we can pound the answer out of him before his tower full of guards and monks descends on us?"

"What else do you want to do? Go door to door asking if anyone's seen an imprisoned captain wandering around?"

Blays rolled his eyes. "Are you even listening to yourself? She's captain of a ship. One that goes where it pleases. We'll go to the *Sword of the South* and see if any of her dozens of crew know where they're holding her. Failing that, we'll check in with the black market. Much easier to buy the information than to track it down ourselves."

"That's not bad at all." Dante gestured to the blank stone wall. "After you."

"I'll give you a knock if it's clear." Blays stepped directly toward the wall. The instant before his nose could smash against it, he dissipated into a vague black cloud. The mist streamed into the stone and vanished. Three seconds later, a low knock sounded from the wall.

Dante lifted his hand to the wall. Stone drew away like rainwater into the dust. He stepped out into the hallway and sealed the gap behind him, leaving no trace of their escape.

He chuckled. "This is almost too easy."

"Quit inviting divine retribution until we're outside."

Blays strode down the hallway, which was lit by a single lantern hanging beside what turned out to be the stairwell. This was a tight spiral that smelled of damp stone. Dante took the lead. The lantern's light faded behind them and he slowed, feeling his way forward step by step. After a quarter turn, the way ahead lightened at a landing.

Dante paused. Hearing nothing, he moved on, keeping the shadows close at hand. They'd taken his boots, which might be a problem out in the street, but proved to be a temporary advantage, his bare soles eliciting no sound. They passed a second landing, then a third.

At the sixth landing, the light was much brighter. Someone murmured from beyond the doorway. Dante edged one eye around the corner, spying a large, open room with double doors at the far end.

Blays shook his head. "One more."

Frowning, Dante moved on. The light waned behind them. The air grew mustier. After several steps of total darkness, Dante conjured the smallest light he could conjure up. The stairwell stopped, feeding them into a windowless hallway.

"Is this the basement?" he whispered.

"Brilliant observation. I knew there was a reason they put you in charge of a city."

"Is there a reason we're in the basement and not dashing away through the streets?"

"Because," Blays said, "the basement has my swords in it."

Without so much as a look around, he headed to the third door on the left. It opened to a room full of shelves of boots, cloaks, knapsacks, bundles of letters, and other personal goods of no great value. Blays headed to the right, pulled down a pack, and passed it to Dante. It was his; at a glance, it was missing nothing besides the shaden. Blays slung on his own pack, belted on his swords, and handed over Dante's.

"Been down here already?" Dante said.

"You were out for two days. I had to find some way to entertain myself."

As they laced up their boots, a shoe scraped from the hall. Dante spun on his heel. A young man bearing a lantern appeared in the doorway. He was dressed in the dark blue uniform of Mallon's common soldiers.

He stared at them, head cocked. "What are you doing down here?"

"Gladdic sent us to pick up the new prisoners' belongings." Blays hiked his pack up his shoulders. "Is he still up on the sixth floor?"

"Think he tells me these things?"

"Then out of my way so I can find him before he locks *me* up."

The young man stepped to the side, then stuck out his lower lip, examining their dingy clothing. "Which split are you with?"

"Which do you think?" Blays said. "The one that gets sent to rummage around a rat-filled basement in the middle of the night."

"You stay here." The soldier moved backward into the hall, glancing down it. "Stay right—"

A spear of shadows struck him in the right eye. He fell to the ground like a toppled fir. The lantern clanked to the ground, spilling oil. Dante swore and stooped to pick it up before it caught fire.

Blays stood over the body. "You should have let me do that."

"I thought you were trying to avoid killing."

"That's exactly why I needed to do this. I'm the one who brought us down here for my blades. Because of that, he's dead."

"He works for people who took us prisoner." Dante stepped over the corpse. "And the way things were going, they would have kept us here for a long time. Or hanged us from a tall tree."

He headed back up the stairwell. Blays fell in behind. At the ground floor, he took another peek at the room beyond. It was fifty feet across. To the right, four soldiers sat around a table dicing for coppers. To the left, two monks were engaged in a vigorous debate.

Dante withdrew around the corner. "Six men. And they're not going anywhere."

"Waiting in the building's only stairway isn't a great way to avoid getting caught. We need to move."

"Don't suppose you can turn me invisible, too?"

"Just myself. And I'm starting to wear out."

"Walk outside," Dante said. "Turn left. Find somewhere to hide. And wait."

"While you do what? Coat the walls with people-jelly?"

"No one has to die. If I'm not out in fifteen minutes, get out of here. Run back to Minn. And forget all about this."

"I found you once. I can find you again."

Without giving Dante the chance to argue, Blays moved toward the stairwell entrance and vanished into thin air. Dante gave him a few seconds, then returned to the basement. He jogged to the body they'd left in the hall, sealed the wound in the soldier's head, and used the blanket from his pack to sop up the blood. There was nothing he could do to restore the man's eye, so he cleaned it up the best he could, then loosened a length of the man's long hair from its tie and draped it over the side of the man's face.

With a surge of shadows, he brought the man to his feet. The body stood dumbly, awaiting orders, just like the tree frog Dante had used to scout the jungle. Dante instructed the soldier to walk forward. He did so, feet shuffling. His arms hung like wet ropes, but he was moving and in uniform. Dante urged the body to walk up the stairs.

They came to the ground floor landing. Dante walked out first, the corpse a step behind him, as if escorting him out. A soldier glanced up from the dice game, tracking them. On the other side of the room, the two monks continued to argue. The soldier stared at Dante until his gaming partner elbowed him in the ribs. He swore, rubbing his side, snatching at the dice.

Dante reached the door first. He opened it and stepped out into the night. It was much cooler than the islands, yet much warmer than the frigid gales blowing in from the north sea of

Narashtovik would be. He stood on the front steps. He hadn't been awake for an hour. His most recent memories before that were of descending into fever, pain, and death. In comparison, the cool wind, bearing the smell of the river, felt like life itself.

A man clacked down the street on a crutch, knocking him out of his reverie. He descended the steps slowly, allowing the dead man to keep pace in case anyone was watching from above. They entered the street and turned left. Sculpted hedges lined the Chenney's grounds. Dante sent the soldier stumbling into the topiary and picked up his pace. As he neared the corner, a man exited the shadow of the shrubs and fell in next to him.

"How did you get out?" Blays said.

Dante didn't look back. "You don't want to know."

"It was something awful, wasn't it? I'm not even going to guess." He glanced at Dante's side and gave him a dirty look. "Don't let your sword flap around like a flag. This is Bressel."

He'd forgotten—the armsman's guilds held heavy influence here, meaning you couldn't wear a sword in public without papers. Blays appeared to have tossed the straps of his blades over his left shoulder and covered the hilts with a thin blanket. This wouldn't have passed in daylight, but it was a few hours after nightfall and the city watch was more willing to look the other way—so long as you made an effort. Particularly if, as Dante and Blays were, you were dressed richly. Once they crossed the street, Dante moved alongside a building, transferred his scabbard to his shoulder, and draped the grip with the only spare shirt in his pack.

They struck east toward the river. Away from the corner, the only light was from the stars and the lanterns spilling from the windows of public houses. It hadn't rained in a few days, at least, meaning the street was dry, hazarded only by the occasional pile of grassy manure.

Dante swerved around the legs of a drunk flopped outside an ironmonger's door. "I don't suppose you know where the ship is?"

"Just a guess, but I'm thinking it's on the docks."

"Of the biggest port town west of the Woduns."

Blays gave him a look. "Maybe you've spent so much time in your little castle that you've forgotten how this works. We're looking for information. Information is often picked up for free. Hence, people are happy to exchange it for hard coin. Particularly the type of people who make their living hanging around wharfs after dark."

"Forget the wharfs, we should head to the university and get you a chair."

With their packs marking them as travelers, they drew more than their share of predatory eyes. As they neared a public house and inn, three men detached from a covered porch. Their leader twirled a cane.

"Don't kill them," Blays murmured. "Escaped fugitives and all."

"Hoy!" the man with the cane called jauntily. "New to the city? May I render my services as guide?"

"Shoo," Blays said. "Before you get the both of us carted off to Darter Lane."

The man paused his cane mid-twirl. "What would you know about the Darters?"

"Last time they locked me up, the only thing that smelled worse than the privy was the food."

The man chuckled and tipped his shapeless hat. "My mistake. You have a good evening, sir."

His trio retreated to their porch. Blays moved on without a glance back.

"Darter Lane?" Dante said.

"Petty lockup. Practically spent half my childhood there, crime school for orphans. Maybe you've forgotten, but I know this city like the back of my hand."

The street began a modest ascent. At the hill's peak, they

crossed an intersection into a neighborhood of whitewashed shops and rowhouses sporting glass-paned windows. Neat cobblestones paved the street. A pair of carriages idled in front of a hotel. They hadn't made it halfway down the block before footsteps picked up behind them. Their pursuer wore a blue hat and sash and a sword at his hip.

"You said you knew this city," Dante said. "So you knowingly led us into a wealthy neighborhood?"

"It's hardly my fault if somebody decided to grow a crop of rich people on this street during my absence."

"Well, how about you lead us back to a place that's too poor for the town watch to care about?"

Blays muttered something obscene. At the next intersection, he hooked to the south. After another block, the houses grew older; the cobbles ceased in favor of rutted dirt. The watchman quit tailing them and entered a tavern. Before Dante could suggest they up their pace, the man reentered the street, accompanied by a second man in hat and sash.

Blays dodged to avoid a pile of corn husks and cobs. "Why did they have to choose *tonight* to be good at their jobs?"

"Need to lose them before the docks. Nobody's going to talk to us when we're being shadowed by the watch."

"Or re-arrested. We're almost at the river. Any ideas?"

"Kill them," Dante said. "Then run."

"Any ideas that don't involve committing capital offenses?"

"But those are much harder." The dirt beneath his next step gave more than he was expecting, stumbling him. "Next intersection, break left. As soon as they cry out, start running and don't stop till we're at the docks."

"And when they follow?"

"They won't."

As they neared the intersection, Dante bit his lip. Shadows rolled toward him. He sent them into the hard-packed dirt of the street. Leaving the surface intact, he loosened what lay beneath, flooding it with water. Blays turned left, back toward the river to the east.

Boots crunched behind them. As the steps neared the intersection, both men cried out, followed by a pair of splashes. Blays laughed and broke into a sprint. They headed north up the first alley they saw, putting a row of buildings between themselves and the guards, then continued east. By the time masts and warehouses showed ahead, there was still no sign of pursuit.

It was roughly ten at night, yet the docks were abuzz, with crews spilling out of newly-arrived vessels while longshoremen flowed toward them. Vendors called from their stalls and blankets, selling meat pies, tea, and beer to the workers. Blays struck up a conversation with the longshoremen at one stall. After handing over a small stack of coins, Blays was informed that the *Sword of the South* was berthed not a half mile to the south.

On their way to it, they got the precise address from another longshoreman who'd been working there the day before. They arrived to find three armed men in blue uniforms standing at the entrance to the pier. Beyond, other soldiers stalked across the deck of the ship, bellowing orders.

The *Sword of the South* had been commandeered.

12

They stood in the muck and gawked at the ship. Dante didn't recognize a single soul on its deck.

Blays gestured to the sentries at the base of the pier. "Shall we ask them what the hell is going on?"

"Did you forget the fugitives thing? We'll hire some street rat. Now let's get out of here before they come over for a closer look."

Dante continued past the pier, ignoring the lingering gazes of the soldiers. The night smelled like fish chowder from the vendors doing a brisk business a hundred yards down the shore. Dante headed toward them, eyeballing the numerous urchins hanging about the crewmen drinking and gambling over cards and dice. He wanted one of the quiet ones. Someone who would parrot the questions he was told to ask without betraying them to the guards or angling for more money.

As they neared the boisterous plaza, a shadowy figure emerged from the corner of a warehouse. "Stop right there."

By instinct, Dante grasped at the nether, but he recognized the voice. "Mr. Naran?"

The man shushed them and beckoned them to him. "This way."

Naran turned stiffly and walked away from the piers. The thuds of cargo being unloaded faded behind them. Dante held his tongue as the quartermaster led them up a flight of stairs, through a rowdy common room, and out to a quiet veranda. Which happened to have a perfect view of the *Sword of the South*.

Mr. Naran closed the door to the veranda. Three men rose with a scrape of chairs; Dante recognized them as crew from the ship.

Naran didn't seat himself. "Where is Captain Twill?"

"That's what we came here to find out," Dante said.

"But she was with you when you were taken."

"It turns out that, as our jailers, they didn't feel compelled to inform us that they were taking her elsewhere. What's going on here? Have the city authorities taken the ship?"

Naran exhaled and slumped back in a chair. He reached for the cup in front of him, inspecting its rim. "After they imprisoned the three of you, they sent soldiers to the dock. They declared that the *Sword of the South* failed to obtain a charter from King Charles and was therefore involved in illegal smuggling. Hence it was forfeit to the crown."

"Smuggling?" Blays said. "How long has visiting the Plagued Islands been illegal?"

The quartermaster shook his head. "It wasn't until recently. But they appear to have retroactively decided to ban all unauthorized contact with the islands. They didn't just seize the ship — they took the crew, too. As indentured servants. They will sail in the crown's navy until their debt has been repaid."

"What a band of thieves! How'd you get away?"

"I was already off the boat. We're attempting to gather all those who avoided capture. Thus why we're watching the pier."

Dante found an empty cup and filled it with beer from a pitcher on the table. "This is about controlling the shaden. That's why they're clamping down so hard."

"Yet they let you loose," Naran said. "Perhaps they'll free Captain Twill as well."

"They didn't exactly *let* us loose," Blays said. "More like they didn't prevent our departure. Because they didn't know about it."

"That bodes ill for Captain Twill. If they've enslaved her crew, as their leader, her punishment will only be more severe."

Dante took a long quaff of the Mallish beer, which was too sweet by half and tasted like old bananas. "No it won't. Because we're going to get her back before they can inflict it."

Naran arched his well-maintained eyebrow. "Why would you do a thing like that?"

"I'm still sick. I need her to take me back to the Plagued Islands."

"She may be an excellent captain, but even she will find that task rather difficult without a ship."

"We'll figure that out later. If we can't recover the *Sword*, I'll buy her a new one. In the meantime, we have to find her."

The quartermaster had been too morose to even sip his beer. Now, though, he leaned forward, cup gripped so firmly it looked about to crack. "And if we do, you will liberate her safely?"

"I don't have a choice," Dante said. "Without her, I'm dead."

Naran set down the cup, drew a knife, and pointed it at Dante's eyes. "Swear it."

"You don't have to threaten—"

Naran sliced open his palm, flipped the knife around, and held it hilt-first to Dante.

Dante eyed him levelly. "You are aware that I'm sick. It could have corrupted my blood as well."

"And you mean to find a cure. In the meantime, let this be proof of how seriously I take your vow."

Dante took the blade and cut his own palm; he'd done so far too often to wince. They shook, wet, warm blood tracing the creases of their palms.

Blays frowned at them. "Now that we've completed the ritualistic shedding of blood, do you suppose we should fashion a plan?"

"We are plying every watchman and tower guard we can find with silver," Naran said. "It's only a matter of time before we find someone who knows where she's being kept."

Dante rubbed his jaw. "Then Blays and I should stick with you. We're escapees. Besides, I don't know how much good we'll do searching a gigantic city we hardly know our way around."

"Don't be daft," Blays said. "We should stake out the Chenney."

"You said she wasn't there."

"She isn't. But after Gladdic discovers we're missing, what do you think he'll do first?"

"Go check on our compatriot." Dante grinned. "He'll lead us right to her."

He finished his beer and headed down to the street. There, he followed his nose to the alley where the pub pitched its trash. A tribe of rats was feasting on the offal. Dante slew three of them with thin bolts of nether, collected the bodies—an intrusion that hardly caused the others to stir from their meal—and revived them as his walking servants. After a quick check of the nethereal bond linking his senses to theirs, he sent them scampering west toward the Chenney.

Back upstairs, the others continued to watch the pier. Longshoremen were now dragging crates and casks onto the *Sword of the South*. Worrisome. They were planning to sail soon.

Dante settled into a chair. The rats were a good three miles from Chenney Hall, but he moved into the sight of their leader on the off chance they'd see something along the way. Twenty minutes later, having encountered nothing more treacherous than boulder-sized horse droppings, the rats gazed up at the Chenney.

While it was a high-profile jail, from the outside, it looked like a barbarian king's first effort building with stone: a blank limestone cube a hundred feet to a side, interrupted by narrow barred windows. It had no wings or turrets, just a small building grafted onto its roof that might serve as the offices of its steward. Dante wasn't well-versed in Mallish architecture, but if it ran similar to what he knew of Gask, the simple building was at least five hundred years old.

He set one rat directly across the street from the broad front doors. He sent a second around the building, stopping it outside a smaller door which, judging from the unkempt grass directly outside it, was no longer used. The third rat scampered up the steps and waited. Twenty minutes later, when a guard wandered outside to light a pipe, the waiting rat trotted inside, hiding beneath a stuffed chair to the right of the doors.

Inside, the tower guards continued to gamble around their table. The two monks who'd been arguing during Dante and Blays' escape were nowhere to be seen. Over the course of the next few hours, only three people entered or exited the stairwell. None were Gladdic.

Dante nodded off in his chair. Jerking awake, he stood, occasionally pacing around the veranda. With his sight embedded in the rats and only a dim awareness of his own surroundings, he was careful not to get too close to the railings. Some time later, a round of cheers stirred him from his reverie; the crew had located another member of their men.

The next thing he knew, bells were ringing. Glassy, piercing. The Odeleon declared it was four in the morning.

"We should relocate," he said. "It won't be safe here after daybreak."

After a brief discussion, Naran departed with him, Blays, and three of the men, leaving two others to watch the dock. They made their way to an inn a few blocks west of the river. There, aided by strong tea that tasted as if it might have been imported from Gallador, he remained awake until dawn. When an unornamented carriage rolled up before the steps of the Chenney and disgorged Gladdic.

"He's here," Dante murmured.

As before, the man was dressed in nondescript robes. Gladdic ascended the steps, entered the foyer, paused as if sniffing, and moved to the stairwell. Wary of dogging the priest too closely, Dante left his rat on the ground floor.

Gladdic descended five minutes later. His face was taut. A second monk accompanied him. An hourglass-shaped brooch declared him a follower of Taim; two blue stripes on his collar announced he was a spalder, a rank that would terrify a parish priest. Before Gladdic, however, he was fluttering like a light-mad moth.

"This room has been watched all night," he explained. "One of the guards wandered off an hour early, but he's a known drunk. Otherwise, there have been no disturbances whatsoever. There is no possible way for the prisoners to have escaped—"

"Quiet." Gladdic stopped in the middle of the room, glaring at the wall across from him. Ether glowed from his fingertips, then dwindled away. Absently, he plucked at a loose thread in his robes, pulling it tight, letting it drop, and repeating. "The captain of the *Sword of the South*. Does she remain in custody?"

The spalder rolled his lips together. "I couldn't say."

"We will go to check on her at once. In the meantime, order the monks to lock the doors. Let no one in or out."

"Do you think they may still be here?"

"If they emerged from their cells without a trace, do you really think they had difficulty walking outside?" Gladdic pulled the thread tight. "I mean to investigate and find out if anyone helped them. And if so, to hang the offenders from the roof."

He moved toward the door. The spalder ran to get there first, holding it open while he shrieked orders at the group of monks who'd silently assembled during the discussion. Gladdic walked outside. With no intention of drawing more attention—besides, it could still be useful there—Dante left the undead rat where it was beneath the chair.

He recalled the one that was stationed at the side door, bringing it around front to join the one that had watched Gladdic arrive. Gladdic climbed into the left side of the carriage, with the spalder circling around to the right and getting inside. The driver bawled at his horses and the carriage rattled forward. Dante sent both rats trotting behind it, concealing themselves by running under debris and alongside the bases of buildings.

In the hotel room, Dante lowered himself to a cot. "Gladdic's on the move. He's heading right to Twill."

Blays paced across the room. "Awfully inconsiderate of him to do this when it's light out. On the other hand, rescuing her in broad daylight will only add to our legend."

"Do you know his intent?" Naran said.

"He's determining whether she's escaped as well," Dante said. "It sounds like he intends to return to the Chenney after that. We'll go for her as soon as he leaves her location."

He shifted his sight back to the rats. The dawn had brought hundreds of people into the streets and the vermin were busy dodging untold feet and hooves. He directed them over to the face of the buildings, where all they had to contend with was the occasional person entering or leaving a shop.

Half a mile later, the carriage turned left. After a few blocks, it stopped in front of a temple of Taim set off from the street by a wrought iron fence. The spalder got out of the carriage, tugging up his blue-striped collar as he walked toward the gate. As the carriage rolled away, the rats trotted after it, sticking close to Gladdic.

The vehicle rambled east toward the river, then turned north on a boulevard snarled with stalls, carriages, and hundreds of pedestrians perusing what appeared to be one of the spring's first vegetable markets. The driver swore, yelling curses at the people clogging his path. It took him ten minutes to disentangle himself from the market and continue north. A few minutes after that, the horses came to a stop. The driver dismounted and leaned through the carriage window. Dante edged the rat closer. The men appeared to be arguing about directions. The driver was blustery and insulted, but Gladdic stayed infuriatingly calm, his voice nothing more than a murmur against the noise of the street. After a lengthy dispute, the driver sighed, threw his hands above his head, and returned to his seat, urging the horses forward. The route took any number of turns.

Someone was nudging his shoulder. In the room of the inn, it was notably brighter, with sunlight spilling through the hearth smoke and over the scarred wooden floor.

"It's been nearly an hour," Blays said. "Where are they headed, East Weslee?"

Dante shook his head. "It's like he's going in circles."

"Could that be because he is?"

Dante's blood ran cold. He ordered one of the rats to race up to the side of the carriage and leap onto its running board. It scrabbled up to the window and pressed its snout to the corner of the screen. Less than a foot away, a man in a plain gray robe sat on the left side of a bench. He had his hood raised, but when he glanced out the window, the rat had a clear view of his face.

It wasn't Gladdic. It was the spalder.

Dante planted his palm on the cot, steadying himself. "He knew he was being watched. He pulled a switch on me. Sent his underling out in a carriage while he snuck off."

Naran lurched out of the window he'd installed himself in. "Where is he now?"

"That's what I'm trying to find out."

Leaving one rat with the carriage, he sent the other dashing back toward the temple of Taim where the disguised Gladdic had given him the slip. The priest must have felt the rats' presence at the Chenney and suspected it was connected to Dante and Blays' escape. Dante had little hope the man was still at the temple, but it was his only lead.

Five minutes later, with the rat en route, and the carriage bearing the spalder still traveling in circles, a fist pounded on the hotel door. Dante came forward from the rats, nether in hand. Blays drew his swords. The crewmen pulled long knives. Naran opened the door.

A man stood outside, sweaty and wild-eyed. He wore the slippers favored by sailors and a beard that couldn't decide between black and red. His name was Jona, and he was one of the two men Naran had left on the veranda.

"They have the captain," he said. "She's down at the dock."

The men sheathed their knives and headed into the hall. Naran jogged at their fore. "Who is 'they'?"

Jona shrugged. "Some creepy-looking spalder. Looked like the walking dead. Accompanied by about half an army and a whole monastery."

"We should be extremely careful," Dante said. "This is probably a trap."

Naran showed his teeth. "They have Captain Twill. There is no more time for careful."

Dante gave Blays a look. The kind that said *Be ready to run*. Blays nodded fractionally. The group poured through the common room and into the street. The morning air was cool and humid, carrying the clang of ships' bells and the squawks of gulls.

While they were still several blocks from the piers, Gladdic's voice pierced the air. "...be laid out before you. The first: trading with the Plagued Islands without writ of permission. The second: transporting the sick from the islands into the city, knowingly putting our citizens at risk of pandemic. The third, and most grievous of all: consorting with blasphemers. Nethermancers. Those who would undermine all for which we stand. Do you have anything to say in your defense?"

The words that followed were strongly voiced, but too faint to make out—Gladdic had been using some trick to project his words. But there was no mistaking Twill's voice. As they neared, she grew loud enough to hear over the clap of their boots.

"...a joke, and not a very good one. You lock me in a hole, beat me for answers, and then charge me without proof on some dirty dock? What happened to Mallish justice, sir? The fairness that was once the envy of every place I traveled? If your goal was to learn the secret of transmuting admiration to mockery, then congratulations, sir. The alchemists will be thrilled."

Naran skidded to a stop at the corner of a closed pub, peered around it, then walked from cover at a too-casual pace. Dante pressed himself to the corner and beheld the plaza he and Blays had crossed through the night before. This morning, its center was vacant, but scores of grubby sailors and locals gathered around the base of the dock berthing the *Sword of the South*.

A row of blue-clad soldiers were lined up between the mob and the dock. There, Gladdic stood apart from Twill. Her wrists were chained. A coterie of monks flanked him.

"Take down the priests," Naran said. "We will handle the guards."

Dante stuttered with laughter. "Should I conquer the entire city while I'm at it? Strike the laws and exonerate her?"

"I thought you were two steps below the gods."

"Those are steep steps. And Gladdic may be standing on them, too."

"I'll do it," Blays said. "I'll shadowalk up to them. Grab her be-fore—"

A hundred yards away, Gladdic strode closer to Twill. "You mean your words as criticism. I hear only praise. We have brought ourselves closer to Taim's will. By defying that will, you are damned. And all others who travel to the Plagued Islands will suffer the same punishment."

Calmly, he extended his hand palm up, as if releasing a butterfly. Pure white light flashed between them. A fan of red gushed from Twill's neck. She crumpled to the dock.

Naran ran forward with a warbling scream. One of his men followed on his heels, but the others jogged, slowed by disbelief. At the foot of the dock, soldiers raised their chins, eyes locking on Naran.

"I'm on it," Blays said. "Do something to help us flee?"

He sprinted after Naran. Dante swore, sticking beside the pub and summoning the shadows from their resting spots behind the building's shutters. Before the dock, the row of soldiers formed a wedge: those in the back planted spears while those at the front drew short swords. Behind and above them, Gladdic watched calmly. Naran's long legs were carrying him toward the soldiers faster than Blays could close. As the quartermaster planted his right foot, Dante shot his focus into the nether inside the cobblestone in front of the man's toe, jerking the stone three inches higher. Naran sprawled on his face.

"Pardon my friend!" Blays slid alongside him and waved off two approaching guards. "He just loves a good execution."

He yanked Naran to his feet. As Naran struggled in his grasp, Blays wrestled his arm back and boxed his ear, grinning cheerfully at the soldiers. Jona flanked Naran on the other side, speaking into the quartermaster's ear. Tears spilled down Naran's cheeks.

The soldiers paused, glancing at Gladdic, who raised his index finger. Dante tensed. Blays, Naran, and Jona slowed, as if slogging through thigh-high water, then stopped fast, goggling at their feet. Gladdic had adhered their soles to the ground. Unhurried, he moved down the dock, ordering his soldiers ahead of him.

Dante had already healed the blood oath wound on his palm. As he drew a knife to cut a fresh one, his hand was shaking so badly he nearly dropped the blade. The trick Gladdic had used was one of the first Dante had learned, but the problem was that the man wasn't using the nether, but rather the ether. While some were able to command both—though rarely with any notable skill—Dante couldn't lift the ether any more than he could hoist a fallen tree.

In Mallon, they positioned the two substances as opposites. Much as they positioned Arawn as the soul-starved god of death who'd do anything to murder the life-giving Taim and claim the world. In treating the powers as opposites, the system encouraged the brute force application of ether against nether or vice versa, much in the way you'd fight a fire by flinging a bucket of water at it.

Long ago, however, his late mentor Cally had taught him that the substances weren't opposites. Rather, they were complements, with as much in common as differences. To this day, Dante was still struggling to absorb this lesson, to learn to combat the ether in ways other than mindlessly bashing at it as hard as he could.

But with the guards closing on Blays and the others, he didn't have time for subtlety. He gathered the darkness into a black scythe and slashed at the glowing white bonds adhering his friends to the ground. They staggered forward, arms windmilling, then caught their balance and dashed toward the street they'd used to come into the square.

Gladdic splayed his palm. Pale lightning flashed toward Blays. Cataracts of nether poured through Dante's veins, as torrential as the boiling springs he'd unleashed on the Dreaming Peaks. A dark spout consumed the forking ether, leaving nothing but a few sparks twinkling in the air.

Gladdic's face, formerly placid, went as stormy as the nether. "Bring them to me. Dead, if you must."

His monks, eight in number, followed behind the charging soldiers, and Gladdic joined them. Dante and the crew of the *South* rushed around the corner and up the street.

"Please tell me," Blays said, "that Gladdic isn't as frightening as he seems."

"Okay," Dante said.

"You're just lying to me, aren't you? That's even less comforting."

"Well, the fact we're running in panic should have been your first clue." They swerved down an alley, navigating single file through debris and brown puddles. Footsteps racketed behind them, along with a gruff voice ordering the pursuing force to split up. Dante swore. "We need somewhere to hide."

"The inn?" Jona said.

"No good. If Gladdic comes around, the innkeep will give us up in a second."

Naran ran in a daze, useless for the moment. Blays shrugged broadly. They turned another corner and found themselves running down a tight alley. The nearest intersection yawned far ahead, seemingly a hundred miles away. With the echo of boots nearing the way they'd come in, Dante touched the nether within the nearest wall and yanked the stone aside like a curtain. He shoved Naran inside. Blays and the crewmen followed. As soon as everyone was out of the alley, Dante sealed the wall shut.

Their heavy breathing filled the room. Dante got out his torchstone and blew on it. Pale light revealed a narrow space half filled with dusty crates. Outside, feet thudded dully, dwindling to nothing.

Naran turned on Dante, mouth twisted in anguish. "Why did you make me run from them?"

"Because Gladdic had a small army with him!" Dante hissed. "You would have been deboned before you got within twenty feet."

"At least I would have died in the service of my captain."

"How would it have served her to die instantly?"

The quartermaster balled his hands into fists. "It never should have come to this. You promised you would save her."

Dante lowered his gaze. "Gladdic outwitted me. I'm sorry."

"He killed the one you swore to protect. It is your duty to kill him!"

"Now isn't the time! He isn't some cutpurse. He's an extremely dangerous sorcerer who is presently on high alert. Any one of his *monks* could kill you with a look."

Naran sneered. "Let me out of here. I can do what you will not."

"You go after him, and you'll die. You know how you *can* honor Captain Twill? By rescuing her crew still imprisoned on her ship. And getting them the hell out of this gods-forsaken city."

"To take you back to the islands, I suppose. Very selfless of you to suggest. Especially now that they have outlawed passage and no other ship will dare help you. Well, Captain Twill is dead. Our deal is annulled."

"Then I have a new offer." Dante got out his knife and cut his palm. "I'll help free your crew. You'll take me to the Plagued Islands. And once I'm cured, we'll return to Bressel—and I will plant Gladdic in the ground."

The quartermaster's dark eyes shifted to the blood dripping from Dante's palm. "You failed our last arrangement. How can I believe this one will go any better?"

Blays got a wry look on his face. "Because if there's one thing this man does well, it's wreak vengeance. Back at the islands, I'm surprised he didn't kill his own father."

Brows bent together, Naran laughed in shock. He glanced between his crew. "You're a part of this, too. What do you think?"

"Still a lot of our men trapped on the *South*," Jona said. "I wouldn't sleep well if we got ourselves killed while they're chained to their benches."

An older man nodded, flashing his wooden teeth in something like a grin. "Besides, they're right. You'd have fought that man and been murdered on your feet. Seems to me these two saved your salty hide."

The other members nodded assent. Mustering visible will, Naran straightened his spine. He extended his hand to Dante.

"I'm not afraid of you, warlock. If you betray me, first I'll kill Gladdic, and then I'll find you."

The moth clung to the side of the warehouse, motionless. Perhaps it was waiting for the night. Or possibly it had recently feasted on a wool sock. It was probably dead, however, reanimated to spy on the dock where, three hours after the execution, Gladdic continued to oversee the comings and goings of sailors.

Dante, Blays, and the crewmen had relocated to a warehouse a half mile from the docks, which likely explained why the building was so little-used. There, while Dante kept watch on the priest as surreptitiously as he could, the *South's* sailors caught naps and sharpened knives. The silver lining to the execution was that it had drawn a great deal of onlookers. Gossip flew like starlings. This had already turned up four more members of the ship's scattered crew, who Jona relayed back to the warehouse.

The plan was to attack the captured *Sword of the South* just before dawn two days hence. If Twill's sailors kept arriving at the current pace, however, they might be able to do so the very next morning.

Around midday, Gladdic finally left the pier, taking most of his retinue with him. Dante sent the moth revenant soaring high above the rooftops, trailing Gladdic all the way to the Chenney. Before Gladdic arrived, Dante dismissed the rat that remained at the prison. To be on the safe side, rather than pursuing the man inside with the moth, he sent it circling around the tower, traveling from window to window until he heard Gladdic's voice wafting from inside.

Over the course of the afternoon, Gladdic interviewed a steady stream of guards, acolytes, staff, and monks. Other than the fact that Gladdic's requests for more tea were delivered in exactly the same tone as his death threats, Dante learned little. As the day departed in favor of evening, he found himself falling asleep.

A rattle awakened him. The windows set high on the side of the warehouse were now dark. A few candles lit the wide space, filling it with the stink of tallow. Blays knelt on the floor, wrapping his swords in a blanket along with several long sticks.

Dante sat up. "Where are you going?"

Blays jerked a thumb at the crew, most of whom were snoring in blanketed piles. "These guys barely have a knife apiece. If we're going to capture the ship, I'd like to be carrying something sharper than our fists."

"And where do you intend to find these weapons?"

"My old stomping grounds. The armsman's guild of Winston Dupree."

Dante rubbed his eyes. "Do you think you'll still know anyone? It's been over a decade."

"Winston might be alive and kicking. He almost never went out on jobs himself." Blays finished bundling his weapons. "Besides, you saw that place. It was nothing but old men and the infirm. They'll be happy to make a quick chuck selling their spare swords and bows. Speaking of, you got any cash?"

Dante handed over what little he had left. Blays got Jona and exited into the night. Dante checked in with the moth. Gladdic remained in his office in the Chenney, but he was alone now, writing notes.

Naran stirred, moving beside him. "Five more of our men have come in. This puts us at fifteen. Counting those we know were detained on the *Sword of the South*, only five of our people are unaccounted for."

"Suppose they ran off?"

"It seems likely. Though it is also possible they are drunk."

"Do you want to strike this morning? Or give your people another day to show?"

Naran clasped his hands, rubbing his palms together. "If your friend can bring back as many arms as he claims, we'll strike tonight. We'll leave word in the taverns for those we've left behind."

Dante stretched his legs, then sat on a crate. Checking within himself, he found the dark spots of his sickness weren't visibly larger. He could feel them, though. He was glad Naran had pushed up the attack. If they left that night, they could be back in Kandak within a week. Dante hoped he'd last.

Well after the nine o'clock bells, Gladdic's door opened. A wizened man entered, completely bald, nose bent like a claw. He leaned on a tall white staff bearing a ruby the size of a walnut. The Eye of Taim. Mark of the Eldor, the highest station in the Mallish priesthood. The staff was so famous it was a stand-in for ethereal power; when children dressed up for Falmac's Eve, any number could be found dashing through the streets bearing a whitewashed branch topped with an apple.

Gladdic leaped to his feet, then kneeled, bowing his head. "Your Righteousness. Forgive me. I did not know you were coming."

"That is because I didn't tell you," the old man said. "So get off your knees already. Unless you find that makes it easier to speak."

Gladdic stood, keeping his gaze lowered. "How may I assist you?"

"Your nethermancer. I hear he remains at large?"

"The fault is my own. I should never have left him unwatched. They are as devious as they are vile."

"Indeed."

"My inattention has profaned the city. My life is yours to take."

The Eldor chuckled. "Your piety, as always, is second to none. Fortunately for your sake, I have been corrupted by the ways of the world, and lack the zeal to destroy valuable assets out of pique. Especially when those assets may be employed to correct their failure."

Gladdic bowed. "If that is your will."

The old man clumped toward the window, looming in the moth's cockeyed vision. "Given our circumstances, however, I think now is a poor time for failure. You will catch this offender. And if you can't? You will *say* you have. Am I understood?"

"Perfectly, Eldor."

"Wonderful. I'm very old, you see. Repeating myself reminds me of how little time I have left."

He smiled and tottered out of the room.

Gladdic closed the door and bolted it. He sat at his desk and closed his eyes, hands shaking. Below, a carriage clattered, drawing away. Gladdic's eyes snapped open. He withdrew a steel scalpel from his desk, pulled his robe past his left shoulder, baring it, and cut a half-inch incision. As blood swelled from the wound, shadows zipped from beneath chairs and rugs, wrapping the priest's shoulder in darkness.

In the warehouse, Dante folded his hands and pressed them against his mouth. Killing Gladdic was going to be even more dangerous than he thought.

Blays didn't make it back until two in the morning. He smelled of rum and looked quite pleased about it. "Sorry for the delay. Winston waxed nostalgic upon my return and insisted we take a tour of the old neighborhood. Were you aware this city is full of pubs?"

"Please tell me you didn't spend all this time drinking," Dante said.

"Of course I did. How else was I going to convince my former employer to sell me an entire armory?"

With Jona's help, he guided a hand-drawn cart into the warehouse. This was laden with swords, unstrung bows, sheaves of arrows, hard leather caps, iron-studded bracers, and pieces of assorted armor that looked as though they would be dashed apart by an angry glance. The sailors had left their hardware on the ship, however, so they spent the next hour trying on bits of boiled leather and testing the balance of the available blades.

Naran sent a runner to a pub Captain Twill's crew had always been welcome at, asking the owner to inform those members who remained in the wind that the ship had departed, but would return in three or four weeks, if they wished to rejoin it.

As soon as the runner returned, Naran stood, holding a saber alongside his leg. "In the last few days, we have lost our ship. Many of our friends. And our captain. One of these things is lost to us forever. But tonight, we will retake the others—and when we return to this accursed city, we will pay them back in full."

His men responded with a compromise between a cheer and a determined grunt. They moved out into the street. Naran's most recent scouting report claimed the city had a mere four soldiers remaining on the dock, and zero monks. Dante could neutralize four guards in a wink. While the crew launched the ship, he and Blays, aided by a handful of the more physically-inclined sailors, would search the boat, do away with any further resistance, and free the indentured crewmen.

They stopped two blocks away, hunkering in the shadows while sending a scout ahead into the square. He paused, sniffing dramatically, as if savoring the redolence of the night air, then disappeared, only to jog back to the group less than a minute later.

"Sir." His voice was choked. "You need to see this."

Naran loped forward. The square was quiet and deserted. Beside the dock, moonlight glinted on the water. The *Sword of the South* was nowhere to be seen.

13

"You have to be kidding me," Dante said.

"I'll be damned." Jona glanced around the plaza. "Could they have moved her to a different dock?"

Naran made a choking noise. He rocked on his heels, then continued toward the only person on the scene, a man sprawled at the base of the dock cradling a bottle.

"The ship that was berthed here," Naran said. "Where did it go?"

The man swung up his head, mouth wide open. "Sailed out less than an hour ago. In a right hurry, too."

"Did you see which way it went?"

"With the current." Clumsily, he swept his arm south. Out to sea. "I suppose they thought that must have been easier than fighting it." He laughed heartily, drunk enough that obvious statements registered as profound wit.

Naran held fast to the hilt of his sheathed saber. "Did they say anything about where they were going?"

"Not that I heard. Then again, they weren't taking me, so what should I care?"

Blays folded his arms, contemplating the dark water. "Should we have a look around?"

"What for?" the quartermaster said. "It's gone. To sea."

"Maybe they're just seeing how she handles. Or they ran into a snag and they're still in the middle of the river. What can it hurt to look?" He jogged south along the esplanade.

Listlessly, Naran instructed his crew to canvass the area to see if anyone knew the schedule for the *Sword of the South*. Dante hung about to provide protection. With dawn approaching and no leads, they returned to the warehouse, where they took off their swords and their piecemeal armor and sat among the cobwebs, eyes downcast.

Naran lowered himself to the cask beside Dante. "The ship is gone. After Gladdic's proclamation, no captain in Bressel will dare take you to the islands. If you wish to survive, I suggest you get a horse and ride to another port at all possible speed."

"You're going to give up, then? What about the rest of your crew? They're still slaves of the king."

"How can I free them when I don't know where they are?"

"Someone must know where they're headed. We just have to figure out who that is."

"Even if we knew their destination, we would have no way to get there. All I can do is wait here for the ship to return. Or for you to come back from the islands, so that we might kill Gladdic together."

He got up and circulated among his men, speaking in low tones. Dante ran through his options. Allingham was the largest city south of the mountains separating Mallon and Gask. He could probably find passage to the Plagued Islands there. However, even if he refreshed his horse with nether, and pushed it to the brink of death, it would take at least three if not four days to get there. It was further from the islands than Bressel, too — at least eight days, and more if the captain didn't fancy sailing as close to the Mill as Captain Twill had. Two weeks or more, then. It would be the death of him.

He'd have to find somewhere closer. And gamble that he

could bribe or threaten a captain into taking him on. He'd have to steal two horses first, though. They'd spent the last of their money on weapons for Naran's men.

He was still sorting through the details when Blays arrived from the docks, looking tired but in reasonable spirits. He drew Dante aside.

"I'm going to present you with a fact," Blays said. "I'm not going to tell you what to do with it, though. That's up to you. Here it is: four piers down, one of the king's ships is tied up. And all ready to go."

"You want to steal the king's ship."

"Why not? I imagine he's lousy with them, considering how casually he snatches them from other people. He already took ours, and we only had the one. So who's the real ship-thief here?"

"We might be able to talk Naran into that," Dante said. "He gets a new ship. I get passage to the islands. Then we come back and stick a knife in Gladdic. A win all around."

"I was thinking more like we use the crown's ship to take back the *Sword of the South*."

Dante crossed his arms. "Aren't we introducing unnecessary links to the chain? If we've got one of the crown's vessels, why bother with the *South*?"

"Because it's full of slaves. Who lost their freedom in the course of helping us."

"They were being paid to do that. If they didn't like the idea of going to the islands, they could have hopped ship."

"Which they well might have, if they'd had any idea they were transporting someone the Mallish legal system considers more dangerous than an erupting volcano. We can't leave them in the king's fetters."

"We don't have time for this. We have no idea where they've gone."

"They barely have two hours on us. And as for where they've

headed, I think you can figure that out easily enough. You once tracked me across the entire continent, didn't you?"

Dante bit his lower lip. "We'll take the crown's ship. If one of the sailors here has something I can use to find the *South*, then we'll go after it. But if not, we'll head straight to the islands. Deal?"

Blays stuck out his hand. "Deal. And let's never tell them that we had this discussion."

Dante moved to the middle of the room. "The *Sword of the South* is gone, but we've still got a chance to find it. Does anyone here have anything that was once owned by one of the members who's been indentured? A personal effect of some kind?"

The men glanced between each other. After a moment of silence, a man rooted through his pockets and produced a folding razor. "This one was Frazer's. I won it playing Pig."

"Exactly the sort of thing I'm looking for." Dante accepted the razor with a smile. If he had any piece of a person's body, he could follow the nether within that portion to the nether inside the rest of them. He found no blood along the razor's edge, however, and when he sank into the few shadows clinging to the metal, he felt no resonance within them. He handed back the razor. "Anything else?"

A sailor handed over a comb that appeared to be made from the spine of a fish, with its ribs serving as the teeth. Hairs snarled the ribs, but when Dante touched the nether within the strands, the pressure that formed in his head pointed straight to the man who'd given him the comb. Someone gave him a coin stamped with the face of a foreign king—a good luck charm given to him months earlier—but this turned up nothing. Neither did the half dozen other trinkets the crew scrounged from their pockets.

That ran them out of objects. Dante sighed and let the nether slip away. "They're lost then."

"Well," Blays said. "Shall we move on? What's next? A little land-piracy?"

"Hold up." A sailor who was little more than a boy shuffled forward, cradling one of the bone flutes they carved at the islands. "This was Kerrick's."

Jona snorted. "So *you're* the one who stole his flute? He didn't shut up about that for three months!"

"Only used it once. Felt too guilty. But if I'd given it back, he'd have known I was a thief. Thought about pitching it overboard, but I couldn't bear the idea. He treasured the stupid thing like it was his own son."

"That's because it was given to him after he saved an island child from drowning!"

The boy blinked back tears. "If he hadn't made such a big deal about it, maybe I wouldn't have taken it."

"Let me see." Dante took the flute. There was nothing out of place on its outside, but a thin sheen of nether clung to its interior, perhaps where Kerrick's spit had dried. Faint pressure bloomed in Dante's skull. Slowly, he turned in a circle. As he came to face south, the force increased. He grinned. "You may be a thief, but Kerrick will have to thank you for it. Because you've saved him from years of servitude."

The eastern clouds glowed gray in the coming morning. A light mist sifted from the river. This wasn't thick enough to provide any meaningful cover, so rather than advancing in a single suspicious cluster of seventeen men, they moved down the esplanade in groups of two to four. The morning's first shifts were already on the move, but the longshoremen trudging toward the docks were too bleary-eyed to pay the small groups any mind.

They stopped two blocks from the Mallish royal vessel. It was a trim-looking caravel, its two masts sporting tall triangular sails. A nice bit of luck. Dante was no grizzled mariner, but she looked plenty fast. Assuming the crew knew how to rig it, he had no doubt they could overtake the *Sword of the South*.

Around him, the men looked eager to try. When Blays had

voiced his plan to them, and Dante explained that he could track the missing ship, they'd agreed without a single complaint. This despite having been up all night and suffering the shock of losing the *South* in the first place. Now, they were on their way to the first of two hijackings. Dante would have expected some of the men to have quietly slipped away, yet not a single one had abandoned the others. Twill's loyalty and respect were paying off beyond the grave.

Dante had already reconnoitered the crown vessel with a dead rat and discovered the sailors sleeping belowdecks were chained to their bunks. They too were indentured or enslaved. This was strange (was Mallon really that hard up for workers?), and not so lucky for the sailors themselves, but it would make Dante's job a little easier.

"Don't get all heroic in there," Dante told Blays. "If things take a turn toward chaos, jump right back over the side."

"Abandon you to your fate. Got it." Blays finished stripping down to his smallclothes, his swords strapped to his back. "See you in a minute."

He strolled down the muddy banks and waded into the water. As Dante kept watch on the ship's deck, Blays swam alongside the dock, approaching the boat in perfect silence. As he neared the hull, he vanished.

Dante nodded to Naran, then walked alone down the dock. A gangplank ran up to the ship. Earlier, a pair of soldiers had stood around it, but it was presently vacant. He crossed the gangplank and descended to the deck. Seeing no one, he cleared his throat.

A man wearing a blue cap and a sword appeared from the crates stacked around the aft cabin. "Stop right there. Who are you?"

"My name is Holton," Dante said, "and I was sent here by Gladdic."

The anger fled the man's face. "Gladdic? What's this about?"

"Yesterday's execution. I need to speak individually with

your troops."

"But none of us were there, sir."

"Then my interviews will be blessedly short. If Gladdic learns I didn't conduct them, however, then the only thing shorter than our chats will be my life."

Two more blue-capped troopers exited the cabin to stand behind the first man, who narrowed his eyes. "May I see your writ, then?"

Dante scoffed. "Why else would I be here at this unholy hour?"

"I'll need a writ, sir. Or I'll need you off this ship. Sir."

"There's no need for this. Get your people up here and I'll be out of your way in five minutes."

"I said move." The man reached for his sword.

Blays materialized behind him and drew the man's blade, whisking it to the side of his neck. "You, meanwhile, should embrace stillness."

"That goes for all of you." Dante gathered the shadows in his hands and made the dark swirls visible. One of the soldiers yelped. "We're commandeering this boat. You have a choice. Keep your traps shut, and we'll drop you off on our way out of the harbor. Or make a ruckus, and I'll drop you off in a hundred miles of open ocean."

They put their hands up. Dante kept eye on them as Blays tied their hands and gagged their mouths.

"I count five free men belowdecks," Blays said. "Only two of them are awake yet. Everyone else must be on shore."

Dante turned to the pier and waved both arms above his head. Naran jogged forward, his men a dim mass in the dawn. Once he arrived, they'd take the hostages downstairs and convince the remaining men to give up without a fight. Naturally, this bloodless scheme was Blays' idea. Killing them all would have been easier and less risky, but Dante had to admit there was a certain thrill to executing their plan so efficiently.

As Naran's men arrived and piled onto the boat, a frantic bell clanged from the mainmast. A silhouette stood high in the rigging. "Help! We're being boarded! For the love of King Charles, send aid!"

Dante swore like the sailor he wasn't and hurled a spear of shadows into the rigging. The alarums and shouting stopped cold. The silhouette leaned backwards, then plummeted to the deck, landing with a crunch.

"I thought you'd checked this thing out!" Blays said.

"I always forget boats have three dimensions." He found Naran's eye. "Get underway. We'll secure belowdecks."

Naran nodded. Boots thumped about below them. The lantern that had been illuminating the lower level went out; a door slammed. Keeping the nether close, Dante started down the ladder. Once he was a few rungs down, he jumped, casting light across the hold as he landed on the wooden floor.

Crates and bins lined the walls. Blays slid down the ladder and drew his swords. Dante moved forward into a bunkroom, hammocks slung from the walls. Faces stared from each one, eyes bright in the harsh glare of his nether-fed light. One man raised a hand and pointed behind them to a closed door set into the rear wall.

Above, Naran's crew called back and forth, stomping around like parade ponies. A heavy chain—the anchor, most certainly—clunked against the hull as it was drawn in. Dante moved to the door, Blays by his side. He tried the handle, but the door was lodged firm, bolted.

"Go ahead and stay in there if you like," Dante said. "But in about ten minutes, we'll be on the high seas."

A wary voice sounded from the other side of the door. "How many of you are out there?"

"Just two. We don't mean to hurt you."

Wood scraped. The door burst open and a man charged forth, leading with his sword. Before Dante could put him down, Blays lunged, parrying the blade and impaling the man's chest. A second thrust put him down for good. Five other men in blue caps waited inside the doorway, swords in hand. One edged nearer.

"Stop it!" Blays shouted. "This is your last chance to not be killed. After that, I turn you over to Mr. Guy You Consider a Demon here."

Taking the cue, Dante spread his palm, enfolding his hand in darkness. The men backed deeper into the room. After a brief discussion, they handed over their swords. Dante marched them to the ladder. While the soldiers were still ascending, the ship swayed, pulling away from the dock.

With all of the sailors engaged in the business of shoving off, Dante and Blays saw to the new prisoners, binding their hands and stuffing them in one of the cabins. The ship cut downstream toward the middle of the river, the pier shrinking behind them.

"You got us out of there in record time, Mr. Naran," Dante said once the man was unengaged from his duties. "Or should I say Captain Naran?"

The man tugged on the hem of his jacket, straightening it. "I never wished for this responsibility. I liked what I did, and what Captain Twill did as our commander."

"Given that I'm hundreds of miles away from the city I govern, maybe I shouldn't be handing out advice about responsible leadership. But I think you're the right man for this. You have a sense of justice and your men respect you."

"Is that all it takes?"

"It also helps to smite your enemies," Dante said. "But that will have to wait until later."

Naran gazed at the gray waters rolling out before them. "Yet you have more than that. You have a second set of eyes. A voice that's not afraid to speak up when you've stepped outside the path."

"Oh, you're free to borrow him if you like. Especially if there's barnacles that need scraping."

"But you see, the role of adviser was once mine. And I'm discovering it's much easier to question orders than it is to give them."

"Well, now that you have your own command, I can let you into the Secret Leaders' Club. The only truth we've managed to confirm is this: none of us has the faintest idea what we're doing."

Naran gave him a look. "I can't tell if you're joking."

"Think about how much confusion your own life provides. Now multiply that confusion by the number of lives under your leadership—and consider that your morass of confusion is just one of thousands bumping through the fog of the world."

"This comparison may be less inspiring than you think."

"It's frightening to sail into such dark seas," Dante said. "But there's comfort in it, too. All you have to do is keep both eyes on the way ahead and a firm hand on the tiller."

Commotion arose along the shore, with blue-capped men running down the esplanade, but the caravel soon put the soldiers behind it. It threaded through the central arch of the Titansbridge and swooped past a number of barges beginning the day's journey upriver. As the sun cleared the trees and buildings, the horizon of the sea spread out before them.

They loaded the captive soldiers into one of the ship's two longboats. Blays untied their hands. The caravel slowed enough to lower the longboat. Once it was clear, they rehoisted the sails and left Bressel behind.

The pressure in Dante's head continued to point south. He didn't have a precise gauge of the distance between them and the *Sword of the South*, but guessing it would be several hours before they closed the gap, he retired to a cabin to grab what sleep he could.

Shouts summoned him from slumber. As shouts went, they sounded excited, but not entirely happy. Out on the deck, the sun stood at roughly 10:30. Men scrambled about, trimming the sails.

Blays strolled toward him, yawning as if he'd been asleep, too. "Guess that head of yours is good for something after all. Naran thinks we've spotted the ship."

Dante touched his forehead. The strain within it had increased significantly. He spotted Naran on the aftercastle and climbed up to meet him. White sails shined on the fringe of the horizon.

"That's the *South*," Dante said. "I have no doubt."

Naran smiled grimly. "Me neither. I'd know it anywhere. I know its limits, too. With this wind, we'll be on them in two hours."

"Do you think they'll fight?"

"We'll offer them the chance to surrender. Given the recent fanaticism in Mallon, I don't think they'll take it."

"What then?"

"We're faster. We'll come up beside them, lash ourselves together, and board them." Naran rested his hand on the grip of his saber. "I'll be glad to have you with us. A boarding action is like an entire war compressed into the space of a ship's deck."

Bit by bit, they gained on the *South*. Naran asked Dante to follow him belowdecks. There, several armed crewmen stood watch over the pressganged slaves they'd found aboard the vessel.

"As of our taking of this ship, you are free men," Naran announced. "You may leave the next time we make port. In the meantime, if you expect to eat, then I will expect you to work."

The indentured crewmen exchanged looks. A gray-bearded man said, "Pardon me, sir. But I couldn't help overhearing that we're headed into a battle. That wouldn't be the work you have in mind, would it?"

"This is our fight, not yours. However, we're about to find ourselves with two ships rather than one. This will necessitate expanding our crew. If you wish to join us, we'll welcome any man who will aid us in the fight."

"Who exactly are we fighting?"

Naran smiled grimly. "The Mallish."

This drew a number of hard looks. Of the fifteen indentured sailors, six volunteered on the spot. Naran instructed his men to arm and prepare them, then climbed back to the deck.

He glanced at Dante sidelong. "Was that all right?"

"Perfect."

"You're sure?" He lifted his chin. "I felt a little stiff."

"Yet six of them signed up to risk their lives in a battle they know nothing about. You must have done something right."

The gap between themselves and the fleeing ship narrowed. Yellow-brown hunks of kelp speckled the waves, as if a recent storm had churned up the sea bed. White birds rode the undulating swells. Around the deck, men strung bows and donned boiled leather armor. Others dragged up ropes and grappling hooks from the hold.

As they came up on the *South*'s starboard side, Jona moved to the prow, signaling with a white flag and a red one. From the *South*'s aftercastle, a white flag answered, indicating surrender.

"Stay ready!" Naran called. "And remember Captain Twill."

The *Sword of the South* let its sails droop, slowing. The caravel did the same. As they neared bow range, Dante cut his arm, holding the nether close.

White light streaked through the briny air and smashed into the caravel's mainmast.

"Ethermancers!" Dante shouted. "To arms!"

Splinters showered to the deck. A deep gash had been gouged into the middle of the mast. A second bolt of whiteness darted from the *South*. Dante met it with a stroke of shadows, sending the bolt careering off into the sky. Naran's archers dropped to one knee, steadying themselves against the roll of the ship, and fired onto the deck of the opposite vessel.

Arrows answered in return, clapping into the caravel's

boards. One landed six inches from Dante's foot, prompting him to dash toward the base of the aftercastle. As he ran, he deflected another bolt of ether, then a third. A gray robe fluttered behind a hastily erected wooden barricade. Dante lashed at it, dashing it apart in a storm of shards. The monk stumbled back.

As he did so, two glittering spears of light stabbed from the fore of the *South*. Both hammered into the wounded mast. Men cried out. The mast groaned like a feverish giant. With a deafening pop, it gave way, thundering into the railings on the caravel's starboard side.

The ship sighed against the waves, slowing. Blays rushed toward Dante, ducking as arrows whisked through the air.

Blays slid in beside him. "Have I ever mentioned how much I hate you guys?"

"I can't protect the sails and attack the sorcerers," Dante said. "It's one or the other."

"And if we try to board while their monks are out and about, our people will be reduced to a salty puree."

Dante paused to knock down an incoming whirr of light. The boat tilted, jarring him into the wall of the aftercastle; the mainmast was dragging in the water, listing the entire boat. Men hacked at the rigging tying it to the ship. The *Sword of the South*'s sails went taut. It began to pull ahead.

"Can you slow them down?" Blays said.

"If I knock out their mast, we'll never make it to the islands before the sickness takes me."

"Then tear down their sails, fool. We can repair those."

"I'd better be able to do that much. If I can't, we'll never see them again."

"Get us close enough to toss a rope across." Blays stood. "I'll take care of their priests."

He jogged toward Naran, who was yelling and pointing, stirring his demoralized men back into the fray. Dante waited for the next bolt of ether to lance forward. He parried it and answered it with a flock of blade-like shadows. These swooped into the *South*'s rigging. Sails dropped to the deck with a whoosh of canvas. With a lurch, the *South* slowed.

Volleys of light flashed toward the larger of the caravel's remaining masts. Dante drew shadows from all sides, dissipating the attacks in a blizzard of sparks. A vest-clad sailor skipped toward the port railing, twirling a many-fluked hook over his head. He let loose. It arced between the two boats and held fast within the railing of the *South*.

Blays vaulted onto the railing, arms windmilling. He steadied himself, stepped onto the rope, and vanished.

Dante was too preoccupied by another flurry of ether to concern himself with trying to cover Blays. On the *South*'s deck, a sailor ran toward the grappling hook, sword in hand. Naran yelled at his archers. Arrows pounded into the other ship, knocking the sailor down.

Sunlight flashed on steel. Blays materialized behind a monk, thrusting both swords into the man's back. The monk screeched and tumbled forward. A second monk stood from behind a bench. Dante splayed his palm, reaching into the nether within the man's heart. The man jumped back, gesturing furiously, severing the cord Dante had sunk into his chest.

While the monk was still flailing, Blays turned, wheeling his swords. The man gestured more, scrabbling back. Blays blinked out of being. The man spun side to side. Blays sputtered in and out. Ether flared past him. The next time he appeared, his right-hand sword was already mid-swing. It cleaved through the monk's neck. The head hit the deck, tumbling toward the railing with the roll of the ship. It caromed into a baluster and splashed into the sea.

Naran's crew threw grapples across the gap, snarling the rigging and the rails. As archers exchanged fire from both sides, the sailors heaved, pulling the ropes tight.

Another bolt of ether winged toward the larger remaining

mast. Dante flung a hasty counter and the bolt clipped the mast a third of the way up, spraying bits of wood. He pointed to the monk hidden behind the *Sword of the South*'s mainmast. Blays nodded and sprinted forward, leaping off the aftercastle and rolling across the deck. He sprung to his feet, swords in hand, blinking out of sight.

Ether plowed from the monk's hands. Blays winked back into being, driven backwards by the raw strength of the attack. He hit the railing and toppled over. With a vexed look on his face, he plunged into the churning sea.

14

Blays hit the water with a spume of bubbles. Dante watched helplessly as the two crippled boats continued forward. At last, Blays broke the surface behind them, pawing at the water.

At the railings, Naran's sailors pulled hard on their ropes, drawing the two ships nearer. It would be impossible to untangle them now. Blays was being swept further away by the moment. On the deck of the *South*, the remaining ethermancer dropped his hands to his side, summoning pure light from the air.

Lacking the finesse to brush the opponents' attacks aside, Dante had been clubbing them down with sheer force. His control of the nether was beginning to waver. If he expended any more, he would be vulnerable to the monk.

Yet if he waited another moment, Blays would be lost amidst the churn of the waves.

Shadows gushed toward him, coating his arms. He channeled them into a ball of kelp floating just beyond Blays. Arms shot forth from the mass, spraying foam into the air. Dante was a piss-poor Harvester, so he made up for this in the only way he knew how: by pouring as much nether into his work as he could summon. Within a blink, a rubbery raft grew beneath Blays, lifting him above the surface. As the two boats cleaved closer, drawn by the sailors' grapnels, Blays raised his arm and waved.

Dante staggered, collapsing onto his rear. His vision went gray, blackening at the edges. Motes of light squiggled across his eyes. On the deck of the *South*, the enemy monk shaped the ether into a spear and swept up his hands.

A barrage of arrows flew from Naran's archers. Distracted by his opportunity to kill Dante, the monk didn't see them coming until the missiles were buried in his body. He dropped to the deck, trying to patch the bleeding with the light, but the ether dispersed into the air, returning whence it had been summoned.

The boats clashed together, rocking Dante's head back. With a roar, Naran led the charge onto the *Sword of the South*. Before the captain landed his first blow, Dante's eyes went dark.

Water dashed his face. He sputtered, pawing madly to get his head above the sea—unconscious, he must have slid over the edge—but his hands waved through empty air. Blays stood over him, laughing. Dante cocked his fist and punched him in the ribs.

Blays rubbed his side. "If that's how you're going to celebrate our victories, remind me to throw the next battle."

Dante lay in a familiar bunk. He was in a cabin on the *Sword of the South*. He wiped water from his face with his blanket. "We won? And you're alive?"

"Quick thinking with the kelp-raft. Naran's retaken the *South*. They came around for me once the melee relented. If you're feeling up to it, Naran's people are sporting a few injuries which I'm sure they'd appreciate being magically erased."

Dante sat up, taking stock of himself. He felt hollow, with a tingling that verged on pain, like a burned finger in the moments after it's removed from the water that's been cooling it. He brought the nether from the corner of the dim cabin. As it neared him, it began to sizzle. He jerked his hand, dispersing it.

"I'm a little thin at the moment," he said. "They're going to have to rely on traditional treatment until tomorrow."

"I'll let them know. Oh, more good news: Naran left some of his crew to patch up the caravel, but we're underway. He expects to reach Kandak within the week." Blays patted him on the shoulder. "So try not to die before then, all right?"

Dante fell back asleep. When he woke, it was still light out—or rather, it was light again. He'd slept for an entire day. He felt much better, but the dark specks within him signifying the sickness' progression had doubled in size. He only had a few days before the symptoms began again in earnest.

Outside the cabin, stretches of railing had been smashed, temporarily replaced with ropes. The rigging had been mended with far greater care. Large, wine-dark spots stained the decks. A young man scrubbed at the blood, but judging by his expression, he knew it was futile. Where life was extinguished, you couldn't erase the stain.

It was a sunny day with a strong northerly wind, propelling the ship through the waves at a steady clip. Dante didn't see Naran anywhere, so he headed belowdecks.

Jona swung out of a hammock. A bandage swathed his left arm. "Look at that. The Shipwrecker's up and out of his cave."

He was grinning. But some of the men recruited from the caravel were watching Dante the way they would if a crated bear had escaped its cage to wander about the hold.

"The Shipwrecker?" Dante said. "All I did was cut a few sails. Taim's priests were the ones who knocked down our mast."

He kept an eye on the strangers as he said this. One of the men softened his expression, but the others remained leery. Dante knew the Mallish had always been hostile toward Arawn and anything connected to him, including the use of the nether, but he'd been away from his home nation for so long that he'd forgotten how deep the prejudice ran.

He had shrugged it off like a sheer robe, but that didn't speak to his broad-mindedness so much as the fact that pursuing the nether had allowed him to rise from nothing to a position of great power. In Mallon, worship of Arawn was banned outright. Now, it seemed as though nethermancers were being hunted down like rabid dogs. Dispelling the crew's ingrained suspicion would take some work.

"I wouldn't discard a nickname as fine as that so easily," Jona replied. "Most people wind up with ones that are far worse." He glanced toward an older man. "Isn't that right, Toothsome Jim?"

The older man sucked in his wooden dentures, scowling.

Dante chuckled. "I didn't come down here to argue nicknames. I heard some of our people were hurt. If they'll allow it, I'll tend to them."

Jona gestured him on. The rear of the sleeping quarters had been cleared out to serve as a makeshift medical station. It smelled like sweat and bandages. Men lay in hammocks, eyes shut tight, brows furrowed in pain. There were seven casualties in total, with wounds ranging from deep cuts, to a broken leg, to two severed fingers.

As he approached the sailor with the broken leg, the man's eyes opened. Seeing Dante, his hands tightened on the hem of his blanket.

"I'm here to fix your leg," Dante said. "Unless you think that would be unnatural."

The man sat up. The movement made him go rigid with pain. Sweat popped up along his greasy hairline, but he forced himself not to make a sound. "You think you can patch it up?"

"In less than a minute, I can make it as good as new. But if you have a problem with what I do, please let me know so I can save my abilities for your peers."

A fat bead of sweat slipped down the man's sun-cracked face. His nose was crooked from an old break and he had heavy, protruding brow ridges, giving him the thoughtful, wary look of a large bird. His eyes hopped skeptically between Dante's. As the man hesitated, Dante's resentment swelled. He said nothing. The only way to change his mind was to show him that the nether could bring good as well as pain.

Besides, they'd had to split the crew between two ships. If Dante was going to make it back to the Plagued Islands, he was going to need every able-bodied crewman they could get.

"Will it hurt?" the sailor said.

"For a moment. Then it will be as if nothing had ever happened."

His eyes lowered to Dante's right thumb, which was still stained black by the time he'd summoned so many shadows it had nearly killed him. "And when the darkness comes…will it leave a mark?"

Dante smiled thinly. "Don't worry. No one will know that I helped you."

The sailor pressed his hand over his mouth, then nodded sharply. "Do it."

He moved to expose his leg, but Dante stopped him. "I have no need for my eyes."

Hearing this, the man's expression grew warier than ever. Dante laughed inwardly and sucked the shadows from the wood of the hull. A dark mist hung over the sailor's extended leg. Eyes bulging at the manifestation, he began to hyperventilate. Dante let the mist linger another moment, then sank it into the man's leg.

The bone came first. It was shattered, but the nether remembered the shape of how it wished to be. As the shards fit together, the sailor screamed, head lolling. Bone knit to bone.

The man straightened his neck, blinking hard. "The pain. It's…"

"I told you it would leave," Dante said. "Now hold still. One wrong move, and I might accidentally merge your legs together. I'm not sure you'd enjoy life as the world's ugliest mermaid."

The suggestion ran counter to Dante's goal of knocking some

sense into the man, but the aghast look on his face was worth it. Dante moved the nether through veins and flesh, tying each strand back together. The man's leg jerked. Seconds later, Dante stepped back from the eagle-browed sailor.

"You're finished?" Gently, the man pulled the blanket free from his leg. "I don't feel a thing."

"That's the point. If you'd prefer, I can re-break it for you even faster than I put it back together."

The sailor stared at him long enough to conclude he was joking. He unwrapped blood-caked rags from his splint, revealing smooth tan skin and a straight shin. He swung his legs off the side of the hammock and slowly extended his leg. He pressed the ball of his foot to the floor, then laughed in disbelief. The other wounded men watched in awed silence as he stood and reeled across the bunk room.

"I'm—" He clapped a hand to his mouth and burst into sobs.

Dante rushed toward him, sprawling forward as the ship pitched down a wave. "What's the matter? Does it hurt?"

The sailor shook his head, tears streaming down his cheeks. "A break like that would never have healed right. Climbing rigging with a warped leg, why, you might as well have asked me to leap over the moon. I've been with the *Sword of the South* for fifteen years—and I thought this voyage was to be my last."

Before Dante could respond, the man hugged him hard. After the battle, the injury, and his subsequent time in the hammock, the sailor smelled gamier than a sack of badgers. Then again, Dante was sure he didn't smell much better.

"Anything I can do for you," the sailor said, withdrawing. "You have only to name it."

"I'll take you up on that," Dante said. "But let me see to your friends first."

After the display put on by the healed man, whose name was Benny, all but one of the other wounded enthusiastically accepted Dante's aid. The single holdout was a young blond man with a deep cut on his forearm. Dante was afraid he'd suffered ligament damage, but the boy shook his head, muttering something about witchcraft.

Dante didn't press him. With his work concluded, he ascended abovedecks with Benny. Compared to the hold, the air was chilly, but much cleaner.

Somewhat sheepishly, Benny grinned, gripping the railing and gazing out to the blue-gray sea. "Now that the moment's passed, I'm not sure what a man like me can do for a fellow like you. But my offer remains."

"You said you'd been with this ship for fifteen years?"

The sailor nodded proudly. "Since Captain Dackers. He's the one who showed Twill—smooth seas for her soul—the passage to the Plagued Islands."

"Has Mallon had a presence there all this time?"

"Not hardly. Now and then you'd see a ship flying the king's colors, but back in those days, they feared the sickness too much. It was mostly outfits like us."

"What changed?"

Benny chuckled darkly. "What else? The Shadow Rebellion."

"The Shadow Rebellion? What was that?"

"The Chainbreakers' War." Blays appeared behind them, speaking around a mouthful of springapple. "That's what they call it down here." He frowned at the sea, then waved to the stern, northward toward Mallon. "I mean, up there. Pretty cool, eh?"

Dante grabbed the apple and took a bite. "What, you knew about this?"

"The giant war that almost killed us on twenty different occasions? If I think very hard, I can recall a detail or two. Now unhand my apple."

"I'm starving. And I mean the timeline. Mallon only started plundering the islands after the war."

"I don't know anything about that. I spent some time in Whetton afterwards, but I didn't hear of the Plagued Islands until you did."

"Then maybe you can quit interrupting the person who *does* know what he's talking about." He turned back to Benny. "Do you know why the crown suddenly took an interest in the islands after the war?"

Benny shrugged one shoulder. "They haven't exactly been champing at the bit to explain. Sorting through the tangled nets of rumor, though, I'd say they were looking to strengthen their fleet. And leverage it to dump a new stream of silver into the coffers."

"I see. Well, if you remember anything more concrete, I'd very much like to hear it."

"What is it that brought you to the islands, anyway?"

"A man named Larsin Galand. Do you know him?"

"Name rings a bell. But I'd bet a week's rum rations that my pal Juleson knows him." Benny gestured up at the rigging. "He's on duty at the moment. Want me to bring him around once he's done?"

"Please."

The sailor smiled, flexed his leg, and did a little jig. "Thanks again for what you've done for me. I won't forget."

He bobbed his head and jogged down the deck, presumably in search of Captain Naran. Blays smirked.

"What?" Dante said.

"I'd accuse you of growing an interest in philanthropy, but I think you just enjoy showing off what you can do."

"How dare you. I would never abuse my powers for anything as petty as vanity. This was for the morally righteous goal of extracting information from people who wouldn't otherwise give it."

Blays' amusement dwindled. "The Chainbreakers' War is the reason Mallon is interfering with the islands, isn't it?"

"It must have scared them. Showed them what a resurgent

Narashtovik looks like. They must have feared they were next."

"And moved to secure a supply of shaden to fight us with."

"The timeline fits. They're more fanatical than ever, too. I doubt it took much to convince King Charles of the necessity of a southern expedition."

"In a way, then, we're to blame for what's happening on the islands. The Mallish wouldn't be backing the Tauren if not for what we did in Gask."

Spray wafted over the railing, leaving the hairs of Dante's arms bright with tiny droplets. "We freed the norren. We did what we had to do."

"Sometimes I have to vomit. I have no choice in the matter, but that doesn't change the fact it makes an awful mess."

"We can't control what the idiots in Mallon do."

Blays leaned over the rails, eyeing a grayish, indistinct lump breaking the surface a hundred feet to starboard. "We're from Mallon. We know what they're like. We could have guessed there'd be a response to their ancestral enemy kicking up dust again."

"So what should we have done? Left the norren in chains because Mallish fearmongers might use their freedom as an excuse to go crush an island we didn't know existed?"

"I'm not saying we shouldn't have done what we did. But we could have been more mindful of the consequences. Sent people south to keep an eye on the place. Or you might have traveled to assure the court you had no designs on their land."

"I was rather busy ensuring *our* land wasn't retaken by the Gaskan Empire."

"So was I, believe it or not." Blays brushed crystallized salt from the backs of his hands. "It's too easy to forget about everything except what's right in front of you. To think you're isolated from anything that's too far away to see with your own eyes. But we're all a part of everything. We can't escape it. And if we ignore it, then we share responsibility for any wrong that comes after."

"It's not that easy. Leading a city or a nation, the weight of history is always dragging you down. There's no way out of the morass. You can't let the fear of how others might respond stop you from doing what's right. Otherwise, the world will stay wrong forever."

"I'm sure it's not as simple as I'd like it to be. But if there's one thing I know for sure, it's that when leaders talk in abstractions, it's usually to rationalize away some horrible misdeed. So let's get specific. We helped drive the Mallish to the Plagued Islands. Are we obligated to help drive them out?"

"Right now, my only obligation is to get myself cured," Dante said. "After that, we'll see where we stand."

"Fair enough. Right now, the only thing *I* want to see about is lunch."

Blays wandered off, ending their talk. After a minute of watching the ocean, Dante began to suspect Blays' departure was actually a fiendishly calculated maneuver to get Dante to continue the discussion in his own head. After how he'd been lied to by his father, Winden, and basically every islander he'd encountered, he was inclined to leave them to their fate. But that was the spite talking, wasn't it? No matter how wretched the Kandeans might be, the Tauren were far worse.

So what to do about the Tauren and their Mallish co-conspirators? Goaded onward by the whips of history and fear, Mallish aggression toward the islands had been precipitated, at least in part, by Dante's rebellion against Gask. If he could boot the interlopers out with a word and a wave of his hand, he'd surely do so. Which meant it wasn't a matter of whether he thought the Mallish should be tossed out—but rather, of how much risk he was willing to absorb to make that so.

He was still thinking of ways to do so without implicating Narashtovik when Benny returned in the company of another sailor. While Benny was middle-aged, thick-browed, and gangly, the crewman beside him looked boyish despite a thick beard, and had the paunch which, on a man as young as himself, suggested he no longer cared. He wore a distant-eyed, taciturn expression that looked more suitable for the solitude of a mountain cave than the cramped quarters of a ship at sea.

"This is Juleson," Benny said. "But you can call him Julie Boy."

"Don't call me Julie Boy." Juleson shifted his feet. "Benny tells me you're off to see Larsin Galand."

"That's right," Dante said. "I'd like to hear what he's like, if you would."

The bearded man squinted. "You're not a close friend of his, then?"

He snorted. "You might say that."

"Good thing. Because Larsin Galand's been dead for nearly a year."

15

Dante cocked his head, examining Juleson's face for signs of a joke. "You must be mistaken. That's impossible."

Juleson didn't waver. "Not two hours ago, Benny here's leg was as floppy as his yard. You went and made it good as new. For all I know, you cured his willy, too. There's magic in the world, sir. You practice it. Yet you want to tell me it's impossible that a man could fall victim to something as common as death?"

"Correct. Because I saw Larsin in the flesh not three weeks ago."

He laughed. "No you didn't."

"Are you calling me a liar?"

"Not necessarily. You could be stu—"

Benny socked Juleson in the shoulder. "Shut your gob, fool. Without this man, my sailing days would be over. Tell him what you know or I'll use you to bait the crab traps."

Juleson stared at him, unswayed, then sighed through his nose and shifted his gaze back to Dante. "One trip here, we made a deal out on one of the swappers. Had everything all squared away with the Kandeans. When it came time to pick up our share, though, Naran discovered the islanders had set out the wrong kind of spice. So he wrote up a note and sent me ashore. I was the newest of the crew, you see. Expendable in case I caught plague. When I came back, though, I thanked him. Because while I was ashore, I met Nassea. My dark-haired beauty."

He smiled to himself. For all his world-weary airs, Juleson seemed eager to unlimber his story. "After that, whenever we came through, I came ashore. To be with Nassea. At the start, this wasn't easy. We had strict schedules, and I don't know how much you know about the islands, but they don't look fondly on foreigners."

"Rixen," Dante said.

"That's right. Well, I didn't give a damn for what they thought of me. All I cared about was my girl. If they'd asked me to, I would have swam the Current all the way from Kandak to Arawn's Mill. Not the one in the sea, either—I'm talking the one in the sky."

"I have no doubt as to your devotion to dark-haired Nassea."

"My apologies for rambling, I didn't realize you were in such a hurry to swim on ahead." Juleson aimed a pointed look at the featureless ocean that surrounded them. "Now, Larsin Galand was once rixen himself, and so they'd assigned him as master of rixen affairs. That meant I had to spend a good long time with him. At first, to explain my intentions. Second, to prove I was worth the hassle. Third, after I had proven myself, to check in and make sure I wasn't causing no trouble.

"We went on like this for almost three years. Every time we came through, I got to see my Nassea, if only for a few hours. When the *Sword of the South* wasn't scheduled to go to the islands, Captain Twill let me crew on a ship that was. Sometimes, when the *South* visited with the intention to return soon, I stayed ashore while it was gone. Not long enough to catch sickness, mind—no more than a few days at a time."

During his recollection of these times, warmth had entered his eyes. He'd even smiled. Now, though, his face became as cold as the crags north of Narashtovik. "Ten months back, we swung through the islands. Normal trip. But when I went ashore, they stopped me right on the sand. Said all rixen were forbidden. I told them I knew Larsin. They didn't care. I tried to storm past them. Would have gotten into a right brawl if Nassea hadn't showed up to explain. She told me Larsin was dead. That a fellow named Niles Ardner had taken over his role. And that he'd kicked all foreigners off the islands.

"I asked her to come with me. Begged, more like. She said she couldn't leave her family. And that was the last time I ever saw her." He blinked, focusing his mile-off stare on Dante. "That's how I knew Larsin Galand. And that's how I know he's dead."

"Not to be indelicate," Dante said. "But these people lie more than a six-year-old thief. You're sure they were telling you the truth?"

"Got another explanation?"

"None that would be polite. But it occurs to me the young woman might have decided she no longer relished your company, and employed this excuse as a way to spare your feelings."

Juleson chuckled darkly. "You almost made that sound like it's not an insult. You claim you've met Larsin Galand. So what's he look like?"

"Black hair streaked white. Dirty gray beard. Blue eyes, like mine. Bit hefty."

"You've just described a million different men who're getting old but ain't yet elderly. This one, were his earlobes stuck fast to the side of his head? Or did they hang freely, like yours?"

"I can't say I noticed."

"Then here's an easier one. Did he have a scar right here, up past his hairline? Where no hair grows?"

"That's right."

"There you go," Juleson gestured. "That's Niles Ardner."

If Dante hadn't already been hanging onto a nearby rope to combat the pitch of the ship, he might have fallen over. "Do you know what happened to Larsin?"

"Died campaigning against the Tauren. Sounds to me like Niles has been impersonating him, eh? Now why would he do a thing like that?"

"You'd know better than I."

Juleson combed his fingers through his beard. "They look close enough to pass, if all you knew was what you've heard of them. Crewed together in days of yore. Came to the islands together. Niles was a natural replacement. Wouldn't have any idea why they'd want him to pretend to *be* Larsin, though." The sailor gave a bitter little laugh. "Like you said, though, they treat lying like an art. Maybe they just wanted him to keep his skills honed."

He turned to go. Dante grabbed his short sleeve. "What was he like? The Larsin you knew?"

"What's it matter now?"

"I'm no rixen. I'm now rixaka, and can come and go as I please. Tell me about Larsin, and I'll tell Nassea anything you want me to."

"Don't know what else I'd have to say to her." Juleson sucked on his teeth. "Then again, I've run my idiot mouth so much here, what's another minute? Larsin was a funny guy. Not like puppet show funny, although now and then he'd come at you with a line sharp enough to gut you. But funny like playing with a sword. Handle yourself correctly, and he'd be right friendly. No harm would come to you." He grinned. "The second you slipped up, though? He'd cut off your hand without a blink."

"He must have had some sense of justice," Dante said. "The way most of them talk about rixen, they would never have let you onto the island. No matter how benign your motives may have been."

"That's what I'm saying. He always treated me fair. From what I hear, he was a hell of a leader, too. Back in the day, he brought everyone together to fight down the Tauren. The alliance might not have been enough on its own, but he pulled off some neat maneuvers at sea. Not easy, given the Currents."

Dante was ready to ask for more, but at once, there didn't seem to be any point. Like Juleson had said, Larsin was gone. So what did it matter what kind of man he'd been?

Besides that—if Dante stayed in public much longer, he was liable to hurt someone.

"Thank you," he said as levelly as he could. "What would you like me to tell Nassea?"

Juleson sniffed. "Tell her 'Hello.'"

"That's it?"

"That's it."

Dante moved to go. This time, it was the sailor who reached out and grabbed his sleeve. "One more thing. Tell her…that I'm still here. And so is my offer."

Dante made something close to a smile, then headed straight to his cabin. As soon as the door was closed behind him, shadows streaked to him so swiftly he thought he could hear them screaming. The entire cabin darkened in a flurry of black snow. His nerves thrummed with a harsh and punishing coldness. It would be enough to burst the cabin apart, to punch a hole in the side of the ship and take them all to the bottom.

Breath by breath, he let it slip away.

The knock came ten minutes later. He'd been expecting it. He didn't open his eyes. "What?"

Blays' voice filtered through the door. "Just checking we're not all about to be sucked down to hell in a typhoon of blood."

Dante didn't respond. The door creaked open. Blays entered and shut the door behind him.

"At least you knocked this time," Dante said.

"Is it true?"

"Juleson has no incentive to lie. He spent significant time around Larsin. And his temperament matches his story: he was kicked off the island, separated from his love, and has been embittered ever since."

"So let me see if I've got this. The Tauren are raiding Kandak again. On a scouting mission, Larsin is killed. With the Kandeans' leader gone, along with all hope of victory, his friend Niles hatches a desperate plan: pretend to be Larsin, then lure Larsin's son—rumored to be all-powerful—to come the island to help defeat the raiders."

"Something like that."

"A plan which would involve getting the entire town to follow along."

The ship rolled down a steep wave; Dante grabbed the edge of his bunk. "Is it that hard to believe?"

"Oh, I don't think it would require the threat of invasion to convince these people to lie to us. I think they'd do it just to get themselves a second piece of pie at dinner." Blays tipped his head. "To be fair, though, I'd lie for pie, too."

"These people are diseased. With something worse than any plague."

"I sense some wrath coming on."

"Niles had better pray I die of sickness before I reach the islands."

"Are you sure you want to get into it with him?" Blays said.

"He lied to me. Lured me to the Plagued Islands to drag me into his fight. Knowing it could take my life in the process. I'm well within my rights to claim his life is forfeit."

"I'm not sure I disagree with you."

"Then why are you trying to talk me out of it?"

Blays folded his arms. "Because I'm not sure."

"Then it's a good thing I have enough confidence for the both of us."

"Maybe you should be glad about this."

"My dad's dead, and his impostor's lies have caused me to become deathly ill. What on earth would I be glad about?"

"At least it wasn't your father who tricked you."

Dante laughed in disbelief. "I can't believe you actually found a way to make me feel better about this."

His improved mood didn't last long. Then again, such moods never did. The day ended in gusty, chilling winds. At least it meant they'd go faster. He woke to a hollowness in his stomach. Outside, it was raining in heavy oceanic sheets. It was cold, but he stayed in the rainfall, hair plastered to his head, a temporary reprieve from the salt that constantly crusted his skin and clothes.

The day after that, he woke to sunshine and fever. He moved about the deck in silence. He remained angry, but with no ability to act on it, his rage settled in his stomach like hot silt.

Day by day, the air warmed until most of the crew worked shirtless, yet Dante found himself shivering. The dark specks inside him expanded inexorably. He slept in later and later. Blays began to hover about, bringing him watery tea and flaky biscuits. Dante studied the illness inside him as best he could, but it remained impenetrable to the nether. His head grew too hot and foggy to focus for more than a few minutes at a time.

He was in his bunk; the door opened, bringing painful light. Blays said, "We're passing the Mill."

Dante got his feet to the floor and shuffled outside, holding onto a rope or a rail at every step of the way. The funnel of gray water connected the sea to the sky. He thought he could hear it roaring, but maybe that was his heartbeat in his ears.

The day after that, he was too weak to lift his legs out of his bunk. All he wanted to do was sleep. Quit. Close his eyes and leave them shut.

But he had to hold on. He had to see Niles Ardner.

Out on the deck, men shouted. Dante's eyes snapped open. He gasped, inhaling—had he stopped breathing? A fluttery strength trickled through his limbs. Outside, a blue shape stood on the horizon. The island.

He sat on a bench at the base of the aftercastle, willing his eyes to stay open. The *Sword of the South* came about the slashing green cliffs of the Joladi Coast and hove into the bay at Kandak, dropping anchor just beyond where the waves broke against the reef. Blays and Benny helped him into the longboat and rowed across the turquoise waters. The tiny waves lapped at the shore with lake-like calmness. Dante stepped onto the sand.

A handful of locals watched, their work forgotten beside them. Winden ran down the path to the beach, arms pumping. She took one look at Dante and reached for his hand.

"The sickness," she said. "I'm so sorry."

"Where is Larsin?"

"Later. Right now—"

"Tell me where Larsin is!"

She swayed back. "This way."

She hiked up the hill. Dante followed, drenched in sweat. His heart pounded. A pair of villagers waved from the shade where they were trimming lengths of bamboo. Winden cut right, away from the houses on their stilts. After a traipse through the jungle, they emerged into the Basket, where Larsin was examining a violet flower. Seeing Dante and Blays, he placed a hand on the small of his back and straightened, smiling sadly.

"Wish I could say I'm happy to see you," he said. "But I know what must have brought you back so soon."

Dante barely heard the man's words. Tottering forward, he drew his sword and swiped at the man's neck. Larsin—Niles—cried out and ducked, falling prone to the purple dirt.

Dante raised his elbow for a downward stroke. Yet with his sword poised to strike, he found he no longer had the energy to swing it. His elbow quivered. Without warning, his legs gave out. He collapsed to his side. People were talking. They sounded concerned, but Dante didn't feel a thing.

Salt. Slime. In his mouth. He sputtered, coughing, sitting up. He was installed in a bed. A wind blew through the open wall, ruffling the gauzy curtain. Winden stood over him holding a wooden spoon full of chopped gray bits.

Dante wiped his mouth with the back of his hand. "What are you doing? Trying to finish me off?"

"The shaden," she said. "It will help you. It already has."

He was in a hut. Quite possibly the one he'd been granted as rixaka. Crystal blue waters shimmered beyond the other wall. He had a faint headache and his limbs were shaky, but his fever had broken.

"The shaden will help me for a week or two," he said. "But what about a cure?"

"A cure." Winden lowered her gaze, loose strands of hair undulating in the breeze. "There is bad news. There isn't one."

He waited for the shock and outrage to arrive, but he was too exhausted. "There's no cure."

"Nothing permanent. There is only treatment. The sickness, it's called ronone. The Damnation. We all have it. We don't know what causes it."

"Is shaden the only thing that helps?"

"That is why we need them so badly. We eat a little bit with most meals."

"That explains the brackishness of the san paste. Do the snails grow anywhere else?"

"No. There is something here that feeds them."

"The Mill," Dante said. "But there must be some way for you to leave. The woman who came to see me in Gallador was from here. My half-sister. Unless that was another lie."

"Her name was Riddi. If you have our water, you can carry live shaden with you, but they last no more than a few weeks."

"That's what killed her. It wasn't the netherburn. She ran out of shaden."

"Probably so."

"It takes two weeks just to sail back to Bressel. The trip to Narashtovik would take nearly a month total. If the shaden only last a few weeks, I couldn't make the trip back." He found her gaze. "That means I can never go home."

She closed her eyes. "I am so sorry."

The curtains stirred in the wind. The hut's ceiling was high, drawing the warmer air away. Dante pulled the sheet from his body and found that he could stand.

"I need to see Blays," he said. "And Larsin."

"Why did you try to kill him?"

"Blays didn't say?"

She shook her head. "He hasn't said a word. Except to ask how you are."

"Show me to Larsin."

"First, promise you won't hurt him."

"I'm stuck on this island for good," Dante said. "If I want to kill him, you won't be able to protect him forever."

Winden pressed her lips together. "You're right. He is the one who brought you here. He will have to answer for it."

Dante's sword stood in the corner. He picked it up and followed Winden into the daylight. As it turned out, Blays and Larsin were right there on the beach. Blays appeared relaxed, but Dante could see the alertness in his stance — he'd been watching over Larsin.

Seeing Dante, Larsin's face went slack with relief. "You're alive. Thank the gods."

Dante drew his sword, throwing his scabbard aside. "If I'd died, it would have been on your hands. So let the gods know who to blame — Niles Ardner."

The older man's mouth fell open. He held an arm out to his side. "How did you find out?"

"One of the sailors knew my real father. And unlike everyone on this damned island, people elsewhere are capable of telling the truth."

"You'll get no more lies from me. Larsin Galand fell in battle with the Tauren. My plan was desperate. But it was the only way I knew how to save our people."

"I'm starting to think they don't deserve saving."

"You want my life?" Niles tugged down the collar of his shirt, exposing his tanned, wrinkled throat. "Go ahead and take it."

Dante's hand flexed on the hilt of his sword. He could imagine the feel of his arm lifting, wheeling the sword across the air and into the softness of the man's neck. Yet something stopped him. It certainly wasn't mercy—this deceiver deserved death, and probably one worse than Dante could have delivered with his sword. Though several people were watching from the shore and from the food stall in a shaded square uphill, he wasn't all that concerned about the publicity of it, either. He had no intention of living with these people. If they came for him in the jungle, he'd cut them down easily enough.

The problem was that he had no intention of staying on the island. Somehow, he would find a cure. Niles Ardner had been able to convince everyone in Kandak to bolster his lie. A man like that could be very useful.

And if he wasn't? Then Dante could always water the jungle with his blood on a later day.

He pointed his sword at Niles' neck. "You will help me find a cure. And to get away from this island forever."

The man inclined his head, careful not to slice his chin on the blade. "I can't promise I can find a cure any more than I can promise to cut down the moon like a coconut. But I swear I'll do everything I can to get you home." He gave Dante an arch look. "And I'll even repeat that vow after you've lowered your sword."

Dante picked up his sheath and put away his weapon. "I've read what little is recorded of the island's history. Your people once left here without worries. All we have to do is rediscover what they knew."

"Back up a ways," Blays said. "What exactly do you need a cure for? Didn't the shells do the trick?"

"There *is* no cure. That's why you have to go back to the *Sword of the South*. Before you catch the ronone sickness, too."

"Let me get this straight. You want me to leave you here to die?"

"I won't die. Not as long as we have a supply of shells. But there's no telling when I'll find my way out of here."

Blays glanced up at a cardinal peeping away on a branch. "Then it sounds like it'll go much faster if I'm here too."

Dante threw his arms wide. "There's no reason to put yourself at risk! What if you get trapped here, too?"

"Nah, I have faith you'll figure this out. Don't you?"

"And what would Minn say about this decision?"

Blays set his hands on his hips. "First off, that is a low blow. Second, inasmuch as Minn loves me, it's because I'm the kind of man who doesn't turn tail and run when my friends are in trouble. If I start doing that now, she'd probably leave me."

"I highly doubt that's how she'd look at it."

"Well, she's not here to ask, is she? And I know her much better than you do. Hence you'll have to take my word."

"It seems to me," Niles said, "that if he wants—"

"Shut up," Dante said. "No one asked for your opinion on this. Blays, I know you think you're being noble, but this has crossed the idiot line. Perhaps you've spent so much time beyond that line that you no longer recognize it. But this idea is so dumb it couldn't feed itself without the help of a team of three servants and a guidebook. I want you to go back to the boat and I want you to do it right now."

Blays took a half step to his right, placing himself entirely within the shade. "If that's how you feel about it, I'll go, then. And I'll take my idea with me."

"What idea?"

"The one that's a thousand times better than anything you'll ever come up with."

"So tell me it. And *then* go to the boat."

"It's really a good idea," Blays said. "But there's no guarantee it'll work. Which is exactly why you need me around. If you get into trouble trying it alone, and fail, then you might spend ten years searching for something else as good. So I won't give it to you unless I'm here to help see it through."

Dante took a rag from his pocket and dabbed sweat from his brow. "If you're that set on this, I don't see how I can kick you out of here. So out with it."

"All right then. You said the histories say the people here used to be able to come and go as they please, right?"

"The older ones, yes. But that seemed to stop at least five hundred years ago."

"That's when the old ways were lost," Niles said. "And no living soul remembers."

"Not a problem," Blays said. "Because we're not going to ask the living. We're going to ask the dead."

Dante laughed, slowly at first, then with increasing heart. "You're right. That's good. That's very, very good."

"You want to travel into the Mists," Winden said. "As they do at the Dreaming Peaks."

"Is there anything stopping us?"

"Yes and no. Anyone can visit the Mists. But doing so, it's not that simple."

"Sure it is," Blays said. "We chew some leaves, go on a magical journey, and ask the old folks how to get the hell away from their beautiful, lovely island."

"Saving our ancestors from the Mists is our most sacred act. We may not even be allowed beyond the Pastlands. The monks may need to go in our stead, but the Peaks have been captured."

"Enough," Niles said. "No more lies."

"We're talking about the Dreaming Peaks!"

"We're *talking* about saving Dante's life. And if he's able to find a cure for the ronone? We wouldn't be bound here any longer. If the Tauren try to destroy us, we can sail away."

Winden's face went stony. "But this is our homeland."

Niles laughed bitterly. "Is it? And if it's a choice between dying on our homeland, and living in a new land, would you really choose the point of a sword?"

"If we tell them, and the townsfolk learn of it, we'll be dead either way."

"I'm not a monster, Winden! And neither are you. We can save Kandak and set Dante free. If our people want to kill us for that, then we'll be waiting for them in the Mists."

They glared at each other. After three seconds, Winden gritted her teeth. "This is the way you want it? Then this is the way we will do it."

"It's a long story," Niles said to them. "Let's find a place to sit down. Somewhere a little more quiet."

He led them a long ways down the beach to a spot in the sand shaded by a roof of overhanging trees. Fallen pods and leaves coated the sand. He swept them away with his sandaled feet, clearing a spot to sit.

"What I'm about to tell you is our deepest truth," Niles said. "It's forbidden to outsiders, rixaka or not. Not even all of our own people know it. By telling you, I can be put to death. I don't say these things to impress you, or to make myself look selfless. I think we're well past that point."

Blays chuckled. Dante didn't. Niles went on. "I'm telling you this because, if we're doing this, there are things you need to know about the Dreamers and the Mists. And so that if anyone asks, you know to keep quiet. And pretend your head's as empty as a faded shell. Got me?"

"Empty-headed is Dante's specialty," Blays said. "As for myself, I'll swear the sky is green if that's what it takes to get us out of here."

"Understood," Dante said to Niles.

The older man leaned forward, hands clasped in his lap. "Five hundred years ago, the Plagued Islands weren't much more than a legend in Mallon. In so much open sea, Mallish galleys were more often lost than able to make it here. And those who stayed too long caught the ronone. Rowing back to Bressel, half the crew would drop dead before making it home. Some ships lost so many men they didn't have the crew to go on. Officers would pack themselves into the longboats and leave the oarsmen to starve. The few who returned told such harrowing tales that only the mad considered braving the trip to the south.

"But the survivors also brought back accounts of riches. Plants and herbs that could cure all manner of ailment. And the shaden, which could turn an ordinary nethermancer into a legend. The king at the time, Jordas of Highhill, poured rivers of silver into his Plagued Islands ventures. Along with funding voyages, he offered a hefty bounty to the captain who found safe passage. But he met with no success. Twenty years later, with Mallon teetering on the brink of bankruptcy, King Jordas earned a dagger in his back, and the woman who ordered his death took his throne.

"Her name was Freda. To separate herself from Jordas' failure, the only interest she took in the islands was to denounce them as a deathtrap. Thing is, if old Jordas had lasted a little longer, his investment might well have saved him. After twenty years of trial by fire—or, more aptly, trial by water—Bressel's captains were starting to experiment with sails. The new sloops they produced were too small to deal with ocean storms, let alone the Mill and its Current. But the ships gained use anyway. Much cheaper to crew a little sailing vessel along the coasts than to maintain a hulking galley full of slaves.

"Ten years into Queen Freda's reign, a woman named Halley Dane arrived in Bressel. The Danes were a noble house. More than wealthy enough to leave each of their children with an estate of their own. Rather than splitting his holdings in this manner, however, the Lord Dane only passed his land to his five sons. Halley was provided with a modest inheritance, but it wouldn't be enough to live out her days on.

"So she hatched a plan. Moving to Bressel, she commission

the construction of a much larger sailing vessel. Her goal: to take it to the Plagued Islands and amass a fortune so vast it would shame her neglectful father's ghost. Two years later, the *Windsplitter* was finished. It was the first carrack in Mallon. But Halley's wealth was exhausted. She'd have the funds for one trip, and no more.

"The *Windsplitter* sailed south. Past the Mill and into the Current. It reached the islands. Halley didn't stay long, but she was able to befriend the people she met here, who were known as the Dresh. And when the *Windsplitter* returned, bore such treasures that Captain Halley nearly recouped everything she'd sunk into her ship. Within two years, she had three more vessels. Within five, she had enough silver to buy herself a title, along with her father's manor from her eldest brother, who'd fallen into rough tides."

A man was walking down the beach toward them. Niles paused to sip from his waterskin, nodding as the man walked by. Once the wanderer was around a bend in the beach, Niles went on.

"But when you land a fish of that size, the gulls come out to grab what scraps they can catch. Others began to travel to the Plagued Islands. They were far less savvy than Halley. Some got into fights with the Dresh. And the sailors brought disease back to Bressel. Queen Freda used this as an excuse to seize the trade lanes. She banned all travel to the islands. When Halley and the other captains continued to smuggle in their goods, Freda put together a grand expedition. Its goal was to capture the islands and build forts on its harbors, ensuring that only those who flew the crown's colors could do business there.

"Her armada sailed forth. A score of ships bearing two thousand men. The Dresh fought back, but as usual, they were divided. One after another, each town fell. But the invasion had a hell of a time with the Tauren, along with the Kandeans. During the fighting, infrastructure was destroyed. Including the small shaden farms both groups had managed to cultivate across generations. Meanwhile, the conquerers set up their forts. Soon, they all developed ronone. And they began to need shells, too."

"Oh hell," Blays said.

Niles gave him a grim look. "See where this is going, do you?"

"In this case, I hope I'm much dumber than I think. Please, go on."

"Well, it wasn't long before the shaden dwindled. At first, Freda's conquerers had the locals collecting them, but as they returned with fewer and fewer shells, the Mallish started harvesting them instead. Soon, there weren't enough to go around. Bet you can guess who got the cure and who got nothing.

"Some of the Mallish chose to sail back to Bressel. They died to a man. The Dresh fared little better. Between the invasion, the poxes brought by the Mallish, and the ronone, almost every native islander died. The few that didn't became servants, or married into the Mallish. Within a generation, their entire people had vanished. And the Mallish invaders were trapped here to live atop the graves of those they'd slaughtered.

"A year after the first expedition, Queen Freda sent a second mission to learn what had happened. The stranded soldiers warned the newcomers away. Told them that plagues cursed whoever traveled here. Trade ceased. Over time, the Mallish survivors became the Dresh. Adopted their clothes, their ways, their harvesting, even what remained of their speech. And we made lying into a virtue. Because that was the only way to hide the horror of what we'd done."

With his story complete, Niles took a deep breath, eyes downcast.

"This is all very extraordinary," Dante said. "But I'm not sure what it has to do with us."

"Winden told you what the Dreamers are up to, didn't she?"

"They travel into the Mists. To rescue the dead who have been condemned as liars by Kaval."

Niles smiled with half his mouth. "That's the story we tell the rixen. Truth is, the Dreamers don't go into the Mists to rescue our people. They travel there to beg forgiveness from the islanders we killed. We believe that, when every single Dresh has forgiven us, they'll teach us how to lift the curse of the ronone."

Dante drew back his head. "The Dreamers have been working on that for hundreds of years, haven't they? We know virtually nothing about this place. How do you expect us to do what your people can't?"

"I don't. The dead wouldn't give a damn and a half about you. I'm telling you this so you understand what you're walking into. The people you want to speak to? They see us as mass murderers. It'll be harder to pry anything out of them than it is to talk the bones out of a live fish."

"I'm sensing a problem beyond the whole angry ghosts issue," Blays said. "According to what you said, the Dresh suffered the ronone, too. So assuming we can get any of them to talk, why do you think they'll know anything about the cure?"

"Because as recently as two or three hundred years before the Mallish arrived, the Dresh sailed freely, without the need for shaden. I don't know what caused them to lose their cure. But that's what we're traveling to ask, isn't it?"

Dante frowned heavily. "If it's that simple, why didn't the afflicted Dresh go and ask *their* ancestors how to lift the ronone?"

Niles lifted his eyebrows a fraction of an inch. "The Dresh's ability to travel into the Mists was very limited. It's said that it was like trying to speak underwater, or to swim in mud. Our Harvesters worked for years to refine the plant until we were able to send the Dreamers all the way in."

"And in almost five hundred years, it's never occurred to *your* people to ask the older Dresh?"

He laughed. "They'd never tell us that. If we knew how to cure ourselves, we could escape here. And leave our crimes behind."

"It sounds like we'll have no chance of convincing them to spill their secret."

"Don't be too sure," Winden said. "The dead, they don't think like we do. And you're rixen. You won't carry the same stain we do. They might be willing to bargain."

"They're dead," Blays said. "What would they want from us? A fresh delivery of worms?"

"We won't know that until we're inside. And through the Pastlands."

"And those are?"

"They take several forms. They may be a cherished memory. Or a wish made real. This place, it seems to be intended to hold the dead fast. Some spend decades there before moving on to the Mist. Others never leave it."

"Come to think of it, I've been there," Blays said. "So maybe I can show the rest of you the way out."

"Everyone goes into the Pastlands alone. It will be up to each of us to navigate through."

"Rougher than it sounds," Niles said. "Once you're there, you forget everything. If you try to remember, it can come back to you, but if you're too far gone, you may not want it to." He stood, brushing sand from his seat. "But this can wait until we're closer to ready."

"How long will it take us to find and speak to the dead?" Dante said.

"There's no telling. Time's funny on the other side. But I can't see it taking less than a few days."

Before hiking up to the temple where Niles had been sick—which he had accomplished, Dante now knew, simply by not eating any shaden, and letting the ronone advance—Dante wrote two letters. The first was to Olivander. He had acted as steward of the Sealed Citadel before Dante had been ready to take his place as the head of the Council. In the letter, Dante warned him that he would need to reassume that role for the foreseeable future.

The second was to Nak. Nak was the least powerful member of the Council—there were several monks of far lesser title who could command the nether with more fluency—but his limits with the shadows had pushed him to excel as a scholar.

And if Dante couldn't find his own way off of the island, he'd need every bit of Nak's talent to come up with other answers.

Benny had brought the longboat back to the *Sword of the South*, so Dante borrowed flags from Niles and waved the rowboat back in. Captain Naran himself accompanied the small crew.

He came ashore and looked Dante up and down. "I'm pleased to see you've stepped back from death's door."

"It's only a temporary reprieve," Dante said. "I've got a sickness called ronone. You pick it up by staying here too long, so you should wrap up your business and cast off as soon as possible."

"You mean to stay, then?"

"I mean to find a permanent cure. Which may be a fool's errand, but I happen to be an expert fool. Could you return in one month?"

Naran's eyes moved up and to the right. "I'll have to adjust our schedule. But this will be no problem. And Blays?"

"He'll be staying as well."

Naran's voice dropped. "So he's sick, too?"

"Only in the head. I have one other request." He held out the letters. "These need to be delivered to Narashtovik. The Sealed Citadel."

"That's a little bit out of our way. By approximately a quarter of the world."

"It isn't *that* far. Just find someone you trust. Please. My city depends on it."

Naran inserted the letters into the inner pocket of his shiny-buttoned jacket. "You have good relations with the norren, yes?"

Dante chuckled. "As far as that's possible. I'm a member of one of the clans, believe it or not."

"A small number of norren have established commerce in Bressel. My understanding is they return to their homeland regularly. I'll see if I can convince one of them to deliver your letters."

Dante thanked him and shook hands. Naran returned to the longboat. Dante watched the crew row across the impossibly clear waters of the bay.

He rejoined the three others and began the trek to the heights. Near the ocean, the air was perfectly nice as long as you stuck to the shade, but as soon as Dante got moving, he was sweating buckets. It felt much better than the cold sweats he'd had during his fever, however, and he kept up easily. They reached the temple by late afternoon. Dante now understood why it looked so old, so worn: the people who'd built it had died long ago. Their Mallish replacements hadn't had any idea how to craft such structures. Instead, they worked with bamboo, wood, woven grass.

During Dante's meeting with Naran, Winden had visited the Basket, acquiring one of the orange flowers the Dreamers used to sink close enough to death to walk in the afterworld. She found a shady spot outside the temple, planted the flower, and harvested it into a full-grown bush. Orange petals bloomed in profusion.

"We can go now," she said. "Or wait until morning. It's up to you."

Dante rubbed his upper lip. It had been an extremely long day. He hadn't entirely recovered from his illness, let alone had time to process the story Niles had told, which seemed to be the key to understanding the whole of Kandean society—possibly the entire island. He was sorely tempted to eat a giant meal and take a long rest.

But the thought of the dark spots growing inside him, lurking within him forever, filled him with a hot and prickly dread.

"We'll go now," he said. "There's nothing to gain by waiting."

"Except a clear idea of what the hell we're getting ourselves into," Blays muttered. "Then again, maybe it's better not to know."

"Very well." Niles reached out and plucked a flower.

"You're coming with us?" Dante said.

"Someone will need to help you navigate the Mists. They can be very deceptive. It's as easy to get lost in them as it is in the Pastlands."

"But I thought the Dresh hated your kind."

"I'll keep myself away from them." Amusement twinkled in his eyes. "Besides, you don't like me any better than they do, do you? So if I'm there, your shared enmity will give you guys something to bond over."

Winden plucked three more flowers, handing one to Dante and another to Blays. They entered the temple and spread blankets and grass-stuffed mattresses across the floor.

"The flower," Winden said. "It will taste very bitter. But eat it all. And when it comes, don't fight it."

"That's all?" Dante said. "No rituals?"

"You might wish to lie down. Unless you are unhappy with the shape of your head, and think it would be improved by a fall."

"And we're all going under? What if this winds up taking days? We'll die of thirst."

"We've arranged for Stav to check in on us. He's the only one we can trust. Are you ready?"

Dante lay back and chewed his flower, releasing a taste as bitter as poison. He swallowed it down as fast as he could. Finished, he lay back on his blankets. He thought he could feel a warmness creeping up from his belly, but it was too faint to be sure.

"How will we find each other?" Blays' voice had a ringing

quality to it. "Once we're through to the Mists?"

Winden shuffled on her mattress. "We're entering the Dream together. This means we'll enter the Mists together, too."

Dante thought he should ask more, but there didn't seem to be any point. Niles had said they'd forget everything in the Pastlands. Nothing he learned now would be useful until they were through to the Mists.

A breeze blew through the many windows of the temple wall. It was cooling, but within a minute, Dante couldn't seem to feel it at all. His body felt odd, as if the border between it and his blankets was indistinct, permeable.

Motion caught his eye. The vaulted ceiling was pulling away from him. Or maybe the temple was growing? No: he was sinking into the floor, he could feel the momentum in his guts. He reached out to grab at the ground, but he wasn't sure his arms were moving. The ceiling went higher and higher. Darkness encircled him.

He sank into the Dream. And saw his father.

EDWARD W. ROBERTSON

16

Larsin Galand galloped through the grass, turf spraying from the hooves of his horse. Clean yellow sunlight slashed through the branches of the forest. Dante could feel the thunder of the hoofbeats through his soles. The beast looked mad—eyes huge and black, lips flecked with froth—but his father was grinning, and so Dante felt no fear.

The horse skidded to a stop. His father vaulted from the saddle, bending his knees as he landed. "There you are. I told you not to run off."

Guilt flushed Dante's face. "I didn't go far."

"You would have been mighty unhappy with yourself if you'd missed me. Mount up. We're going for a ride."

His father slung himself back into the saddle and helped Dante up behind him. In a blink, the horse was galloping. Dante hung on tight, jostling up and down. Branches ripped past them, but not a single one touched his father. Dante loosened his grip and laughed. He'd never gone so fast in his life.

The trees ceased. Just ahead, the land ceased in a cliff. Green hills and black rocks stood hundreds of feet below. Dante's breath caught. His father dismounted and walked right up to the edge of the cliff. Dante didn't want to get so close, but he did anyway, and he was okay.

"Do you see how big it is?" His father pointed to the ridges on the far horizon. "And when you cross this plain, and stand on those heights way over there, there's another view just like this. So it goes around the world."

"How big is the world?"

"No one knows. That's the beauty of it. And that's what I needed you to see. Tomorrow, I'm going on a journey south. I'll take a boat. I could be gone a long time, because there's so much to explore. But I will come home."

"Where are you going?"

"I'm going to earn our fortune. But I'm going to bring something else back, too." He beamed. "Your mother."

"You're going to find Mom? But I thought she was dead!"

"We all did. There was a mistake. It turns out she'd just gone very far away. That means I'm going to have to travel just as far to find her. But don't be scared, okay?"

"I'm not."

His father examined him. "You aren't, are you? That's good. Because if I'm gone too long, I'll need you to come find me. You can never stop searching, okay? As long as you keep looking, you'll find me. I promise."

"I'll find you," Dante said. "Even if it takes me until I'm as old as you are."

Larsin laughed and ruffled his hair. "You'll never be as old as I am. Every year you get older, I get older, too. Now come on. We've a long ride ahead of us."

They turned around and galloped back through the forest. The horse seemed to be able to run forever. Dante felt as light as the wind. His dad was going to find his mom. And if he took too long, he wanted Dante to find him. Pride rose in him like a marble pillar.

Night came on fast, like they were riding into the darkness. Dante fought to stay awake, to be there on the horse with his father, headed off on the start of something great together. But before he knew it, he was asleep.

He woke on a cot in a small, unfamiliar room. The floorboards were cold. He dressed and walked out into a close, tidy house with books on the shelves and inkwells on the table. He walked out onto a cobbled porch shaded by an overhang. The full moon hung in the sky, pale white against the washed-out blue morning.

A man walked in from the side. He handed Dante a cup of yeasty smallbeer. "You're awake! My name is Tod. Your father's left you in my care while he's away."

The man wore a gray robe and his hair was cut close on the sides. Every other monk Dante had met had been haughty, grumpy, or strict, but Tod was kindly and quick to laugh, even when Dante couldn't remember yesterday's lesson. These occupied the afternoons—Tod wanted him to become wise and smart before his father returned.

Every morning, Dante walked out to the porch. The full moon hung in the air like a stone tossed upward and suspended at the height of its arc. Every morning, Tod brought him breakfast with a cup of smallbeer. And every morning, after Dante ate his sausage and tomatoes, he went out and explored.

The house was alone in the woods and he could walk for miles and never see a soul. Birds swooped from the branches, following him as he ran down the dewy trails. Mist flowed down from the hills, vanishing as quickly as his breath on a cold window pane.

One morning early in his stay—he thought it was his third day there, though it could have been his fifth, or maybe a week—he headed north, running and running until his lungs gave out. He stopped, folding his hands behind his head. The birds had gone quiet. Leaves crackled ahead. He froze. Were there bears in this wood? Or was it the wolves he'd heard howling at night? He cast about himself and picked up a damp branch fallen by the trail.

Something pale moved through the trees. Dante gripped his staff. Not twenty feet away, a stag stepped onto the trail, its fur as white as high clouds. Its antlers spanned the path. Its blue eyes locked on Dante. Steam trickled from its nostrils. It lowered its head and pulled at the grass. A minute later, it turned and walked back into the woods.

Every morning, he searched for the stag, but he never saw it again. His travels brought him many other wonders instead: owls, yellow-eyed and patient; baby rabbits like tufts of mobile fur; deer and mice; a waterfall, and the pond below it; the fish within it and the dragonflies above it.

Back at the house, Tod led him through the *Account of the Events at Nine's Crossing*, then the three-part story of the *Fabriosic*, then the *Compleat History of the Kingdom of Eritropolis*. Every day, Dante felt a little wiser. A little more capable of making his own way in the world. He couldn't remember why he was doing so much reading—or even, come to think of it, how he'd come to the cottage in the forest—but he knew he liked it very much. He felt destined for something great. He wasn't sure he wanted more than he already had, though. When he went exploring, pushing past the brush and into the tall grass of a clearing, he felt as though he might be happy here forever.

One morning, he walked out onto the porch. The moon hung like a stone. Tod came to give him his smallbeer and his sausage and tomatoes. Finished, Dante walked toward the pond beneath the waterfall, his favorite place. There, the stream poured down the cliff, battering the deep end of the pool. Rainbows flitted through the haze. He walked to the shallow side where moss swayed on the rocks, stopping to pick up a twig. As he moved on, he poked at the dragonfly larvae clinging to the weeds where the stream fed out of the pond. Halfway around, a snake slithered away, startling him so badly he laughed.

In time, as always, he came to the right side of the falls, where the cave hid behind the sheets of water. As always, he stopped there. He wanted to go inside, but he had no source of light. Besides, the rocks were slippery, and with the water gushing down on his head, he might fall into the pool. Tod was much too far away to hear him.

He turned to go, rocks clacking under his feet. Something was trying to swim up from the deep places of his mind. He stopped and waited, letting it come. He was supposed to keep exploring, wasn't he? To keep searching. He didn't know why; that part didn't seem to want to come back. He only knew that it was important.

He lowered himself to his knees and crawled forward. Stones shifted under his weight, grinding against each other. After a few feet, they turned mossy. The knees of his pants soaked through. Mist clung to his eyelashes. It was very cold. He could feel the thunder of the water in the hollow of his chest. Droplets began to strike his face. The curtain of water was right in front of him, so whitely churned he couldn't see through to the other side. He closed his eyes, held his breath, and scrambled forward.

Ice cold water drenched him to his bones, battering him, threatening to knock him off the rocks and into the depths. He felt his way forward. The curtain fell behind him. He wiped his eyes. The cave opened before him.

It was cool and smelled musty, but in a clean way. A soft glow emanated from the back, revealing a cavern thirty feet deep. Was there a hole out to the other side? He picked his way across the pebbles and sticks lining the floor.

Eight feet ahead, a shadow moved along the floor. Goosebumps swept his skin. But there was no animal there. Just a patch of darkness, swirling within itself and holding position. A gathering of shadows. They moved like water or fire or a school of fish. The way they flocked and flowed, they reminded him of something, but he couldn't say what. He stepped back, heart bumping. The shadows retreated. But rather than feeling relieved by their withdrawal, he felt sad.

He stepped forward. The shadows advanced. He reached out and so did they. His fingers touched darkness. It felt right.

Another memory broke the plane of his consciousness, bobbing up like a piece of wood dislodged from the rocks it had been trapped beneath.

His father was gone. And had been for a very long time.

He ran back to the house. Tod was sweeping the porch. Dust motes swirled through shafts of sunlight.

Seeing him dripping water everywhere, Tod's cheeks pursed in a frown. "What happened to you? Get thirsty and decide to drink the whole creek?"

"How long has my dad been gone?" Dante said.

The monk stopped and leaned on his broom. "I'm not sure. No more than a week or two."

"It feels like it's been months."

"It hasn't been that long, has it?"

"Think of all the books I've read since then. It must have taken weeks. I'm worried."

The monk resumed sweeping. "Well, I think you should forget about it. We're about to start *The Book of the Soaring Vale*. You'll like that one. Plenty of adventure."

"I think I was supposed to find him."

"Give it a few more days. If he hasn't shown up by week's end, then we'll see what we can do."

Dante wanted to argue, but the monk's smile was so kindly he acquiesced. And Tod was right: *The Book of the Soaring Vale* was so wonderful he felt he could get lost in it for years. Yet every evening, when the sun stole away and they folded up the book, Dante reminded himself of what he had to do.

Week's end arrived. That morning, as Dante accepted his cup, he looked Tod in the eye. "I have to find my father."

Tod licked his lips. "That could be dangerous. It would be a shame if you went out and got hurt or lost, and he returned and you were nowhere to be found."

"He told me I had to search for him. I can't let him down."

"Very well. I won't try to stop you."

"Will you help me?" Dante said. "I don't even know where he went."

"Larsin went to the west," Tod said. "But wolves prowl that way. You'll never get past them."

"I have to try!"

The monk snapped his fingers. "I've just remembered. He left a sword for you. It's in a chest in the basement—but the chest is locked."

"Where's the key?"

"Oh, it's hidden somewhere. You'll have to find it."

"If my dad wanted me to have the sword, why would he hide the key?"

Tod blinked. "Well, of course he didn't hide it. I meant to say it was lost. But you can find it, can't you? Or else you'll never be able to search for him."

"Then I better get started."

Dante put on his boots and a cloak and found a tall, straight branch that Tod helped him cut into a walking staff. Thinking his father had dropped the key on the way to the west, Dante headed down the path that way, checking the trail and the grass to either side. By day's end, he'd found nothing.

The next morning, he tried the north. Then the east. Then the south, which was a quiet meadow he'd never found anything special in and rarely visited. He came back to the house and searched the grounds around it.

"It's no use," he said. "I could search for years and never find it."

"But the key is bright gold. When you're close, it will shine like the sun. All you have to do is keep looking."

The encouragement lifted Dante's spirits. That day, he hunted for so long that twilight was upon him before he knew it. Eyes glittered from the shadows. A wolf howled from so close that his bladder tried to let go. He dashed back to the house as fast as he could, looking over his shoulder all the way.

"You were out late," Tod said. "You missed all our reading." He held up the leatherbound copy of *The Book of the Soaring Vale*. "To make up for it, we'll have to start first thing tomorrow."

Chagrined, Dante went to bed. Yet try as he might, he couldn't fall asleep. Shadows played on the ceiling. Why had he been out so late? He'd been looking for something, hadn't he? He punched his pillow and rolled on his side. Well, if it was that important, he'd remember it in the morning.

The howl of a wolf pierced the shutters. He sat straight up in bed. The key! He'd been traipsing around all day, yet somehow, he'd forgotten to look for it. Which meant he'd forgotten to look for his father. Heart racing, he went to his desk, hunting for a quill and parchment. He couldn't trust his memory. He had to write it down before it could be lost again.

His desk had parchment, but no quills or ink. He went to Tod's desk in the main room. Again, there was parchment, but nothing to write with. Dante pulled the drawers open a second time, as if to force the inkwells to reappear, but the desk stubbornly remained empty.

He backed away from the desk. The table by the fireplace was vacant. But he didn't need ink, did he? He rushed to the hearth, meaning to grab charcoal and scrawl his message with that, but the fireplace had been swept so clean he could have eaten off it. He ran to the door to go outside and get some dirt to smear on his wall, but the door was locked. He banged his shoulder into it until he cried out with pain.

"Tod!" he called. "Tod, I need something to write with!"

No matter how hard he yelled, the monk's door stayed closed. Dante bashed his small fist against it. Hand aching, he staggered back and sat on the floor. Tears washed down his cheeks.

The candle in his lantern sputtered, then steadied. The

lantern's glass was bubbled and unevenly thick. He gazed at it, tears stopping. Everything he could use to write had disappeared. But they'd missed one thing.

He removed the candle from the lantern and set it on the table, then smashed the lantern to the floor. Setting his parchment beside him, he picked up a large triangular shard and pressed it to the back of his arm. Blood welled from the wound. He dabbed his finger in it, intending to scrawl his message to himself in crimson.

Shadows flicked from the corners of the room, coating his hand. As they touched him, he remembered. He looked up. Tod stood before him, mouth agape.

"My dad didn't go west," Dante said. "He went south. Toward the sea."

"You can't go south. Past the meadow is the Racing Woods. You can't enter it at anything less than a run. It's miles and miles across. And if you slow down, even for a second, you'll be spit back out to wherever you started your day."

"My father must have made it through."

"He had a horse to carry him across the forest. You'll never make it on two legs."

"I have to try."

Tod reached out his hand. "At least wait until morning. It's too dark, and you've broken your lantern."

Dante looked at him a long moment, then nodded. "Okay. Don't worry about the lantern. I'll clean it up."

Tod kept watch on him as he swept up the broken glass and dumped it into a bucket. As he finished, Dante picked up two small slivers, tucking one between his fingers and dropping the other into the bucket so it would make a sound. Back in his room, he cut himself again, and wrote himself a note in blood.

When he woke, it was still there on his table. He went outside. The full moon peered from the morning sky. Tod brought him his drink and his food.

"Well," the monk said. "Ready to return to *Soaring Vale?*"

"I'm going south," Dante said. "Into the forest."

"I'd forgotten all about that. Just be careful."

Dante walked out of the yard and into the meadow. It was a long ways to the forest, but he had to save his strength. Crickets chirped from the grass. Doves called sadly. Flies buzzed. The forest rose ahead. He stopped at its edge, took four deep breaths, and jogged into it.

The noise of bugs and animals faded behind him. Within a minute, he could hear nothing but the wind in the trees and the rasp of his boots in the fallen leaves. He saw no squirrels, mice, or spiderwebs. He was the only living creature in the Racing Woods.

Tod had said the forest was miles across, but Dante was fit from so many days of hiking and exploring. A path ran south, firm and mostly clear. Good for running. Five minutes in, and he was barely breathing any harder. After ten, he'd crossed at least a mile and he still felt good.

His heart beat faster. A stitch started in his side, hurting worse by the moment. A hundred yards ahead, an oak tree leaned over the trail. He promised himself he'd stop when he reached it. He passed it and kept running, telling himself he'd stop at the stand of birches ahead. He meant to trick himself again, to keep on going like that until he was through the entire forest, but his side hurt too badly. He grimaced, slowing.

Around him, the woods warped. Light flashed.

He was in his bed. He threw off the sheets. Out on the porch, the moon was still out, but it had climbed higher; it was still the same day. He felt exhausted.

"So?" Tod said. "How far did you get?"

"It's hard to tell," Dante said. "But it had to be two miles."

"It's at least twenty! You'll never make it through. You should look for the key."

"I could search forever and never find it. Besides, I don't have to cross the forest tomorrow or the day after. I just have to make it a little further each time. Until I make it to the other side."

Tod looked skeptical. "Well, you can't go back today. It'll kick you right back out. So we might as well read, hm?"

He agreed. He fell asleep early and slept straight past dawn. In the morning, he ate, drank, and went back to the forest. This time, he ran more slowly, pacing himself. By the time he reached the oak, he was breathing hard, but he felt good enough to keep going. He made it past the birches. His legs were so tired. When he reached an outcrop of limestone, he stopped.

The warp of the forest. The flash of light. And he was back in his bed. Too tired to get up, he fell back asleep, drenched in sweat.

The next day, he made it past the outcrop. The day after that, he made it at least another half mile, all the way to a burbling stream. The morning after that, though, he hadn't even gotten to the outcrop before a stitch stopped him short. Before he knew it, he was thrust home to bed. He lay there, miserable at his failure, then went out to see the monk.

"This is foolish." Tod did nothing to hide his peevishness. "He'll be back in time. Why don't we go swimming at the falls? You used to like that."

"I have to keep searching."

The following day, with his only audience the man-in-the-moon smiling overhead, Dante ran all the way to the stream and kept on going for another two miles. The day after that, he barely made it as far, but he'd reached a new peak. By week's end, he could run for a full hour without stopping.

Each day, he ran further and further: sometimes no more than an extra hundred yards, but sometimes as much as a mile. His heels were callused, his legs lean. He reached ninety minutes straight. Then two hours. Then three. And one day, he ran on and on, breathing calmly all the way, with no aches or weakness in his legs. The disc of the moon slipped behind the trees to the west. He kept going. The sunlight grew more and more yellow, then red. He kept going. It sank away and the forest turned blue and gray.

He kept going.

Full night. There were still no crickets. No owls. Only the thump of his feet on the trail. The Racing Woods were even wider than Tod knew, but it didn't matter. Because Dante could run forever.

The night was cool and windless. It seemed to pass in no more than two hours. With the coming dawn shading the world gray, the land sloped up. It was the first change in elevation he'd encountered on his entire run. Around him, the trees thinned. A smile broke across his face. The ground leveled. He ran free of the woods.

And found himself in the yard outside the house. The moon hung in the sky like a stone. Tod wandered onto the front porch, cup of smallbeer in hand.

Dante stopped, sank to his knees, and wailed until he passed out.

When he woke, he was in bed and it was three days later. Tod entered the room and patted his knee. "Are you okay?"

"It's over," Dante said. "I'll never find him."

"Now, that's not true."

"I ran all the way through the forest. And wound up right back here. I know he went south. If I can't go that way, then there's nothing I can do."

"Not so." The monk's eyes twinkled. "I found something while you were out." He extended the first two fingers of his right hand. Between them, he held a golden key. "Want to give it a try?"

Fresh hope rose in Dante's chest. They went outside to the staircase down to the basement. There, a long, narrow chest sat in the middle of the floor. Dante put the key into the lock. It fit. Tumblers clicked. He opened the chest. A brilliant steel sword rested on a bed of red velvet.

"Go ahead," Tod said. "Pick it up."

He seemed very eager. For Dante to move on? Or for him to forget what he'd just been through? He reached for the sword. There was something else in the box: a shadow coiled around the blade. Tod didn't seem to be able to see it.

Show me, Dante willed it. *Show me the way.*

The shadow fell into the sword. The blade shortened by three inches. The ends of the crossbar curled into little balls. He knew this sword, didn't he? It wasn't his, or his father's. Instead, it had once belonged to a friend of his. A friend whose father had died when he was a child.

"I remember now." He closed the chest. "He's gone."

Tod screwed up his face. "Well yes. That's why you need to pick up this sword. So you can go slay the wolf. And start the business of finding him."

"And after the wolf, there will be a bear. Or a bad man. Or I'll have to find a shield next. It will never end. Because he's gone."

"You can't say that. Or he *will* be."

Dante slowly shook his head. "He already is. No matter how long I go on searching, I'll never find him. I'll just be wasting my life reaching for something I can never touch."

Tod's face went as cold as a tomb. "You could have been happy. It's in your blood to try to climb heights you can never attain." He moved forward, looming over Dante. "I can make you forget. You can read. And explore. And search. Forever."

"I can't do that. Because it's also in my blood to know the truth. No matter how much it hurts."

He turned his back on the monk and climbed up the stairs from the basement. Halfway up, the steps shot upward, expanding for hundreds of feet. The exit was a pinhole of light. He turned around, but there was nothing behind him. He climbed on. There was no sound but the thump of his boots on the treads.

The light ahead brightened, expanded. A cold wind rolled

down the stairs. The light beyond the doorway was too bright to make out anything on the other side. He stepped out.

He stood in a white valley. Mist flowed to all sides, blocking out the sky. To his left, a gap looked down on the craggy crown of a mountain, black rock capped with snow. To his right, and hundreds of feet above him, another gap looked up on a wind-tossed sea. Struck by vertigo, Dante staggered back a step, holding up a hand as if to stop the onrushing upside-down tide.

He was disoriented by more than just the ocean in the sky. He was a grown man again. And he remembered.

He turned in a circle, taking in his surroundings. Figures walked toward him, silhouettes in the blowing mist. Dante reached for the nether. Nothing came. Heart racing, he drew his sword.

"About time you showed up," Blays said. His cloak billowed behind him like the hero from an old poem. "Now what say we go grab us a ghost?"

17

Dante ran his hand down his face. "It felt like I was in there for months. How long did you have to wait?"

"Er," Blays said. "Well, apparently you don't have to sleep here. Unless you want to. And there doesn't appear to be a sun. Not one that moves, anyway. Also, time's kind of funny here. So…"

"So the answer is you have no idea."

"Approximately two relative days," Niles said. "Long enough for the three of us to figure out where we're going next."

Dante folded his arms. "Why did you have to figure that out?"

"Do you think the afterworld has maps? The geography of this realm is no more fixed than its sense of time."

"But don't worry," Blays said. "Time goes a lot faster here than for our bodies back in the real world. So we probably haven't pissed ourselves yet."

Dante continued to hold Niles' gaze. He'd spared the man's life, but the decision had done little to quell Dante's anger with him. "You spoke like you'd been here before."

"Years and years ago," the older man said. "They don't like us to come here. The Dreamers spend years building up enough trust to get the deceased to talk to them. If I'd visited more often,

I would have disrupted their work."

"I don't suppose we could go back to Kandak and find someone with more experience to guide us."

"We may be able to do that. Though if word gets out that we've let you come here, they'll tie rocks around our ankles and toss us in the bay. So we can risk that, if you like. Or we can move our damn feet and get underway."

Anger spiked up Dante's spine. "Let's move, then. The sooner we find the cure, the sooner I can leave your wretched island."

Wordless, Niles turned and walked ahead. Their movement stirred the fog, revealing bare black rock with one step, spongy green grass with another, and inch-deep tide pools with the next. In such a place, it was hard for Dante to care about Niles' deceit. For years, he'd wondered about what lay beyond the mortal realm. Now, he walked in that place.

"This is much different than what's described in the *Cycle of Arawn*," he murmured.

"Your accounts may not be wrong," Niles said. "This place seems to be for the island alone."

Buffeting winds tugged at the mists, revealing glimpses of palms and pod trees, then soaring, knife-like green cliffs. The air had been a neutral temperature, odorless, but it began to warm. On occasion, Dante smelled the briny tang of the sea, or the pleasant scent of sunlight on leaves.

"So," Blays said. "What was so fascinating about the Pastlands that you had to stay there for months?"

Dante stepped over a thick root that didn't appear to be connected to anything else. "Mostly the fact that I could hardly remember that the socks go on your feet and not your hands. Let alone that I was adrift in a dreamworld."

"What did they show you, then?"

Dante was about to give a glib answer about visions of short dresses and high winds, but something stopped him. The Mists were, as far as he could tell, as real-feeling as reality, with none of the swimminess or fuzziness that came with normal dreams or his time in the Pastlands. Yet despite the clarity of the Mists, there seemed to be something about the place that compelled him to be more truthful. Less hidden. Separated from his life, the cares of that place seemed less real.

He explained how his father had sailed off on a journey to find his mother. How Tod the monk had looked after him, but seemed to be trying to keep him stuck there. And how, after a long search for Larsin, Dante had realized there was no finding him, and had finally been able to step out of the trap.

"Huh," Blays said. "Was this the same monk who raised you?"

Dante shook his head. "Not exactly. It was a lot like a dream. Some things were true, but others were more like wishes or fears. What about you? What did you see?"

"I was a kid running around in the hills saving smaller kids from trouble," Blays said. "Same as the last time I died."

Niles led them onward. After several seconds, Winden spoke up. "I was with the Tauren. I was a great warrior, but I'd lost my way. I had to find it again. And lead my people to honor."

Blays made a thoughtful noise. "Your big dream was to be a member of the Tauren? You mean the guys who drop babies off by the riverside to fend for themselves? I'm afraid you just lost my support for mayor."

"You don't understand," Winden said. "I *was* one of those babies. The Kandeans took me in."

"Aha. Dante, you're quite the physician, aren't you? Don't suppose you know any way to remove the foot I've lodged in my gullet?"

"That place seems to be about fixing the parts of us we wish were better," Dante said. "But you have nothing to be ashamed of, Winden. You're one of the Kandeans. You bear no blame for anything the Tauren do."

"It's one thing to know that," she said. "It's another thing to feel it."

They walked on. Dante gazed at Niles. "And what about you?"

Niles didn't look his way. "I was back with Larsin. In the days when we united the island against the Tauren. When we were brothers."

He didn't seem inclined to go on. Soon, the path descended. The air warmed further. The crash of waves sounded from afar.

Blays craned his neck at a tree floating high in the sky and upside down. "Place is a bit quiet, isn't it? What happened to the millions of dead people?

"Most have passed out of the Mists," Niles said. "To the deep place Dreamers can't go. We call it the Worldsea."

"Do the gods ever come here?" Dante said.

"Not that I'm aware of. Though who can say what happens beyond."

Dante had any number of other questions, but Niles knew very little beyond the basics. From what he could gather, the Mists were a sort of waiting room between the Pastlands (where people usually forgot they were dead) and the Worldsea (where, from the sound of it, people forgot they'd ever been alive). The Mists were a sort of conscious and collective dream where people could play out lives similar to the real world, but with fewer restraints. According to Niles, most of the dead got restless and moved on within a few years or decades, but some—like the massacred, grudge-holding Dresh—lingered far longer.

While Dante was still trying to tease all this out, the fog thinned. A green meadow spread before them, leading to a beach of dark purple sand. Houses of black stone hugged the shore, their open walls screened by sheets of lightweight cloth. Canoes bobbed on the turquoise sea. Further out, small round islands sprung from the water, domed like mushroom caps.

A few hundred people scattered the fields, the beach, and the water. Some were up to nothing obvious, but others hacked at plants, scraped canoes, or cast lines into the water.

Blays squinted. "How odd. These people appear to be *working*."

"Working makes people feel useful," Dante said. "I expect those with no interest in it soon move on to the Worldsea."

"Well, when I die, I hope I have the good sense to travel to Hammockland."

"Time to cut the chatter," Niles said softly. "We won't be welcome here."

They entered a field of san, the long green stalks rising from shallow pools. A hundred feet away, a man poked at the roots with a narrow wooden shovel, dislodging the plants and tossing them up onto the bank.

Seeing the four of them, he stood and stared. His skin was the same medium brown as the people on the Plagued Islands, but while most of the living had blue, green, or gray eyes—signs of Mallish stock—this man's were a light brown. His features were smaller, too, except for his jaw, which was more angular. Niles nodded to him. The man turned and walked toward the shore.

Without exchanging a single word, the people in the field followed him. Those along the path joined the flow. By the time Dante and the others reached the village of stone structures, it was deserted.

"We're off to a great start, Niles," Dante said. "What's your next suggestion? Set their houses on fire?"

Niles' brows lowered. "I'm doing the best I can."

To their left, an old woman approached along the sand, supporting her weight on a gnarled cane. Her back was bent like the claws of the bright orange parrot that sat on her shoulder. Her face was heavily wrinkled, but her eyes were lively, contrasting with her utterly plain clothes. She stopped in front of them. Her expression was lightly amused. Closer up, her face appeared to be perfectly symmetrical, right down to the crinkles around her eyes and mouth. She too was small-featured and sharp-jawed. One of the Dresh.

Niles bowed his head. "Good morning."

"Is it?" she said. "What are you doing here?"

Dante stepped forward. "We'd like to speak to your leader, if we could."

The woman glanced at her parrot, as if sharing a joke. "You're troubling my people. Leave us, please."

"We would never have disturbed you if it weren't absolutely vital. If you'll let us speak to whoever's in charge here, we won't trouble anyone else."

Her smile waned. "I ask a second time: leave us."

"All we need is ten minutes of—"

The old woman's eyes expanded like pools of oil. Her irises were light brown, overlaid by a braid of darker lines. Dante felt as if he were falling into her pupils, that they were growing and growing until they'd swallow everything: the round little islands, the san fields, the fogs—

He splashed down into water, plunging below the surface. He thrashed, choking. Salt slipped down his throat. Somehow, he broke into the open, coughing up fluid. The other three bobbed beside him in a calm, warm sea. Banks of clouds surrounded them on all sides.

"Help!" Dante yelled, pawing at the water, dragged down by his boots, sword, and pack, all of which had accompanied him into the world beyond. "I'm sinking!"

"Oh, for gods' sake." Blays grabbed his arm and steadied him. "Just move your arms and legs. It's salt water. You have to *try* to drown."

"Will yourself to float," Winden said.

Dante calmed his motions, paddling steadily. "What do you mean, will myself?"

"The people who stay here have agreed on the same laws of nature we're used to. But these laws, they'll bend. All you have to do is want them to."

He focused his mind on staying above the water. He rose several inches. After a few moments, he found he hardly had to paddle at all. "What just happened?"

"Same principle," Niles said. "The old woman willed us away."

"Let me get this straight. If someone's bothering you, all you have to do is wish it, and they'll drop right into the ocean?"

"Aye, that's right. When we return to the village, we'll have to will ourselves to stay, or she'll do this again."

Dante slicked the hair from his face. "Can you will someone to die?"

"We're already in the land of the dead. There's no second death."

"But can the dead will us out of the Mists?"

Niles blew his nose into the water. "I don't think that works. The only way we'll leave is if we fall asleep. It'll still take time for the drug to wear off, but we'll pop back into our bodies next thing we know."

Blays screwed up his face. "Can you will someone into a volcano? Or a pit of snakes?"

"Conceivably."

"And keep them there forever?"

Niles glanced at Winden. Winden said, "To keep you in such a place, no one could do that by themselves. To overcome your will to such an extreme would require the focus of hundreds of people."

"Holy shit. Then it is possible?"

"To keep you there, those hundreds of people would have to constantly think of it, and nothing else. They would share the same hell they put you in. It would never last for long."

Blays treaded water with casual skill. "Well, if it's a pit of snakes, any amount of time is long enough."

Dante glanced up, but the fog was so thick he couldn't even find the sun. "How do we get out of here?"

"It's just as we've been discussing," Niles said. "We will ourselves forward. Back to the town."

"Well, why didn't you say so?" He closed his eyes and imaged the village of stone buildings. When he opened his eyes, nothing had changed. "One flaw: I'm useless."

Winden touched his arm. "This willing, it's easiest to pair it with physical motion. Moving the body helps the mind to understand."

Dante exhaled, chose a random direction, and started swimming, concentrating on keeping his head above water. When this proved simple enough, he began to think about the town. The islands. The pale blue water. He swept forward, crying out in surprise as he gained speed, a chevron of water spraying away from his chest.

Blays drifted up beside him, stroking cleanly through the neutral water. "This," he said between breaths, "is a very strange place."

Niles and Winden matched their pace. Within minutes, the fog thinned. A blue hump of land materialized ahead, resolving by the second. Dante soon found himself wading through the shallow breakers onto purple sands. The town was less than a quarter mile to the north.

"I envisioned the town," he said. "But we wound up outside it. Because they don't want us there?"

Niles grunted. "Keep your mind on staying put."

"And if the whole town comes for us?"

"Then focus on running as fast as you can. And this time, let me do the talking. Don't you realize the old woman *was* the chieftain?"

Dante went red. He'd been so annoyed with Niles' presence and awed by the strangeness of the Mists that he'd been acting like a fool. He had to settle down. To let Niles take the lead. The older man was already walking north, shedding water from his clothes with each step. Dante fell in behind him, willing the water to leave his sopping shirt and trousers. It obeyed, leaving a damp trail in his wake.

The town remained deserted. There were no longer any canoes in the shallows between the islands. As they neared, a middle-aged Dresh woman walked toward them, dimpling the sand with a tall walking staff. A golden-furred monkey loped along beside her, regarding the four of them with human suspicion.

"I told you to leave us be," the woman said.

Her voice sounded nearly identical to the old woman's. She had the same symmetrical face, the same light irises shot through with dark brown. With a jolt, Dante realized she *was* the old woman.

Niles lowered himself to one knee. "Lord of this land. Forgive our intrusion."

"I reserve my forgiveness for those who deserve it." The woman was handsome, made moreso by the easy command in her eyes. "I don't know which is worse. That two usurpers have come to us, or that they've brought two outlanders with them."

Niles blinked at the sand, cheeks flushing. His jaw worked, but he couldn't find any words.

"We're not any happier to be here," Blays said. "We're trapped on the island. If you don't help us, sooner or later we're going to die, and then you'll *never* be rid of us."

The woman leaned on her staff. "You think you'd be allowed here? Have you seen any of the usurpers in our city?"

"Well, no. But I've been a little distracted by the flying oceans and floating trees."

"Here's a question for you," Dante said. "Do you want to spend the rest of your time here fighting to keep us out?"

She smiled tightly. "At least you're more amusing than these weeping toadies." She flicked her hand at Niles, who remained kneeling; her monkey mimicked her gesture. "What do you want?"

"To learn how to lift the ronone."

"I am glad to tell you in truth I don't know."

"Those who came before you knew. You've never asked them about what wiped out your people?"

"I know the cause: the Mallish."

Dante tensed his jaw. "But surely you were curious about the sickness."

"I'm happy to be dead. Why should I care what killed me? When a bird sings for you, do you ask it why? If so, it's no wonder the birds don't speak to you."

"Those who came before you knew, didn't they? Couldn't you ask them?"

She drummed her fingers against her staff. "That would be in my power."

"Then what can we do to convince you to aid us?"

"I don't know. Make me an offer, outlander."

"In my world, I'm a sorcerer. One of the most powerful there is."

"And this matters to me how?"

Dante gestured at the air, groping for answers. "I could help your descendants. Heal them, if they're sick. Or build them stone fortresses to keep them safe. Do you know what they're using now? Wooden shacks. At the mercy of fire, storms, enemy attacks."

"That's because their brains have been made stupid by Mallish blood," she said. Dante would have sworn the monkey chuckled at this. "Besides, I don't care for my descendants' lives. I'd rather they die. The sooner they're brought to the truth, the happier they'll be."

"I've traveled far. I've seen wondrous things and know many secrets. I can tell you about parts of the world you never knew."

"And will never see. So what's the point?"

"Then I could…" he trailed off, shooting a glance at Blays.

"Don't look at me," Blays said. "She's got a pretty good point."

Dante turned to Winden. "Please tell me you're more help than he is."

She pressed her lips together, regarding the sand. "If your god stepped down before you, what would you offer him?"

"My devotion. I have nothing else."

The Dresh woman laughed ringingly. "Your devotion interests me about as much as the sand fleas that used to bite my ass."

She drove her staff into the sand. Her eyes ballooned to the size of plates, then stormheads. Dante willed himself to stay on the beach. As her eyes engulfed him, he launched into a stream of invectives. He was cut off halfway through by the clap of water swallowing him up.

He shot to the surface of the cloud-wrapped sea. "Son of a bitch!"

Niles glared at him, water streaming down his goatee. "I told you to hang on!"

"I tried! It was too slippery."

"What was? Your attention? The rest of us were doing fine."

"Then why are *you* here?"

"Because we're together," Niles said. "All part of the same dream. The same will. So do your damned job!"

Dante kicked at the water beneath him. "And you're quite the teacher, aren't you? Such a marvelous leader. No wonder that, now that my father's gone, you're about to lose the entire island to the Tauren."

A knife appeared in Niles' hand. Dante felt a pang of fear. He reached for the nether. When none came, the fear doubled—and then he remembered Niles couldn't hurt him, either. And he laughed.

"This arguing," Winden said. "Is it getting us closer to our answers? Or are you two like the south wind: hot air we can only pray will go away?"

Niles put away the knife, cheeks as flushed as they'd been beneath the Dresh woman's judgment. "You're right. Anger will get us nowhere." He shifted his gaze to Dante. "And you're right, too. I'm not the man your father was. But I was his friend for a very long time. He had more patience than either of us. That's part of why he was such a good leader—and a fine teacher, too."

"There was a time when I might have cared," Dante said. "The Pastlands cured me of that."

"Good for you. As for me, I figure I owe him one. I will get you off these islands. Right now, that means getting this right. Are you ready to listen?"

"If it helps me out of here? Absolutely."

"Very good." Niles shut his eyes, visibly composing himself. "When you're willing yourself across these waters, or to stay put in the village. What are you doing?"

"Is this a trick question? I'm willing myself."

"Are you willing yourself to float right now?"

"Mostly, I'm willing myself not to punch you. But yes. I'm floating."

"Look to where your body is in contact with the water," Niles said. "What do you see?"

Dante dropped his eyes to the sea. "Water."

"Drop your brattiness for one second and *look*!"

He glanced up, startled, then looked back to the water. Light danced around him. At first he thought it was the sun, but that was obscured by the fog. He went still, keeping himself propped up with thought alone. Pure white light ringed him, surrounding his trunk and legs, glowing beneath the waves.

He'd seen such light before. The last time had been less than two weeks ago in Bressel.

"This place," Dante said. "It's made out of ether."

18

Dante gazed down at the light. Stupefied. Dazzled.

Beside him, Blays snorted. "This is some big surprise? Doesn't the *Cycle* claim the whole heavens are made out of ether?"

"Yes," Dante said. "But I'm controlling it. We all are. Just as we move the nether in our world."

Niles drifted nearer. "Your will is what shapes it. When you float here, or swim toward the village, or try to stop the woman from tossing you out, this is what you must grab tight."

Hesitantly, Dante reached for the ether the same way as he would the nether. It came reluctantly, a fraction as readily, but a bit pooled in his hand, shining like mercury lit from within. Now that he called to it, and knew where to look, he saw it everywhere: on the surface of the water, on his clothes and skin, in the tiny droplets of the fog. Everywhere the nether wasn't—rather than hiding in the cracks, like the nether did, ether seemed to line and coat things. Though it was possible that that was simply how it worked in the Mists, where *everything* was ether.

He dismissed it, summoned it, and repeated. He felt as feeble as a man taking his first steps after battling off consumption, yet at the same time, he felt impossibly strong, shot through with power. Before this, he'd never so much as seen the ether unless someone else had summoned it. Now that he'd broken through, though? He thought he might be able to do so back in the world as well.

He continued his practice. Summoning. Releasing. Around him, the others chatted with each other. Bobbing in the middle of the ocean, it was unnerving to divert so much of his attention to the ether, but the water wasn't cold, there was no danger of currents, and as far as he knew, any sharks in the Mists subsisted on wishes and light.

He'd long ago given up any hope of ever being able to grasp the ether. If he'd been on his own, he could easily have continued his study of it for hours, if not days. Knowing that time was passing slower to his body made that thought even more appealing. If this was a breakthrough, though, he could return to it later. In the meantime, he had a death curse to lift.

"I'm ready," he said. "This is the last bath we'll take today."

They swam forward. The ocean rushed past them, its low waves sheened with a light of their own. As they traveled, Dante delved into the ether, feeling its malleability, its ties to this place.

Land resolved ahead. They'd hardly waded ashore before the Dresh woman emerged from the banyans lining the beach. Three jone trotted beside her, tusks jutting from their maws, heads bullishly thick. This time, she was no older than Dante, her face hard and unlined, her muscles lean and cat-like. She carried a tall spear tipped with a six-inch saw-edged tooth.

"This is the third time I ask you to leave," she said. "If you come here again, I'll bring my people with me—and you'll spend the next nine years fermenting in an eel's belly."

Dante moved to face her. "That's how you and your people want to spend your days? Torturing us? Your every second spent trapped with us in our pain?"

"We're here forever. What does a few years matter to us?"

"Do you think it matters any more to me? I'm trapped on this island. I'll spend my entire life fighting to get out of here."

"And it will be wasted."

Her eyes expanded, filling his vision. Dante reached into the ether in the sand and the air, holding on with everything he had, insisting to the Mists that he stay there with his friends on the beach. The Dresh woman's eyes ceased growing. They wavered, flickering like the frenzied beat of a mouse's heart against its ribs, then contracted.

The woman fell back a step. She cried out, drew back her spear, and slung it at Dante's chest. He asked it not to touch him. Somehow, it wound up behind him, massive tooth buried in the sand, shaft wagging up and down. He was beyond glad he hadn't had to find out how much that would have dream-hurt.

She pressed her palm to her brow. "Why don't you just *die*?"

"It sure would be easier than this," Blays said.

"All your cares would fall from you like a leaden robe. Do you have any idea what it's like? How free you could be? You see what we have here. Why would you choose to struggle and ache when you know the peace that awaits you?"

The sun broke free of the mists, warming Dante's skin. A breeze blew off the water, cooling him perfectly. The air in his lungs refreshed him like the first drink of water in the morning. At once, the woman before him was so beautiful it hurt to look at her. By comparison, he felt shabby, shopworn. Why *did* he fight on? There was no nobility in suffering, was there? If he was bound for this place anyway, why not cut to the chase?

"Odds are we'll be back here sooner than we'd like," Blays said. "Until then, we've got business in our world."

"You don't have to." She reached out and touched Blays' face; tines of jealousy pierced Dante's heart. "You can choose death at any time."

Dante found his voice. "We don't belong here. Not yet. The gods must have created the two worlds for a reason. We'll stay in ours until they decide it's time to take us."

"Your world exists to make this one feel like a blessing. You can feel it's true, can't you?"

Blays folded his arms. Steam rose from his sleeves. "Why are *you* still here? Why not move on to the Worldsea? That's what you're supposed to do, isn't it?"

She smiled at him. "Hate. Hate for those who flensed us from our land."

"And we hate the Tauren," Niles said. "That's why we have to go back."

The woman's smile fell away. She moved before him, gliding, and stuck her finger in his face. "You lie. You tell yourself tonen so you don't have to face the darkness. It isn't the Tauren that propels your struggle."

His voice was a whisper. "No."

"Then why? What drives you to come here where you don't belong?"

"Because we hate ourselves! For what we did to you! We've devoted everything to your forgiveness and it's still not enough."

She sputtered with laughter. "How could it be? All your pleading and sobbing, has it brought any of us back? Returned the island that was taken from us?"

"We know we can't do that," Niles said, voice ragged. "Sometimes I don't know why we try. None of us were alive when it happened. Why do we still feel responsible?"

"You didn't just kill us. You took our skin. You're still wearing it today."

"I think we—they—did that to honor you, in their way. To let you live on in the only way they knew how. They would have undone it, if they could. But they couldn't. Neither can we. But we'll do anything to make it right."

The Dresh woman sighed out all her anger, turning to face the sea. "You say this. Yet you let the Tauren profane our sacred place."

"The Dreaming Peaks?"

"The only part of your world that still matters to us."

"Do you want us to clear them out?" Dante said. "And then you'll tell us what we need to know?"

"We're getting so tired of this." She crouched beside the waves, letting her fingertips dangle in the lapping water. "All the bowing and scraping. The Dreamers—so patient. So kindly. So exhausting. Maybe it's time we set the past aside." She clawed her fingers into the purple sand, scooping up a handful and casting it into the waves. "Toss the Tauren out of our place. And I'll find out what you want to know."

"But they're too strong," Niles said.

"No—you're too *weak*. Until you've proven your strength, you'll have nothing." She picked up her spear and stood. "Don't come back until then. If you do, all of the Dresh will pass into the Worldsea. And all forgiveness will go with us."

She walked down the shore. The three jone padded beside her, nosing at the shells dotting the beach.

"Well, we still don't have answers," Blays said. "But we weren't dropped into anything hideous, either. I'll count that as a win."

Winden shifted her feet. "I don't know if we can trust her to keep her end of the bargain."

"We have to," Niles said. "If we had any better options, we would never have come here in the first place. We have to take back the Dreaming Peaks."

Dante eyed him. "Is this why you're helping me? To continue your fight against the Tauren?"

Niles folded his arms. "Like I knew what they'd ask of us? Coming here was your idea."

"Still, it's mighty convenient. To get what I want, I have to help you get what you've wanted all along."

"This is the path we've been given. If you'd rather walk it alone, that's your call."

Overhead, the fog returned, blocking out the sun. "We'll deal with whoever's in the Dreaming Peaks. But that's as far as I'll get involved."

"If we hit them there, you know they'll retaliate," Blays said. "They might even come for Kandak."

"They'll do that eventually no matter what we do. By hitting them in the Peaks, at least we'll have softened them up for the Kandeans."

Niles had said that all they had to do to go home was to fall asleep. They headed into the shade and lay down. Despite the dense atmosphere, there was plenty of light. Between that and everything swimming through his head, Dante was afraid it would take hours to fall asleep. But after a few minutes, it greeted him as if it had been waiting for him.

He inhaled through his nose, taking in the dewy mountain air. He opened his eyes. He lay on the blankets in the temple. Outside, it was dark. He felt so hungry and shaky that he could have believed they'd been under for days.

The others stirred on their blankets and mattresses, groaning. While they stretched and rubbed their eyes, Dante extended his hand and reached for the ether. The room remained dark. His heart beat faster. Frustration twisted a cold knife in his heart.

And then light glimmered on the back of his hand.

He grinned. "Winden. I need paper and ink."

She sat up, massaging her temples. "And I need a minute to recover before I start taking orders."

Blays stood, planting his palms in the small of his back and stretching backwards. "You have got to be the most boring person I know. We just got back from the underworld, where we were tasked with casting down an awful villain, and the first thing you want to do is write in your diary about it?"

Dante got up to search the room. "I have to get this down. What we saw there—it's worthy of a *Cycle* of its own."

He found quills and a pot of ink—possibly the same instruments Niles had used to write him the fraudulent paternal letter of summons—and located a blank book among the volumes on the shelves. He retired to one of the back rooms and began to write. An hour later, the light of his torchstone faded and he ignited a candlefruit. Hours later, this dimmed and he used it to light another.

Before the second fruit faded, daylight crept through the open walls. Dante finished, leaving some thirty blank pages for later notes, and sat back. His hand was cramped and his back wasn't much better off, but he felt energized. At last, some small good had come from traveling to the islands. Even if he couldn't leave here, his work could. And what he'd learned would change everything they knew in Narashtovik.

The others had gotten some sleep, but were soon woken by the cardinals cheeping from outside. After a meal of san gruel, the four of them gathered in the shade of the porch.

"Do we know how many people the Tauren have in the Dreaming Peaks?" Blays said.

Niles pursed his lips. "Both our scouts have been lost. We had to pull back behind the Broken Valley. Before that, reports were they had some twenty men there. And at least one sorcerer at all times."

"That doesn't sound like much."

"They may be counting on us not wanting to fight on sacred ground. Or they may believe we wouldn't dare provoke them. It's also possible they intend to use it as a staging ground for more raids, but don't want to commit too many troops there before they're ready."

"Can we call on your warriors for help? Or do we still need to keep our endeavors a secret?"

"I'll tell our people we have to drive the enemy out of the holy peaks." Niles smiled wanly. "It won't even be a lie. It's a strategical maneuver, too. Seizing the overland route will make it much harder for the Tauren to strike Kandak."

"We need hard numbers," Dante said. "Or planning is pointless."

"I might be able to drum up thirty troops. Would that be enough?"

"If your reports on the Tauren are accurate. How soon can you have them ready?"

"This same afternoon. It will take time to cross the valley, though. We tore down the ropes to keep the Tauren from using the crossing against us."

Dante nodded. "Winden and I will deal with that. You bring your troops up to us as fast as you can. If you can spare any shells, I'm sure we could use them."

"What about me?" Blays said.

"I think it's time for you to deal with your fear of narrow ropes over high places."

Niles headed down the trail toward town. Dante, Blays, and Winden traipsed deeper into the mountains, crossing the bridge above the raging ocean on their way to the Broken Valley.

There, as promised, all the ropes had been torn down. But vines hung from the branches like leafy cloaks, trailing down the sides of the plateaus and mingling with the roots holding tight to the cliffs leading to the bottom.

Dante gazed down into the thicket crushing the passage between the plateaus. "Any idea where the ropes wound up?"

"Most were hauled away," Winden said. "Those that weren't? Tossed down there." She pointed to the right. Below, ropes and tackle tangled the brush.

"Want to be useful?" Dante said to Blays. "Go get those."

Blays eyed the ravine. "Know what, I don't think this is where my talents are best spent. I want Niles' job instead. I can walk down a hill and go yell at troops with the best of them."

Tree roots held fast to the sides of the rock. Blays worked his way down, aided in a handful of spots by harvested vines. He carried a machete with him.

"There won't be nearly enough ropes to cross," Winden said.

"You mean to harvest across the gaps?"

"That's right." Dante moved to the cliff's edge. "It'll be hours faster than getting the ropes back up. Now let's find out how strong these vines are."

They tested several, hanging from them with all their weight. Some of the single vines snapped, dumping them to the ground, but two vines together was more than enough for one person, and three braided could hold both of them at once.

Dante kneeled by the cliff's edge and drew the nether to a length of vines. They extended, tumbling down like rivulets of water. They snaked across the tops of the brush, wriggled up the roots on the side of the next plateau, found hold in the nearest tree, and pulled taut.

By the time he had the first gap bridged, Blays had climbed back up with the first of the ropes, which they used to haul up the others. Methodically, they worked their way across the valley. Where the ropes were long enough to cross, Blays tied them to a tree, climbed down into the ravine below, and then climbed back up the neighboring plateau, securing the end of the line there.

Dante had been hoping to span the entire valley that same day, but Winden's hold on the nether flagged less than a quarter of the way across. He still wasn't all that skilled at harvesting, but he made it almost halfway before his own strength gave out. He tried feeding what little ether he could draw to the plants, but they didn't so much as budge.

Warriors started trickling in by mid-afternoon. They carried spears and knives, some metal and others bone. Their arrows were tipped with bone or obsidian. Unlike the armies in Mallon and Gask, there were as many women as men, their hair pulled back into braids. Some bore ropes and climbing gear they used to span several more gaps. As night neared, Niles arrived with a final band of four more soldiers, putting their numbers at 23.

"It was as many as I could muster," he said. "The people are scared to strike back. They know it will provoke a war."

Blays scratched his neck. "Then why did any of them agree to fight?"

"Because if we give up the Dreaming Peaks, then we've already lost."

They camped on the plateaus overnight. During all the thrashing about down in the ravines, Dante had stumbled on any number of dead animals. He raised a rabbit and something that resembled a ring-tailed squirrel to stand watch on the far side of the valley.

By morning, they'd seen no sign of Tauren scouts. With the help of Blays and several soldiers, Dante and Winden finished crossing to the other side.

It took a day and a half of travel to reach the fringe of the jungle. Beyond, the trees thinned, replaced by grass and rocks.

"Blays and I will scout ahead," Dante told Niles. "Be ready to march after sunset. We'll strike in the middle of the night."

He and Blays continued on, with the rabbit and the ringtail scouting ahead. As the undead vermin neared the colorful, bubbling pools, a man carrying a short bow and a thin sword made his way down the slopes. He wore iron bands around his joints and moved from rock to rock with the fluid lope of a lifelong scout. Dante grabbed Blays' sleeve and pulled him behind a shelf of basalt.

"Please tell me you're not about to try to kiss me," Blays said.

"Scout ahead," Dante said. "Quarter mile."

"Then let's leave him be."

"Don't tell me you think we're getting out of this without killing anyone."

"We shouldn't kill this one right now. Because if we do, we'll tip off the others before we're ready to strike."

"Oh. Right."

The scout jogged onward, pausing on outcrops to survey the long downward slope. Dante shadowed him with the rabbit. The man stopped well short of the jungle, turning back for the mountains. Dante and Blays continued upward toward the high single peak and the pass running beside it. The steam from the flatulent-smelling pools obscured them, providing decent cover.

They crossed a small ridge. In the dip below, flies buzzed as thickly as rain. No less than thirty of the golden-furred monkeys lay strewn across the rocks, hacked and bashed. Judging by the smell (bad, but not gut-turningly so) and the level of bloat (minimal), they'd been dead less than a day.

Blays kneeled beside the nearest. He reached out and touched the beast's golden fur. "Why would they do this?"

Dante pointed to the pieces of a broken shaden shell scattered around one of the bodies. "Looks like they were thieving."

"I'm going to pretend we were sent here to get their revenge."

"I think we're close enough. Let's hunker down and I'll send in the spies."

They stopped in a hollow. Dante sent the ringtail and the bunny the rest of the way up the slopes. The Tauren had been busy since claiming the Dreaming Peaks. Rocks had been dislodged from the heights, clogging the entry from the north. A wooden hutch had been built on both sides of the rise overlooking the rubble. Both structures contained a sentry. As the ringtail advanced past them, Dante made sure to make it stop to poke around the pebbles, flick its tail, and otherwise not look like it was a puppeted zombie.

Beyond the wall, the fields of flowers were empty of workers. A single warrior walked down the path to the great hall where the Dreamers had slept. The ringtail followed the man inside. There, a dozen soldiers snored in the beds or kneeled around low tables playing dice games that looked like woten, but involved the exchange of iron coins rather than truths.

"Counting at least fifteen soldiers so far," Dante murmured. "No sign of sorcerers."

Outside, the rabbit hopped languidly through the grass. It

came to a trail at the base of the cliffs. Dante directed it up a switchback too narrow for two people to pass each other. Very easy to defend. Dante wasn't that surprised when the rabbit emerged on a shelf of rock where two soldiers sat before a round wooden structure. Small branches stuck from the building's sides, sprouting leaves. It was new—probably to keep out the monkeys—and had been harvested here. A door stood in its face, but the rabbit found nothing to crawl through. The windows were placed too high for monkeys to get to, let alone a bunny. A stem-like chimney jutted from the middle of the roof.

Dante still hadn't seen any of the Dreamers or their monk wardens. He sent the rabbit back down the slopes and the ringtail up the rocks behind the harvested structure, meaning to search for a way in.

While the ringtail was still working its way up the crags, the rabbit entered a grassy field. There, people in plain clothes dug listlessly at sprouts and weeds, their bodies rickety from disuse. They appeared to be preparing fields to grow crops for the occupiers. When Dante had last seen the place, there had been roughly forty Dreamers. Now, there were only a dozen, with no sign of the monks. The laborers were overseen by three armed soldiers seated in the shade, along with one of Vordon's nethermancers, a hefty man who wore short pants and no shirt.

While the ringtail searched fruitlessly for a way inside the round structure, one of the two guards rose and opened the door. The creature scampered in beside him. Seamless wooden bins were grown to line the sides of the walls. They were covered tightly with nets. The soldier grabbed a sack from a shelf, tossing shelled nuts into his mouth.

After he walked out, the ringtail hopped on up one of the bins. A foot of water filled its bottom. Shaden oozed across a layer of sand and rocks.

Dante withdrew from the eyes of his scouts and leaned back against a rock. "They've got roughly twenty soldiers and, as far as I can tell, a single nethermancer. On numbers alone, we could take them."

"Then what's the wrinkle?" Blays said.

"Shaden. They have a storehouse full of them. We can't go against that. With that many shells for them to draw on, our people could be torn apart."

"So kill the nethermancer first."

"That might work," Dante said. "But if they've got another one I don't know about, we'll be walking into a deathtrap. And you know how I feel about deathtraps."

"Then the solution suggests itself. We steal the shaden."

"Can you shadowalk in?"

"Depends. What are they housed in?"

"A house."

Blays rolled his eyes. "And what is this house made out of?"

"Harvested wood. Basically seamless."

"No good, then. I can only walk through stone."

"How is it you can move through rock—proverbial for its hardness—but a few boards will stop you in your tracks?"

"Don't ask me. You're the expert in mystical doings, Sir High Priest of Arawn. And if the People of the Pocket haven't figured this out in the last thousand years, I doubt whether we'd be able to do so in the next few hours."

"So we sneak in together," Dante said. "I'll heat the lock. Break it off. And you shadowalk through the door."

Blays squinted at him. "Why do I need to be invisible to walk through an open door?"

"For one thing, it will be a lot harder to see you."

"But not you. Is there any other way inside?"

"It's got a few windows," Dante said. "But they're barely a hand's span wide. Way too narrow to squeeze through."

"For a person, maybe." Blays grinned. "It's time for the revenge of the monkeys."

~

Under cover of darkness, twenty golden-furred monkeys climbed through the heights to the right of the sentries, picked their way across holds far too small for human hands, and came to the bluff above the Harvested building.

Below, a single sentry watched the switchback trail. The monkeys were reanimated corpses, prone to clumsiness, but they retained some of their long-limbed grace in death. They formed a chain down to ground level, descending in silence. The windows were too high for them to jump to, but at the back of the building, they assembled a simian pyramid. Once this was several monkeys high and in reach of the window, the other monkeys climbed up their peers and squeezed through. Inside, they plucked the snails from their bins and used the shelves to climb back up to the window. Any rustling they made was covered by the steady winds.

They reformed their chain up the cliffs. At the bottom, one monkey dispensed the shells, which were passed on from monkey to monkey to the top of the bluff. Finished, they assembled at the top and withdrew, each animal clutching several shells to its furry chest.

Once they were out of the Tauren-occupied land, and heading back down to Dante, he withdrew from their vision.

"Got the shells," he said. "And still not a peep out of the Tauren. Know what? I think we can do this by ourselves."

"Oh sure. We've got two dozen troops, but why not take on all the risk personally?"

"I think there's less risk of waking the enemy if it's just the two of us rather than twenty-plus people trying not to step on any twigs."

Blays chuckled without much humor. "What's the plan? Take out the guards, and knife the others in their sleep?"

"They'll never surrender to the two of us."

"Probably not. Still feels a bit unsavory."

Dante tucked his hair behind his ear. "If we do it this way, there's less chance they'll be able to hurt the Dreamers they've captured."

Blays shifted his sword belts. "That's reason enough. Let's do this."

Dante went to Niles to tell him the plan. "Blays and I should be able to handle this on our own. After I take out their guards and clear the path in, bring your people over the rubble, but keep them back."

Niles stuck out his lower lip. "You're sure you don't need help?"

"It'll be so easy I might even feel bad about it."

He and Blays headed uphill, moving from rock to rock. It was a clear night and the stars shined like raw ether. A half moon provided a little more light than Dante would have preferred. He pulled the nether around Blays and himself, darkening the air around them. His monkeys ran up to him. He took two shells from them and sent the others downhill to Niles.

Dante's ringtail was perched on the cliffs to the right of the blockade of rubble. As he neared, he used the animal to watch the sentries for any sign they'd spotted him. He closed within five hundred feet, then three hundred. He stopped behind a boulder.

Two lances of shadows streaked toward the guards. Both men fell, voiceless, slumping back against their hutches.

The rubble was now unguarded. Dante picked his way across the rocky scree. Once he and Blays were on the other side, he sent the rabbit bounding back toward Niles.

Before heading to the great hall, Dante detoured to the harvested shaden vault, dispatching the single sentry there with another bolt of nether. He and Blays crept back down the switchback. At the hall, the skin that had once been used to cover the entrance had been replaced with a wooden door. Dante didn't have eyes inside the building, but from the outside, it was silent, at peace.

Blays drew his swords and walked toward the stone wall. Shadows shimmered around him. He moved into them, disappearing. Five seconds later, the bolt scraped from the other side of the door, which swung open with a creak.

Dante moved inside, stopping beside the doorway to watch for movement and let his eyes adjust. The vast space was darker than it had been outside; on the far left and right walls, a single lantern hung from a hook. The space was broken up by pillars and drapes, but Dante didn't see anyone up and about.

"Person to person," he whispered. "If they mount a resistance, get out and wait for our people to back us up."

Blays moved forward. His posture wasn't proud, but it bore the sturdiness of someone who knows what he has to do. A worm of shame turned in Dante's gut, but as he neared the pallets of the sleeping soldiers, his nerves went calm. These beds had once held the Dreamers. Who gave up their lives to seek the forgiveness of those their people had once wronged. And most of whom had almost certainly been put to death by the Tauren.

He moved from bed to bed, spiking each soldier's brain with nether. Blays worked across the other side of the hall, muffling mouths and slicing his blade across their throats. After tending to four of the occupied pallets, Dante still hadn't seen the portly nethermancer among them.

Faint light glowed to his left, then faded. Dante turned, scanning the hall, but he couldn't see any sign of Blays. He approached the light, keeping the nether close. A heavy curtain hung over a doorway leading into a silent courtyard surrounded by ten-foot rock walls. Dante took two steps out, but saw nothing. The wind had stirred the curtain, letting in a sliver of moonlight.

To his right, a shadow detached from the cover of the wall.

THE RED SEA

Dante whirled and looked into the eyes of Vordon.

EDWARD W. ROBERTSON

19

The man laughed raspily. He wasn't wearing his helmet or the guards on his forearms and shins. Instead, he held an oblong blue fruit, half-eaten. Despite the casualness of the scene, he looked no less formidable. He was broad-shouldered and exuded lazy arrogance.

Vordon smiled. "Had a change of heart? Decided to surrender to me after all?"

Dante moved half a step, putting himself between Vordon and the doorway. "And I brought tribute." He condensed the nether into a black blade.

Vordon clucked his tongue. Darkness enfolded his hands. "Don't."

Dante eased back. Every second he could delay the man was another second for Blays to conclude their dark business. "I made a trip to Bressel. While I was there, I learned a few things. The Mallish are using you."

"Oh, do you think so?"

"They want the shaden. For now, they're happy to let you gather them up for them. But that won't last. Eventually, they'll want to take the source for themselves."

"They'll try."

"I know they've taken these islands before. They can do so again."

Vordon took a bite of fruit and spat a seed at Dante's feet. "So they come here. We let them have the shores. Soon enough, they'll get sick—and then they'll die."

"Unless they know the shells hold back the ronone. Then you'll be trapped in the hills, with them on the coast between you and the shaden."

"Do you bring me a proposal? Or are you just here to warn me of dangers you don't understand?"

Dante's mind raced. "Withdraw from the Dreaming Peaks. Declare an island-wide truce. This fighting only weakens you all. United, the Mallish would never be able to take it away."

The man tossed the spent fruit over his shoulder. "The Mallish bring me steel. That is good of them. I will use it to take this island. And if they come for me? Then I will kill them with their own blades."

"You have no idea how big Mallon is. To them, the Plagued Islands are nothing but a speck. If they want this place—"

"Help!" a man shrieked from inside. "We're being—" His voice cut off.

Vordon clenched his jaw. "You have sneaky friends."

"You have no idea," Dante said. "We took your shaden, too. Give yourself up now and the Kandeans might let you live."

Vordon laughed. He jabbed the nether at Dante's heart. Dante deflected it easily. But this was just a feint; as he moved to counter, Vordon poured nether into the seed at Dante's feet. Leaves erupted from the ground. Before Dante could stagger back, something cool, damp, and fleshy engulfed him head to toe.

Liquid clogged his mouth and nose. It tasted sweet. Sticky. It was the juice of a fruit grown to massive size, engulfing him in its sturdy pulp. In another situation, he might have laughed. But he couldn't move his arms or legs. He couldn't even draw breath.

Nether speared at him from outside. Instinctively, he tried to jerk back, but he didn't so much as wobble. He struck at the incoming shadows and felt them disperse. When the next thrust came, he parried it much more calmly. The attacking nether withdrew. He felt it massing outside. With a squelching noise, the substance engulfing him grew heavier yet.

He held his breath for several heartbeats, awaiting a new attack. None came. Shouts pitched up from back in the hall, muffled heavily. Dante tore at the shadows within the fruit around his head, smashing the sticky, fibrous matter down into itself until a space was cleared around his face.

He breathed deep. The air tasted like the fruit, humid and thick. He squished down more of the pulp, freeing his hands. His breath echoed hollowly. He dug forward, fingernails scraping against a shell that felt as hard as rock. The air was already starting to taste stale. He spiked the shadows forward. They hit the shell with an arrow-like rap. A small crack appeared, pierced by a beam of moonlight.

He pressed his mouth to the hole and drew clean air. Once his lungs felt less panicked, he backed off and struck again at the crack, widening it an inch, then three. A few more blows, and a chunk of shell as big as a shield fell to the ground, rocking back and forth.

With a slurping noise, Dante pulled his feet free and stumbled out of the fruit. As soon as he was clear, he stopped, listening. Hearing nothing, he moved toward the curtain.

Blays materialized in front of him, swords in hand.

Dante called out in surprise. "Don't *do* that to me! I was about to knock a window straight through you."

Blays kicked at a shard of shell. "Holy shit, you were inside that thing?"

"What do you think happened? I decided to take a juice bath?"

"What a waste. You'd have to take a normal bath right after."

"Vordon was here in this courtyard. Either I missed him earlier, or he showed up after we were done scouting."

"Well, he's not here anymore." Blays swept the curtain aside with his sword, eyeing the silent hall. "He ran out of here like the building was on fire."

In the vast space, Dante saw nothing but bodies. "So he's gone? That's good."

"What do you mean, good? He escaped. Absconded. Got away!"

"We aren't here to kill him." Dante moved to light more lanterns. "We're only here to take the Dreaming Peaks. We've done that. As soon as this place is secure, I'm going back into the Mists."

In all, fourteen men lay dead, including the portly nethermancer. The room that had once smelled like incense and flowers now reeked with the metallic tang of blood. Dante sent the rabbit and the ringtail down the path south from the great hall. They reached the river without incident. Since Dante had flooded out the old bridge, Vordon and his people had harvested a new one, a solid arch with roots on both ends that dug deep into the soil.

He kept watch on the place while Blays went to call for the others. The twenty-odd Kandean warriors helped make a more thorough search of the area. Dante posted sentries at the bridge and gathered Niles, Winden, and Blays.

"First, the good news: I don't think Vordon will be back soon. Not without more men. And more shells."

"But he will be back," Niles said. "This is merely a reprieve."

"Could be." Dante gestured south. "But if you knock down that bridge, and fortify this side, you'll make him pay dearly if he wants to reclaim these peaks."

"You said there was also bad news," Winden said.

"I spoke to him. He knows the Mallish are using his people. He doesn't care. All he wants to do is conquer the island."

Niles grimaced. "Then why doesn't he do so already? None of us can stand against him."

Dante shrugged. "He's gathering steel. And shells. I think he's hesitant to make a move until he has enough strength to stand against the Mallish, too."

"Then I dearly hope you learn to lift the ronone. If the Tauren gather that much power, we may have no choice but to sail away from Kandak."

"That might be for the best. Between the Tauren and the Mallish, I'm afraid the coasts could turn as red as the Bloodfalls."

Winden opened her mouth like she smelled something foul. "These lands, we know they weren't those of our ancestors. But the Tauren have no respect for those who once lived here, and the Mallish don't even know who they were. If we leave here, the Dresh will truly be dead for good."

Niles reached for her arm, glancing about the hall, where some of the warriors were dragging out the corpses. "Keep your voice down. If the others learn what we've told Dante and Blays, then we'll find ourselves cast into the Mists permanently."

She pulled from his grasp, but held her tongue.

"Speaking of," Dante said. "I think it's time we went back."

Niles raised a brow. "Right now? We've just taken this place."

"Vordon won't be back for at least a few days. We have to make them count."

"And we'll need every minute we've got to fortify the peaks."

"Fortify away. With or without you, I'm going back to the Mists."

He exited through the northern door, heading for the fields of orange flowers. Blays went with him.

Niles said something to Winden and jogged after them. "You still don't know the ways of the Mists. I'll go with you."

Dante glanced over his shoulder. "You're sure they won't miss you?"

"I've put Winden in charge of the defense. She's capable of

handling the fortifications."

They reached the fields and plucked three flowers. It wouldn't do to pass out right there in the field. Nor could they lie down in the hall without revealing their activity to the warriors. Niles brought them to a shed full of hoes and shovels. They spread out blankets that turned out to be incredibly coarse.

"What are these made out of?" Blays said. "Hog fur?"

Niles popped his flower in his mouth. "Do you see a lot of sheep around here?"

Dante swallowed his plant before its poisonous taste could permeate his mouth. "Is there anything I can do to get through the Pastlands faster this time?"

"It shouldn't be as bad. Once you've made it through them once, the heart remembers even if the mind doesn't."

The edges of Dante's vision started to close in. This time, he didn't fight it. He sank into the floor.

He woke. The room looked the same, but the bed was so small that his feet jutted off the end. His feet had a dusting of hair on the top. This time, he wasn't a child.

Stranger yet, this time, he remembered the last time.

He walked out. The house was vacant, but embers burned in the stove. Dante went to the porch. The full moon hung in the morning sky. Tod walked in from the side carrying two mugs. He passed one to Dante.

It tasted stronger than before, more bitter. There was nothing small about this beer. Tod gazed out on the meadow.

"What are you?" Dante said.

"It doesn't matter."

"When I'm not here, do you still exist?"

The monk smiled slightly. "If I don't, I don't remember it."

"I can't stay long," Dante said. "But I'll finish this drink."

Flies flitted about the meadow, chased by birds. Dante sipped unhurriedly. The place was peaceful, he'd give it that. It wouldn't be so bad to rest here a while. To take a break from the travel and fighting and hardship. He could stay a week, and to the others, it would only feel as though a few minutes had passed.

With a jolt, he stood, then slugged down his beer. "Good to see you again. But I'd best be on my way."

Tod watched him solemnly. "Don't be too pleased with yourself. You are no longer tied to here. But only because a piece of your dream has died."

"If it makes my vision clearer, it deserves to be dead."

He clomped down to the basement, took a look around, then headed back up the stairs. They extended before him. The doorway filled with light. He walked out into the land of clouds.

He was the first to arrive. Under different circumstances, he would have done some poking around, but he stayed put. A few minutes later, Niles walked out of the Mist as abruptly as when Blays walked out of the shadows.

Dante watched him. The man looked away, smoothing his shirt, which in this realm was cleaner than the version he'd worn in the Dreaming Peaks.

"What did you see this time?" Dante said.

Niles shook his head slightly, as if to brush off the question, then gazed up at a jungle passing through the fog. "I was fighting the Tauren again. But this time, I was alone."

Blays showed up seconds later. "Ah good, no waiting around this time."

"I had to wait," Dante said.

"Yes, but as it turns out, you're not me. Which I'm thankful for in a number of ways."

Niles led the way forward. Mist gushed around them, stirred by each step. In less than five minutes, the fogs parted to their left, showing a brilliant blue sea. A lane of purple sand divided the water from the land. The Dresh woman strolled toward them. She was still young and carrying her spear, accompanied by the three hogs.

She regarded them coolly. "It's said that many Tauren were ushered into the Pastlands less than an hour ago."

"We drove them out of the Dreaming Peaks," Dante said. "The space is sacred once again."

"I wonder how long this will last."

"The Kandeans are digging in as we speak. They won't give it up easily. Our agreement was to boot out the Tauren. We've done that. None of us can guess what the future holds from here."

"I know what our agreement was." The woman planted her spear in the sand. "Remain here. I will ask those who came before me how to lift the ronone."

She walked away, fading from sight. The three jone vanished with her. A thrill tingled up Dante's belly. He'd been trying not to think of the prospect of being stuck on the Plagued Islands for good. Even his optimistic forecasts of finding a cure involved months of research and interviews with the island's various peoples. The idea that he might have his answer in minutes was more than he could have hoped.

"So where exactly did she go?" Blays said.

Niles sat down in the sand. "The Worldsea, I'd wager. To speak to her ancestors."

"The dead in the Mists can move back and forth?"

"Aye, in very limited fashion. Like leaning through a doorway without crossing the threshold."

"So what's it like in the Worldsea?"

"Can't tell you."

"Another one of your secrets, eh?"

"It's not my secret," Niles said. "The dead don't speak of it often. Sometimes the Dreamers hear things, but the way they talk, the Worldsea's less like a place and more like a mood."

"Aha. And how exactly does one search a mood? Are we going to be sitting on this beach until our bodies are covered by the dunes?"

"I don't think the passage of time in the Worldsea has much to do with time here. I can't rightly say if they *have* time."

While Dante tried to make enough sense of this to form questions of his own, the air condensed before him. A gray cloud drifted toward them, joined by three others, lower to the ground. These drew together into the shape of the Dresh woman and her three hogs of war.

"I have been to the Worldsea." Her voice was soft, her expression jagged. "And I have nothing for you."

Dante tilted his head to the side. "But they were once able to cure the sickness. They have to know how that was done."

"All those who knew about the ronone, they left to sail the Worldsea long ago. They've forgotten their mortal lives. No one from that age remains here in the Mists."

"Surely you didn't have time to ask everyone!"

The woman lifted an eyebrow. "Do you think I had to go from village to village, asking them one at a time? I asked them all. And they all knew nothing."

"I don't understand. You said they would know."

"I said I would ask."

"Knowing they wouldn't have what I wanted?"

"I had no way to know that," she said. "The ancestors, some might have held on to their pasts. Or been living in the Mists until recently. It was a good idea to try. But the knowledge is lost."

Dante lowered his gaze to the sands. "Then so are my hopes."

Blays clapped him on the shoulder. "We're a long way from done. The solution existed once. That means we can find it again. Maybe the Boat-Growers will know. Or one of the peoples on the west side."

Dante turned to Niles. "Is there anyone on the island who doesn't need shaden?"

The older man pinched the bridge of his nose. "Everyone I've ever seen has eaten the snails."

"They'd only do that if they had to. No one knows the secret."

Blays was staring hard at the Dresh woman. Noticing his attention, she rearranged her expression.

"What was that?" Blays said. "You looked like you'd just swallowed a live bee and were banking on it forgetting how to sting."

"Go from here. The dead have no answers for you."

"Everyone remotely related to this island lies like it's their job. So pardon me if I don't take your word." He gestured toward the distant mists. "Do you know what's happening back in the land of the living?"

The woman regained her glass-hard expression. "You squabble and you die. Just as you always do."

"The Mallish are coming back to the island. They want the shaden. They'll kill everyone who doesn't help them and enslave those who do. If you know something more, and you let that come to pass, you're damning these people to the same fate as yours."

"Sounds like justice to me."

"The people alive today had nothing to do with that! They need to be cured of the ronone so they can leave. Or freed to use the shells to defend themselves. How can you condemn them like this?"

The woman closed her eyes. Wrinkles deepened across her face; the skin of her neck slackened. Within seconds, she'd aged twenty years. One by one, the three jone disappeared, leaving her alone.

"You're not like the others," she said.

Blays inclined his head. "I know. I'm much better looking."

"I wasn't lying. All the Dresh who might have known have sailed away on the Worldsea. But not all the Dresh are dead."

20

Niles' jaw dropped. "It's been four hundred years since the invasion. There's no way a settlement of Dresh could have survived on the island without being seen."

"You're right," the woman said. "They're not on the island. They're on Spearpoint Rock. That's where they fled when they knew their land was lost."

Niles stared dumbly. Dante waved a hand in his face. "What the hell is Spearpoint Rock?"

"It's a small island just off the north shore. But the Current's so strong there it's impossible to reach."

Dante locked eyes with the woman. "Do they have the cure?"

"They don't," she said. "But they've survived all this time. They may remember how it was once done."

"Are any of their dead here?"

She shook her head. "You'll have to visit the rock itself."

"So all we have to do," Blays said, "is go to the place it's impossible to get to. Normally I'd laugh at you, but considering we're gabbing around in the afterlife, I'm sure we'll figure something out."

"Thank you." Dante turned away from the woman.

She grabbed his arm. Her fingers were as hard and cold as iron railings on a November night. "If you harm them. Or cause any harm to come to them. When you come to the Mists for good, we'll keep you in a hell that will make you beg for a second death."

He tried and failed to extract himself from her grasp. "If they're as friendly as you, they have nothing to worry about."

The woman released him, watching him as he walked into the trees.

"I need to oversee the defense of the Peaks," Niles said. "Winden knows the way to the north coast. She'll take you there."

"Think we'll actually be able to get to this place?" Blays said.

The man laughed. "Anyone else, I'd tell you to give up now. But after seeing what you lot can do, I think you should leave at first light."

They stretched out in the grass and slept. Dante awoke in the tool shed, head pounding. The moon had only moved a few degrees across the sky. They returned to the great hall. While Niles gave his men their orders, Dante drew Winden aside and told her what they'd learned.

"I can get you to the shore," she said. "But I don't know how to get you to the island."

"Leave that to us."

Feeling suddenly generous, he went to the river on the south side of the grounds. There, he raised a line of waist-high ramparts on the north bank. Once he was done, he returned to the great hall, found a pallet in a quiet corner, and slept.

He woke before the sun. Unable to sleep, he returned to the river. Niles was there, looking haggard.

"Been up all night?" Dante said.

"I don't have any hours to waste." Niles stirred, inhaling deeply. "Not if we're to stop them from retaking this."

"I've seen their raids. I don't think you could stop them if you had a hundred years to fortify."

The other man looked Dante in the eye. "Be angry with me until your dying day. But my people have done nothing wrong. Please don't wish for harm to befall them."

Dante wasn't certain the Kandeans were blameless—they'd been complicit in Niles' lies, after all—yet he felt rebuked. Niles had helped them navigate the lands beyond. As a result, Dante was on the verge of finding his answers. It was becoming more difficult to be angry with Niles. He'd been duplicitous, yes. He'd taken a tragedy and shamelessly turned it into a pillar of his strategy.

And it was for that very reason Dante felt a perverse measure of respect for the man.

He readied for the trip, appropriating a small amount of food and supplies from what the warriors had cached at the Dreaming Peaks. Just in case they needed to revisit the Mists, he packed six orange flowers, too. By the time he was done, Blays and Winden were up. Winden requisitioned eight of the captured shaden. As sunlight streamed in and struck the heights, the three of them left the compound, heading north.

The slopes commanded a view of the upper lobe of the island. As they maneuvered through the steaming, odiferous pools, Winden pointed to the northeast.

"That curve," she said. "That is the way to Kandak. To reach the Joladi Coast, we veer northwest."

Dante had seen the Joladi Coast from the deck of the *Sword of the South*, but in all their wanderings, they'd never gone further north than Kandak. "Whose territory are we entering?"

"Several peoples inhabit the way to the coast. The largest are the Gauden. They lived on Gaudel Bay in the northwest. Good shaden there."

"Lived?" Blays said. "What happened to them?"

Winden stepped down a shelf of purple rock. "The Tauren killed many. Drove the survivors into the jungle."

"What about the others?" Dante said. "If they've been fending off Tauren raids, are they going to be happy to see outsiders tromping around their territory?"

"It won't be hard to avoid them. Most live on the coasts. And the further north we go, the less the coasts can be used for travel."

"What about Spearpoint Rock? Is it really that hard to get to?"

"For birds? No. It's half a mile from Joladi. But for people? It's directly in the Currents. They'll sweep you south faster than you can paddle toward it. Smash you into the rocks."

Dante got out a rag to dab his neck and brow. They were in direct sunlight and he sweated freely. "What if you sail around to the side? Come at it from the north?"

"Then the Currents will smash you on the reef that grows there."

"Well, it can't actually be impossible. Apparently the Dresh made it there in one piece."

"We have a story about their passage," Winden said. "I always thought it was just a fable. It's from the time of the invasion. As the last days neared, and the Dresh saw that the Mallish couldn't leave, the great chief Durado took his canoe and sailed from beach to beach, gathering up all those who'd hidden themselves. It took him forty days, but in time, he had an army. They marched on the Mallish, who had fortified themselves in the High Tower behind their unbreachable gates.

"The battle lasted six days. On the seventh day, Durado led a charge against the gates. Countless other charges had failed, but this one tore them down. But when Durado tried to take his people through the gap and into the tower, one of his Harvesters betrayed him. Paid off by the Mallish, he snarled the gap with thorns. Durado and all his best warriors were ensnared. There, they died by Mallish arrows.

"Seeing the battle was lost, Durado's daughter Eleni led their people in retreat. But the Mallish, they didn't stay fast in their tower. They chased Eleni north, into the high country, through the Dreaming Peaks, past the Boiling Fields, and around the Jush Backbone.

"Finally, Eleni and her warriors came to the Joladi Coast. Knowing their enemy could run no further, the Mallish honed their metal swords, preparing to finish the murder of the Dresh. But Eleni found a way to walk further yet—into the sea. She marched her people toward the crashing waves. As they neared, Mora, the god of the sea, grew furious. The ocean boiled. Steam filled the skies. Eleni walked into the mists along with all the Dresh. And when the steam cleared, the Mallish couldn't find a single trace of those who'd died."

"That's it?" Dante said. "They walked into mists? Like *the* Mists?"

"That's how I always took it."

"So maybe they crossed into the land of the dead, then reemerged on Spearpoint Rock."

"But when you Dream, your body stays in this world," Blays said.

"Maybe they found a walk to walk into the ether." Dante stopped to pick burrs from his sock. "The same way you shadowalk."

"When I shadowalk, it sure as hell isn't into the afterlife. I'm still right here. You just can't see me."

"Winden, are there any other stories of Eleni? Or Spearpoint Rock?"

She made a thinking noise. "According to the story, every last Dresh died there. Eleni, she's never mentioned again. As for Spearpoint Rock, there are stories of shipwrecks there, but the sailors always die in the Current or on the reef."

That sounded less than promising, but Dante had her recount the stories anyway. They reached the jungle later that day, following the main path for several hours. It was good to be back under the canopy. They made camp by a stream. The next day, shortly before noon, the path veered east around the Jush Backbone, a series of knife-like ridges running north-south. Winden diverted west down what appeared to be a game trail.

This was far more winding than the eastern trail down to the Broken Valley. Some segments were washed out; others had to be hacked clear of growth. Progress was beyond slow. By the end of the day, they were filthy, scratched up, and exhausted.

Dante soothed the worst of their aches and pains with nether, then turned his attention to the ether. If he quieted his mind, he could make it appear to him, but he still couldn't do anything with it. He tried to recall the lessons his former mentor Cally had tried to instill in him back when he'd been on the run in the Mallish forests, but after Dante had shown no ability to summon the ether whatsoever, Cally had given up in disgust. Dante couldn't recall a single thing the old man had tried to teach him.

The following day, the trail smoothed out. Winden warned them that they were entering the territory of the Cadren, a people who followed the fruiting of the jungle's figs and used jone to hunt down mushrooms to trade for shaden.

The forest floor was hopping with red-furred rodents. Dante slew two of them to scout the way ahead. He saw a few midden heaps and chewed-up fig trees suggesting the Cadren's presence, but saw no people. After a few hours, the path widened, leading into a rubble of purple-black stones numerous enough to have once been a village or a large temple complex.

Before, Dante had taken the ruins as a simple point of fact. Everywhere in the world carried remnants of long-lost people. Now, knowing these structures had been built by the Dresh, he felt a reverence similar to what he felt when he entered the church of a faith that wasn't his.

As the sun dropped, clouds piled against the heights. Squeezed against them like a dark, misshapen fruit, they drenched the forest with rain. The clay trail grew so slick they called an early day. By morning, the clouds had cleared out, leaving the scent of rain behind, along with deep puddles filmed with rainbow-colored oil.

They hiked onward, meeting up with a noisy stream that made frequent drops down shelves of rock. Falls splashed into deep pools, churning the smell of fresh water into the air. They detoured inland around a village of wooden houses on stilts, then reconnected with the river, which had a clear pathway beside it.

The sky darkened. The rain returned, hissing onto the canopy. The trail hadn't had time to dry out from the previous evening. With the clay squelching at each step, yanking on their shoes, they found it easier to stomp through the rain-beaten grass and weeds beside the path.

Behind them, birds squawked raucously. Winden stopped, straightening her back. The river had gone brown-purple. An uprooted sapling sped through the water, spinning crown over roots.

"High ground," she said. "Hurry!"

Dante broke from the bank, slogging to the right, uphill. He slipped every few steps. His knees and hands grew caked with clay. The sound of rushing water became a low roar.

Glancing over Dante's shoulder, Blays' eyes went wide. He grabbed Dante's arm and pulled him up. "Less falling. More running."

Dante ran on. Water surged through the trees, frothy and brown. The leading edge looked no more than ankle deep, but further up, it rose six inches up the trunks, then a foot. Leaves and branches tossed in the flood. It was more than enough to sweep them away. If it didn't drown them, they'd be battered to bits against the rocks and trees.

He redoubled his efforts, pumping his legs without regard for his footing. The floodwaters sluiced forward faster than any human could run.

"We're not going to make it!" he yelled over the thunder of the water.

Winden pointed at a tall tree heavy with long and slender leaves. "Into the tree!"

Its trunk was thick, but it was also smooth, with no major branches until twelve feet up. She gestured, nether gushing from the damp clay into the trunk. Wrist-thick branches shot out from its side, stout and strong, spaced vertically every three feet. Winden hopped onto the lowest and grabbed the one above it. Clay fell from her sandals as she scrambled higher.

Blays flung himself into the tree like a golden-furred monkey. Water trickled past Dante's feet. By the time Blays got up to the next branch, the water was an inch deep and rising fast. Dante grabbed a branch and hauled himself up. His boots skidded on the smooth bark. He scraped off as much clay as he could and climbed higher. Water swirled below him in a solid sheet.

Winden came to a stop twenty feet up. Blays laced himself into the boughs. Dante seated himself, holding fast to the branch above him.

"Should have known," Winden said. "I almost got us killed."

Blays slicked back his hair. "We do that all the time. The important thing is you also got us un-killed. Keep that up, and it'll be a regular day."

Rain pounded through the trees. The flash flood continued to sweep down the hillside. Just as Dante began to fear they'd have to lash themselves into the tree overnight, the waters ebbed, slipping down the trunks. The rain weakened to a steady patter. Soon after, the ground became visible again.

They made their way down. Whole patches of plants had been yanked away, the earth scoured down to purple clay and black rock.

"I'd say the trail has departed this world for the Pastlands." Blays jabbed at the earth with a broken branch. The tip sank three inches deep. "Maybe we should have brought a boat."

"We'll spend the night on high ground." Winden gestured

above them. "It will be better come morning."

The following day, everything remained waterlogged. However, the floods had torn away much of the undergrowth, and they advanced through the jungle with reasonable speed. Near the end of the day, Winden found a trail snaking along a plateau. Beneath it, blades of land slashed at the sky, impossibly green. Beyond, the ocean spanned until the edge of the world.

"We're close now," Winden said. "Just past those peaks."

The ridge she gestured toward looked about as surmountable as a pane of glass. The next day, though, the trail led to a pass through the worst of it. Within two hours, they looked down on the north shore.

"The Joladi Coast." Winden pointed to a small green island a half mile offshore. "And Spearpoint Rock."

It looked close enough to swim to. But the Current was visibly enraged, white-capped swells rushing past the small island and destroying themselves against the disintegrating cliffs beneath them, the wild spray slicking the rocks. The cries of shorebirds lifted on the wind. Carefully, the three of them made their way down from the heights. They emerged onto a narrow beach stretched between the two surrounding ridges like a hammock of white sand.

Winden stepped out of her sandals. She smiled. "We're lucky. This beach isn't always here. In the winter, when the storms are worse, it washes away."

At the moment, the waves looked relatively gentle—a small reef or break was buffering the shoreline—but they hammered the cliffs to either side of the barrier. The tideline was littered with kelp, coral, shells, bones, and sticks, producing a thick smell of salty marine rot. Thousands of crabs scuttled among the debris, clawing up the shreds. Hundreds of birds were there, too, but the refuse of the sea was so plentiful they weren't even bothering to go after the crabs.

"Is this where Eleni led her people?" Dante said.

Winden walked closer to the waves, inhaling deeply through her nose. "That is what they say. But it's my people saying such things. So maybe we should be skeptical."

She said this lightly enough that Dante didn't feel bad about laughing. He could feel the waves slapping into the coarse, pebble-strewn sand at the water's edge. Not only was there the Current to contend with, but also a steady wind out of the north. He soon gave up any idea of attempting to sail or paddle out to Spearpoint.

He didn't have to, though. Not when he could build a bridge there.

He moved to the left side of the cliffs. There, he cut his arm and fed his blood to the nether. The shadows moved as swiftly as baitfish, as if enlivened by the fury of the ocean and its obvious wish for everything on land to die. He sent the shadows into the rock where the cliffs met the shallow ocean floor, softening it and lifting it, meaning to extend it foot by foot toward Spearpoint Rock.

As soon as he softened it, though, the waves and tides dashed the earth away, scattering it across thousands of gallons of moiling water. Leaving him with nothing.

"Something wrong?" Blays said. "You look like you just caught the wife you don't have in bed with the friend you don't have."

Without a word, Dante moved to shape the stone again. But again, the water churned it away, the particles as fine as dust.

"I was going to build a bridge," he said numbly. "A causeway to Spearpoint. But the tides are sweeping it away."

He'd never encountered anything like it. Then again, he'd never tried to work the stone underwater before, with the exception of the boiling channels at the Dreaming Peaks, where it had been his goal to remove the rock. He backed off and tried another route: softening the rock beneath the surface and lifting it up, leaving the top layers hardened.

At a certain point, though, the part of the rock doing the lifting—the fluid part he shaped with his mind—had to be exposed to the violence of the waves. As soon as the fluid rock emerged, water slashed in, rasping away every non-solid trace. The shaped block fell down, collapsing back into the bed of the ocean.

He tried as many variants of this process as he could imagine. After a while, he moved to the right side of the beach to see if the Current was any weaker there. This failed as well. So he couldn't go through the water—but what if he could go under it? He dropped his focus into the rock beneath him, beginning a tunnel outward. But the rock was porous, shot through with fissures, seams, and plugs of material that felt solid, yet turned out to be loose sand. Sea water gushed into his tunnel, rendering him unable to continue.

He tried again and met the same result. Conceivably, he could back up into the hills where the rock was solid, dig down as deep as he could, and make his way across the strait. To advance the tunnel, though, he'd have to be inside it. Any flaw in the stone could flood the passage, drowning him. And the closer he got to the surface of Spearpoint, the weaker he feared the rock would become.

As his command of the shadows grew fainter and fainter, he trudged up the beach and plopped in the shade.

"I can't do it," he said. "The water's too strong to go through. And the stone's too weak to go under it."

Blays sat beside him. "Then it's a real shame you're such a one-trick pony."

"If you have another idea, what will be faster? Telling it to me? Or making fun of me?"

"Sure, but which one will I enjoy more?" Blays plucked a piece of grass sprouting from the sand and held it at arm's length, eyeing its tip. "Think you could grow a living bridge across it?"

Dante rubbed his arm, which was crusty with salt from the mist tossed ashore by the surf. "I expect it'll be bashed to splinters. But it's worth a shot. I'm spent, but Winden should have some oil left in the lantern."

Winden was staring out to sea, shaking her foot whenever a small crab climbed across it. Dante moved beside her. "Blays has an idea."

"Grow a bridge across it?" she said.

Dante chuckled. "That would be it. Think you can do it?"

"Bridging something that far, it would take me multiple days. The water would destroy it in the meantime."

"I can help you after I've had some rest. And what if we used the shells?"

She nodded in thought. "I'll try. See how far I can get."

Winden walked away from the swarms of crabs and toward a twisted banyan growing at the base of the slopes. Dozens of roots were driven into the soil. She opened a small cut on her hand. Nether winged to her. She diverted it into the banyan. Rope-like branches slithered across the turf, then the sand. As they neared the surf, they elevated to climb over the waves, extending over the water.

With the branches drooping under their own weight, Winden sent roots questing down into the waves. Their tips had barely sunk below the surface when a sharp crack rang across the beach. One branch snapped in half. It was flushed ashore in moments. A second followed. So did all the rest.

Winden muttered a Taurish curse. "Did you see that?"

"You mean, was I paying attention to my only hope for salvation?" Dante said.

"This won't work. If I make the tree longer and thicker, that will only give more area for the water to press against."

"I don't suppose you know any friendly dolphins who'd carry us across."

She eyed him. "You're speaking to me like you speak to Blays.

Does this mean we're friends?"

"I think you're about the only person on this island I could be friends with."

"That answer, it wasn't an answer."

He moved his gaze to the waters, which stubbornly refused to be agreeable and part down the middle. "I'm sorry. It's hard to think of any of you as friends when I'm fighting for my life to get out of here. But maybe I'll never be able to leave. If so, then I hope you would be my friend."

She was quiet for a moment. "Maybe we could try again. Or try to grow something beyond the breakers. The water there, it's less violent."

Blays crouched down to poke a stick at a white-shelled crab. It waved its claws back and forth like a pugilist. "What if we're taking the wrong side here?"

Dante looked up. "Wrong side of what? Surely you're not suggesting we try to make a treaty with the Tauren."

"The Current is basically a god. Not one of the happy ones, either. More like the kind who has just been awakened from an eternal slumber. Why try to fight a guy like that? We should be trying to buddy up with him."

"You're talking about extending a bridge from Spearpoint."

"I was thinking a vine-rope. Like we used to cross the Broken Valley." He stood and bent backwards, stretching his back until he could touch the sand behind him. "The more flexible you are, the less likely you are to break."

"And then what do we do?" Dante said. "Drag ourselves along it all the way to the island?"

"Sure. If we get tired along the way, we can tie ourselves to it and take a quick rest."

"That sounds beyond dangerous and firmly into suicidal."

"If we'd ruled out every suicidal idea we've ever had, we'd be dead a hundred times over by now. There are no bad ideas. There are only ideas you don't have the balls to attempt."

Dante snorted. "That sounds like famous last words. But there's no harm in seeing if we can extend a vine across."

He had all but exhausted himself, but they still hadn't tapped their supply of shells. He got one out of the black wooden box they were using to keep the snails alive and summoned the nether from one of the shaden. He gazed across the water, homing in on the trees along Spearpoint Rock's southern shores. They were close enough that he could separate each tree from the ones next to it, but even with the shaden's power, he couldn't reach into the nether inside the branches. He groped blindly, casting about for any feeling of the death that existed in all things. He felt nothing.

"It's no good," he said. "It's like when the loons broke. It's too far away to work."

Winden tried her hand at it, drawing from the same shell he'd used. Sweat popped up along her brow. Five minutes later, she stepped back, shaking her head.

Blays crossed his arms. "I hate to see a great idea ruled out by a little thing like the fact it's physically impossible. Well, maybe if we sit here long enough, the Current will shove the entire island over here."

Dante ground his teeth. "It was a good idea. But it failed. So what else do we have?"

"I don't know. Grow wings and fly there?"

"A *real* idea."

Blays glared at him. "I just gave you two. That's as many as you've come up with."

"And we're still not there. So what else do we have?"

"Increasingly strained patience?"

"I have one," Winden said. "Spearpoint Rock. We don't have to reach it to speak to the Dresh there. All we have to do is go to the Mists. And wait for one of the Dresh to die."

"Which could take years," Dante said. "Longer, if only a select few know about the history of the ronone."

Blays poked at another crab. "That's really not a bad thought, though. Maybe we're being too narrow-minded."

They discussed this and several other possibilities, but as the day wore on, Winden's idea remained the only one remotely plausible. In time, Dante's mind refused to process anything at all. The only thing he could do was stare dumbly at the distant island.

"There's no point staying here," he said. "We should go speak to the other people along the coasts. Some shred of lore may have survived with them."

Blays glanced at the sun. "It's the middle of the afternoon. We're not going to have more than two hours to travel."

"Then we'll be two hours closer to our answers."

"We just got here. I don't think we should give up this fast."

"Everything we've tried has failed. We could spend ten years here and still not come up with a plan. It's like you said: we need to stop being so narrow-minded. Come at this from another approach."

"We have failed," Blays said. "But that's nothing new. Sometimes, it feels like all we ever do is fail. But we've never given up. No matter how foolish we feel. And that's why we win—because long after everyone else has gone home, we're still here, pounding foolishly at the solution."

"There's a point at which bashing your brain against a wall results in nothing more than scrambled brains."

"Do you really think we've hit that point?"

Dante licked his lips. His skin was hot from too much sun, which was doing nothing to improve his mood. "We'll stay here overnight. I'll be able to work with the nether again come morning. I'll try again to build another bridge. Make another run at a tunnel. But if the sun goes down tomorrow and we're not any closer, I think we should move on."

In case the rains returned, they moved to higher ground and built a lean-to. Dante used the rest of the daylight to explore their surroundings, searching for inspiration, or any clue as to how the Dresh had crossed the channel all those years ago. With no fresh insight in hand, he returned at sunset to eat some of the mashed san they'd carried with them, then slept.

Hours later, the cry of a bird stirred him half awake. He couldn't bring himself to get up yet, but as he lay there, with the waves washing in and out below their camp, it sounded as though someone had set fire to the inside of the world and the entire sea was boiling itself away. A pleasant thought: if the water were gone, they could simply walk to Spearpoint Rock.

As intrusive as a stranger in a dark room, a thought appeared in his head. He couldn't boil away the sea any more than he could leap across it. Quite recently, however, he had boiled an entire river, flushing away the Tauren as the enemy had pursued them into the Dreaming Peaks. That had involved channeling water. Hot water. As he'd coaxed open the rock holding it back, he thought he'd felt the source of that heat: the rock itself.

And according to Winden's story, when the Dresh had walked into the ocean, the water *had* boiled.

He jumped up from his bedroll. It was dark out, the stars blazing like condensed drops of heaven. He got his torchstone from his pocket and blew on it, illuminating his way down the makeshift trail to the beach. There, the birds were gone. Thousands of crabs crawled over the detritus in a living blanket, shrinking away from the light.

He cut his arm. Brought forth the shadows. And plunged them down into the rock beneath the sand. The stone felt cool, immobile. He went deeper. Not far below the surface, what felt like a jumbled column of rock was embedded within the rock around it. He touched its edges, confirming its shape, and followed it downward.

After a long ways — impossible to judge the true distance — his touch weakened. But the stone was warming. He delved until his hold went feathery, prone to slip at any moment. There, he softened the rock and melded it into the walls of the tube it had plugged. Fluid rose to fill the gap.

Unlike in the Dreaming Peaks, though, this fluid wasn't water. It was rock. Rock so hot that, somehow, it formed a liquid.

Up on the surface, his hands were shaking. As subtly as he could, he drew away more and more of the plug, allowing the heated rock to flow upward. After several minutes, he stopped for a break. The eastern horizon was turning gray-blue. He'd barely scratched his reserves of nether, but knowing how much work lay ahead of him, he returned to their camp to grab the pack containing the shaden.

Back on the beach, he returned his focus to the depths of the earth. Foot by foot, he brought the liquid rock up the tube. As he moved through it, he could feel this tube had multiple forks and potential exits. He chose the one that looked to be the shortest distance from shore. The rock pushed upward as if it were alive. As it neared the surface, Dante withdrew up the slope, distancing himself from what was to come.

Steam bubbled to the surface of the water in great vents, carrying the stink of sulphur. The seabed glowed an eerie red-orange, brighter and brighter. Within a minute, a glob of red-hot rock broke the surface, barely visible beneath the clouds of burningly hot vapor. Virgin land. Already cooling in the constant wash of the ocean.

Dante shaped the stone around the mouth of the vent, moving it further out to sea. Fifty feet. A hundred. The eastern sky was glowing now, too, the oranges and reds of the sun mirroring the hues burning beneath the waves. The bubbling of the steam was thunderous, even louder than the tides.

As the arm of stone stretched further from shore, the water deepened. Dante widened the vent's exit, allowing more and more lava to glurp forth. As he felt his hold starting to go slack, he shifted his attention into another shaden, adding its strength to his.

By the time he'd forged halfway toward the island, the wind had cleared the air at the start of his bridge. While the rock still steamed, it was no longer alight from within. Instead, it was a deep purple-black.

He pulled the shadows from another shell. As the column of steam approached Spearpoint Rock, the seabed climbed closer to the surface. The trail of rock traced itself forward faster and faster. Though in theory the shaden could grant him limitless power—assuming he had an unlimited supply of them—his body could only channel so much nether before it gave out. As the bridge of stone closed on the southern reaches of Spearpoint, Dante swayed back, shaking bodily.

"Now that," Blays said, "was awesome."

Dante jumped. Lost in his work, deafened by the turmoil of the water, he hadn't heard or felt the others approach. Beside Blays, Winden gazed in sheer wonder at the steaming seas and the squiggly line of black stone.

She turned to him. "Loda. You're Loda."

"Loda?" Dante said.

"Mora's sister. The goddess of the fire from the earth."

"Flattering, but I'm missing a few of the right bits to be a goddess." He wiped the sweat from his dripping face. "Now let's wait for this to cool down. It's time to see the Dresh."

21

He walked out onto the path of black stone. Waves beat against both sides, splashing up the gentle slopes, but for the most part, the incoming tide was parallel to the bridge. Few swells made it all the way to the top of the fresh rock.

Even so, as Dante advanced further from shore, his heart beat like it had a race to win.

Blays and Winden were right behind him. For all of Blays' recent difficulties crossing narrow spans over high places, he strolled across the water as casually as if he were traversing the path along the pond at a prince's manor. Every time a wave threatened to roll over the top, Dante hunkered down, holding fast to the warm rock.

Step by timorous step, he drew nearer to Spearpoint Rock. Its name was a bit of a misnomer. Far more than a single jut of stone, it was at least a thousand feet across east to west, and when he'd seen it from above, it looked close to half a mile north-south. Not large, by any means. But large enough to believe it hosted a people who'd kept themselves hidden for four hundred years.

The land was completely covered in trees. At the edges, the underside of the rock were scored away by the ruthless Currents, leaving the land above jutting several feet outward. He spotted a single beach. The island was crumbling too quickly for more.

Dante crossed from the causeway to the island. As soon as he stepped foot on Spearpoint Rock, dozens of people emerged from the forest.

Armed men and women stared with clear hostility. They carried spears tipped with shark's teeth or obsidian chipped as sharp as any steel. Others had short bows or clubs far more sophisticated than any Dante had seen. These had a knob below the leather-wrapped grip and a flared wooden guard above it. The clubs' heads were studded with small rocks.

Winden brushed past Dante. She lifted her left hand, opening it so her palm faced inward. A few of the people glanced at each other.

"We know this land is yours." Winden's words carried an air of formality. "We walk humbly through it."

A woman edged forward, bow aimed at Winden's chest. She spoke. The words had the rhythm of Taurish, but they bore a thick accent Dante found hard to parse.

"Their speech," Winden said. "It's like the Gauden. This woman, she says we've profaned their island. That we're rixen."

"We need to speak to their king." Dante's face twitched as he remembered his mistake with the woman in the Mists. "Or queen. We'll explain everything."

Winden turned back to the Dresh. She repeated Dante's words in an accent similar to the one the other woman had. He didn't pick up every single word, but he was familiar enough with Winden's speech to get most of it.

The woman with the bow shook her head sharply. Her words were low yet heated.

Winden stiffened. "She says we're dead. That we became so as soon as we stepped onto Spearpoint."

The woman adjusted her bow at Winden's chest. Her people

cocked their spears.

"Stop!" Dante gestured to the rope of rock connecting their island to the much larger one. "I built that. I can destroy it just as easily. But if you kill us, it will stay here until the Current tears it away. Until then, you'll never be safe."

Winden translated hurriedly. The woman replied. Winden said, "She asks if you will destroy the bridge."

"If we speak to their ruler?" Dante said. "I swear it. On my life."

Winden relayed this. The woman replied, pointing at Dante, then the ground.

Dante cut Winden's translation off; he was starting to get the rhythm of the Dresh's speech. "She wants me to prove it? That I can take away the bridge?"

Winden shifted her weight. "That's right."

He'd had the nether in hand since the instant the Dresh had appeared. He reached into the ground three feet in front of him, elevating a foot-high pillar of rock. With a flourish of shadows, he shaped it into an approximation of the weathered statues in front of the temple in Kandak, whose small features resembled those of the Dresh.

The woman got a strange look on her face. Beside her, a man said a single word. This was repeated by several others.

Dante cocked his head at Winden. "Did he just call me Loda?"

Winden laughed, though it was more of a release of tension than an expression of mirth. "No. But the concept is similar. One who moves the rock."

Most of the Dresh still looked hostile, but several now appeared curious. The woman lowered her bow and spoke.

"We are to lay down our weapons," Winden said. "And follow her. If we step off the path, we'll be killed."

In Mallish, Blays said, "We're not about to be killed, are we?"

Dante unbuckled his sword belt. "I think if they wanted to do that, they'd do that."

"I don't have a great feeling about this." Blays smiled charmingly at the Dresh and began the lengthy process of disarming himself. "If something goes wrong, take Winden and run as fast as you can. I'll shadowalk in and out of them. Cut them to ribbons."

"I can handle myself."

"Against a volley of arrows? Maybe, maybe not. Even if you can, I'm not so sure about Winden."

Winden tucked down the corners of her mouth. "I will be fine."

"Wonderful. New plan: if something goes wrong, we just massacre them as fast as we can."

He handed over his two swords and copious knives. The bow-carrying woman said something. Her people parted. She gestured Dante forward onto a path worn into the dirt. She kept her bow in hand. Eight warriors surrounded Dante. The rest fell in behind Winden and Blays.

In less than a hundred yards, the wild jungle gave way to a cultivated orchard of yellow, orange, and pink citrus fruit. The trees didn't look orderly enough to have been harvested. After the orchard, the land cleared into a grassy field broken up by shade trees, benches, and some cleared spaces that had the look of ball courts or playing fields. This was screened off to the left and right by more orchards, rendering any evidence of inhabitation invisible to observers at sea.

Ahead, a swampy san field sprouted thickly. Past this, a few dozen black stone homes clustered around a small, circular bay. The shallow water was an aquamarine that took Dante's breath away. It opened to the sea, but the entrance was hidden by two tree-encrusted arms of rock, one extending from the south shore and the other from the north. Twenty feet high, the breaks kept out the Currents.

"Stay," the woman said.

She jogged toward one of the houses, leaving the three outsiders surrounded by warriors. There were only two people down at the lagoon. The village itself seemed deserted. Most likely, after seeing the steaming ocean coming their way, the Dresh had pulled everyone out to sanctuary. Judging by the number of buildings, however, there couldn't be more than three hundred people in the village.

Yet the lagoon and its enclosure looked perfectly engineered. Dante might have been able to believe this was the simple result of hard work, except that the houses, despite some wear and tear, had a smoothness and a regularity to them that suggested the Dresh had once had an earth-mover. Interesting. From what he'd learned, earth-moving had originated in Narashtovik long, long ago. Then, following a great cataclysm, all those who knew its ways had walled themselves off in Pocket Cove, where they'd remained hidden for the last thousand years. Either the Dresh had discovered the ability on their own, or one of Dante's sorcerous forebears had found their way to the islands ages before the Mallish invasion.

The Dresh earth-mover must have died, however. And not been replaced. Or they wouldn't need Dante to do away with the bridge.

The woman reappeared from the stone houses accompanied by a middle-aged man and woman. Both wore green wraps. He was portly, balding, and bore an amused look. She was tall and thin and as severe as a bamboo cane.

The trio stopped before them. The stout man raised his left hand, gesturing in the same way Winden had on arriving. The thin woman swatted his wrist. He rubbed it, frowning at her.

Winden and the woman with the bow made introductions. The man's name was Sando. The woman was Aladi.

Sando looked Dante and Blays up and down. His eyes glittered. "It seems we have a problem. You see, you're here."

"You brought the land to our island," Aladi said. "Why?"

"I'll answer everything you want to know," Dante said. "But

before we get too deep, I want you to swear you'll speak truth. Before your people and your gods."

Aladi's face darkened with fury, but Sando merely laughed. "You expect us to lie to you? You've spent too much time among rixen."

"I won't swear a thing." Aladi was the same height as Dante, yet she managed to look down her nose at him. "You disgrace yourself by asking."

Sando rolled his eyes. "Can you blame him? Look where they came from."

"Pardon me," Blays said. "Are you two married?"

The man laughed until his eyes began to water. Aladi gave Blays a stern look. "Of course we're married. If you can't handle a relationship with your spouse, how could you handle one with your entire people?"

"I imagine you have more than your share of assassination attempts, then."

This finally put a crack in her reserve. She gestured to take in the island. "Why are you here?"

"I am the leader of Narashtovik," Dante said. "A city thousands of miles to the north. Tens of thousands of people depend on me. But because of the ronone, I might never see them again."

"The ronone is everywhere. What does this have to do with us?"

"There was once a cure, wasn't there? On the main island, it's been lost for centuries. No one even remembers how it was done. You're the only surviving Dresh. We hoped you might know how to lift the sickness."

Sando's expression went grave. "Do the rixen know we're here?"

Dante shook his head. "We're the only three people who know. We didn't hear it from anyone living on the island. We had to travel into the Mists. There, we learned it from a Dresh woman who died during the Mallish invasion."

The two leaders exchanged a shocked look. Aladi said, "How did you convince her to tell you we were here?"

"By being royal pains in the ass." Blays swept his hand north. "The Mallish are returning. If the people on the island can't learn how to cure themselves, they'll have no hope."

Sando and Aladi gave each other another look. Sando stepped back. "Give us a moment."

They retreated from the group and held a hushed conversation. Sando no longer sounded jovial; Aladi no longer sounded hostile. They concluded their talk and returned.

"We know how to lift the ronone," Sando said. "If we show you, will you leave? And tear down the bridge?"

The hair stood up on Dante's neck. "Of course."

"And all three of you—you'll never tell another soul that we are here."

"We have no desire to harm you. We'll take your secret to our graves."

"Swear it," Aladi said. "Before your friends and your gods."

Dante did so, joined by Winden and Blays.

Aladi bowed her head. "Then come this way."

She walked along a path ringing the village, heading for the far side of the bay. Sando reached for her hand.

"I'm not stuck in the Pastlands or something, am I?" Dante said. "We're really about to get our answer?"

Blays eyed the woman who'd first spoken to them, who was still carrying her bow. "It meant something to them that we'd met with the dead. Maybe we should befriend a few more ghosts."

The path curled around the bay and up a low ridge. On the other side, the crumbled remnants of another jetty did little to block the Currents, which poured into a second bay, churning it too violently for fishing or the farming of mussels. A dike of stones and earth had been built along the bay's south shore, but the tides had eaten through this, spilling into the field beyond.

Dante could just make out the orderly squares where san roots had once grown, but the plants had been killed by the salty water.

After another citrus orchard, they passed into the jungle. Birds twittered from the branches. Lizards scuttled over sunny boulders and climbed the trunks of palms. Trees soared eighty feet high, fighting for their share of the light.

The path spat them into a clearing a hundred feet across. In its center, a gray tree stood alone. Its leafless branches arced over the clearing. There was a steady wind, but it wasn't moving. Branches lay shattered around its trunk.

"The Star Tree," Sando said softly. "Its fruit cures the ronone."

Dante drifted forward. "It looks like Barden. The White Tree of Narashtovik."

"I don't know of those things." Aladi matched his pace. "These trees, they were harvested this way. Ages ago. To be rid of the ronone for good."

He scanned the branches. "Where are its fruit? Is it out of season?"

She laughed sadly. "It is dead."

"*Dead?*"

Sando tipped back his head. "They are nothing like the trees they were cultivated from. Very difficult to keep alive. Need constant attention. Years and years ago, our last Harvester died. And so did our Star Tree."

In a daze, Dante kneeled and touched one of the fallen branches. It wasn't rotten. It didn't even feel like wood. More like bone—or shell. He picked up a fragment. The outer layer was gray, faded, but where it had broken, the edge was pearlescent.

He let it fall to the ground. "How do you regrow a new one?"

"Like all things," Sando said. "With a small seed."

Blays broke into a grin. "Great news. Winden here's a Harvester. Give her one of the seeds. She can grow you a new tree."

"She can't," Sando said. "The seeds, they're all gone. When this one died, our old ones tried to grow more, but their Harvester was dead too. Most of the seeds were lost then. The others were ground up and eaten to cure the ronone."

"Well, that wasn't very forward-looking."

"Our people always hoped to find a new island. But none of our sailors ever returned. After the tree died, they continued to search. They needed sailors who could travel for weeks without dying of sickness."

Dante turned to Winden. "Have you ever seen anything like this?"

"Never," she said. "There is nothing like this on our island."

"Can you regrow a new tree from a piece of this one?"

She shut her eyes. Nether flickered around her hands. She shook her head. "This tree. It's dead. I can only Harvest what lives. Or seeds that yearn to."

Blays pointed at the grayed trunk. "Where was the tree that grew the seed for this one? Was it on the main island?"

Sando gritted his teeth. "The other trees, they all died in the tribal wars before the Mallish came. When our people came here, they had a single seed. They used it to grow this Star Tree."

"So we'll search this entire island," Dante said. "There must be a lost seed somewhere."

"We've shown you the tree." Aladi's voice was firm again. "That was our deal. Now go. And tear down the bridge."

"We can't go yet. We still don't have the cure."

"We promised we would show you the answer. There was no promise you would leave with a cure."

"She is right," Sando said. "We showed you our land. Now be gone from it."

Around them, the warriors moved toward their weapons. Frustration pulsed in Dante's veins. At last, he had his answer, but the path had led him to a cliff's edge. Nothing lay below but vacant sea. His hope was wearing thin.

But hope wasn't the only thing being eroded.

"This land," Dante said. "It won't be yours for much longer."

Aladi stepped in close, face inches from his. "Do you threaten us?"

"I'm telling your future. You once had an earth-mover, too. Someone like Loda. That's how your people built this place. Only that sorcerer passed away like the Harvesters."

She slitted her eyes. "How do you know that?"

"Your lagoons. The protective jetties. It's obvious this place was sculpted. Except the Currents are starting to wear it away. You haven't been able to repair what's been damaged."

Aladi stepped back. "Make your point."

"The Currents will devour this place. They'll eat through the rocks and spoil the lagoon. Next, they'll flood your fields. Spear-point Rock won't last forever."

"Much longer than I will."

"How much longer? Fifty years? A hundred? Surely not a thousand. Look how much wear this place has taken since its creation. Boot us out, if you want. But you're damning your descendants to a miserable end."

"What do you care for them? You only want your cure, yes? So that you can get away from here."

"I can make this place bigger for you. Rebuild your barriers. Just let us search the island."

"And if you make it bigger, then what? It holds a few hundred years longer? What you said, it's true. This island won't last for long."

"Come back to our island," Winden blurted. "*Your* island."

Aladi and Sando exchanged yet another of their looks. Sando turned back to them. "Then we will have it back. All of it. The sons and daughters of Mallon will take the cure—and then they will leave."

Silence fell across the clearing. Dante looked to Winden, but she was staring at the ground.

"There's a minor problem here," Blays said. "We can't make a promise like that. Are you aware of the charming people known as the Tauren?"

Aladi smiled thinly. "We keep watch. We know they make war."

"And their goal—backed by Mallish steel—is to take the whole damned island for themselves. They'll never give it back to you."

"But you would?"

"Sure. *I* don't own the place. If you want, I'll give you all of Mallon, too."

Aladi laughed with genuine happiness. "You are more honest than most. But we need more than hollow words."

"I hate this," Winden whispered. "But I hate what my ancestors did to you more. The Kandeans will leave. Our lands, they're yours."

Around them, the warriors murmured. Sando chuckled and raised a brow at Aladi, who nodded.

Sando reached for Winden's hand. "I have made a decision. You are not a rixen. So perhaps you will deal fairly and honor your bargains."

"What will you have us do?"

"We don't want Kandak. You have made it your own. But we will have our piece of the island. Promise me that you will defeat the Tauren. That you will make it safe for us to return. And I will tell you where you might find another Star Tree."

Winden eyed Dante. "If you want your cure, you will need to help us face the Tauren."

"If that's what it takes?" Dante said. "I'm yours to command."

"It is good to agree." Sando smiled. "Well then. Do you know of Durado?"

"Winden told us the story. He led a rebellion against the Mallish. When that failed, his daughter Eleni brought the Dresh here."

The portly man chuckled. "It is also good to hear their names have lived on. When Durado brought all the peoples together, they found they had much knowledge they thought had been lost. With the help of all the chieftains, Eleni cultivated a plan. They would come here, cure the sickness, and wait for the Mallish invaders to die.

"So they stole the seed—our seed—from where they were kept. No one knew how to grow it, but they brought dreamflowers as well. When they came here, they traveled into the Mists. Spoke to the ancestors. And learned how to grow the seed. Our people no longer had the sickness. But the Mallish refused to die.

"Our people, they were too few. Not enough had the talent to call out to the darkness or the light. To Harvest the trees or the rocks. When our sorcerers died, there were none to take their place. The Star Tree died, and the generations that came after were stricken with sickness. This island, this haven, it became a prison."

Dante licked his lips. "Do you know where Eleni stole the seed from?"

"The First Basket."

"And where is that?"

"You'll soon be on your way there." Sando seemed to find this very funny. "The First Basket—it is within the High Tower of the Tauren."

22

Blays groaned. "Should have guessed. The object of desire is *always* in the enemy tower."

"How do we know the Tauren haven't used all the seeds?" Dante said. "Or that the Basket is even still there?"

"The Basket remains," Winden said.

Sando shrugged. "The Mallish, they had no idea what the seeds were for. But they knew the tower was of great value. As was the Basket inside it. They preserved everything."

Dante let out a ragged breath. "Yes, but it's been *four hundred years*. Surely someone's done a little spring cleaning since then."

"It might be a long shot," Blays said. "But so what? There are no seeds here. Besides this one, there haven't been any living Star Trees for what, six hundred years? Seems to me this First Basket is the likeliest place to find what we're looking for."

Dante took another look at the dead husk of the tree. "True enough. Then we'll head to the tower."

Sando and Aladi led them back to the village. There, Aladi trekked to one of the houses. She returned with a smooth purple stone that fit in the palm of her hand. One side of the stone was etched with a star. One of its five points wasn't quite closed.

"The Star Tree," she said. "This is what its seeds look like."

"I will find one," Dante said. "And once it's grown, the Dresh will have the cure, too."

They continued back to the bridge Dante had summoned from the heat within the earth. From its edge, it looked as though a god had taken a quill to the map of the world and drawn a line connecting Spearpoint to the main island.

"Stop," Aladi said. "Before you go. You will remove the bridge."

Dante frowned. "Those two acts would be mutually exclusive."

"If you die at the tower, we will fall to the Tauren as well. Erase the bridge. You will take a canoe home."

"How about we cross, and then I get rid of the pathway?"

"Because I don't trust you."

"It's possible to sail," Winden said. "We'll be moving with the Currents, not against them."

"Which means there's only *some* chance we'll be drowned."

It was an unnecessary risk. Dante had the information he needed and had every intention of dismantling the bridge once he was across it. He was tempted to walk right on out of Spearpoint.

It seemed, though, that after centuries of lies, a fragile trust was blooming across the islands. Niles and Winden had shared the secret of the Mallish invaders. The dead woman in the Mists seemed tired of their ancient grudge. Here, the surviving Dresh had given them the key to changing everything. The bloom of trust needed a thoughtful Harvester. Walking out would be safer, but it would stamp the seedling into the dirt.

"Go get the canoe," Dante said. "And I'm going to need more shaden."

Erasing the bridge was a much simpler affair than creating it. All he had to do was soften the stone to mud and let the tides take care of the rest. Even so, he didn't eradicate every inch of the passage. Only the upper ten or fifteen feet of it. More than enough to render it impossible to cross by foot. He made a mental note to inform Captain Naran of this change in the local coastline.

With his work complete, he made his way down to the island's only beach, a strip of sand on the south side of Spearpoint protected from the worst of the Currents. The Dresh's canoe was long and very narrow, with outriggers bracing it to either side.

"I've always known everyone here," Sando said as they climbed aboard. "This is the first time I've ever met a stranger. Or said goodbye to one."

Aladi looked down on them. "What you've seen—keep it safe. If you've been to the Mists, you know there's a hell."

Inside the canoe, Blays stood and bowed to her. "Your secrets will never leave our skulls. Not even if the Tauren crack them open and use them for chowder bowls."

The Dresh helped push the canoe into the water. The currents swirled crazily, threatening to toss them back ashore; the Dresh extended long poles, their tips padded with cloth, and pushed the canoe away. Dante grabbed a paddle and thrashed at the water. Winden and Blays were both considerably more skilled. They directed the boat away from the rocks. As soon as they were out of the island's lee, the canoe straightened and tore south, borne along by the madness of the Current.

"Where are we going?" Dante yelled into the wind. "Joladi?"

Winden gestured along the coast. "This is far faster than our feet. We could be at the High Tower by day's end."

"Is that remotely safe?"

"We just booted the Tauren out of the Dreaming Peaks," Blays said. "How safe do you think we'll be if we try to hoof it across their lands?"

Dante's paddle slushed through the water. "Canoe it is. But if we wreck, I reserve the right to ride your corpse to shore."

Swells jarred them, rocking the outriggers. Spearpoint shrank behind. Ahead, the jagged green cliffs waited to smash them to bits and feed their remains to the crabs. Dante was clumsy with the paddle, but what he lacked in skill, he made up for in terrified enthusiasm.

He soon got into the rhythm of it. The tides pushed them steadily toward the cliffs, but by paddling hard on the same side of the canoe, they kept their distance. Within fifteen minutes, they were rounding the northeast side of the island. There, the Current ran parallel to shore. They pulled in their paddles and rested. The canoe skimmed along. To their right, a massive turtle broke the surface, blinking at them.

Blays watched it pass. "Are we really going to battle the Tauren?"

Dante smiled. "We made a promise, didn't we?"

"Yet for some reason I suspect your other promise carries more weight."

"Which promise is that?"

"The one to yourself to never, ever die."

Dante glanced at Winden. "I'm not sure what we'll do. I know this much: it doesn't make any sense to regrow a Star Tree only to die before we can make use of its fruit."

Winden wiped spray from her face. "You swore an oath."

"And before we came back here, I swore an oath to kill a man named Gladdic. If I die here, I won't exactly be able to fulfill that, will I? So which takes precedence?"

"The one that allows you to leave here and see to your other one."

Dante reached for his oar, meaning to take out his frustration on the waves. "If all of your people aren't enough to take on the Tauren, what difference will the two of us make?"

"There's nothing to say we have to destroy them in battle," Blays said. "It seems to me we've got two other approaches. The first is to cut off the head. Specifically, Vordon's."

"And the second?"

"To cut off the arms. Without Mallish steel, they can't conquer this place."

"Ah yes. Defeating the Tauren is too hard, so we'll take on the entire nation of Mallon instead."

"We don't have to wipe them out, either. Just their interest in the Plagued Islands."

Dante tapped his nails on the paddle. "Winden, when did the Tauren start dealing with the Mallish? Before or after Vordon came to power?"

"During," she said. "Their support was what let him kill his enemies and seize the High Tower."

"If he's dead, do you think his armies will continue to fight?"

"The Tauren, they're very proud. They may keep warring simply to prove Vordon was right."

Blays scratched his neck, which had gone stubbly over the last few days of travel. "If they're that proud, surely some of them are less than pleased to be under the thumb of the Mallish."

"You want to back one of his rivals," Dante said. "Bump off Vordon in exchange for a promise of peace."

"It would sure beat trying to bump off hundreds of troops in the field."

"What do you think, Winden? Feasible?"

"The city of Deladi—this is where the Tauren live—it's ruled by many tolaka."

Dante crinkled his brow. "War-families?"

"They squabble just as much as the name suggests. Very rare that they're united. That's why the Tauren don't rule the island already. There will be cracks in their front."

"Then it's a good thing we're accomplished chisels," Blays said. "I say we go to work on one of these tolaka."

Something the shape of a giant kite was swimming to the right of the canoe, flapping like a bird. Dante watched it pass. "Pulling off a coup could take weeks. Our first goal is getting the Star Tree seeds. Once we've got those out of Deladi, then we'll go to work on throwing a rod into Vordon's wheel of war."

"We need to stop in Kandak." Winden looked at them in distaste. "Your clothes, they're for rixen."

Hurried along by the Currents, it was less than an hour before they looked on the arm of land embracing the Bay of Peace. They took up their oars and paddled hard, drawing the canoe into the calmer waters of the outer bay, then crossed right over the reef. To Dante's relief, Kandak didn't appear to be on fire or otherwise under siege.

They put in at the shore, drawing glances from the fishermen and the shell-divers. Winden led them to a wooden house where a man, a woman, and their many children were beating fibers and stretching out cloth. Dante and Blays were soon kitted out in the short pants and simple shirts favored by the islanders, along with long green garments that were more than a cape and less than a cloak. They were lightweight, but the woman went to great lengths demonstrating how well they kept off the rain. For the final piece, they swapped out their boots for rugged, strap-heavy sandals.

Before they left, Winden asked around about the Dreaming Peaks, but there had been no new developments since their party had struck out for Spearpoint Rock. They returned to the canoe and shoved off, continuing south along the coast. The land ramped up. Waterfalls spilled straight out of the jungle, disintegrating to mist before they reached the sea.

Once they were back in the Currents and relieved of the need to paddle, Dante grilled Winden about Deladi and the High Tower. According to her, the city was the largest on the island. Located on the south coast (which was actually the translation of its name), it was in the lee of the wind, rain, and Currents, making it one of the few places on the island where it was possible to sail around freely.

"During the Dreshi civil wars, Deladi was the capital of the entire island." Winden gazed up at the Dreaming Peaks, which stood so high they looked like they were already a part of the heavens. "That fighting, though, it ruined so much. That must have been when the Star Trees died. The Dresh never recovered. Before that, the Mallish would never have been able to conquer them."

"I've been to many places," Dante said. "The history's the same everywhere. A people rises to greatness. They overreach and get bogged down in wars, or they're stricken by tragedy. And another people cuts them down. Like that, they're lost."

"It's a wonder anybody's alive at all," Blays said. "Sometimes I think the hermits have the right idea." He smiled at Winden. "Then again, if the Mallish had never taken this place, you wouldn't be alive, would you?"

She chuckled uneasily. "I don't think I find that comforting."

The High Tower, she said, predated the Dreshi wars by a few hundred years. A lighthouse and a fortress, the Basket within it rendered it and the city virtually invulnerable to siege. Some claimed the tower had been built during a wager between Loda and Mora to prove which was stronger: mountain or sea. Loda had attempted to raise a peak to pierce the skies, but Mora sent wave after wave into Loda's work, washing it away. At the end of seven days of fighting, Loda relented, but Mora hadn't been able to destroy all her work. The core of Loda's mountain remained: a pillar of stone that the Dresh later shaped into the High Tower.

Dante wasn't so sure about that. He was starting to suspect that some branch of the Narashtovik diaspora had found its way to the Plagued Islands and joined the Dresh. Perhaps the sorcerers had been drawn by Arawn's Mill or tales of the shaden. Or perhaps the Dresh had made all these discoveries on their own. He'd never seen anything like harvesting before, either in person or in his years of research.

The timelines kept matching up, though. It called out to be studied. He wasn't sure when, though. Even if he was able to cure the ronone and topple Vordon, he still had to go take vengeance on Gladdic for the execution of Captain Twill. And after *that*, he surely needed to return to Narashtovik and catch up on whatever had been happening in his absence.

But perhaps he could dispatch a team of monks to the islands. Or carve out time to come back himself. Between the wars, the clash of kingdoms, and the fall of empires, so much knowledge was lost. This tragedy was more than a historical notation. The Dresh had once known how to grow the Star Trees. When that knowledge had been torn up and scattered, it had trapped the islanders here for centuries. It was possible there *were* no more seeds and never would be again. You had to preserve wisdom and history where you found it. Otherwise, the Currents of time and strife would erode it to obscurity.

And if those forces ever grew stronger than those who preserved what had come before, the entire ship of civilization might slip beneath the sea.

They passed below the Dreaming Peaks by early afternoon. After that came the highlands, then Iladi Forest, the jungle where the Boat-Growers made their home. With the Current slackening, they paddled as their stamina allowed. With the sun still three hours from the horizon, the canoe slipped past the hills containing the Bloodfalls.

"When we made this trip overland, it took us a week," Blays said. "And by water, it's less than a day?"

Winden's cheeks flushed. "We still would have had to walk back. Besides, it's as you guessed. Niles wanted you to see the Tauren's crimes. To grow angry enough to wish to fight against them."

"Well, he's going to receive a giant bill from my cobbler."

The coast bent to the right. Following its curve, the canoe was soon headed west. After a bit of jungle, the land cleared out into grasslands of shrubs, with trees clustered around the furrows winding down from the heights. The Current shifted toward the southwest, its speed reduced to a walking pace. Canoes and sailing rigs dotted the blue sea. Villages perched on beaches, the structures a mix of stone and wood.

None of the locals paid them any mind. The sun drooped to the west, silhouetting a tall tower standing above a thriving town.

"I say we do this tonight," Dante said. "Check out the Basket, locate the seeds, and get out of here before Vordon knows we're here."

Blays laughed. "That sounds idealistic. Besides, if we're going to rouse the rabble against him, it's going to take much longer than an overnight trip."

"One scheme at a time. Star Tree first."

"I suppose restoring a sacred tree will bank us a little divine goodwill before we return to commence with our murdering."

They paddled on. When they tired, Dante refreshed them with the nether. Winden warned them that the city's bay was lit at night. To minimize the attention they'd draw, they beached the canoe three miles east of Deladi, hauling it up into the weeds and continuing on foot.

By then, it was fully dark. It was even warmer on the south side of the island, though, especially compared to an all-day voyage on a windy sea. On their way to the dirt trail worn into the turf above the beach, Dante spooked a rodent. He dispatched and raised it, sending it up the path to make sure they weren't about to stumble into any hordes of armed men.

After half an hour of walking, they topped a ridge and looked down on the city less than a mile away. Lanterns burned in intersections and above the doors of larger buildings. Both the city and the fields around it were terraced. Moonlight glinted on watery fields of san. A faint chorus of wooden chimes carried on the breeze.

A great deal of the buildings were the black island stone, ranging between two and four stories. There were enough to house several thousand people. A river wound through the center of Deladi, dispersed into a great many canals that fed into a bay teeming with small vessels and voluminous orange lights.

"Candlefruit," Winden explained. "Harvested to massive size. Helps them keep watch on the bay."

Blays made a skeptical noise. "And impress the neighbors, I'd wager."

Half a mile up the shoreline from the bay, the High Tower overlooked it all. Its lower levels showed lights in the windows, but its upper floors were completely dark.

"Let me guess," Blays said. "The upper portion, that's the First Basket?"

Winden nodded. "Baskets are sacred. Especially this one."

Dante continued forward. "And it's a good way to keep it out of the hands of the hungry peons."

"I think it will be less suspicious to cross the edge of the city than to bypass it."

"We can stroll right in?"

She frowned at him. "Your cities, they're built to keep people out?"

"The larger ones tend to have walls. Does wonders to deal with rampaging barbarians and enemy nations. Along with anyone too poor to buy anything."

"Here, walls would be stupid. Your enemies would just come by sea."

They entered the city. The scent of grilled fish and chicken carried on the wind, reminding Dante he'd eaten little but san mush for several days. People walked about freely. Almost everyone carried a club at their waist, women included, and some bore spears or swords.

Wooden chimes clonked musically, stirred by the wind. Mosquitos whined in his ears. As he neared a set of chimes outside a public house, he saw they were actually the still-growing seed pods of a willowy tree. Harvested, probably, but in this land of bizarre flora, who knew.

They crossed a wooden bridge arched over a brackish-smelling channel. People paddled canoes, slicing along at jogging speed through the canals, which were as numerous as the streets. Some neighborhoods fronted small lakes. Artificial islands sat in the lakes' centers, claimed by stone temples with steep, triangular roofs. Outside the temples, groups of men and women moved in choreographed unison, barking out noises halfway between a grunt and a chant.

"What's that?" Blays said. "Some kind of dance?"

Winden laughed dryly. "Of war, maybe."

Dante's Taurish was more or less fluent, but his accent lagged, and he spoke as little as possible on their way through the city. Pairs of soldiers patrolled the streets, carrying swords and dressed in mismatched armor.

"Can we find a public house?" Dante murmured. "I'll explore the tower while the night settles down."

"You can't just walk inside the High Tower," Winden said.

"I won't. But I'd like to see them keep out a highly determined moth."

She homed in a set of chimes, the presence of which seemed to indicate a public structure. The building she brought them to was stone, implying it was pre-Mallish, but its bar, tables, crowd, and performing minstrel could have been shipped straight from Bressel. Which, in a sense, they had. Dante and Blays hung at the back of the common room while Winden secured lodging. They headed upstairs.

Like almost every room on the island, the windows were large and held no glass. Out in the street, a candlefruit lantern summoned flying insects of all kinds. Dante used the smallest pin of nether he could muster to impale a moth. He raised it and sent it flapping toward the High Tower.

The grounds around it were open and clear, well-lit by a bevy of lanterns. The main tower was at least two hundred feet high, accompanied by shorter spires and squat, round-capped towers.

Warriors stood outside the front entrance. Dante sent the moth above it all, winging its way toward the darkened floors that began halfway up the tower's body.

The moth careened toward a black window. And struck something solid.

Dante pulled his sight from the moth's spinning vision, squeezing his eyes shut and pinching the bridge of his nose. Once he'd recovered, he ordered the moth onto the windowsill and walked it forward. Again, it bumped into solid matter. Angling for a better look, he made it fly back a few feet and do its best to hover.

"The window," he said. "It's covered in wood."

"You mean it's shuttered?" Blays said. "Those fiends!"

"It's not a shutter. It's solid. Seamless. Like it's been harvested."

"Harvested? But aren't there supposed to be plants in there? How can they grow without any sunshine?"

"I don't know." Dante sent the moth to the next window, but ran into the exact same barrier. He flapped up to the next story and found more of the same. It took ten minutes to make a complete search of the darkened half of the tower. "They're all closed off."

"The windows," Winden said. "They must harvest them shut at night."

"Why would they do that?"

"To keep things out. Much like your cities and their walls. They can reopen them easily enough when it's light out."

"Oh, all right then. So we'll just break in under cover of broad daylight."

Blays wandered toward the window of the inn. "This seems rather excessive. The Basket's already on the top of a fortress. How safe does it need to be?"

"I told you," Winden said. "It holds food. Medicine. Spices. With these at hand, a strong Harvester can supply everyone in the tower. The Basket is vital."

"Well, if we can't get in through the windows, I have a radical suggestion: we take the stairs."

Dante laughed in embarrassment. "Right. On my way."

Plenty of the windows on the lower floors were open. The moth flapped into a dining hall, then out into the hallways. After much confused meandering, it located a stone staircase. The next landing was illuminated by a lantern. But the one above that was blocked off by a seamless sheet of wood.

"Stairs are out, too," Dante said. "Covered in wood. So no shadowalking, either."

Blays put his hands on his hips. "It's almost like they knew we were coming."

"Except for the part where we're not in jail. Or being separated into various pieces and waved about on the points of spears."

"Look, the windows are harvested over, right? So why don't you and Winden just un-harvest them?"

Dante stood. "It'll be pitch black in there. We won't be able to see anything. As long as we're close enough to crack it open, we may as well harvest down a vine, climb up, and take a look for ourselves."

"Nothing conspicuous about rappelling up the side of a guarded tower."

"The back side is practically right against the cliffs. There's nobody out there."

"Sounds like we have a plan," Blays said. "Let us sally forth!"

They headed back downstairs, under close scrutiny from the innkeep. Dante walked north over a number of canals. The tower loomed hundreds of feet to his left. He continued on, heading into an orchard west of the tower. The air smelled of pollen and citrus. Dante circled back toward the shore and hunched in the brush at the edge of the grove, watching Vordon's sentries patrol the cobbled grounds around the tower. It would have been simple enough to strike them all dead and pitch their bodies off the cliff, but within fifteen minutes, Blays spotted a gap in the patrol pattern. They waited, confirming it. When the gap appeared a third time, they stood and walked briskly toward the tower.

Dante moved into the cover of the wall. They crept along it toward the south face. A hundred feet away, waves boomed on the cliffs. Dante sent the nether into the wood sealing the lowest of the blocked-off windows. It lived. Gently, he pulled it apart, drawing open an aperture wide enough to crawl through.

He sent the waiting moth inside. Moonlight revealed a wide room overflowing with trees, shrubs, and flowers. Plenty of vines, too. He moved the shadows into the one nearest the window, thickening it and two others, especially where they held fast to a tree. The vines slithered toward the window, braiding together. And snaking down the side of the tower. A minute later, they dangled a foot above the cobbles.

He gestured to Blays. "You first."

"Not sure it'll hold, huh?" Blays gave it a tug, eyed the lower windows—many of which were lit—and scrambled up, bracing his feet against the side of the tower.

Dante kept watch on the grounds. With monkey-like dexterity, Blays reached the window, hauled himself inside, and waved. Winden was next. When she was fifty feet up, a silhouette appeared in the window just above and to her left. Dante's heart pounded. He held the nether in his hand. The silhouette receded.

Winden got to the Basket and swung inside. Dante started up. The vines were springy, offering a good grip. The rain-roughened walls made good footing for his sandals. At the window, Blays reached for his wrists and helped him inside.

"Here we are," Blays said. "Now how about we find ourselves some seeds?"

23

Keeping both eyes on the grounds, Dante grabbed hold of the vines and hauled them up the side of the tower, assisted by Winden and Blays. The room was cavernous but the air was thick with the scents of flowers and leaves. Once the vine rope was coiled in a heap, Dante grew the wood back over the window, sealing them in darkness.

He fetched his torchstone and warmed it with his breath. Pale light beamed across the space. They stood on an elevated platform rimming a wide, round room, which would allow the Basket's minders to move about and tend to the countless trees and shrubs growing from the dirt-packed floor. The ceiling was twenty feet high. He'd seen many of the trees here grow much taller than that, but the Harvesters clearly kept them in check.

Every surface that wasn't covered in dirt was sheeted over with smooth, grained wood. An odd touch, but Dante supposed that allowed Vordon's harvesters to do things like seal up the windows, or grow chairs, furniture, or tools wherever they pleased.

"So," Blays said. "Do we have any idea what we're looking for?"

Dante held up the torchstone, slashing light through the

branches, which cast shifting shadows. "Storage of some kind. How are seeds traditionally kept, Winden?"

She peered into the foliage. "In Kandak, care of seeds is the duty of the Archivist. To keep them safe from insects and water, they're stored in sealed bins. In case something were to happen to the Basket, these are often kept elsewhere."

"Meaning a where that's else than here? So the seeds might not even be in this tower?"

"In Deladi, there is nowhere safer than the tower. If it has fallen, then so has the entire city. I think the seeds will be here."

"Maybe the seeds are here and maybe they're not," Blays said. "But we're never going to find them by arguing about it."

Blays climbed down the steps from the platform and disappeared into the trees. Dante recognized most of the trees from his traipses through the jungle, but there were many he'd never seen, including one that was nearly all trunk (for easy firewood or fortifications?) and another that grew finger-thin, perfectly straight branches ready-made for the shafts of arrows.

Curious, but beyond the focus of his search. They made a quick circuit of the room and found no storage of any kind. An enclosed staircase took them up to the next level. This was all fruit trees, shrubs, and vines.

Winden frowned at a waxy yellow berry. "Poison. So are the ones over there. These things, they shouldn't be kept so close to the food."

"Think we should leave them a note?" Dante said.

A shack had been grown from the eastern wall. Dante opened the door and shined his stone inside, but the small room was filled with trowels, rakes, and snips. There were candlefruit lanterns, too. He lit three and put away his stone.

They ascended to the third floor of the Basket. This room was the most odiferous yet, with flowers and herbs filling the air with so much sweetness, pepper, savor, and mint that Dante found himself sneezing repeatedly.

Anxiety tightened his chest. Judging by the windows on the outside, the Basket was only five layers deep. They'd already exhausted three. On reaching the fourth, they found it divided into three sections. One held saplings, cuttings, and sprouts. The second was devoted to mushrooms and fungus, which Winden claimed were notoriously hard to harvest.

And the third was filled with growths that would be described kindly as "oddities," and less politely as "weeping sores on nature's face." A tree with matte black bark. A vine with an open maw feasting on a chunk of what Dante hoped was raw pork. A flower whose petals dangled like dead worms.

"Experiments," Winden said. "The Harvesters search for new plants."

Blays made a face. "Looks more like they search for ways to make grown men cry."

This floor also sported a shack. It was filled with tools, too, though they were so strange Dante couldn't begin to guess their purpose.

The staircase terminated at the fifth level. While the previous levels had been filled with a dazzling diversity of species, this was dominated by a monotony of squat trees with thick trunks and spiky branches. Heart sinking, Dante made a circuit of the walls. He saw no bins of any kind.

He rubbed his hands down his face. "They're not here."

"They must be somewhere in the tower," Winden said. "Maybe the basement. It will be cool there. Protected."

"So all we have to do is descend through all the inhabited levels, find a way into their safehouse, and pray *that* is where they keep the seeds."

"Suppose they'll have the basements harvested over?" Blays said. "If not, I could shadowalk in."

"If the seeds are that valuable, I have no doubt they're enclosed at night, too."

Blays moved toward the grove of identical trees, testing the point of a thorn against the tip of his finger. "Maybe we should go hole up in the inn. Throw some cash around to find out where the seeds are hidden. And *then* go after them."

"That would make a lot more sense than blundering around this place." Dante was aware that coming up here in person had been his idea, but that only made his annoyance worse. "Is there anything we're missing? Is this the highest floor? Could there be a secret level above us?"

"You're the one with the magic moth."

Dante moved to one of the windows and harvested a crack in the wood covering it. His moth fluttered outside and up the tower. Its top was only five feet above the ceiling of the fifth floor of the Basket. It was possible there was a chamber in that space, but if so, it would be very cramped. There were no obvious entrances on the roof, either. Unless they had a nethermancer capable of opening a hole in the stone—something he'd seen no evidence of—he doubted there was anything to be found there.

As he explored these things, Blays walked up to one of the stubby trees. "This is a bit odd, isn't it? Why these?"

"Who cares?"

"On every other level, there was only one or two of each subject. One walnut tree, one verberry bush, and so on. But this is an entire grove of the same thing."

Dante slapped at a fly on his neck. "Maybe they just love fat little trees. Winden, are these ceremonial?"

She wrinkled her brow. "These are damans. They grow in the driest lands. They have hollow trunks for the storage of water."

Blays' eyebrows shot up. "Hollow trunks?" He knocked on the one next to him, producing an empty rap. "Well, probably nothing to it. Best be on our way."

Awash in nervous heat, Dante brought himself beside one of the damans. He took hold of the nether within its trunk and peeled the wood apart. Inside, shelves held dozens of polished wooden boxes.

"Genius!" Winden laughed. "You would never look here if you weren't a Harvester yourself. And the trunks, they insulate the seeds from light, bugs, and rot."

Dante drew out one of the boxes. When he shook it, it rattled. It appeared to be a single piece, and he was on the verge of harvesting it open when his fingernail scraped over a seam. He pulled it open, revealing nine separate chambers filled with seeds.

"That's one down." He regarded the tiny forest. "Only hundreds and hundreds to go."

Blays and Winden joined the search. Each tree contained up to forty boxes, and each box held anywhere from four to sixteen different chambers, depending on the size of the seeds, nuts, or slice of fungus inside. There were easily a hundred trees within the level. Some were empty, but even if only half the trees were filled, they still held something like twenty thousand different varieties of seeds. Perhaps some of those were harvested variants of other species, meaning the number of truly discrete plants was closer to a few thousand.

Even so, the number was boggling. This was a storehouse of knowledge just as great as the Library of Bressel or the archives in Narashtovik. Perhaps even greater. Books held ideas—but the plants here could feed the hungry or treat the sick.

Pawing through them, then, made him feel like a looter. Like he was betraying one of his dearest ideals. Going forward, he was careful neither to spill anything or to mix the seeds between compartments. And when he put back a box, he made sure to replace it from where it had been removed.

Blays lifted his head from a box. "Did you hear something?"

Dante went still. No wind could penetrate the Basket. The only noise was their own rustling, currently paused. "Nothing."

"Still got your moth around?"

"It's outside. Everything looks fine."

Blays set the box back on the shelf within its trunk. "I'll be right back."

Dante nodded absently. Each tree was taking about five minutes to search. The empty ones would speed the process up, but at their current speed, it would take up to six hours to check every last box. Six hours would run them uncomfortably close to dawn. It was possible the tower's Harvesters would arrive to open it before then. He could kill them, if he had to, but—

A piercing whistle drifted up the stairwell. Dante shoved his open box back on the shelf and ran for the stairs, drawing his sword. Further below, steel swashed against steel.

Dante's curse echoed off the walls. The candlefruit lantern flickered on the next landing down. There, Blays ducked under a flash of metal and flicked his sword into the attacker's forearm. The man shrieked and dropped his weapon. He wore a chain mail jersey and iron helm. Blays threaded his sword into the man's neck.

He fell, joining the bodies of three others. Without an instant of hesitation, Blays lunged into the next warrior, pinning the man's sword against the wood-lined inner column of the stairwell and slashing his second sword straight though the man's collarbone. As the man dropped, Dante shot a streak of nether into the warrior behind him.

But two more rushed up to take the dead man's place. And others swarmed up behind those.

"How did they know we were here?" Dante said.

Blays feinted at his opponent. "Must have seen us climbing up."

Horror gushed through Dante's veins. "We still haven't found the seeds. We need more time to search!"

"I'll just hold them off for the next eight hours, then." Blays parried an incoming strike with such deftness it looked like he might actually be able to do so all night. A soldier jabbed with a spear from the second row and Blays pivoted, the spear whisking past his head.

Dante fell back a step, delving into the nether in the wooden stairs, casting about for any stone he could plug up the entrance with. But the stairwell appeared to be entirely wooden.

Winden brushed past him. She rolled her hand forward, gesturing at the steps. "Blays, get back!"

Blays hammered at his foe, driving him down the stairs, then danced up beyond Winden. Shadows streaked from Winden to the wooden floor. With an audible rasp, branches shot upwards, twisting and tangling around each other, filling the stairwell from top to bottom. She continued harvesting until the growth was three feet thick.

"Well done," Dante said. "Blays, stay here and—"

Nether flickered within the wall of wood. A branch shot forth, its tip as pointed as a spear. It struck Winden in the ribs and punched out the small of her back.

"No!" Dante cast his mind along the trail of shadows, following them past the wooden wall and to the Harvester who must be lurking on the other side. With an ice-cold surge of nether, he reached into the man's heart and squeezed.

A gasp. The thump of a body against the steps.

Blays cradled Winden's limp body, taking the pressure off the makeshift spear she was impaled on.

"Don't move her," Dante said. "Hold her just like that."

Blays braced himself beneath her. Dante's mind was squealing like quenched metal, but he breathed deeply and sent his mind inside the spear. It withdrew from her body, moving back into the tangle. Blood spurted from Winden's back and chest. Shadows glommed onto her wounds. Dante took them up and shaped them into her flesh, knitting it back together.

The bleeding stopped. Blays held her aloft, face coated in sweat. Winden took a juddering breath. Her eyes remained closed, but she breathed.

Dull thuds sounded from the other side of the barricade. By the sound of things, it would take the Tauren many minutes to hack their way through. Dante gave Blays a hand carrying Winden back upstairs.

"Will she live?" Blays said.

"I think so. I'll keep an eye on her. You watch the barricade and let me know if they're close to punching through."

"Don't tell me you're going to keep searching."

"We can't leave now," Dante said. "They'll know we were after their seed archive. Either they'll move it, or lock this place down so tight we'll never get in again."

They reached the top level and its forest of damans. Dante ran back to the boxes he'd been searching previously.

"What's the plan, then?" Blays said. "Stay up here until we're completely surrounded?"

"I don't know! I don't even know if the seeds are here."

"If we stay here much longer, even if we find the seeds, we won't get out with our lives."

Dante moved to the next tree, parting its trunk down the middle. "Then quit griping at me and come up with an idea."

"First step is to assess what we've gotten ourselves into. Block the stairs to this level and open a window."

Dante turned from the boxes and did as he was told, sealing the stairs off with a crush of branches grown from the living floor, then pulling the wood away from a window.

Blays moved to it, gazing below. "Yup. Guards down there, too."

"Wonderful. Since they're already aware of our presence, we may as well keep up the search."

After another minute of window-gazing, Blays came to join him. Dante no longer had any regard for keeping the boxes orderly—when he lifted a lid and confirmed there were no Star Tree seeds inside, he cast the box away. Even though this archive was the work of the enemy, it hurt to wreck it. Dante consoled himself with the thought that the Harvesters could rebuild it from what they had in the Basket.

Anyway, not all knowledge was created equal. The Tauren had been sitting on the seeds for centuries, clueless as to the treasure they possessed. Surely the ability to free an entire people was worth destroying a storehouse of fruits and herbs.

He paused, box in hand. If the seeds were that old, then maybe the box that held them was, too. Some of the boxes differed in color and size, obviously created at different times. Dante moved from tree to tree, peeling each one open.

"Time to get smarter," he said. "Grab any box that looks faded or dusty."

Blays caught on, rifling through them. An axe thunked into the barrier at the top of the stairs, startling Dante. He moved to it, reinforcing the branches, lashing them at whoever was on the other side, producing a yelp of pain.

The northern edge of the grove held a number of boxes scuffed with age. Dante opened one after another, tossing them aside. The process became so routine that he was in the act of casting away an opened box when he registered the five-pointed star on the side of a round, flat pit.

He laughed, delirious. "I've got them. I've *got* them!"

Blays moved to his shoulder, looked down on the seeds, and thumped him on the back. "I was starting to worry Sando and Aladi sent us here just to stir up trouble between the Tauren and the Kandeans. Now let's get the hell out of here, shall we?"

Most of the boxes contained at least ten of each seed. The smaller seeds were piled up by the dozen. But there were a mere four of the Star Tree pits. As if the Tauren Harvesters had destroyed most of them in a futile effort to grow more trees, then set the remainder aside to wait for new information. And hundreds of years later, they were still waiting.

Dante put two of the seeds in separate pockets, then stuck the box in his pack. Blays moved to the open window on the tower's south face. Dante checked on Winden, who remained breathing but unconscious, and joined Blays. Lanterns glowed far below them, illuminating ten warriors covering the grounds between the tower and the seaside cliffs.

Axes chopped at the wood snarling the stairs. Closer now. Dante thrust his hand at the branches, pouring the nether from a shell into them. They burst downward. A man screamed. The chopping stopped abruptly.

Blays gestured at the other windows. "Open those up, too?"

Dante did so, tapping one of the shaden in order to preserve his strength. Even more soldiers stood watch outside the north, east, and west sides of the High Tower.

Blays grimaced. "Don't think we can fight through all of them."

"Especially not if we're carrying Winden."

"Don't tell me you're thinking about leaving her."

"If it's the difference between living and dying? Wouldn't she rather we get the Star Tree seeds back to her people?"

"I think," Blays said, "she would *rather* not be chucked aside like a worn-out sock."

They stared at each other for a long moment. Dante knew he could perform such an act with no great inner turmoil. It was what logic commanded: when you were given the choice between losing your arm or your head, then you chose your arm, no matter how painful you knew it would be. He liked Winden, but with her in tow, he saw no hope of escaping Deladi.

But leaving her wouldn't only cost Winden. Once, years ago, Dante had let someone close to Blays die. Her death had saved not just Narashtovik, but also the norren. Without question, it had been the right move. Even so, it caused Blays to leave the city. It had taken years (and a new threat to Narashtovik's existence) to mend the friendship.

Dante knew Winden didn't mean as much to Blays. Leaving her behind wouldn't necessarily smash their friendship anew. But he thought it would crack it. Were friendships like bones, where cracks mended over time, and could even make those bones stronger than ever? Or were they more like rock—once they began to shear, there was nothing you could do to stop them from falling apart?

"We'll take her with us," Dante said. "But please, please have an idea with any chance of success."

Blays jogged back to the southern window overlooking the coast. "There aren't as many of them down there."

"Any of them is too many. If a single one spots us climbing down with Winden, they'll have a hundred people on us before we reach the bottom."

"Think you could run a vine down there without it being seen?"

"That's a tall order. People tend to notice things flapping around at eye level."

"Then don't grow it all the way down. You can stop about twenty feet from the ground."

"Could work. The rock's black. But they'd spot us coming down."

Blays grinned. "Not if I'm not there."

"Finally decide to run out on me?"

"Thought I'd drop down and cause a little havoc. They'll have no reason to guard the tower if they think we've escaped it."

"That might actually work," Dante said. "And it beats trying to jump."

He brought the lanterns to the north side of the room and left them there, then returned to the southern windows, which were now in almost total darkness. There were only a few vines draped across the squat daman trees. He coaxed out two, twining them around each other, then slithered them out the window.

He waited for any reaction from the soldiers below. When none came, he grew the vine onward, letting it wind into the folds and crags of the tower. A minute later, it was forty feet long, snaking past two levels of enclosed windows. The axe-men still hadn't resumed their attack on the barrier across the stairs. Either they'd given up, or they'd gone in search of another Harvester.

"Twenty feet from the ground." Dante moved back from the window. "You're sure you can handle the drop?"

"I'll be fine. Weight's weird in the shadows. Meet me at the canoe, all right?"

"Here." He handed the seed in his right pocket to Blays. "In case I don't make it out."

Blays weighed the pit in his palm. "I'd like to assure you this is an unnecessary gesture. But there *is* half an army down there."

"Take it to Kandak. If they can't grow it, find some way to get it to Spearpoint."

Blays pocketed it, glanced out the window, then hugged him. Blays stepped back and vanished.

Dante stuck his head in the corner of the window. From what he could see of the vine rope, it was barely wiggling. He waited there until Blays had likely gotten to ground level. With the warriors showing no signs they'd seen a thing, Dante went back to Winden.

Her condition was unchanged. His supply of nether was getting thin, but he still had some left in the shells. He harvested forth another length of vines, winding them around Winden's arms and legs. He carried her to the window, set her beside it, and waited.

Something heavy slammed into the branches enclosing the stairs, startling him. A man yelled orders from behind the barricade. An axe went to work for a while, replaced in time by the squeak and crack of metal bars leveraged against the growth.

A shout rang out from outside the tower. Down in the yard, men moved about in confusion. The voice went on: "They've escaped! To the west! For Kaval's sake, they're killing—"

Blays' Taurish was accented, but the soldiers were listening to the words, not the person delivering them. A sergeant dashed in, gestured broadly, and ran west toward the woods. Soldiers streamed after him. A bell clanged from the west, though Dante had no way to tell whether that was Blays, or the reaction to him.

The attack on the staircase barricade redoubled. With no desire to tip them off to the fact that some of the interlopers were still in the tower, Dante made no effort to stop them. He scanned the grounds below. Only two soldiers remained on sentry. Concluding these were the best odds he was likely to see, Dante lifted Winden to the window, wrapped a vine around his left arm, and swung his legs over the side.

Shadows arced from his hands. Below, both guards crumpled. Hanging tight to Winden, Dante poured nether from the dwindling shaden into the vines, extending them as fast as he could. He reeled down the side of the tower. Palms sweating like mad, he tightened the plants around his arm, dangling like a spider nearly two hundred feet in the air.

He dropped past one set of windows, then another. A lot of yelling was going on to the west, but the southern yards remained clear. Halfway down, he started paying more attention to the top of the tower than the bottom. If the soldiers hacked through the barricade and found the vines out the window, they could dash him to the ground with a single hack of their axes.

He was still looking up when his feet touched the bottom.

He untangled himself, then withdrew the vines from Winden and heaved her over his shoulder. He circled toward the east, away from the hubbub. The only people who'd seen them inside the tower were now dead. If he could get back to the inn, he could rest there until Winden woke up, then rendezvous with Blays where they'd stashed the canoe.

A warrior trotted around the east side of the tower. Dante pierced the man's skull with a bolt of nether, dropping him like a sack of onions. Winden was slipping down his back. He bounced her higher up and got a better grip.

Feet scuffed on stone. A squadron of soldiers rounded the

tower, halting in surprise.

"Intruders," Dante said in Taurish. "To the west!"

He pointed that way. One of the men took a half step, but a second trooper was gazing down at the warriors Dante had just killed. Dante gathered the nether.

"All hands!" the trooper bellowed. "All hands to—"

Dante silenced him with a spear of nether that entered his mouth and exited the back of his neck. But the others were already calling out, drawing swords. Dante sprinted west. If he could get into the woods, he might be able to slip away. He hadn't taken two steps before another squad appeared from that side.

Men charged him, swords drawn. He drew the last of the nether from his shell and lashed out. The nearest six men flew backwards, their heads rolling away like coconuts. This was a needlessly horrific gesture, but Dante hoped it might dissuade the others from following.

He was growing weak. He couldn't kill them all. Even more would be upon him in moments. There was only one option left. He turned south and ran as fast as Winden's weight allowed.

"The cliffs!" he yelled in Mallish, his voice echoing across the heights of the tower. "I'll be at the cliffs!"

An arrow whisked over his head. Uselessly, he ducked. Winden's weight shifted forward and he nearly toppled over. Another arrow clacked off the stones ahead of him. Most of the soldiers were content to hang back and let the archers do the work, but a few swordsmen sprinted after him. The cliffs were forty feet away now. He threw daggers of nether over his shoulder with his free hand, slaying two more pursuers. He reached the edge of the land before the others could catch up.

It was a twenty-foot drop to the sea. Dante bowed his legs and leaped.

24

He plummeted toward the surf. Waves smashed into the rocks below, sending spray dozens of feet into the air. If he landed in the water, he'd be pulverized, flushed out to sea to feed the fish and the crabs.

Dante sent his mind into the base of the cliffs. A stone ledge flew outward like a dresser drawer. He landed hard, ribs creaking. His left arm went numb at the shoulder. Pain flashed up his spine. Winden rolled toward the edge of the shelf. He grabbed her and hauled her back toward the cliff. At his insistence, the rock receded, forming a hollow. Dante crawled inside, Winden in tow, and withdrew the shelf back into the cliff.

His left arm throbbed with pain. Every breath was a stab in the ribs. He couldn't spare any nether to heal himself. If something else happened, or Winden's condition worsened, he might not have enough strength to go on.

Light shined on the waters. Voices yammered back and forth, words lost in the boom of the waves. Spray spattered inside the hollow. The air was warm enough, but he was getting soaked. The wind wasn't helping. He strained his ears, fighting to hear as many words as he could. He couldn't make out much, but they didn't sound orderly or directed. They sounded confused. He didn't think anyone had seen him land on the shelf.

Lights continued to flash across the waves. After a few disorganized minutes, a beam cut down from above, illuminating a precise section of ocean. The beam lingered before slowly moving on, enacting a methodical outward sweep from the base of the cliffs. Now and then a man called for it to stop and it held position for several seconds before continuing.

When it was closer, Dante used its illumination to investigate Winden. She hadn't suffered any visible injuries in the fall. He moved into the nether within her organs, confirmed nothing was fatally wrong, and withdrew.

In time, so did the light. The voices above him persisted. The ache in his shoulder and arm dulled somewhat, but the hitch in his side was still as bad as the moment after he'd landed. It was hard to focus.

He frowned. His hold on the nether was slipping, but he hadn't so much as touched the ether. Supposedly, it was even better for healing. He was able to summon the tiniest bit, but try as he might, he couldn't figure out how to make it patch the crack in his ribs.

He used his surplus of time to sort through his options. There was no chance of swimming away. Even without Winden weighing him down, and his ribs hampering his every stroke, the ocean's surges were far too powerful. He couldn't climb up; the grounds were still patrolled and surely would be until morning. After a good rest, he might be able to tunnel away to the forest west of the tower or the city to the east of it.

That would require hours of sleep. Between his physical aches, the cramped location, and the crash of the waves—which was irregular but ceaseless—he wasn't sure sleep would be possible.

Then again, what else could he do?

He arranged himself in the least uncomfortable position he could attain, wrapping his islanders' cloak around himself. If he died now, would he find himself in the Pastlands? If so, he suspected it would be a new incarnation of that realm—he suspected that death would alter the state of his mind enough to conjure up a fresh set of dreams and worries. Likely, he'd find himself in an unfamiliar place, with no recollection of how he'd come there, or even that he was dead.

He didn't like the idea of that. The Pastlands were a lie. A trap that preyed on the weaknesses of the human mind. Sooner or later, though, he'd riddle his way out into the Mists. Would he emerge into the Mists of his people, the dead of Narashtovik? Or would he find himself among the Dresh and the islanders? If so, was what they called the Worldsea the place where all souls mingled? It seemed as if you lost your memory there too, however. Possibly your entire personality. If he died, then, one way or another, he would be lost forever.

Death wasn't an option. As he combed through the possibilities for survival, he drifted off.

His feet. They were wet. He sat up, momentarily afraid he'd pissed himself in his sleep. But the water was cold. As he processed this piece of information, a wave splashed against the entrance, flooding the cubby with a thin layer of sea water.

His heart jolted. The tide was rising. Another few minutes, and they'd be swept out of the shallow cavern altogether. Seeing no lights searching the darkness, he risked poking his head out of the cave. No silhouettes watched from above. He reached for the nether, but he hadn't slept nearly long enough to tunnel away.

He could only see two options. First, carve a few handholds into the rock, climb west of the tower, and try to slip away through the woods. Doing this, there was no chance he could carry Winden. He was so tired and banged up he wasn't sure he'd make it himself.

Second, he could use his remaining strength to elevate the cavern. And give Blays that much more time to find them.

He moved back into the hollow and gazed down at Winden. "It would be a great help if you chose to wake up." She did no such thing. He sighed, squeezing his eyes shut. "You're flinty-eyed. A realist. You'd want me to go, wouldn't you? There's no sense in *both* of us dying, is there?"

She continued to breathe in and out.

"Really, it's your own fault we're in this mess. If you hadn't participated in Niles' lie, things would never have come this far." He rubbed his sore shoulder. "Besides, there are a lot more lives at stake than ours. We have to get the seeds out of here. And I have to help grow them."

He bowed his head and moved toward the entrance. Another wave sloshed inside, seeping over the stone toward Winden's sandaled feet. Another ten or twenty minutes, and the tides would take her away.

Dante stepped back from the entrance. Swearing steadily, he raised a layer of stone over the lower two feet of the opening, blocking out even the unruliest waves. With nothing else to do, he gazed out to sea.

Ten minutes later, a pebble sailed through the cave and plunked him in the forehead.

He leaned outside. Below, a man on a canoe did battle with the waves. Seeing him, Blays flashed a grin, put a finger to his lips, and gestured up at the cliffs.

Dante nodded. He pointed inside the cave and mouthed the word "Winden." Blays squinted, then nodded back. Dante had suffered a few scrapes in the fall, but they'd scabbed over. He cut his arm and summoned every shadow that would listen. He sent them into the stone, rebuilding the shelf he'd used to catch himself. It grew over the water like a branch. Blays maneuvered beneath it, paddling hard to prevent himself from being lobbed against the rocks.

Dante went in for Winden. When he took her up, pain blazed in his ribs like a flaming spear. He dropped to one knee, hissing.

Catching his breath, he gathered his strength. And lifted.

Blays was right beside the shelf. The higher swells threatened to batter his canoe against it. Dante moved to its ledge, waited for the canoe to rise, and stepped over the gunwale. He collapsed to the bottom in a controlled fall, holding tight to Winden. When the stars of pain faded from his eyes, he took up an oar, paddling one-handed. Blays drove his paddle into the sea with military precision. The cliffs drifted away behind them.

Lanterns burned around the tower, but the search of the sea had ended. Blays and Dante fought free of the eddies closer to shore and hove southeast, putting plenty of space between themselves and Deladi's bay.

"What took you so long?" Dante said.

Blays glanced over his shoulder. "First there was the matter of stealing the boat. Then came the business of waiting for the hundreds of people hunting you to move along."

"Did you hear me, then?"

"Hear you? I spotted the cave. You have a habit of seeking them out to hide in. Not unlike a number of other nasty creatures."

"Before I jumped, I yelled for you," Dante said. "I said I was going to the cliffs."

Blays laughed. "I didn't hear a damn thing. But it was hard to miss the million-odd armed men shining their lanterns down at the sea. There were so many lights it looked like the stars had come down to see what all the fuss was about."

"Well, I'm glad you got here before the tide could finish us off." Dante winced and set down his paddle.

"You all right?"

"A little beaten up. You?"

"Same." They were sailing past the bay now and Blays kept up his water-eating pace. "I suppose the assassination attempt is off."

"After tonight, there's no way we can get near Vordon. I say we hike back to Kandak and grow us a Star Tree. By then, Deladi may have settled down enough to come back and take a shot at him."

Blays turned and gave him a long, assessing look. "Agreed. Before that, though, we need to find a place to sleep. You look like something the dog coughed up."

Despite the day's hardships, Blays was able to paddle for another hour before finally relenting and turning toward shore. They landed on a gritty beach and dragged the canoe into the trees. Dante's mind and body were leaden. He helped lift Winden out of the damp canoe, broke off a few fronds to sleep on, and fell unconscious.

The pain in his ribs awoke him hours later. Surf washed on the beach. The sun was up. And so was Winden.

"Blays told me what happened," she said. "Thank you for getting me out of there."

Dante shrugged. Pain stabbed his ribs; he clutched at them. This provided a nice distraction from the guilt of having almost abandoned her.

"We're not above all kinds of dirty tricks," he said. "Not if it means living to see the next sunrise. But once you're with us, we're behind you all the way."

She turned west, toward Deladi. The trees were much too thick to see the tower. "You want to go back to Kandak?"

"For now." Dante gestured to the nether and found it renewed. Shadows zipped from the undersides of the leaves and sank into his shirt over his damaged ribs. The pain eased. "Our first order of business is to grow a Star Tree. Once that's accomplished, then we can throw our newly-saved lives at Vordon."

"About that." Blays padded up to them, eyelids puffy. "Growing a Star Tree would be a pretty big deal, wouldn't it? The kind of thing that might convince other peoples that we're on the side of right."

Dante drew back his head. "And if they're not impressed by

the accomplishment, we could offer them a deal: if you don't support the Kandeans, you don't get any fruit."

"That sounds less like a deal and more like blackmail."

"Why do they deserve the fruit? It's a fair exchange. If they can cure the ronone, they won't have to trade for shaden anymore."

"I didn't say I disagreed. I just like to know the difference between shaking someone's hand and twisting their arm."

Dante raised an eyebrow at Winden. "What do you think?"

She considered this. "Control of the Star Tree would finally give others a reason to ally with Kandak rather than the Tauren. But it would also give Tauren a reason to take Kandak for good."

"I can't tell if that's a yes or a no."

"This idea, we should bring it to Niles. He knows more about the others than I do."

Dante prevented his eyes from rolling. "I have some experience with warfare. To beat a more powerful foe, you isolate them from their allies while finding ways to enlist more of your own."

"This sounds wise," she said. "But he is the one who negotiates Kandak's alliances."

"He's wanted our help all along. He should take our advice."

She tipped her head in a way that neither agreed nor argued. Dante healed his sore shoulder, then tended to the numerous cuts and aches the others had suffered. They'd left some of their packs in the inn and the rest in the tower, including almost all their food. All they had left was a box of san paste spiked with shaden. They gathered fruit from the shore, then began the hike up the long slopes toward the Dreaming Peaks.

Dante hadn't gotten as much sleep as he would have liked, but compared to the absurdly long, insanely dangerous activities of the previous day, the march through the grasslands felt like an outing to the beach. As the afternoon waned, they veered toward Iladi Forest to make camp in the cover of the trees.

After they'd hacked out shelters and fed themselves, Dante

got out one of the Star Tree seeds and sat next to Winden. "Want to give this thing a whirl?"

"We can't grow this so close to Tauren territory," she said. "But you mean to learn how it's done?"

"Exactly. The Dresh made it sound like harvesting the Star Trees is a real process. It'll take us days to get back to Kandak. We might as well make use of them."

He laid out the four seeds. They were all roughly the same size. Each bore a star on one side. With no obvious difference between them, he put three away and set the fourth between himself and Winden.

Dante sent his mind into the curve of the seed. The outer layers held traces of nether, no more or less than an average rock, leaf, or bone. But he found a small chamber inside the seed. Filled entirely with shadows. There was another chamber beside it. And others after that.

They were arranged in a spiral. As he moved inward, he counted eleven shadow-filled chambers. A twelfth lay at the very center of the seed. This chamber was no larger than the pip of an orange. Unlike the others, it was empty.

He withdrew and gestured to Winden. She send her focus within it, exploring. A minute later, she sat back, lips pursed.

"Remind you of anything?" Dante said.

"A shaden. The spiral, it's just like it."

"The Star Tree on Spearpoint looked like it was made out of shell. Is it possible the ancient Dresh harvested the shaden into the tree itself?"

Winden laughed. "I should know this? If so, I could have saved us a great deal of time."

"It makes sense, doesn't it? Did you see how the central chamber is empty? If we fill it with nether, I think the seed will sprout."

"Could be."

"All the others are filled. Isn't it the obvious step?"

"That's what it suggests," Winden said. "But it may not be so straightforward. Harvested plants—the further they are from their origins, the more difficult they are to grow. If the Star Trees are truly part shaden, nothing about the seeds will be as they seem."

"Fair enough. But we have to start somewhere. May as well rule out the direct routes first."

He cut the back of his hand, pooling nether in his palm. He eased it into the seed, channeling it toward the center chamber, feeding it in drop by drop. As soon as the space filled completely, the nether bled away, escaping from the seed like steam, lost to the dirt around it. Dante withdrew, heart pounding. And watched helplessly as the nether evaporated from the other chambers as well. In seconds, the seed was empty. Nothing remained but the typical nether that lurked in all things.

Winden sucked in a breath. "What did you do?"

"You tell me. You're the Harvester!"

"I think one thing's clear," Blays said. "Whatever you did, you shouldn't do it again."

Dante turned his head. "You saw that, too?"

"To my eternal disappointment."

"I don't suppose you have any insight."

"You suppose correctly."

Dante poked and prodded at the seed with the nether, refilling the chambers, but the shadows simply leeched back into the surroundings. The night air was still and heavy. Dante sat back, layered in prickly sweat.

"Winden, why don't you try harvesting it?" he said.

Winden narrowed one eye. "Because it's dead."

"Then that means there's nothing to lose."

She looked dubious about that, but gave it a try, feeding the nether into the seed. It didn't so much as stir. After several efforts, she shook her head.

"Maybe that one was flawed," Dante said. "What if we tried

another?"

Winden scrunched up her mouth. "I fear it would be the same. It's like I said—plants as extreme as these, they're very delicate. They may only grow in certain places. The one the Dresh had was in the lowlands. Perhaps like the snails they're grown from, the trees prefer to be near the sea. I think we should wait until we're back in Kandak to try again."

This wasn't at all what he wanted to hear. She was the Harvester, though. And as far as he knew, the three remaining seeds were the last ones on the island. He couldn't allow his impatience to rob him of the cure.

They slept, rose, and continued uphill. The day was another quiet one. After the last week of nonstop troubles, Dante welcomed it. As they walked, he thought about the seeds. When they rested, he attempted to reinfuse the empty seed with nether, but it was like Winden said. By all indications, he'd broken it.

"The twelve chambers," he said after they'd made camp that night. "In Gask and Mallon, we believe in the Celeset. The River of the Heavens. Twelve gods reside there, dividing the sky between them. Do you have anything like that here?"

Winden chewed on a mealy, bulbous fruit that tasted like stale bread. "Here, there is no River of Heavens. But there is Kaval and His Eleven. I've told you of Mora and Loda. There are nine others, too. Each commands a piece of the land, the sea, and the air. But Kaval is the only one who can reach the heavens and what lies beyond."

"In that context, does the seed's shape mean anything to you?"

"Nothing leaps to mind."

"Is there a hierarchy to the Eleven? Or are they all equally subordinate to Kaval?"

She rolled her eyes up and to the right, thinking. "The least of them is considered to be Doga. He who cares for the toads, the snakes, and every creature that people despise. The central chamber, it's the smallest. Perhaps it is his."

"If it was, would that mean anything to you?"

"Such as?"

He gestured searchingly. "Perhaps we need to fill it with the nether from a toad."

This time, Winden's eye-roll was pure exasperation. "Does that really sound like it could possibly be true?"

"This is your land, not mine. I'd like to see *you* navigate your way around Narashtovik."

The following day, as they neared the Boat-Growers' territory, they veered west into the open plains. Dante patrolled the forest's edge with a team of dead hopping rats, ensuring they weren't being watched. The day after that, with no new progress on the seeds, they ascended the Dreaming Peaks.

On its southern approach, the bridge spanning the river had been torn from its moorings. Instead, they'd strung a rope across, which the Kandean guard used to convey a small raft to them. By the time they ferried themselves along the rope to the north side, Niles had arrived to greet them.

"You left from the north and returned from the south?" he said. "No wonder it took you so long."

"We made it to Spearpoint Rock." Winden's face shined with wonder, as if she couldn't believe her own words. "And then climbed the High Tower itself."

Breathlessly, she relayed the story. Niles' response switched between laughter and drop-jawed disbelief. By the end, he was looking at all three of them as if they'd stepped down from the stars.

"This was why we needed you," he said, gripping first Dante's arm, then Blays'. He turned to Winden, smiling. His eyes brightened with tears. "And you. You would have made Larsin so proud."

Blays' eyebrows vaulted up his brow. "You're Larsin's daughter?"

"Adopted," Winden said. "When I was found in the Tauren wilds, he was the only one who'd take me in."

"So that means you and Dante are siblings?"

Dante snorted. "Don't look so surprised. Knowing my dad, he probably left bastard Galands in every corner of the world."

Niles' brow furrowed. "Don't speak of him that way. It was the ronone that kept him here."

"He could have visited."

"For what? A few days, only to leave again? He was afraid you'd follow him back here. And that you would get sick, too."

"None of this matters," Dante said. "What happened, happened. It's behind us. What matters now is growing these seeds—and curing the island."

Niles pressed his lips together. "You could do that here in the Dreaming Peaks. After all, the people of the Mists are the ones who gave us the answers."

"I don't think they'll grow here," Winden said. "We'll take them to Kandak."

Dante motioned to take in the islands. "We're thinking you could use the fruit as bargaining tokens to rally other people to our banner. If so, best to keep the Star Tree close to home."

Niles rubbed his jaw. "Aye, that does seem practical."

"We'll be on our way, then. Our raid on the High Tower may have stirred up the Tauren. Best to move as fast as we can before they marshal a response."

"Did you see any sign of pursuit?"

"None. Keep your eyes sharp, though. Vordon knows us. Too many of his people saw us to think he won't connect the raid to Kandak."

They resupplied and headed on. In the great hall, the Dreamers were back in their beds, lost in the Mists. Some of the Kandean warriors had been swapped out for others, but they were no more numerous than when they'd reclaimed the Peaks from the Tauren. After seeing the city of Deladi, and the forces at Vordon's command, Niles' garrison looked paltry. Dante wondered if they'd be able to put up any resistance at all.

Three days later, they arrived in Kandak. The town looked more or less the same, but on their way down to the beach, they passed a woman cutting the thin, perfectly straight branches from a harvested arrow-tree. A team of fletchers trimmed off twigs, notched the branches' ends, and affixed arrowheads and the white feathers of sea geese. Most of the tips were obsidian, flaked to a razor's edge, but others were shiny iron, likely acquired in trade from one of the *Sword of the South*'s earlier visits.

Dante glanced at the bay. "Given any thought to where we should plant the tree?"

Winden padded through the shade. "On the coast. Not too close to Kandak. Somewhere secret."

"Sounds like you have somewhere specific in mind."

She smiled but would say no more. She acquired a trio of machetes, however, then led them south past the bay, following a trail into the jungle. When this petered out, they hacked their way forward, taking game trails where possible. Within minutes, Dante was sweaty and filthy.

When they came to a stream, he was ready to dive in. Yet he barely had time to wash his face before Winden directed them upstream. The growth was so thick it was easier to wade through the shallows.

"You're sure this is a good idea?" Blays said. "Remember, you're going to have to come out here all the time."

Winden swept back her sweaty hair, securing it behind her head. "Then we'll just have to clear a trail."

A low roar sifted through the trees. The stream led to a round pool overhung by a waterfall forty feet wide and ten high. Trees crowded the banks, but a small island in the middle of the pool held nothing but shrubs and grass.

"There," Winden pointed.

Dante eyed the island. "You mean the only place that trees *aren't* growing?"

"The Star Tree is no normal tree. And look." She nodded to the rocks around the pool's edges. Dozens of crabs sunned themselves, harmoniously picking their way between small snails studding every damp surface. "Everything with a shell loves this place."

"She's the Harvester," Blays said. "We're two city folk who barely know where corn comes from. I say we trust her."

Something in Dante wanted to argue, but he suspected that was nothing more than a desire for control. "Lead on."

Winden tossed her cape aside and waded into the pool, which Dante discovered was much colder than her indifference implied. Holding his pack above his head, he walked until the water reached his throat, then paddled toward the island. Winden climbed ashore, wringing the water from her shirt. It clung to her tightly. Under other circumstances, he might have enjoyed the scene, but knowing his father had helped raise her, he felt compelled to look away.

Blays heaved himself onto the island. They moved toward its grassy center. This was in direct sunlight, defraying the chill of their sodden clothing.

Dante got out the three living seeds. "Well?"

"I've been thinking," Winden said. "The twelfth chamber, maybe it means nothing. Maybe we should simply harvest the seed the way we would any other."

"You know more about this than I do. Let me know if you need a hand."

She got a copper trowel from her bag, its surface worn and green. She dug a shallow hole, placed the seed inside, and covered it loosely. Dante moved his mind within it. Winden drew nether from the grass, surrounding the seed with it. The shadows moved oddly, swooping back, as if wary of what hid inside. Dante could see her urging them forward, but only a trickle of them would touch the seed's surface. And none would enter.

They went still. Winden frowned. "Something is wrong. It's like the seed doesn't want to grow."

"Or the black gunk is afraid of getting eaten," Blays said. "What *is* this thing?"

Dante massaged his forehead. "Maybe the nether knows it isn't natural."

Winden returned to her work, probing the seed with the shadows. Twenty minutes later, she stood, hurling her copper trowel down with a clang.

"I don't understand," she said. "I can't find a way in."

Dante crossed his arms. "You shouldn't *have* to find a way in. They should just absorb."

"I could force them to."

"And that might kill this one, too. Try some more. Maybe we're missing something."

She exhaled and got out her water skin. After pacing around the island, she came back to the patch of overturned dirt and resumed her attempts. She lasted another thirty minutes before swearing, standing, and stamping to the island's edge.

After she calmed down, Dante took over, with Winden providing instruction. She might be the Harvester, but he was far and away the superior nethermancer. A part of him was sure he'd find a way inside the seed in seconds. Thirty minutes later, he was still searching for a way in.

"There," he said. "I think I see a seam."

Winden squinted. "I don't see it."

Keeping an eye on the shadow-filled chambers, Dante forced the nether into the hair-fine crack he'd found. As it penetrated the surface, a fissure formed in the largest chamber. It burst open, followed in turn by the chamber next to it, and then the one after that. He watched as the seed died.

"Son of a gods-damned bitch!" He lurched to his feet. "I thought I had it."

"This isn't working," Winden said.

"You don't say! Well, we have two more chances to not fail. After that, everyone on this island is stuck here forever."

She glared at him. Dante grabbed his temples, squeezing hard. At the island's edge, a crab crawled up a rock, waving one oversized claw back and forth like it was leading a sing-along.

"That crab there." Dante was instantly calm again. "Could you harvest it?"

"Of course not," Winden said.

"Why not? If the Star Tree is part shell, then maybe it has to be harvested as a shell, too."

"Animals, they're different. They're born knowing their size. But a plant can grow forever."

"So you say. But maybe it's just difficult. And that's why growing Star Trees was so difficult for the Dresh." He hissed air through his teeth. "They knew what writing is, right? Would it have been that hard to make a permanent record of the most vital knowledge on the island?"

"Here's an idea," Blays said. "Let's go for a swim."

Dante glanced at the pool. "How's that going to help grow the tree?"

"By cooling our boiling heads. Come on."

Before anyone could voice objections, Blays peeled off his shirt and leaped into the water, landing in a ball. It seemed pointless, but Dante was hot and sweaty. A quick dip would improve his mood; mood, in turn, had a great deal of influence over the efficiency of the mind. Muttering profanity, he dived into the pond. The water was bracingly cold. He swam beneath the falls, letting the water batter his head. Shivering, he paddled a loop around the pool, then returned to the island.

He felt much better. The physical activity had stirred his brain as well. As the others climbed ashore and dried off, he paced about, letting an idea take shape.

"I think we should try the chambers again," Dante said. "It

can't be coincidence that there's twelve, and only one is empty."

Winden wrung her hair over the grass. "The last time we tried to fill the empty chamber with nether, the seed broke."

"Correction: it broke when we filled it with *outside* nether. But these seeds probably came from the same tree. That means they're like the loons—part of the same whole. The nether within them will be linked."

Blays flicked a lacy fly from his bare shoulder. "So what? You want to try drawing the nether from one of the seeds into the empty chamber of the other?"

"Exactly! The others are filled, yet they're stable. Maybe that's how we keep the last chamber stable, too."

Winden insisted on a detailed rundown of the loons. After Dante explained how the parts of a body could be separated, but the nether within those parts remained sympathetic to itself, she dug out the dead seed and replaced it with the two live ones.

"Be careful," she said. "If anything starts to go wrong, stop at once. Or we'll lose everything."

As carefully as he knew how, he sank his mind into the nether within one of the seeds' chambers. When nothing smashed into pieces or burst into flames, he touched it, then pushed it forward. It moved easily enough. He reeled a thread of shadows from the chamber, directing it toward the the empty chamber of the other seed. The first drop landed. A second. When the third hit, a tiny fissure formed in the chamber's wall.

Dante dropped the shadows like they were a pot left on the stove all day. Winden bit her lip. The drops of nether frittered away from the chamber. But its wall held.

"That's not going to work," Dante said. "It was right about to break."

Winden touched the dirt covering the seed. "I didn't see any sign it was ready to grow. I don't think this is the way."

"What are we missing?" Using his hand, he dug out one of the seeds. "Maybe we should regroup. Go speak to other Harvesters.

The Boat-Growers do some wondrous things, don't they? Maybe they'd have insight."

"The Boat-Growers have chosen to ally with the Tauren. Besides, I've seen their work. It's nothing like this."

"Then let's try another angle. Are there any other trees similar to this one?"

"You're asking if there are other trees with bark like a seashell, seeds like a shaden, and fruit that cure a fatal disease."

"The Star Trees had to come from somewhere," Dante said. "If we know what type of tree was used as their base, we may be able to extrapolate answers from the seeds of that tree."

"They were created at least six hundred years ago. How would we know their lineage?"

"Easy. Look for anything else with a five-pointed star on its seeds."

Blays grunted. "Who says that marking wasn't harvested?"

Dante cocked his head. "What purpose would that serve?"

"To instantly identify the seeds? Or maybe just to look fancy? These trees are completely fabricated, aren't they? Harvested to hell and gone. Maybe the Dresh named them Star Trees and *then* changed them to grow the marking."

"This is getting away from…" Dante trailed off. Gears in his mind clicked into place. "Then why would they be named Star Trees?"

"Once again, I am bereft of answers. Maybe they wanted something that sounded grand."

"I think they had a reason. Winden, you said that of Kaval and His Eleven, Kaval's the only one who can reach the heavens. Right?"

"That is so," she said. "What of it?"

"The heavens and the stars are the seat of the ether. Its source. Maybe the empty chamber represents Kaval. Maybe it needs to be filled with ether."

"That's a pretty story," Blays said.

"Why not? The nether can't do anything to help with the ronone. But back in Bressel, the priests were able to soothe my symptoms with ether."

Winden quirked her mouth. "As Harvesters, we all use nether. Ether is virtually unknown. If it's needed to grow the seeds, maybe that's why the Star Trees were lost in the first place."

"We have two seeds left," Dante said. "I want to give this a try. If we lose one, then we'll save the other one for after we've done more research on the Star Trees."

Winden nodded. So did Blays. Dante kneeled beside the dirt. Nerves thrumming, he reached out to the ether, pulling it from the light and the air into a glowing bead. He sent this within the still-buried seed, guiding it to the empty chamber.

It flashed with blinding white light. Nether flowed out of the eleven other compartments. Dante cried out in panic. But the shadows weren't leeching out into the soil—they were moving inward. Congealing around the innermost chamber. And sinking into it.

A white sprout curled from the dirt.

25

Dante laughed, a rushing exhalation, releasing all his worry and stress. Winden grinned with the beatific glow of a mother looking down on her newborn. Blays jumped up and did a quick dance. Between them, the sprout unfurled a head of teardrop-shaped leaves with a pearlescent shimmer.

It grew four inches high, then stopped. Hesitantly, Dante peeked inside the seed. All the nether had been absorbed.

"I can't believe it," Winden said. "The first Star Tree in centuries."

"It's used all its nether," Dante said. "Should we harvest it higher?"

"It might not grow as other plants do. We could kill it by mistake."

"We have a spare seed. Left on its own, it could take years for this tree to grow fruit."

Winden tapped her chin. "I will try. But if it's damaging the tree, we'll have to let time take its course."

They had picked up two more shaden in the Dreaming Peaks. Thinking the fledgling Star Tree might be more sympathetic to nether drawn from a shell, Dante got one from his pack and handed it to Winden. She sat cross-legged by the seedling and closed her eyes. Shadows flickered between the shell and the sprout, bringing light, air, earth. The tree wound upwards, leaves unfurling and shaking. It climbed six inches, then a foot. Small white flowers bloomed. As the last of the nether left the shaden, the Star Tree stood as high as Dante's navel.

"Look." Blays pointed to the underside of the largest leaves. There, three white berries had formed from the flowers. "How long do you suppose until they're ripe?"

Dante smiled and passed Winden the remaining shaden. "Let's find out."

She closed her eyes again. The tree crept upwards, branches extending on all sides. By the time the nether gave out, the Star Tree was taller than Dante, its trunk wrist-thick. The pale, rainbow-filmed tree held a mesmerizing beauty, but there was a wrongness to it that made Dante want to look away.

The berries had ripened disproportionately, swelling to the size of lemons, their skins lightly pebbled. Dante reached out and plucked one, careful not to damage the branch. The fruit felt heavier than it should. Unable to get his thumbnail into the skin, he cut it open with his knife. The pale flesh smelled faintly of the sea.

"And we're sure this isn't poison?" Blays said.

"There's only one way to find out." Dante took a bite. It tasted lightly salty, but also sweet. He swallowed. Winden and Blays watched him with the intensity of dogs waiting to be fed. He rolled his eyes. "Quit staring. If something's going to happen, it's going to take a few…"

Goosebumps shot down his arms as coldness flowed through his veins. But it wasn't a painful cold. It was a cleansing one, like an interior form of the swim they'd taken around the waterfall-fed pool. Ever since the ronone had taken hold of him, he'd felt a vague weariness. Over the weeks, he'd grown so used to it that he'd forgotten he'd ever felt different. Now, though, it lifted, leaving him so buoyant he felt as though he might drift off like a milkweed seed.

He turned his sight inside himself. The dark specks were still present. His heart sank. As he watched, though, one shrank, contracting on itself until it disappeared.

"It's working," he said. "We've found the cure."

As it turned out, Blays had been inflicted by the ronone as well. He'd shared the same shaden-laced food that everyone ate, though, meaning he'd seen no symptoms. He ate a bite of the fruit—a generous mouthful seemed to be enough—and pitched the remaining piece to Winden. As she felt the sickness leave her, tears tracked down her cheeks.

"We should get more shaden," she said, voice catching. "People will be eating them to treat the ronone. We should use them to grow more fruit instead."

Dante nodded. "Blays and I may be rixaka, but I doubt your friends will just hand us their shells. We'll stay here and watch over the tree."

She smiled, then hugged them both. "Thank you for this. A cure—I never thought it was possible."

She picked another fruit, tucked it in a pouch, and swam away from the island. Dante watched her recede into the trees.

"We have a decision to make," he said softly. "The *Sword of the South* will be back in a week."

Blays tipped back his head. "You're thinking about leaving."

"Thinking. I haven't decided."

"What about our promise to the Dresh?"

"Winden can use this tree to cure everyone. To unite the other villages against the Tauren. But accomplishing that could take months."

"We could always ask the *South* to come back later," Blays said. "Then again, outside of returning to the tower to put a blade in Vordon's heart, I'm not sure how much more help we can be."

"You sound like you're ready to go, too."

"We still have to deal with Gladdic. You have a major metropolitan area to govern. And I have to get back to Minn at some point."

"We don't have to figure this out now. We can see how the next week goes, then either leave with the ship or ask them to return in a few more weeks."

Blays scowled at the placid waters. "I really don't like the idea of running out on them. Even if Niles brings some allies on board, there's no guarantee the coalition will be able to stand against the Tauren."

"Do you want to take another shot at Vordon?"

"What if we take the *Sword of the South* back to Deladi? We kill Vordon, then make a big show about leaving on the boat. That way, the Tauren will blame us awful rixen rather than the Kandeans."

"And that would let you feel like we'd discharged your duty to the Dresh?"

"If casting down the tyrant driving the Tauren to war won't stop them, what else are we supposed to do? Murder every last one of their soldiers? There's limits to what we can accomplish."

Dante laughed. "I thought you were supposed to be the good one."

Blays shrugged. "If the Dresh were that good, they would have helped us find the Star Trees just for the sake of lifting the ronone. They're lucky we don't skip out on them right now."

The tree provided the only shade on the little island, but standing beneath it felt unnerving. They swam back to shore to get out of the sun. Two hours later, Winden returned with a handful of shells. They used them all to grow the tree and its fruit. If they'd spent that much nether on a palm or a pine, it might have grown high enough to pierce the Mists, but by the end of their efforts, the Star Tree was still only fifteen feet tall, generating a mere twenty fruit. Winden was going to have her work cut out for her.

"Could try growing more trees," Dante said. "Then again, it's probably more productive to focus on this one than to coax a bunch of seedlings to adulthood."

Winden gazed up at the branches. "We have many seeds now. More importantly, we have the knowledge. We can grow more later for everyone."

"Then you know what our next step should be? Writing that knowledge down. So it can't be lost again."

Winden made another trip back to Kandak, returning with three spearmen she trusted to keep silent. She posted them at the banks of the pool, then walked back to town with Dante and Blays. There, Dante wrote deep into the night, scrawling down everything they'd learned regarding the Star Tree's history and cultivation. In the morning, while Dante returned to the tree to harvest more fruit, Winden translated his Mallish notes into a Taurish copy.

When he came back to town, Winden sent a runner bound for the Dreaming Peaks. The messenger carried several of the lemon-sized fruit. With any luck, Niles could use them to convince the other groups to rally to the Kandeans.

Dante didn't yet have the heart to tell Winden that he and Blays would be gone before the coalition could take shape. But the timing might be a good thing. If they were able to strike Vordon down, that might fracture their alliances. Weakened on all sides, they'd be more apt to strike a truce with the other islanders. In the meantime, Dante would continue to grow more fruit.

The runner should have been gone for at least a week. But the very next day, he burst into the house where Dante, Blays, and Winden were discussing the logistics of curing all of Kandak. His face was so sweaty and red it looked like he'd been running all morning.

"The Tauren," he panted. "They march on the Dreaming

Peaks. Their army is two thousand strong. And they'll be there in two days."

Winden's jaw dropped. "Who told you this?"

"Jolo. Niles sent him to warn us. But he was exhausted from running. When he told me, I turned back."

"What does Niles intend to do? He has two dozen men. He can't fight two thousand."

"He asks for all the help we can send," the runner said. "Vordon, he says we attacked the High Tower. He means to take the entire island. To pacify us for good."

Winden's face grayed. She thanked the man and sent him to spread the word.

"So we got a Star Tree," Blays said. "And in doing so, we sparked the Tauren into waging war."

Dante massaged the back of his neck. "This isn't our fault. It's always been Vordon's intention to take the whole island."

"Could be it was inevitable. But we're the ones who lit the fire under his ass."

"You think we have to fight them."

"It doesn't sound like we have a choice. They could be here in days."

"But we don't have to be," Dante said. Blays hesitated, rubbing his mouth.

"You mean to escape." Winden glanced between them, expression flat. "On your boat."

Dante's face reddened. "Would you blame us?"

"You are right. The Tauren, they would have come eventually whether or not the three of us had attacked their tower. My people will fight. But you have a choice."

Blays ran his hand through his hair. "What will you do?"

"Abandon the town. We can't let the Tauren find the tree. We'll fight from the jungle. Faced with destruction, the other peoples might join us."

"You could do that. Or we could stop the Tauren from ever

getting here."

Dante sputtered with laughter. "How do you intend to do that? Break the island in half?"

"Kind of the opposite. To reach Spearpoint, you called up a bridge of red-hot rock. What do you suppose would happen if you dumped that stuff on the Taurish army instead?"

"I can't do that anywhere. Most of the land isn't alive like that." Dante's eyes widened. "But the Dreaming Peaks are filled with hot springs. There must be melted rock there, too."

"Think we can make it there in two days?"

Dante moved to the door. "Grab your things. And make sure your sandals are tight. We've got a lot of running in our future."

Winden bent for her pack. "Two days might not be enough time to reach the Peaks."

"That's why you're staying here. Gather as many warriors as you can and lead them toward the Peaks. If we don't make it in time, we'll fight the enemy for every inch of the jungle."

She nodded. "Go. I'll see you there."

Dante grabbed his pack and his sword, belting it on as he strode through the sunny morning. Blays fell in beside him. As soon as Dante had his sword on, he broke into a jog. The path out of town was all uphill, but at least there was shade. At first he didn't think he'd last five minutes, let alone forty-odd miles of uneven ground, but he soon fell into a rhythm.

"Two thousand troops," Blays said, breath huffing lightly with each step. "That's a lot of men. Like two thousand of them."

"They always exaggerate the initial numbers. I wouldn't be surprised if it was fifteen hundred. Maybe even a thousand."

"And how many do you think the Kandeans can muster? Two hundred? Three, tops?"

"I might be able to cripple Vordon's army. But there's no way I can wipe it out completely."

Blays flicked the sweat from his forehead. "Vordon doesn't strike me as the type to lift his boot once it's on your neck. We need to be thinking of contingencies for after he makes it through the Peaks."

"There's a lot of ground between here and there. We'll make the most of it."

They alternated between running and walking. When their muscles declared there would be no more running, Dante used the nether to wash away their exhaustion. They reached the rope bridge on the way to Niles' temple.

"This might be a good spot for a stand," Blays said once they'd crossed over. "Though they'd probably just harvest a bridge across it. Or detour through the ridges there."

"Know where that won't work so well?"

"The Broken Valley."

Dante nodded. "That's our fallback."

As they ran on, they discussed logistics. As usual, Blays was a font of ideas. Dante picked at them, refining some and discarding others. They passed Niles' temple and crossed the up-and-down terrain to the Broken Valley. They stopped at its edge to catch their breath, sketch a quick map, and do some scheming, then crossed the ropes and vines to the other side. By day's end, they were more than halfway to the Dreaming Peaks. There was enough moonlight to see by, though, and they continued another few miles before packing it in.

Dante woke halfway through the night. He was so exhausted he mistook the sound of water for the surf. Which was several miles away. It was raining. Harder and harder by the moment.

Between the noise and the dampness, his sleep was interrupted a dozen times. By morning, the ground was absolutely sodden, the trail slick, sucking at their feet with every step, rendering it impossible to run. A sour node hardened in Dante's stomach. By late morning, things had dried enough to allow for fitful jogging, but they were losing time.

Up the washed-out trail, feet squelched through the muck, swishing through branches. Blays gestured into the shrubs. They withdrew from the path, crouching under the wet leaves.

A score of men appeared ahead, carrying long spears and longer faces. Niles marched at their head. His face bore any number of cuts and scratches and his clothes were filthy with mud.

Dante emerged from cover, waving his arms above his head. "Niles!"

The man reached for his sword, recognized Dante, then trudged forward. "You came."

Dante pressed his lips together. "Too late, by the look of it."

"They came straight to the Peaks. They outnumbered us a hundred times over. We had no choice but to retreat."

"There's no shame in not throwing yourself on the enemy's swords. Winden's gathering your troops as we speak. We'll meet her on the way back."

"It won't be enough." Niles grabbed his elbow. "Your ship's coming in soon, isn't it?"

"A few days. More than enough time to stick our boot up Tauren ass."

"You have to leave. We'll take to the jungle. Cure as many of our people as we can. And sail away."

Dante drew back his head. "You can't possibly be serious. We can fight them, Niles. And we can win."

The older man smiled sadly. "Heart and spirit can't beat raw numbers. You've already done more than I could have asked. With the Star Tree, we have the chance to live on. It just won't be here."

"Run away, if you think that's the best use of your legs. As for us, we'll meet Winden. And we'll make our stand."

"Why?" Niles crinkled the corners of his eyes, mouth a taut line. "This isn't your fight, Dante. It never was."

"You're right," Dante said. "Maybe this entire island deserves to burn down to ashes. Not just for what the Mallish did. The Dresh were slaughtering each other long before the invasion swept them away. That's how they lost the Star Trees in the first place. My people are no different—a thousand years ago, after decades of fighting, we all but obliterated an entire people. The history of humanity is the history of the strong killing the weak. The warlike killing the peaceful. It's probable that every one of us alive today is here because of some atrocity committed by our ancestors. Maybe there *are* no good people left. If there ever were any innocents in this world, I expect the guilty massacred them long ago.

"But despite everything, I'll help you. Because whatever your sins, the Tauren are much worse. They show no signs of an impending change of heart, either. Fighting them is our chance to restore some small piece of good to the world. And to finish my father's work."

Across from him, Niles' eyes were bright. He blinked back tears. Resolve spread across his face. "I don't know if we stand any chance to win. But you're right. We'll fight them. We'll fight to the very end."

"The Broken Valley," Blays said. "That's where we'll ground our spears. We'll fill the ravines with so many of their bodies you'll be able to walk across them."

Niles burst into laughter. "Remind me never to get on your bad side."

They turned and headed back the way they'd come in. Now that Niles was into the spirit of the thing, he spoke professionally and analytically, discussing how best to hold the valley and stall the Tauren without exposing their own troops to the danger of being cut off on one of the plateaus.

With the land continuing to dry out, they made good time, camping overnight and reaching the Broken Valley the next morning. There was no sign of Winden yet, but with so little time to spare, they prepared to hold the valley anyway, tearing down the ropes and vines near its southern edge. The work stirred up a number of rodents. Dante dispatched two of them, sending them miles south to watch for the advance of the Tauren.

That afternoon, they moved to the north side of the valley to take it in as a whole. Most of the little plateaus were distributed regularly, but here, there were two clusters large enough to hold scores of men, while being close enough to the north rim to minimize the risk of being cut off during a retreat. If the Tauren were foolish enough to engage them there, the Kandeans might be able to hold them off indefinitely. Niles' men went to work on the platforms, chopping down branches and small trees to build barricades. Dante strung multiple lines of vines between each one, along with others trailing down the sides of the plateaus to allow for a hastier withdrawal.

"I'd like to harass them for every foot of the valley," Niles said. "But it won't be easy. We don't have enough men to hold a line across the entire southern front. The Tauren could climb down whatever part we're not defending, bypassing our skirmishers altogether."

Blays scratched his jaw. "They'll have two options: descend to the floor and hack their way through the growth, or cross from platform to platform. Either way, they'll be slow enough for us to outmaneuver them."

"They will have the numbers, though. We'll have to be very careful not to get flanked."

"We'll hurt them as best we can." Dante gestured to the northern cliffs they were standing on, which were far narrower than the southern approach, no more than five hundred feet across. "But here's where they'll be most vulnerable. Trying to cross from the platforms to the cliffs. They won't be able to bring their troops across fast enough to hold out. We'd slaughter each man as he came over. They'll have to hike up the cliffs, where we can fire down on them all the while. Will they even be able to get up?"

"Look, they'll post their archers on platforms near enough to fire back. We won't be able to shoot at their advance without exposing ourselves." Niles turned in a circle, surveying the area. "I wish we had some high ground to fire down from."

"What, you mean like this?" Dante nicked the back of his arm and plunged a swath of nether into the earth. The dirt swelled, raising five feet high. He shaped it into a rampart ten feet across and twenty feet long.

Niles' men watched, wide-eyed. When Dante stepped back, Niles laughed, smacking himself on the thigh. "How much more of that can you do?"

"That depends on how many days they give us."

"Say they occupy a platform with a hundred archers. Would you be able to topple the whole thing?"

"Only if there were no other nethermancers," Dante said. "If there are, they'll be able to stop me. Besides, if this battle goes like our previous ones, I think I'll be too busy negating their attacks to make many of my own."

During this, Blays had wandered off on his own, inspecting the cliff and the ground around it. He returned, smirking.

"I know that look," Dante said. "About to suggest something fiendish?"

"Barring miracles, we'll have to fall back eventually. So why not make that part of the plan?"

"To do what? Hand them a faster victory?"

"We'll hold them off for a while. But before they've got enough people up here to overwhelm us, we'll retreat. They'll want to seize the rampart at once. Almost certainly before they've got everyone up here. Unfortunately for them, however, they will discover they've advanced into a field of harvested candlefruit."

"Which we'll set on fire," Dante said. "Splitting them off from their reinforcements. We'll massacre them."

Niles brows raised. "That might win the battle on its own. At the very least, they'll have to regroup, giving us time to get out of here."

"And then what?"

"That depends on how fortune rewards us, doesn't it? If we're in good shape, we can press the attack. If that would be too risky, it might be best to retreat all the way to Kandak. It will stretch their supply lines while contracting our own."

Under Niles' direction, Dante expanded the rampart several more feet. Finished, he got a candlefruit from one of the men and grew a thick line of candlefruit shrubs in front of the cliffs. He kept the plants squat, heightening the grass around them to conceal them.

With a few more days and a heavy supply of shaden, he might be able to make the north end of the valley nearly impregnable. Then again, if he fortified it too well, the Tauren might choose to detour around the other side of the Jush Backbone. Dante had to strike a delicate balance between a defense strong enough to give them a chance of winning, but not so obviously strong that the Tauren would bypass them altogether.

That afternoon, a pair of scouts trotted in from the north. Winden was on her way. She had close to two hundred warriors with her. A small reserve remained in Kandak in case the Tauren tried any advance raids. She arrived within an hour. Her people carried an array of spears and bows, along with a handful of swords and pieces of armor.

Winden greeted Niles, then sized up Dante and Blays. "Then there was no engagement at the Peaks?"

"We didn't make it in time," Dante said. "Vordon's army is untouched. We'll have to break him here."

They met with the men, familiarizing them with the points of defense and the general plan. For the most part, the warriors were able-bodied, but few had seen combat. They all had some training, however—the last few months of Tauren raids had been good for that much—and many were capable bow hunters. They spent the rest of the daylight drilling, with special emphasis on quickly climbing across the ropes between plateaus.

As dusk neared, Dante's rodent scouts located the Tauren. They were less than ten miles to the south. And still on the move. He perched a rat beside the path, counting soldiers. Some were spread out through the trees, making a precise count difficult, but he believed two thousand had indeed been an exaggeration.

Fifteen hundred was not far off, however. A full quarter of that with swords and some bits of armor. Vordon walked near the head of their column, face printed with a self-satisfied smile. A few dozen personal guards, commanders, and advisors clouded about him.

"They're on the march," he told the others. "There's no chance they'll be here in time to fight, but their scouts may be in the area. They could be on us tomorrow."

Niles grunted. "They will be. Every day they wait is another day they have to feed themselves. And another day for us prepare."

Dusk fell. The Tauren walked on. He was sure they'd stop when the daylight ended, but they stayed on the march, guided by the trail. Another hour, and they were upon the valley's southern cliffs. There, scores of camp fires sprung up, studding the darkness with shimmering orange light.

26

Perhaps the fires were meant to intimidate the Kandeans, but Dante appreciated their cheery glow. They announced that the Tauren were finally making camp for the night. He kept one of his rats close enough to Vordon to catch snatches of conversation. Aware that the Kandeans waited across the valley, Vordon sent scouts out on the nearby rocky islands protruding from the ground, harvesting vine ladders to link them to the cliff.

He talked surprisingly little strategy. Either he'd anticipated a battle here and had already discussed it, or he thought his army was so much larger it didn't matter where he fought. By the time Vordon lay down to sleep, all Dante had learned was that the Tauren seemed to be planning to hack their way across the valley floor.

After that, there was nothing to do but watch the firelight flicker.

"He's right over there," Blays said. "Think we should take a run at him?"

"Too dangerous," Dante said. "Even if you shadowalk up to him, he'll be able to feel you. If we die before the battle, the Kandeans are doomed."

"I don't suppose there's much point, is there? Plant him in the dirt, and we'll still have to contend with his fifteen hundred friends."

Since the arrival of the Tauren, Winden and Niles had been speaking with the warriors and dispatching scouts. With this concluded, they joined Dante and Blays in staring across the valley.

"Morning's eight hours away," Winden said. "That means you still have eight hours to run."

Blays laughed first. "I'm afraid you're cursed to be stuck with us. The good news is that the curse might not last another 24 hours."

"I've never seen them in such numbers," Niles said.

"The fires always make an army look bigger," Dante muttered. "They probably camped in plain view intending to give us a poor night's sleep."

Blays stretched his arms. "We'll have to thwart them by turning in early."

He soon made good on that threat. Winden departed a few minutes later.

"I know you don't think much of us," Niles said. "But if we make it through this, you'll be remembered here forever."

Dante rubbed his eyes. "Then I'll try extra hard not to die tomorrow."

They said their goodbyes. Dante slept as best he could, which turned out to be better than expected. There were no alarums from the scouts, and every time he woke up and checked in on his rat, the enemy camp looked at rest.

He got up for good around three in the morning. The Kandeans rose, preparing quickly. Within twenty minutes, they were climbing across the ropes and vines. These were stretched horizontally, meaning the going was much slower than on his first visit to the valley, when they'd used the handlebars to skim from tree to tree. Now, however, they had several different lines, allowing the troops to advance steadily. As dawn neared, they arranged themselves on four platforms just out of bow range of the southern cliffs.

After their long march the previous day, the Tauren were slow to get moving. Sun shined across the rocky islands. With his troops arming themselves, Vordon walked to the edge of the cliffs and stared out at the Kandeans. It was too far to see his expression, but Dante was sure he was smiling.

"Is this all of you?" Vordon called in his Deladi-accented Taurish. "Maybe I don't even need Kandak."

"Feel free to turn around," Dante yelled back.

"I don't think so. I think I will walk straight through you, take your town, and kill anyone stupid enough to have stayed there."

Niles moved to the edge of the platform and jabbed his finger at Vordon. "We'll bury you in this valley. Your loss today will be your final legacy."

Vordon laughed and pulled down his trousers, waggling himself at them. "This will be one of the last things you ever see. Enjoy it!"

He returned to his people, who were lighting fires and cooking food. Completely unhurried. Dante's head throbbed from lack of sleep. They'd eaten a breakfast of cold san paste. At that moment, he would have traded all his other skills for the ability to conjure up a plate of hot bacon.

At nine o'clock, Vordon's commanders moved along the many tents. The warriors rousted themselves. Archers formed up along the bluff. One man fired a single shot, testing range. It fell well short of Dante's platform.

A mass of Tauren moved two hundred yards to the east toward a trail zagging down to the valley floor. Niles yelled to his people. Dante, Winden, and the two lesser Kandean Harvesters sent vines flying between the pillars of land, bridging a path to the east. Warriors climbed along them, supported by loops of rope slung over the vines. Dante queued up, among the first twenty to make the crossing. He grabbed hold of the vine and swung off the ledge, legs dangling.

He reached the next platform, continuing immediately to the next. Directly across from it, Tauren soldiers made their way down the trail. Dante reached out to the dirt and rock within it. Before he could shift a single pebble, a light-haired woman on the top of the cliff splayed out her hand, knocking away his grasp.

He tried again, testing her. Again, she dislodged him. Her attacks didn't feel especially refined. More like she was swinging a mallet around. She was probably drawing on the shaden. Pointless to exhaust himself against that. Besides, even if he were able to kill a few of them on the switchback, ruining it in the process, they'd simply go harvest another way down. He could only watch as the Tauren descended to the valley floor.

There, the Tauren hacked their way forward with machetes, clearing a path. Niles' archers crowded onto the island with Dante, along with the platform beside it.

Blays squinted. "It can't be this easy, can it? They're like cows leading themselves into the slaughtering pen."

With the exception of some tall brush, they'd have a clear shot down on the enemy. Slowed by their work, they'd be easy marks for the archers' arrows. Even as Dante thought this, runners moved along the cliffs, carrying broad, curved shields. These were clearly lightweight, but they had no doubt been harvested for impenetrability. Dante lobbed a bolt of nether at the lead runner. Again, the light-haired woman deflected it.

With the shields delivered to the valley floor, soldiers took them to the front of the path and fanned out to hold them over the machete-carriers' heads. Two minutes later, Niles gave the order to fire.

Forty archers unleashed a volley. The arrows soared through a low arc, striking the shields in a cluster of sharp raps. But there were a pair of screams, too. A shield faltered. The archers nocked a second round. As they drew back their strings, the female sorcerer unleashed a blast of shadows toward the bowmen. Dante sucked in breath, slamming nether into the incoming strike. Black dust exploded from the contact, twinkling into the open air and fading away.

Under steady fire from the archers, the path-cutters veered to their right, working their way around the back of a plateau across from the Kandeans. The woman on the cliffs gestured. Dante saw no result, but he could guess what she was doing: harvesting a ladder up the back of the plateau. His suspicion was confirmed when a line of soldiers jogged down the cliff, followed the trail, and reappeared on the platform. Taking cover in the trees there, they opened fire on the Kandeans, driving Niles' archers back into the cover of the vegetation.

Which allowed the trail-cutters to push forward under minimal fire. A few dropped to the Kandeans' arrows, but the path advanced steadily. The female nethermancer attempted the occasional attack on the archers, but she, like Dante, appeared to be conserving her strength.

A second group of enemy soldiers descended the bluff and made their way up the plateau next to the one they'd already claimed. Now fired on from two angles, the Kandeans were reduced to erratic sniping. Niles called for a withdrawal. The harried archers retreated across the ropes to the platform behind them. Dante was among the last to leave. This process repeated across the Kandean lines until all four groupings had retreated.

The Tauren's strategy was sound. Rather than advancing more quickly across the platforms, where a mistake or a Kandean gambit might cripple their entire army, they were taking the safe route through the ravines. It would be slow going, and they'd concede a trickle of casualties for the lengthy duration of the advance. But they had more than enough troops to sustain those losses.

And it granted them zero risk of an unfavorable outcome. Soon enough, they'd cross the valley. And there would be nothing left to stand between them and the Kandeans.

Blays found his way next to Dante. "This is less like a battle and more like a life-sized game of Nulladoon. The only thing missing is the mad king ordering us around. Unless that's you."

"You know how these things go."

"Do I? Because I don't remember ever swinging from platform to platform, outnumbered ten to one, while all the other guys are doing the work."

"We're feeling each other out. I doubt there'll be a major engagement before the north cliffs. If there is, then either they've made a major mistake, or we have."

Over the next several minutes, the Tauren pushed them back another row of islands, and then a third. Only half the Tauren were actively engaged in the assault. The other half, including Vordon and most of his court, remained on the southern cliffs, which were now several hundred yards away. The only sorcerer on the front lines was the light-haired woman.

"Good news." Dante smiled. "They've made a mistake."

The Tauren were presently occupying three adjacent plateaus and the two behind those, overlooking and defending the advance of their soldiers through the thickets below. The enemy nethermancer was on the frontmost central platform. Across from her, Dante flung shadows at the archers sharing her position. She clubbed aside each strike, as aggressive as always. Drawing on one of his shaden, Dante sent a second salvo at the archers. While the light-haired woman contended with these, he moved into the tree above her. Branches stabbed down at her head and shoulders. She shouted a curse, sending the nether into them, bending them aside.

Giving Dante the opportunity to split the earth she stood upon.

With an ear-piercing crack, the rim of the plateau cleaved beneath her. She turned, jumping toward solid ground, but Dante rooted her feet in place, sticking her to the falling rock. The woman's scream punched through the clatter of stones. The shorn-off rim slammed into the ravine below, rattling the ground beneath Dante's feet. A hemisphere of dust erupted from the impact.

And with no friendly nethermancers within range, the archers were now painfully acquainted with Dante's wrath.

Shadows whipped across the divide, felling one Tauren soldier after another. They broke from cover, rushing for the ropes at the rear of the platform. Dante homed in on a knot of five men, picking them off one by one. After he'd slain the first four of them, the lone survivor swerved to the edge of the rocky island and leaped out into open space.

In less than a minute, he'd killed some thirty men, draining one shell and starting in on another in the process. A contingent of replacements was scurrying along the ropes from the southern cliffs. As when he'd lifted the land bridge to Spearpoint, the quick use of the shaden left Dante's nerves feeling frayed, implying he couldn't keep it up all day.

Still, with no one close enough to resist him, he went after the archers on the plateau next to the one he'd destroyed, slaying just enough of them to flush them from cover, exposing them to Kandean fire. Together, he and the warriors shredded their way through another thirty of the enemy before the first black bolts raced to intercept his.

Vordon had arrived, his helm gleaming in the afternoon sun. Backed by two men and a woman—nethermancers, certainly—he stomped to the edge of the outcrop, pointing at Dante.

"You think you're so strong?" he bellowed. "My men fight clean, and you kill them like ants?"

Dante moved from behind a tree, keeping the nether at hand. "For years, you've used your armies to squeeze the life out of these people. But you've never faced someone like me. As long as you hide in the rear, your people will die."

Vordon clenched his hands into fists. He drew a knife and

slashed it across the skin of his bare stomach, feeding his blood to the nether. He lashed across the gap, hammering Dante with a barrage of blows, any one of which would have torn his flesh to the bone. Dante drew hard on his second shaden, barely keeping up his defense.

"Don't just stand there!" Blays yelled at the warriors. "*Shoot him!*"

The awestruck archers nocked arrows, firing on Vordon. He danced back, harvesting a wall of shrubs in front of him.

His three nethermancers dispersed across the nearby platforms, attacking any archer who rose to take aim. Dante was so busy battling them off he had no time to strike back. Winden assisted him, along with her two Harvesters, but they were modestly talented. In rapid succession, the Kandeans were forced back three rows of plateaus, struggling to regroup. With each retreat, Vordon and his sorcerers hurried along the ropes to the newly-vacated platforms, pressing the attack.

Throughout this, Blays kept busy giving orders to one of the divisions of archers. During a lull, he crossed over to Dante's platform, sweaty and dirt-streaked.

"Well," he said, "if your mission was to make Vordon fall in hate-love with you, you've succeeded wildly. Which has given me an idea."

Dante kept both eyes out for any sign of incoming shadows. "Which is?"

"Next time we retreat, I take a stroll into the nether. And stay right here. Until Vordon delivers himself to me."

"Which will leave you surrounded by Tauren soldiers. And probably at least one other nethermancer."

"I'll be cutting his throat, not making him dinner. I'll be invisible again within two seconds."

"Unless one of their sorcerers shoves you out of the shadows. Like the Minister did back in Spiren."

Blays waved a hand. "Then I guess you'll just have to keep the others off of me."

Dante glanced across the platforms. So far, their own losses had been extremely light. But other than his unfettered assault on the Tauren following the death of their nethermancer, the enemy hadn't lost more than a few dozen men.

"Killing Vordon might crack them," he said. "But it might not. They'll still outnumber us many times over. I'm not sure I see them retreating."

"If they're that much stronger than us, then the only way we can win is by rolling the dice. They're playing too conservatively to exploit. By the time they push us out of the valley, I don't think we'll have reduced their numbers sufficiently for the candlefruit scheme to be a death blow."

Dante swore. "I've been thinking the same thing. Take your shot. But if anything goes wrong, you run away like your feet are on fire."

Blays grinned, loosening his swords in their sheaths. As the trail-cutters advanced below them, the Tauren archers intensified their fire. The Kandeans began crossing to the next plateaus. Blays tucked himself into the growth on the middle of the island. And disappeared. Dante pulled himself along the ropes to the next island, sticking to its southern side to keep close to the action.

A few Tauren shock troops were the first to cross to the vacated platform. They made a fast search, securing it, then beckoned to Vordon, who waited behind. Vordon lashed himself to the ropes and pulled himself along beneath them. Once he was a quarter of the way across, a gangly nethermancer Dante had seen earlier followed after him.

Dante's eyes skipped between the two climbers. Would Blays have the sense to take out Vordon, then light out for safety? Or would he try to take out two birds with one stone? If so—

Halfway along the ropes, Vordon came to a stop. Dante was hundreds of feet away. Much too far to make out the specifics of what the man was doing. What he wasn't doing, however, was clear: moving onto the platform.

Dante cupped his hands to his mouth. In Mallish, he yelled, "Blays! Blays, he *knows!*"

With no trees above Vordon, he hung in broad daylight. And there was no mistaking the flock of darkness forming around his hands.

At the far end of the plateau, a figure shimmered into being. Blays swung his sword at the ropes with all his might, severing them. Vordon and the long-limbed nethermancer dropped into the canyon below. The shadows sizzled from Vordon's hands: not toward Blays, but at the upcoming ground.

Tauren soldiers charged toward Blays, firing arrows. He blinked away. Dante lobbed nether at the soldiers' backs, but only two bolts made it through the defenses of the two sorcerers watching from the platform where Vordon had fallen. With no idea where Blays had gone to, Dante could only watch helplessly as Vordon's two Harvesters grew vines to replace the cut rope. Tauren soldiers stormed across, slashing swords and spears through every square inch of grass and brush.

At the edge where Blays had disappeared, one of the Tauren shouted. Others clustered there. A great cheer went up from their people. The crowd parted. A man strode forward, sunlight glinting from his steely helmet.

"Is that all you have?" Vordon yelled. "This snake of yours, he's dead. And now I come for you."

He followed this with a brutal assault of shadows, occupying every whit of Dante's attention. As Vordon's troops moved onto the other platforms, the Kandeans withdrew once again. Dante held position as long as he could. With arrows and nether flashing past him, he turned and ran for the ropes. Halfway across, he paused, seized by the sudden urge to let go and let the fall take care of the rest. He'd see Blays again soon enough in the Mists.

But nearly two hundred Kandeans were watching him,

yelling for him to cross over. Back home, tens of thousands awaited his return to Narashtovik. There were many times in life, especially one as turbid as his, when it would be easier to let go. For all his loss, though, and all his pain, he couldn't. Too many people needed him. To keep them safe. To carve out a small slice of the world and make it better.

And he needed revenge.

Fast as he could, he swung along the rope, drawing himself to the other side and dropping to the ground amidst the defenders. As he took a long breath, Blays walked out from the trees. He was scratched up and grimier than ever, but wholly intact.

Dante laughed out loud. "Lyle's balls, he said you were dead!"

Blays shrugged. "You know all these people are liars. I had to do a bit of running and a lot of climbing, but strenuous though it was, I wouldn't claim it was a fate on par with death."

"Did you see how Vordon survived?"

"Grew a giant mattress of grass beneath him. Looked like he might have broken a leg in the fall, but he appeared to have dealt with that."

"What about the gangly man?"

Blays chuckled. "Our tall friend made a very long splatter."

"So at least some good came of your little adventure. No sense in trying it again. Vordon's wise to your tricks."

"That's about the only area he's wise. I mean, have you seen his hat?"

The battle quieted to a steady pattern. Each time the Kandeans retreated from a platform, Tauren archers claimed it, allowing them to cover the termite-like advance of the troops down on the ground. As these closed on a Kandean plateau, the archers there were able to pick off a few of the enemy, but not nearly enough to make a difference in the overall numbers.

By early afternoon, the Kandeans had been pushed halfway across the valley. They might have kept on in this way all day, slowly whittling down the Tauren, but they were having increasingly large difficulties removing their own wounded from the scene. Their stock of arrows wasn't getting any larger, either. They hastened the retreat, falling back two or three platforms at once, offering token resistance, then moving back again. In less than two hours, they stood on the last plateaus clustered along the northern cliffs.

There, Niles found Dante. "The warriors are getting tired. I don't think there's much sense in trying to hold this position."

"Agreed. We should save our strength for our stand on the cliffs. Let's go get dug in as fast as we can."

Niles bellowed the orders. Kandeans streamed across the ropes, found their footing, and shuffled off toward the ramparts. The warriors moved sluggishly, sweating freely. Dante regretted not having grown a few shade trees along the fortifications, but it was far too late for that now.

Besides, they wouldn't be out in the direct sun for long. The plan was to "break" after the briefest of encounters — to spring the trap.

Archers lined up along the raised arm of land. Spearmen planted themselves in front, supported by skirmishers equipped with a variety of clubs, swords, hatchets, and slings. Over in the valley, the Tauren seized the closest platforms. The trail-cutters angled toward the eastern edge of the cliffs, where their ascent would be out of range of the fortified archers. Reaching the base of the cliffs took the enemy a good half hour, allowing the Kandeans some much-needed rest.

While this was going on, Dante tracked down Winden. She was as dirty and sweaty as everyone else, but showed no major wounds.

"How are you doing?" he said. "Got any arrows left in the quiver? Nether-wise, I mean. Not real ones."

She tipped her head from side to side. "Less than I'd like. The shaden, I can use one more, maybe two. Any more, and I'll be burned."

"Don't be afraid to use almost all of it. Save a bit for some final emergency, sure. But if we can't break them here, I don't think we ever will."

"I've never seen anything like this. So many dead. And it's only begun, hasn't it?"

"I'm afraid so." He put a hand on her shoulder. "If it's any comfort, we're doing this so your children never have to face something like this themselves."

"Do you think so? The years are cruel to memory. They erode it like the Currents of Spearpoint. The new generation forgets. And fights new wars of their own."

He withdrew to the ramparts to discuss final tactics with Niles. The first of the Tauren scaled the cliffs to the left, hastily digging in, supported by the archers on the plateaus behind them.

"If I were them," Niles said, "I'd wait to blow the horns until my whole army was up here. They do that, and we'll have to be as precise as the stars. Too many of them get past the candlefruit, and we won't be able to resist them."

"But if we let in too few, we might not kill enough to drive back the rest." Dante sighed, swabbing sweat from his face. "I suppose we'll have to play it by ear."

"Play it by ear?" Niles laughed. "Is that how you conduct all your wars?"

"Eventually, yes. If you have a problem with that, feel free to go find your own war."

"Is something the matter? Normally when you say something like that to me, it's spoken like an insult. That, though? That sounded like a joke."

Dante chuckled. "I must be tired."

The Tauren piled onto the bluff, showing no sign of haste. They seemed to think—quite rightly—that the pace of the battle was now theirs, and there was no sense mounting a charge before they were damn good and ready.

Blays jogged up, eyeing the growing number of enemy soldiers. "Think we ought to do something about that?"

"What, the army?" Dante said. "What do you want to do, *fight* them?"

"How many of them do you think we're going to be able to take out with this little trick? Two hundred? Three? That still leaves a thousand of them. Who, by nature of the fact they'll have just been outwitted, will be apt to be considerably more disciplined during the next engagement."

"Probably."

"So we need them to come for us before their whole army's up here. That way, if everything goes well for us, we can run over to the cliffs and smash up whatever they've got *there*. Before they've got enough men up top to hold us off."

"Optimistic," Dante said. "But the only way to do this is to keep putting ourselves in position to succeed. So how do we coax them over here now?"

"Stage an argument. Make it look like most of us are storming off, with the rest remaining to make a suicidal stand."

"What's to stop them from waiting anyway?"

"Nothing," Blays said. "Except they've just spent the last five hours cutting their way across a miserable valley while getting their noses bloodied at every turn. At this point, they'll be starving for blood."

"Or they might want to seize the moment before we think better and regroup. Well, there's no harm in trying."

"Excellent. I'll start: your ego is of troubling size, and you don't bathe enough."

Dante folded his arms. "You're too impulsive. And prone to running your mouth. As proven by your readiness to launch into this without letting the others know the plan."

They spoke with Niles and Winden, who jogged off to spread the word to their people. After the argument peaked, Winden and Niles would storm off with a hundred and fifty of the warriors, leaving two score with Dante and Blays—only to return to the field once the Tauren were committed.

This settled, Dante and Niles went at each other, shouting back and forth in Taurish. Blays and Winden joined in, their tone raising by the second. Their warriors exchanged uneasy glances. It wasn't long before their shouting match was drawing attention from the soldiers on the fringe of the Tauren.

After an appropriately apocalyptic exchange of curses and insults, Niles spat at Dante's feet, then turned his back and walked away. Winden followed. So did a trickle of warriors, then a flood. Dante gave a sloppy speech about the virtues of bravery, loyalty, making a stand, and so forth. A few dozen troops stayed put or returned from the exodus, establishing a defensive formation on the rampart.

At the cliffs, the Tauren stirred, pulling together a mixed force of archers, swordsmen, and spearmen. Vordon moved among them. Within five minutes, he'd assembled a troop of some three hundred. More than enough to squash the paltry resistance Dante headed.

They moved through the thinly-wooded ground between the cliffs and the rampart. Some of the Kandeans looked terrified—faces tight, eyes wide—but the number coming for them was perfect. Many of the Tauren would be hurt or killed by the candlefruit. The rest would be thrown into disarray. If Blays could dash through the shadows to Vordon, and cut him down early in the engagement, Dante, Winden, and Blays could carve through the rank and file. In one stroke, the Tauren would lose a quarter of their force, along with their leader.

At the cliff's edge, more warriors climbed up from the ravines. Vordon's vanguard was spread into ten loose rows. The first ranks crossed into the field of candlefruit. They marched on, oblivious to what lay within the grass.

"Something's off here," Blays said. "He's not sending off any scouts. Or trying to flank us. Either our steel-worshipping friend is very confident in his coming victory, or we're missing something."

"Find it fast. As soon as the third-to-last row is into the fruit, I'm lighting the fires."

The front ranks were now within bow range, but the Kandeans held their fire, as if waiting to make the most of their shots. Behind the rampart, a harsh crackle filled the air. Dante whirled. At the rear of their lines, a thick line of brown and green matter burst from the earth, congealing into a dense hedge six feet tall. Before he knew what was happening, the harvesting was complete. His force was enclosed on the rear. And cut off from all aid.

27

Nether winged from the oncoming Tauren, streaking toward a Kandean archer. Dante's mind raced. They were separated from their main force. The exact thing they'd meant to do to the Tauren, over a hundred of whom were now through the strip of concealed candlefruit. He needed to open a path through the hedge that hemmed them in, but more importantly, he had to stop any more of the enemy from being able to reach them.

Which meant lighting the fruit sooner than he'd intended. Even if, by some miracle, they survived this encounter, it wouldn't be enough to break the Tauren. But that objective was now lost. Pursuing it would mean the death of them all.

Ignoring the incoming nether, even as it spun the archer from his feet in a spray of blood, Dante delved into the candlefruit running across the middle of the oncoming Tauren. And set it aflame.

With a great whump, white light flared across the line. Some of the oily fruit were so ripe they burst, setting aflame those beside them. Tauren screamed. Those caught within the fires rushed about in panic, slapping at their clothes, some driven so mad by their pain they did nothing but run aimlessly, as if they could outdistance the oil-fueled flames clinging to their skins.

The two groups were now caught in an arena of death: ringed on one side by fire, and on the other by a wall of wood. Dante turned, meaning to blast a hole through the hedge, but bolts of nether streamed directly toward him. He had no choice but to stand and counter the attacks. He stood within a haze of shadows, dark blots arcing through the sky like the inverse of the sparks soaring from the fires.

A small group of Kandeans rushed the growth, hacking at it with machetes and axes. But the Tauren were already charging, swords and spears lifted as they yelled a wordless rallying cry. Blays lifted his swords and rushed them. The Kandeans jolted forward, more than a few looking shocked to find themselves moving toward an enemy who, despite the anarchy of the back rows, still outnumbered them at least two-fold.

Blays met the first of the Tauren, cutting him down without slowing. He spun deeper into the ranks, holding off three at a time as the Kandeans caught up and engaged. Erratic arrows hissed back and forth. Dante exhausted the nether within one shell and tapped into the next. His nerves were starting to waver. On neutral ground, he might have been able to batter Vordon down, but he'd already spent much of his strength while the Tauren leader had largely let his sorcerers do his fighting for him.

If Blays were to shadowalk, he might be able to behead Vordon while the man engaged with Dante. But the outnumbered Kandeans were barely holding the line. If Blays left them, they'd collapse in seconds. And Dante would die as well.

The field stank of the greasy smoke enfolding it. Within the pall, it was increasingly difficult to make out Vordon's strikes. Dante knocked aside a flurry of three. The fourth lagged behind. He didn't spot it until it was an instant away. He swung a clumsy bludgeon of shadows against it, deflecting and blunting it, but a splinter drove through. It struck him in the ribs with the bite of frozen iron.

He gasped, staggering back. A rock turned under his foot and he sat down hard. Ahead, Blays dropped back a step, swords slapping away a forest of spears.

A cheer went up behind him. Dante risked a glance at the hedge. There, Winden sprinted through a hole gouged in the growth, followed by a column of her warriors.

"Regroup!" Dante called. He found his feet, parrying another volley of Vordon's strikes.

Blays led a disciplined retreat up the slopes of the rampart. The Tauren, outnumbered for the first time in the battle, hesitated. The attacks on Dante ceased. Aided by Winden's nether, the Kandeans smashed into the waiting Tauren, obliterating the front line in seconds.

Niles ran to Dante, eyes dropping to the blood seeping through his torn shirt. "We have to get out of here. Their reserves are circling us already."

Dante peered into the smoke, but he could see no trace of Vordon. Corpses and the injured were strewn across the field. "Get our wounded out of here. We'll be right on your heels."

Niles ran off, accompanied by a growing knot of warriors. Some joined Blays in the assault while the others gathered up any of their fallen who weren't obviously dead and hauled them through the portal in the hedge. Dante used the reprieve to draw the darkness into his wound and stanch the bleeding. The remaining Tauren trapped inside the fires were wavering, on the edge of a rout, but if the Kandeans stayed any longer, they'd wind up routed in return. Dante called to Winden and Blays. They led their people in an orderly withdrawal. The Tauren didn't so much as pretend to give chase.

Dante filed up with the others and jogged through the cleft in the wall of growth. Seeing them coming, Niles ordered his people to retreat to the north. Dante moved up beside Niles.

The man glanced at him, soot-streaked and haggard. "What happened back there?"

"Their Harvesters must have circled around," Dante said. "Sprung their own trap on us. It's a small miracle any of us made it out."

"Too many of us didn't."

Dante regarded the mass of troops moving along the trail to the north. They'd managed to stave off total disaster, but they'd lost at least fifteen on the spot, with an equal number of freshly wounded. Such casualties would mean nothing to the Tauren. But it represented nearly a fifth of the Kandeans.

"What's the plan?" Dante said.

Niles sighed lengthily. "Get away before the Tauren give chase. After that…" He shook his head.

"We're down a quarter of our people. We gave much better than we got with the candlefruit, but we didn't take down half as many as I was hoping for. Vordon's still out there, too."

"We can't risk another battle today. Our troops have exhausted themselves and most of theirs haven't yet taken the field." Niles ran a hand down his face, smudging the sweat and ash. "It's over, isn't it? That was our best chance. The only thing left is to go to Kandak, gather our people, and flee into the woods."

"We fought hard. Made them pay in blood for every foot of ground they took. You should be proud."

"I am. But sometimes pride isn't enough."

They trudged on. Blays and a few of the less-exhausted warriors prowled the forest to their rear, wary of the Tauren. The enemy still had to maneuver the remainder of their army up onto the bluff, at which point they'd spend some time regrouping, but the Kandeans wouldn't have much of a head start.

Especially the way they were slogging along. Many of their wounded had to be carried. Others limped heavily.

Less than ten minutes into the retreat, Blays jogged up next to him. "This is no good. At this pace, they'll be on us by nightfall."

"I was just thinking the same thing. Niles!" Dante waved the man over. "Gather all the wounded. Everyone who's not going to be able to march for the rest of the day."

The other man narrowed his eyes. "We're not going to leave them."

"I have no intention of doing that. Now quit being an asshole and do as I say."

Niles tipped back his head, but moved off without another word, bringing together all those hurt the worst, from gut wounds to broken legs to split scalps that wouldn't quit bleeding.

"Keep the column moving," Dante said. "We'll catch up once we're fit to do so."

Niles adopted an appropriately sheepish look and led the march on its way. While Blays and his scouts roved to the south, Dante performed hasty triage, starting with those with leg wounds. He moved on to the pair of scalp wounds, saving for last those with deep injuries to the guts.

The shadows came more and more slowly. He pushed through it, fueled by a mounting anger at the resentful nether. Not all those he patched up arose from unconsciousness. In that case, he directed two or three of the healed to take up the sleeping man or woman and carry them to Niles. At last, he saw to the final casualty, then lay back in the shaded grass.

Someone was shaking his shoulder. He jarred awake, punching at the air.

Blays bent like a reed, ducking the blow. "It pains me to criticize anyone taking the time for a nap. But in this case, it's probably not wise to do so less than a mile distant from the army of a thousand foes."

With Blays' help, Dante got to his feet. They moved to rejoin the column. Dante didn't have the strength to do more than walk. The shadows kept their distance. If he forced them to come, even if he used the shaden, he'd burn himself. He might not wake for days, if ever. That meant he had to walk on until his legs gave out, too. If they faced the Tauren again that day, none of them would come out of it alive.

Some of their people still couldn't wake up, let alone walk on their own power, but these were now far fewer. Few enough to be borne along by those who still had some strength left. The sun dwindled. They rested briefly, then moved on, continuing by the moonlight shining through the canopy before making camp in the jungle.

They ate, drew up a scouting schedule, and slept. A warrior nudged Dante awake well before dawn. Every piece of him ached, from the arches of his feet to the brain in his skull. The nether had returned to him, however. He soothed his pains. As the camp stirred, he visited the injured he hadn't been able to treat the day before.

Groggily, they got on the move. At rougher spots in the trail, Dante delved into the nether and tore up the ground behind them. Shortly after first light, Blays loped in and reported the Tauren were on the move. The Kandeans had a comfortable three-mile lead on them. Driven by the need to return home and get their civilians to safety, the warriors continued to push themselves as hard as they could.

That afternoon, they passed by the mountain temple where they'd first met Niles. Beside the rope bridge, which would have taken their people an hour to cross, Winden and Dante harvested a platform of trees across the gap overlooking the sea.

Blays shot them both a look. "We couldn't have done this the *first* time we came here?"

Winden shrugged. "We've never wanted it to be easy to reach Kandak. Now you know why."

Once the last warrior was across, they knocked down the growth and chopped through the rope bridge. It wouldn't slow the Tauren any longer than it had stalled them, but every minute mattered.

"So," Blays said once they were back on their way. "What's our plan?"

"We've done all we can," Dante said. "The *Sword of the South* should be back tomorrow. Unless you intend to make this your new home, I say we go."

He expected an argument, but Blays merely nodded. "Do you think things would have been better if we'd never come here?"

"Sooner or later, the Tauren would have pushed to take the island. At least we gave these people one last chance to stave them off."

"I think the Kandeans would have mounted a defense of their own. If they'd had a few more months or years to prepare, maybe they would have pulled it off."

"Maybe someday I'll learn to tell the future. Until then, all we can do is what we've done: make each choice the best we can. And hope, in time, that takes us where we want to be."

He believed this, yet the words seemed to fall away into a space as meaningless as the ocean in the Mists. Defeat stole everything. Within a few more days, it would steal the Plagued Islands, too.

With the day growing short, they entered the upper bounds of Kandak. Townsfolk trickled out to meet them, but one look at the warriors' faces told them everything they needed to know. Men and women dispersed to their houses, packing whatever they could carry. There was no sign of the *Sword of the South*. Dante intended to hike north that night, find a beach sheltered enough for longboats to navigate the Currents, and stay there until they spotted the ship.

They'd hardly been in town twenty minutes when fearful shouts went up from the beach. Dante and Blays ran for them, joined by a hodgepodge of warriors. A small armada of canoes sailed into the quiet waters of the bay. Niles barked to his people, ordering them into defensive positions in the homes along the shore. One of the canoes broke formation, paddling in. Niles, Dante, Winden, and Blays jogged to the surf to meet it.

The woman in the bow wore a leafy green cape curled around her shoulders. The Harvester from the Boat-Growers.

Dante summoned the nether to his hands. "What's this? Come to stab us in the back to impress your Tauren masters?"

"Our people, we're here in peace," the woman said. "May I step onto your land?"

Niles glanced at Winden, then nodded. "Why are you here?"

The Harvester waded ashore. She gazed south, eyes hard. "The Tauren. They've lied to us. We do all they say, and still they keep our children hostage. If you wish, our boats will take you out of here."

"To where?"

"North. South. Anywhere that will give you more time."

Winden and Niles gave each other a long look. Eventually, she nodded. He turned back to the Harvester. "Aye, we'd welcome that. But we'll have to leave tonight. The Tauren will be standing here by tomorrow morning."

"Before we go," Winden said. "We have to destroy the Star Tree. I won't leave it for Vordon."

As Winden spoke, the face of the Boat-Growers' leader underwent a transformation as dramatic as anything Dante had ever seen on a stage.

"My ears," the Harvester said. "They heard you say 'Star Tree.'"

"Would that mean something to you?"

"They are the miracle of the Dresh. Proof of Kaval's favor. But they haven't grown here in hundreds of years. Not since the wars and betrayals caused Kaval to turn away."

Dante raised an eyebrow. "What do they mean to you? Do you know what they're capable of?"

The woman looked at him like she'd caught him vigorously pissing on an idol. "They connect us to Kaval. With them, we no longer have to fear his judgment in death. There is nothing more sacred." Her expression darkened. "Which is why you rixen could never grow one."

"Turns out Kaval doesn't share your blind prejudice against foreigners." Dante swung his pack around and dug out one of the white, pearlescent fruits. He cut it open and dug out the pit, revealing the five-pointed star.

The woman reached out hesitantly, as if afraid to touch it. "If this is true. How did you do this? Star Trees, they have been dead for half a thousand years."

"We traveled into the Mists." Dante chose his truth carefully. "And found those who used to know the ways."

She took the seed, lifting it to her face, then rushed to her canoe. A lively conversation ensued between her and the others in the boat.

When the Harvester walked back, her expression bordered on furious. "We can't take you from here."

Winden curled her lip. "Then go. We don't need the help of the Tauren's servants."

"We can't leave because we can't forsake this place. Kaval would never forgive us. We will join you—and we will fight."

Niles broke into relieved laughter. He gestured to the bay. "How many people do you have here?"

"Eighty who can fight."

"I appreciate your offer like a beer at the end of a long day. But we've only got twice that many. Combine our forces, and the Tauren will still outnumber us four times over."

The woman jabbed her finger to the south. "It doesn't matter! You won't fight? Then we will. And when you reach the Mists, you will explain to Kaval why you rejected his greatest gift."

Niles scratched his beard. "It might be enough. Dante, what do you think?"

"This is your survival you're thinking of risking," Dante said. "It's your decision."

"I want to fight. Without you, though, Vordon will carve us like a hog."

Dante gazed across the Boat-Growers' canoes. "All right. I'm in."

Winden cocked her head. "That simply? But we've already lost once."

"That's exactly why I want to do this. If there's one thing I hate more than tyrants, it's losing."

Niles reached out and clasped his hand. "I promise you. This time, we won't fail."

Dante eyed him. "That sounds like tonen to me."

This drew a loudly appreciative chuckle from all the islanders present. Before officially committing her forces, the Boat-Grower Harvester, whose name was Dess, asked to see the Star Tree. Winden and a contingent of warriors led her into the jungle. While they were out, and with Niles' scouts jogging off to keep tabs on the Tauren advance, Blays walked across town, assessing a potential defense.

"Those canoes of theirs," Blays said. "They're as strong as they are light. I think they'd make pretty good mobile shield walls."

"A little bulky," Dante said. "Suppose they'd let us chop them in half?"

"The way Dess reacted to the Star Tree seed? I think she'd let us chop *her* in half."

"That's a good start to our defense. But we're dealing with a thousand soldiers. We're going to need a lot more than a few shields."

Blays pointed up the road. "Archers behind the shields. Withdraw whenever the Tauren get too close. We can fight them all the way into town. To that temple there." He gestured to the large, blocky temple that sat in the middle of Kandak. "It's stone. Fireproof. Cut down the trees around it, and it'll make for a pretty good keep."

"Which means Vordon will just surround us and starve us out."

"Who says I mean for us to hide in it? I want him to *think* that's what we're up to. You, meanwhile, will have made use of the town's local hot springs."

The wheels turned in Dante's head. "Now that just might work."

"Work" was the operative word of the night. After having seen the Star Tree, Dess was happy to let the Kandeans chop her canoes into portable shield walls. While the warriors drilled with these, learning how to pivot them and to retreat while covering the archers within them, citizens and soldiers chopped down the trees and shrubs around the temple, stripping away the Tauren's cover. And Dante prepared the field.

He went to sleep while many of the Kandeans were still laboring to convert their home into a battlefield. It felt like he'd hardly closed his eyes when he woke to Winden poking him awake.

"Your friends in the ship," she said. "They're here."

He glared at her, utterly confused, then put her words together. Outside, dawn broke, and the *Sword of the South* sat at the mouth of the bay—along with the Mallish navy ship they'd captured in Bressel.

Dante asked for the flag to indicate the rixen should come ashore, waving it back and forth. A longboat launched and stroked its way to the beach.

Naran waded onto the sand, resplendent in his many-buttoned jacket. "You're looking hale. Don't tell me you've found your cure?"

"Sure did," Blays said. "That's the good news. The bad news: we've also found a war."

They summarized the details of the Tauren assault, including the previous battle and the one they now faced.

At the end, Naran smiled wryly. "Decided to get involved in local politics, have you? Don't you get enough of that back home?"

"Clearly, I haven't learned my lesson," Dante said. "We've chosen to make a second stand. It should be decided within two days. Can I ask you to come back then?"

"You may not."

"Naran, we're too deeply entangled to leave now. But if I survive this, I swear to you that my next act will be to end Gladdic's life."

"I like that part," Naran said. "And that is why we will be fighting alongside you."

Dante snorted. "Don't be ridiculous. You have nothing to do with this."

"But I have much to do with *you*. I require your help to avenge Captain Twill. To my mind, you are an investment, and one not easily replaced. Hence I'd be a fool to watch you die against overwhelming odds."

"And what about your crew?"

"Most of them owe you their freedom, if not their lives. I won't force them to fight. But I expect I won't have to."

Dante gestured at the lightening sky. "Better hurry. The Tauren are camped less than five miles from here. Once they get on the march, they can be here in two hours."

Naran got back in his longboat and headed back to the two ships. As he was out speaking to his people, the scouts came in. The Tauren were on the move.

"No waiting until afternoon tea is finished?" Blays said. "I'm afraid they're finally taking us seriously."

Most of the citizens had already left Kandak, but Niles sent the few who'd stayed into the temple. Scouts dashed every which way. Warriors ate breakfast, dressed themselves in their various bits of armor, and did some last-minute practicing with the Boat-Growers' shields.

Naran returned with a squad of 36 irregularly-armed men, putting their numbers close to three hundred. Half again as many as they'd had at the battle of Broken Valley. The Tauren, meanwhile, were down at least two hundred troops, plus two of their nethermancers. The scales were still grossly imbalanced, but as Dante made last-minute preparations, he found his anxiety mingled with hope.

The Tauren came within three miles, then two. Kandean warriors installed themselves in houses along the road. Archers lined up behind the shields, which were so long they had to be carried by a man at each end.

A mile out, the enemy army came to a halt, detaching a large contingent that angled to the north. Anticipating a pincer attack, Niles shifted a few score defenders to the northern road toward the temple plaza.

Minutes later, a scout dashed in from that direction, face anguished. "The Basket. They're destroying it!"

Winden clenched her jaw. "We have to stop them. Niles, we have enough warriors!"

Niles reached for her hand. "To fight back that arm of their troops? Could be. But then we'd be smashed by their main force. The Basket will burn either way."

"It took years to grow that. Some of those plants, they've been here for generations!"

"This is the cost of war," Dante said softly. "Things that should last forever are torn to the ground. But you can rebuild."

She whirled on him. "Do you think I don't know that? Is it supposed to be comforting that, if I devote years of my life to it, I might one day regain what we've lost?"

He flushed, embarrassed to have offered such platitudes. "You're right. There is no good here. Only death. For them, or for us."

Smoke climbed from the Basket up the coast from the city, drifting inland on the seaborne breeze. Other columns sprung up on all sides. The Tauren were burning fields and orchards. This gave them no tactical advantage, but the destruction wasn't for the Kandeans. It was a message to the other people on the island: resist, and your earth will be scorched.

The defenders could do nothing but wait. Once the Tauren finished pillaging the outskirts, they regrouped and marched on the city proper, burning everything that would take flame. Though it wasn't necessary to the Kandean strategy for the enemy to advance along the main east-west road, Niles dispatched his army there to entice the Tauren to do so. Vordon obliged, concentrating his troops several hundred yards from the front lines of Kandean skirmishers and shielded archers.

Vordon stepped out from his troops, shoulders swaying. He surveyed the resistance. "Did you bring your friends out? I'm happy to see this. It means I won't have to march as far to kill them."

"Destroy us, and you'll never know what you've lost," Niles called back. "But that's your way, isn't it, Vordon? You'd rather rule an entire wasteland than live peaceably in a slice of paradise."

"Old man, your judgment is as tired as you are. Time to put you and your people to bed."

Vordon threw out his arms. His army marched forward, enveloping him. It split to either side of the road, advancing in two wide columns.

Niles cupped his hands to his mouth. "Open fire!"

Kandean archers popped from behind their long shields, launching a volley at the front lines. Tauren fell and lay still. Their archers returned fire, but the Kandeans had already ducked back behind the shields. The incoming arrows whacked into solid wood.

Vordon shouted orders. Archers moved into the cover of buildings and trees, sniping on the defenders. Led by Vordon, a body of men split from the left-hand column, circling behind a closely-grouped stand of houses. On the other side of the road, the right-hand column mirrored the maneuver, the flankers accompanied by two other nethermancers.

"They're surrounding us," Niles said. "We'll have to fall back. We can't let it degenerate into a rout."

Dante nodded. The plan was similar to that at the Broken Valley: concede ground, but make the Tauren bleed for every inch of it. Whittle down the enemy to more manageable numbers and make a final stand at the temple keep.

But if the retreat grew too disorganized, the Kandeans might be crushed right there in the field. And if they withdrew too early, the Tauren might disengage, besieging the keep and starving the Kandeans out—be it through food, or through the shaden the mostly-uncured locals still needed to ward off the ronone. The battle would be another dance, then. Like before, if there was any stumble or misstep, everything would fall.

"Send Winden and Dess to support the right flank," Dante said. "I'll hold off Vordon."

He ran left, Blays at his side. Two hundred feet up the slope of the city, the frontmost archers retreated, covered by those behind. A squadron of armored Tauren swordsmen swung around a stone building, charging the archers' flank. The Kandeans pivoted their long shield to meet the threat. Blays broke into a dead run, swords in hand. Dante fell behind with each stride.

The swordsmen plowed into the shield, hammering at it. The archers had dropped their bows to poke at the enemy with short spears; pressed by the swordsmen, they staggered back. Skirmishers rushed forward to support them, but a withering volley of Tauren arrows forced them into the shelter of a house. One of the shield-carriers staggered, dropping his side of the modified boat to the ground.

Swords reaved into the archers. As they broke and ran, Blays tore into the swordsmen's flank, knocking one soldier to the ground. The dead man's partner jabbed at Blays' gut. Dante sent a spear of nether plunging into the man's eye. Darkness streaked toward Blays. Dante grunted, parrying it awkwardly.

"Vordon's here!" He scanned the buildings, but Blays was already running for the closest house. Shadows crunched into its corner, showering Blays with splinters. He dived behind it.

The archers had made use of the confusion to join up with the pinned-down skirmishers. Behind his incoming troops, Vordon weaved in and out of trees, shacks, and houses, striking at any Kandean who straggled too far from Dante's protection. Eyes out for arrows, Dante moved up behind the front line of battling Kandeans.

As before, his personal battle with Vordon became a stalemate, with each feint and thrust of nether negated in turn. The other man was too swift to overpower and too canny to trick. Tauren maneuvered between the houses, claiming one row at a time. Those at the rear of the advance set fires, hazing the air with acrid smoke.

The Kandeans dropped back in disciplined turns. The Tauren had metal blades and superior armor, but the Kandean's constant archery, use of the houses for cover, and bouts of vicious resistance left three enemy soldiers dead for every warrior they lost.

But they were running out of space. And even a three-to-one margin would see the Kandeans annihilated long before the Tauren.

To the right side of the road, men and women were crying out in panic. Through gaps in the buildings, Dante watched as the right flank crumbled, the Kandeans running away in all-out retreat. There was nothing he could do. If he left to assist them, Vordon would crush the left side unopposed.

"Pull back!" Dante yelled. "To the temple!"

"We've hardly dented them!" Blays said, swords slick with blood.

"We have no choice. Another minute, and the right flank will collapse."

He called orders to the Kandean sergeants, who relayed these to their people. The withdrawal hastened, with warriors hanging onto each house just long enough to cover the retreat of those in front. Sensing the Kandeans were at the breaking point, the Tauren flowed into the gaps heedlessly, daring the Kandean archers to stay put and fire at them.

But there was no time for that. The right-hand ranks were streaming into the open ground surrounding the temple. They poured inside, archers appearing in the windows of the upper floors. The windows on the lower level had been plugged with boards and debris. These barriers wouldn't be strong enough to resist determined men with axes and sledges, but they'd hold out long enough.

Ensconced in the keep, the Kandean archers poured arrows into their Tauren pursuit, keeping them at bay in the buildings beyond the plaza. Niles stood in the temple's entrance, guiding his troops inside. As the warriors from the left side ran to the converted fortress, Dante stayed near the front, countering Vordon's attacks.

Vordon hung back, reuniting the two wings of his force at the west edge of the plaza, which was slightly uphill from the temple but provided no meaningful tactical advantage. Keeping one eye on Vordon, Dante ran up the steps, Blays at his side. Naran was right inside, bearing a gash on his forehead that trickled blood into his eyes. Dess was there, too, the tatters of her leafy cape flapping behind her as she gave orders to her people, who had prevented the enemy's sorcerers from eliminating the right-hand column.

Dante exited out into the hot sunlight, finding Niles. "Where's Winden?"

Niles shook his head, threatening to spill his tears. "She went missing in the retreat."

"*Missing?* How could you let that happen?"

"Their sorcerers were too strong. They sliced right through our lines. Winden tried to sneak through a house to hit them from behind, but we broke too fast."

Dante gazed across the city. Most of the Tauren were gathered in the square, but others patrolled the abandoned portion of the town, setting fires and rooting out anyone in hiding.

"She might still be out there," Dante said. "We have to hold them back as long as we can. Give her a chance to get back to us."

"They were going door to door. Either she's already slipped away, or..." Niles was unable to voice his conclusion.

Shadows rippled at the far end of the plaza. Prior to the attack, the defenders had torn out almost all the vegetation around the temple, but they'd left scattered grass and shrubs deemed too small to bother tearing out. Now, fed by the nether of the Tauren Harvesters, the remaining plants crept upward inch by inch. The stumps of trees sprouted fresh branches that tangled together, squeezing out the daylight between them. The growth snaked across the plaza, nearing the temple. Ample cover for an advance.

Dante couldn't stop them. Slowing them down would burn nether he couldn't spare. Tauren soldiers filtered into the harvested maze. Dante yelled at the archers, urging them to rain down hell. But few arrows found their mark. Dozens of Tauren infiltrated the field, their archers taking aim on the entrance. Dante and Niles retreated inside.

The Tauren shot into the windows, forcing the fortified archers behind cover. At least a hundred of the enemy hunkered in the trees and bushes. With the Kandeans pinned down, unable to offer more than trifling fire, Vordon bellowed, his voice echoing across the square. Scores of men trotted from the safety of the buildings.

Blays brushed Dante's shoulder, angling for a view out the debris-choked window. "This is going to work, isn't it?"

"It might," Dante said. "But Winden's still out there somewhere."

Blays froze. "Alive?"

"We don't know."

"We know this much: she's not in that field." Blays gestured to the square, which was now nearly as full of the enemy as it was with the harvested bushes. Vordon moved into the ranks, eyes locked on the temple's open doorway. "This isn't the same as in Narashtovik. Vordon's right there. We can't wait any longer."

In his heart, Dante knew this was true. He might not be sacrificing her. Not as he'd once done to save his city.

Yet as he reached deep within the earth, removing the plugs from the tunnels he'd shaped the night before, he couldn't help feeling as though he was reliving the worst moment of his life.

Steam shot from cracks across the plaza. Tauren cried out in shock. A spume of yellow lava erupted into the air.

EDWARD W. ROBERTSON

28

After being held in place all through the night, the freed lava rushed across the square in rivers of molten rock. Trees erupted into flame. Men wailed, the noise unearthly and paralyzing, cut short as the fires stole the breath from their lungs. They sank into the lava, their flesh combusting as they melted away.

Heat wafted through the temple entrance, carrying the smell of roasted pork and rotten eggs. The Kandeans gasped. Some retched. Out in the plaza, the patches of solid ground shrank between rivulets of orange-red rock. Dante poured shadows into the earth, opening the lava tubes wider.

Near the left edge of the field, his nether went dead. Someone was arresting his work. Through the steam, flames, and smoke, he couldn't identify a soul, but he could feel the hand behind the shadows. Vordon.

But it wasn't enough to stop the flow. The rock had a mind of its own, beyond anyone's control.

Panicked Tauren fled away from the lava and toward the temple. The archers in the windows shot them all down. At the right edge of the chaos, two men stood on a dwindling island of rock, separated from escape by a fiery stream. One of the men backed up, then ran to the right, leaping as far as he could. His feet landed in the lava and sank to the shin. He screamed, toppling face-first and bursting into flame.

A few of the Tauren on the fringes slipped away from the flaming rivulets, but some three hundred soldiers had burned away like a morning mist. Around the perimeter, men screamed senselessly. Troops began to break from the main force, running off into town, portions of which were burning as wildly as the plaza. The trickle of deserters became a flood.

"We've done it!" Niles thrust his fists in the air. "We've broken them!"

Blays grimaced at the scene. "Along with every law of the gods."

Vordon's voice rang out from the clamor. Dante homed in on a smoke-hazed figure on the periphery of the square who was gesturing furiously at the temple. The stream of deserters ceased. Vordon motioned sweepingly, as if he were ushering something along. His lines recohered.

"Son of a bitch," Dante said. "Are they that scared of him? *I'm* the one who just melted a quarter of their army."

"And a few dozen more ran off." Niles set his jaw. "Let them come for us. See how long their mettle lasts when they're dying at our walls."

"If the lava wasn't enough to shatter their spirits, I don't think a pitched defense will be enough to do the job."

Blays wandered toward the entrance. "I don't think he's urging them on. I think he's telling them the lava's about to do their job for them."

Dante stared into the red-hot rock. It was still flowing out of the ground, making its ultimate path difficult to gauge. Yet his blood ran cold. When he'd been preparing the ground the night before, it had looked and felt level—but the lava was oozing toward the temple.

He drove his focus into the molten rock, attempting to shape it, but it was like trying to shape the earth in the midst of the

Currents. Every time he tried to give it form, the heat of the surrounding rock melted away his work. After the third failure, he shifted his mind to the earth between the magma and the temple, raising a three-foot-high wall between them.

He wasn't nearly familiar enough with the properties of melted rock to know whether the dam would hold. But it didn't matter. Vordon was already leading his people to the left of the square, circling around on the temple.

"He's smart enough not to attack us directly," Dante said. "He'll hem us in and let the lava do the rest."

"You can't boss that stuff around?" Blays said.

"It's much harder than with cool stone. If I'm busy preventing our fiery demise, Vordon can hit us from the rear."

"A siege is bad enough without a field of red-hot stone creeping up your backside. We need to get out of this place and we need to do it now."

Niles spread out his hand. "Then what? Fight them in the open field?"

"We'll take to the jungle. You know this place far better than they do. You can elude them until they run out of food and have to go home."

"Our citizens are out there, too. If the Tauren find them, it'll be a slaughter."

Dante peered through a gap in a window on the left side. "They'll have us surrounded in another five minutes. If we can't run away, our only choice is to charge them."

Niles rested his hand on the hilt of his sword. "They still outnumber us three times over."

"Meaning they've lost a hell of a lot of people today. One more blow could break them."

The older man laughed. "I'm starting to regret ever inviting you here. But you're right. It's a bad play—but it's the best one we've got."

He called out orders to his people. Naran did the same, but

his face looked as brittle as badly cast glass. By contrast, Dess looked furious, as though she couldn't believe Kaval could favor them with the Star Tree only to let them fall to their foes.

Warriors tore down the boards and rubble they'd used to block up the rear doors. Soldiers spilled onto the temple's shaded back porch. Ash blew about in gray eddies. A wide road or small plaza separated them from the next row of buildings the Tauren were presently moving behind.

"Do we have a plan?" Dante said. "Anything else we can throw at them?"

Blays wiped the sweat from his eyebrows. "Every time we've met them, we've dumped a bag of tricks on their heads. I say we rush straight at Vordon and do our best to take him out. This time, the trick will be that there *is* no trick."

"You and I will lead a column around to meet them head on. Niles, you drive straight forward, into their side. Take Dess in case they've got a sorcerer."

"My crew will go with you," Naran said. "The Tauren seem hesitant to fight us."

"Most of you are Mallish. They're probably afraid of offending the people they do business with." Dante inhaled deeply. "Go at Vordon with everything you've got. Don't give up an inch. If he falls, we'll break their back. But if he holds? Then everything is lost."

Niles assigned him half the remaining troops. Dante cut left from the rear of the temple, heading for the buildings there. Cries arose from the Tauren, who halted. Arrows streaked between the shops and houses. They were answered by the archers still posted in the temple's upper windows. Dante reached the first row of buildings. Down the street to his right, a smattering of Tauren scouted ahead; the bulk of the troops were to the right of them, blocked from sight by a mix of stone and wood edifices. Dante slashed nether at the scouts, felling three of them. The others sprinted around the corner to rejoin their vanguard.

Dante jogged onward, Blays, Naran and crew to one side, the Kandean warriors to the other. The Tauren yelled to their archers to form up.

"Shield crews!" Dante said. "Take the lead. Drive straight at them. We'll be right behind you."

Most of the repurposed canoe shields had been lost in the retreat, but they'd retained enough for a single rank. At the corner, they formed up, then pivoted out into the street beyond. A Tauren officer bawled an order. Arrows flew down the street in a flat arc, pummeling the shields. Yet their bearers ran toward the hundreds of soldiers awaiting them.

The side of the Tauren formation rippled—Niles and company were approaching from the flank. Dante ran with the shield-bearers, searching for the glint of Vordon's shiny helmet.

Shadows darkened around a figure thirty feet behind the Tauren lines. Vordon was bare-headed. Red skin and bubbly blisters traced where his helmet had been; it must have been heated during the fires, burning him. If he felt the pain of it, though, he didn't show it, striding back and forth among his men and launching a bolt of nether toward the center of the shield-bearers.

Dante battered the bolt aside, answering with a slew of his own. There was no more need to hold back. Any strength he tried to save would only wind up wasted.

Seeing him coming for them—or perhaps it was Naran's foreign crew of many lands, or simply the fearlessness of the charging Kandeans—the Tauren front lines hesitated. The oncoming wall of shields plowed into them with a hollow bang, driving the enemy back six feet before the scrum grew too fierce to press forward. Swords and spears jabbed back and forth. The shields were dropped or wrestled away.

Dante fired raw nether at Vordon's head, then reached for the ground beneath his feet, softening it in preparation to swallow him up. Vordon deflected the obvious strike. Beside him, a thin, short woman moved into the shadows within the earth, disrupting those as well.

Blays hit the front lines, swords whirling in perpetual arcs that only arrested when one of the blades was parried or met an opponent's flesh. As bodies piled around him, the Tauren shrank back, creating a void in their ranks. Naran's sailors and the Kandean warriors rushed into the gap.

For a moment, it looked like they might break through and kill their way to Vordon and his fellow sorcerer. But as Vordon drew back, fresh soldiers moved up to support the bowing line. Inch by inch, the Kandeans were shoved back.

Blays cried out in pain, staggering back from the melee, clutching at his chest. Dante saw no blood. Blays winked, then fell. Before he hit the ground, he vanished.

Smiling, Dante redoubled his attacks on Vordon. But the small woman beside him was making no attacks of her own. Too late, Dante understood: she was a bodyguard. Her eyes darted to the space ten feet in front of Vordon. The air shimmered as she forced Blays out of the shadows.

A hundred of the enemy were clustered between Blays and Dante. As those nearest to Blays turned, raising swords, Dante enfolded them all in a sphere of darkness. Blinded, the Tauren shouted in surprise. Vordon dismissed the sphere with a wave of his hand, but Blays was gone once again.

Seconds later, he materialized beside Dante. "It's no good. That pet sorcerer of his is making sure nothing gets close to him."

Dante nodded, firing off another blast of shadows; these too were dispersed by his foes. "I don't have much left. Vordon may be a violent despot, but he's a hell of a nethermancer."

Tauren officers yelled commands. A hundred men detached from the middle of their force, moving down a side street.

"They'll be on our backs in a minute," Blays said. "Got any last tricks?"

To Dante's left, Naran reeled away from the lines, holding a gash across his sword arm. His crew edged back.

"We've used everything and then some," Dante murmured. "There's only one question left."

Blays smiled grimly. "Do we want to die here?"

Dante nodded. Blays didn't reply. The Tauren pushed the Kandeans back another two feet. This last charge, it had been a fool's errand, hadn't it? Vordon was arrogant, but he was too canny to let himself be exposed to real danger. Standing against him—today and at the Broken Valley—it had all been hubris. Dante should have insisted the Kandeans take the fruit of the Star Tree and sail to a new homeland.

He never should have come to the Plagued Islands in the first place. What did he care about Larsin Galand? It hadn't bothered Dante to learn his long-lost father was actually dead. His time in the Pastlands had shown him his hunt for the man was futile, a waste of focus and emotion.

Mistakes were so easy to make. In normal times, it was simple enough to brush them off or minimize the damage.

But when you played with strife and war, any error could be your last.

The Kandean lines slipped back another foot. The detachment of maneuvering Tauren were almost in position to hit Dante's soldiers from the side. Furious, he sucked every shadow from the shaden he'd been using and drove them at Vordon. Vordon shuffled back, burned face hardening with concentration. The woman beside him weaved her hands in an intricate pattern, helping him to turn aside the flurry of nether.

The space around Vordon was now empty, his soldiers fleeing the battling storms of darkness. Behind him, a warrior in patchwork armor limped into the open space, raised a spear, and slammed it into Vordon's back.

He pitched forward, catching himself on his palms. Beside him, the female sorcerer faltered. The patchworked warrior ripped his spear loose from Vordon and shoved it into the woman's gut. The shadows on her hands flickered.

With both sorcerers turning on the traitor, Dante sent two dark streaks above the clashing lines. One struck the woman in the temple. The other took Vordon in the back of his head.

Blays lifted a sword and roared, slamming into the Tauren. Dante followed, lashing about with blade and nether. A massive cry of triumph arose from the Kandeans. Outraged Tauren swarmed around the traitor. But with no one to protect them from Dante's shaden-enhanced wrath, the defenders fell as quickly as Dante could shift the shadows. Blays' swords dealt death nearly as fast. A spearhead of sailors and Kandeans punched through the enemy lines and penetrated to the soldier in the patchwork armor.

"Who are..?" Dante's question died in his throat. The traitor turned. Beneath her iron cap, Winden's eyes met his.

Together, they pressed forward. The Tauren held fast. Dante's arms and legs were shaking; each summoning of the nether was weaker and slower than the last. Another few seconds, and he'd be no more than a man holding a sword.

He drew forth everything he had left. A great wreath of darkness formed around him, darting and swooping like a flock of ten thousand crows. They were no more harmful than a dapple of shade—but at last, the Tauren collapsed, dashing away into the streets.

To the right, Niles' people broke forth, aligning themselves beside Dante. Behind them, the maneuvering Tauren had been on the verge of a charge. But they no longer had the numbers. The remaining enemy drifted to a halt, then turned and dispersed through the smoky streets.

Within moments, the Kandeans stood alone.

29

Smoke rose from the cinders that had once been homes. The wounded lay within the temple by the dozens. Scores of the dead were being dragged down to the shore. Exhausted to the core, Dante could do no more than witness the damage. As night fell on Kandak, Niles found him and told him the Tauren had continued to retreat.

"They still have the numbers," Dante said. "If they rally, they could launch another strike."

Niles grinned, his teeth bright in the darkness. "They won't have enough to take the town. Not with Vordon and so many of his Harvesters lost."

"What about when they get back to Deladi?"

"Many of the High Tower's tolaka have no interest in Vordon's conquest of the island. Or in his dealings with the Mallish. Now that he's dead, the alliance he built will crack like a nut." He nodded to the contingent of Boat-Growers stoking their camp fires on the beach. "And ours will grow."

All those who weren't out on watch or tending to the wounded began a slow migration to the Boat-Growers' fires. Inevitably, a feast broke out. It wasn't much of a meal—san paste, dried fish, and fresh fruit plucked from the surrounding jungle—but people passed around stoppered gourds filled with fermented fruit juice. Others sang songs and told stories about what had happened that day or during wars long past.

Dante joined them, glad for the reprieve from responsibility. As he listened to them sing and tell stories, he heard someone call a name he'd all but forgotten: Nassea.

A young woman turned, dark hair spilling down her back. Dante crossed the sand to her, waiting as she concluded her conversation with the woman who'd called to her.

"Excuse me," Dante said. "You're Nassea?"

The young woman nodded, folding her hands in front of you. "I knew your father. He was fair to everyone."

"That's what brings me here. We have an acquaintance in common. Juleson, of the *Sword of the South*."

Nassea's eyes seemed to shrink. "Juleson, he's your friend?"

"I wouldn't go that far. But I owe him a favor. He wanted me to tell you hello. And that the offer he made you — it still stands."

"And what am I supposed to do with that?"

Dante shrugged. "Nothing, if nothing's what you want. But he fought in the battle. If you want to speak to him, he's here."

Nassea glanced over his shoulder, as if Juleson might be lurking right behind him, then nodded. "Thank you for telling me."

She smiled tightly and walked off. As she departed, Winden limped up beside him. Between scouting, triage, and assessing the state of the lava (which had threatened to absorb the temple, but was now cooling and purple-black), he'd hardly seen her since the Tauren retreat.

"You know Nassea?" she said.

"Just passing along a message." Dante jerked his chin in the direction of the temple plaza. "Neat trick back there. I was sure you were dead."

"I almost was." She took a swig of fruit-based spirits. "But I saw my people falling back. I ran into the jungle. Snarled the way so the Tauren couldn't follow. While I was there, do you know what I saw?"

"Trees?"

"A fox ant. Most ants form great colonies, but fox ants live alone—unless they are threatened, or they want to steal the grub of other ants. Then, they walk into a swarm just like they belong there. Fox ants don't look that much like the other ants, but they must be close enough to fool the swarms, because they come and go as they please. Even when they are carrying off the colony's young."

"So rather than rejoining us, you thought it was wiser to try to sneak into the middle of an enemy swarm?"

She shrugged, waving one hand. "Your grand maneuvers, none of them were working. Neither was our magic. I thought I would try something simpler."

"Well, try not to get a big head about this," Dante said. "But you and your fox ant won us the war."

"Don't be stupid. If you hadn't been attacking them on two sides, I never would have been able to get close. If not for the Boat-Growers and your sailing friends, we wouldn't have been able to counterattack in the first place." She gestured toward the trees down the shore. "Those trees, do you think the trunk is all that matters? They need their leaves, too. Their roots. Their branches. Their fruit. All of these things work together. Take one away, and soon enough, the trees will die."

"Are you always this philosophical?"

"Only on days when I've almost died five times."

"Ah, so now you understand why I'm always so opinionated."

Winden smiled. Smoke blew past them, but it had the welcoming smell of a cook fire, not the acridity of painted planks. "He fought for years for this. Dedicated his life to it. He would have been proud of us."

Dante nodded, gazing out on the gentle waters of the Bay of Peace. He wouldn't say he'd forgiven his father. He wasn't sure he wanted to—or that he needed to. He'd been fine with things for a long time. Much more so than he'd known.

But after seeing the island—its beauties and its horrors—he understood, at last, all the things that had taken the old man away.

For as much as Blays tended to sleep, something about a battle had him up early the next day. That morning was no exception. The sun had hardly lifted itself from the eastern sea before Blays ran up to the house the two of them had been granted and knocked stridently on its frame until Dante stirred.

"Latest from the scouts," Blays announced. "The Tauren camped five miles from here. They struck out at first light. Heading south."

Dante absorbed this the best his war- and liquor-addled mind could manage. "Which is toward Deladi."

"With such a keen mind for details, it's no wonder they put you in charge of Narashtovik. Their retreat could be a ruse of some kind, but if they keep it up for another few hours, they won't be able to strike back today, at least."

"I don't think it's a gambit. They've made too many other enemies. If they lose any more of their army, they might not be able to defend their city."

"Probably right. Either way, I thought the news would help you sleep easier." Blays walked away, oblivious to the daggers Dante was staring in his back.

With his command of the shadows renewed, Dante saw to the wounded in the temple, aided by Winden and Dess. They were more skilled at growing plants than mending flesh, but there had been so many injuries that every bit helped. It was somber work. Some of the warriors' limbs were so mangled there was no fixing them. Others had suffered rattled minds Dante couldn't soothe, which he hoped were only temporary.

Despite this, they were able to restore most of the injured to full health, or at least close enough for their bodies to handle the rest. Outside, the mood in Kandak was one of quiet resolve. The storm had hit. Much had been ruined. But it had passed. Now, they would rebuild.

The magma at the temple lay dormant, but after seeing how pressure could grow beneath the ground, Dante spent his remaining strength sealing up subterranean tubes and fortifying the layers of rock. He'd just about finished when Naran padded up to him. The man had a bandage the size of a sail wrapped around his head, but appeared hale. They exchanged greetings.

"Pardon my haste," the captain said. "But when do you expect to be ready to weigh anchor?"

Dante smiled crookedly. "We're still cleaning up the wreckage of the last battle. You're that eager to go feed Gladdic your sword?"

Naran shrugged his narrow, well-appointed shoulders. "I'm in charge of two ships now. Sixty men. I need to set my schedule."

"Assuming the Tauren are gone for good, there's only a few things left for us to do. It shouldn't take more than a few days."

"This cure of yours. You're positive it works?"

"I took it days ago and I still don't see any sign of the sickness." Dante tipped his head toward the bay. "But if you're afraid for your men, I'm sure no one would be offended if you'd rather wait at sea."

"Your word on its effectiveness is all I need. But I have something else in mind. This morning, I was approached by Niles and an old man with curly white hair. For our assistance in the battle, every man in my crew has been granted a station known as 'rixaka.'"

"Foreign family. You can come and go in Kandak as you please."

Naran raised one kempt eyebrow, nodding significantly. "If so, and if we no longer have to fear the sickness, that opens up some rather intriguing possibilities for trade."

Dante chuckled. "Sounds like you and your crew are only a lot of hard work away from being rich men. Would that change your mind about pursuing Gladdic?"

"I'm afraid not. Whatever our future, I could never accept it knowing it was purchased with Captain Twill's death."

"Fair enough. I'd like to build these people a few fortifications. After that, there's someone I need to visit, but maybe you can help with that. Ever heard of Spearpoint Rock?"

While Naran set to work on finding a less strenuous approach to the northern island, Dante hunted down Niles, who was busy arranging a mission to bring the evacuated citizens back to Kandak.

"The Tauren are gone for now," Dante said. "But it only takes one lunatic to drive them back here. I'm thinking it's time this city had a wall."

Niles tugged on his goatee. "Walls aren't much use against a nethermancer, are they?"

"That depends on whether you have any to defend it."

"True enough. Well, we might as well put ourselves in position to succeed, eh? Do as you will."

Enclosing the entire town would have taken a week, if not more. Instead, Dante took a cue from Narashtovik's Ingate, which encircled the city's inner core. Under normal circumstances, it wouldn't have been easy to erect a wall within a built-up city. But the silver lining of the battle was that so many houses had burned down that Dante had plenty of open space to make use of. Foot by foot, he raised a line of purple-black stone, shaping gaps for gates as well as flood paths to accommodate the tropical rainfall.

While he worked on this, Winden and Dess harvested the Star Tree. This remained a slow process, yielding no more than ten fruit per day. With patience, though, all those afflicted by the ronone would be cured. With nothing else to occupy him, Blays made use of the many swords left behind by the dead or fleeing

Tauren to set up an informal training ground, showing every warrior who was interested the basics of combat with a blade.

Four days after the battle, as Dante put the finishing touches on his simple wall, an exhausted scout returned from the south. The Tauren had crossed through the Dreaming Peaks, taking their occupying troops with them. Niles sent a group of warriors into the wilds of the mountains to inform the monks and the Dreamers they could go home.

"I have similar thoughts," Dess said to Dante. "I should be back with my people. We live too close to the Tauren. There's always the chance of treachery."

"You certainly don't need my permission," he said.

"But so few of my people are cured."

It would have been plausible to establish an ongoing trade route. The Boat-Growers found it easier than most to reach Kandak—to get there as fast as they had, they'd carried their ultra-light canoes up into the mountains, then followed the rivers to the northeast shores and sailed the Current into the Bay of Peace—but the journey was no trivial matter.

Dante considered her. "Do you have a proposition?"

Dess lowered her eyes. "Kaval's favor was given to the Kandeans, not me. But I have to ask. Will you show me how to grow the Star Tree?"

"You risked everything for us. So I henceforth declare that Kaval favors the Boat-Growers, too."

With Winden's help, he showed Dess the inner workings of a seed. As he filled the innermost chamber with ether, and the pale sprout broke free from the dirt, Dess' eyes filled with tears.

Using her copper trowel, Winden dug up the sapling and potted it in a small wooden box. Finished, she held it out to Dess.

"Without the strength of the Boat-Growers, the Kandeans would be gone," Winden said. "With this plant, the Kandeans hope to make the Boat-Growers even stronger."

Dess accepted the box, holding it in both hands. She glanced at Dante, anxious. "The Star Trees, what if they die again? And we have no one who can use the ether?"

He lifted one shoulder, a half shrug. "Guess you'll have to kidnap a Mallish priest."

Dess nodded thoughtfully.

"Don't actually kidnap a Mallish priest," Dante said. "I have several monks versed in the ether—and far more skilled with it than I am. Once I'm home, I'll send one of them here to offer training to your Harvesters."

"Thank you. There is no finer gift than freedom." She turned to Winden. "That is why I pledge to help you regrow your Basket. So the Kandeans will always have everything they need."

Winden broke into a smile. "This is how it should always have been."

Dess gathered up her people. With the Boat-Growers' canoes having all been bifurcated to be used as shields, they borrowed Kandean boats, with the promise to replace them with the lighter harvested versions on their next visit. Many of the Kandeans halted their work cleaning up the town to see the Boat-Growers off. As their new allies departed, the Kandeans broke into their farewell song, bone flutes carrying on the wind.

With the Boat-Growers gone, the Dreaming Peaks restored to the Dreamers, and Kandak under reconstruction, there was little to require Dante or Blays' assistance. Though a part of Dante yearned to move on and begin his travels home, the thought of leaving the island caused him to consider it anew, as he had the first time: as a paradise. One that rivaled anything he'd seen, be it in the lands of the living or of the dead.

He allowed himself a single day to enjoy it. Swimming in the tranquil turquoise bay. Lying in the sun. Bathing in the hot springs. Hiking out into the jungle, both to check on the Star Tree, and for the simple desire to spend a few final hours in a forest of unsurpassed greenery and vibrancy. When the modest rasp of the surf woke him in the morning, it was the most rested he'd ever felt.

After asking around, he learned Winden was out tending to the Basket. He hadn't seen it since the Tauren had pillaged it, and despite having heard of the damage, when he saw it in person, his heart sank. Trees had been hacked down, piled up, and torched. Flowers lay in great wilting heaps. Fruit had been smashed with mallets and—unless his nose deceived him—defecated on. Winden was among a handful of people raking out the wreckage to clear the circle and start anew.

"We'll be leaving tomorrow," Dante told her. "Before we go, I've got two last tasks. The second is to visit the Dresh, let them know what happened, and grow them a new Star Tree."

"As for the first?"

Dante bit his lower lip. "Do you have any dreamflowers here?"

She motioned to the shredded trunks and moldering leaves. "They ripped up everything. There's nothing left. But there may still be some at the temple above the city."

"Thank you. I'll go take a look."

"Are you going into the Mists? Do you want me to come with you?"

"I'll be fine." He tipped his head at the remains of the Basket. "Your time is better spent here."

Back in town, he located Blays at his fencing grounds, where he waited until they concluded the morning's training.

"I need to go into the Mists," Dante said. "Alone. But I'd like you nearby in case anything goes wrong."

Blays toweled the sweat from his face. "The Mists? Don't tell me there's more we need to know about the Star Trees."

"I'm going to find Larsin."

His eyebrows shot up. "Yes. Of course. Whenever you're ready."

They headed up the main road, which had been stomped

down by the passage of a battalion. Dante was afraid the Tauren might have sacked the temple, but it stood unmolested. After a short search, they located a bush of the orange flowers growing in the woods behind the building.

Dante arranged himself on one of the pallets inside the temple and consumed the flower. "Let's hope I know what I'm doing."

Blays snorted. "When has that ever stopped us?"

Dante closed his eyes. Before he knew it, his world faded behind him.

He woke in the bed. As before, it was much too small. As he swept off the sheet, it tore apart in a shower of crusty fragments. The bedroom was festooned with cobwebs and mouse droppings. Outside, the overhang had collapsed onto the porch. The mug he'd taken his smallbeer in was smashed beneath the rotten beams, half buried in the dirt like the shards of pottery he sometimes found in the norren hills.

There was no sign of the monk, living or dead. Dante descended to the basement, prodding his way down the moldy steps. Three of them snapped. At the bottom, he turned around and hiked back up.

He exited the blank white portal into the vaporous land beyond. There, he walked forward, picturing his father's face. Trees began to jut from the all-encompassing clouds. Minute by minute, the mist thinned. He was in a dense deciduous forest that smelled of dew and shade. A path resolved from the dirt. He followed it.

And found himself facing the exact cabin he'd just left. It was much newer, though. Well-maintained. Like the first time he'd come to the Pastlands.

His heart raced. If he was stuck, would he be able to remember the way out? What if his mind faded as it had before, and this time, rather than hours of real time, he lost years here, adrift like the Dreamers on their beds?

Something rasped from the side of the house. He headed for the sound, ready to accept his cup of beer from the waiting monk.

In the side yard, a man straightened, leaning on his broom. He was nearly as young as Dante. Disbelief, shock, and recognition filled the eyes of Larsin Galand.

30

Larsin drifted forward. As he neared, Dante saw the man wasn't quite as young as in his memories. Nor as he'd appeared on horseback in the Pastlands; his dark hair was starting to recede from the temples, and as he smiled in awe, the corners of his eyes crinkled deeply.

But it was, without doubt, him.

"You're here." Larsin's smile collapsed on itself. "Then are you..?"

"Dead?" Dante said. "No, despite everyone else's best efforts. I'm Dreaming."

His father laughed in relief. "But you're there? On the Plagued Islands?"

"And we've defeated the Tauren. Not only that, but we rediscovered the Star Trees. The cure for the ronone."

"Then he was right," Larsin murmured. "Did you come here to tell me this?"

"Preserving your people's freedom was your life's work. I thought you had the right to know it's been fulfilled."

"You're sure the Tauren are gone? We've beaten them back before only for them to return."

"Vordon's dead," Dante said. "Along with at least half of his soldiers. The return of the Star Trees has forged a new alliance between the Kandeans and the Boat-Growers. I wouldn't be surprised if others join them soon."

"Aye, that would do it. Incredible. Once the Mallish started arming the Tauren, I didn't think we had a chance."

"There's more. The Dresh aren't all dead. We found a town of them on Spearpoint Rock. After this, we'll be inviting them back to the main island."

Larsin gawked. "Is there anything more? I'm quickly running out of shock."

Dante tipped his head to the side. "That's everything. Relevant to you, at least."

His father nodded slowly. "I'm sorry. I'm at a loss for words. I long ago got used to the idea that I'd never see you again. I'm sorry. For everything."

"I don't need your apology."

"I can see that. But I need to make it. If you'll allow me."

This sounded familiar. Had Larsin and Niles had become such good friends because of their similarities? Or in order to manipulate Dante, had Niles become exceedingly adept at imitating Larsin's thinking?

Dante nodded. "I know you couldn't have come back. You'd have had to turn around for the islands within days. And me being me—prone to ignoring anything resembling authority—I would have found a way to follow."

Larsin smiled, eyes crinkling again. "So I left you with that much, at least. As for the cleverness, that's all your mother."

Dante gestured around the glade. "Is...she here?"

Larsin's mouth formed a tight, crooked smile. "If so, I haven't found her. Rebuilding the cabin we used to live in is the closest I've got."

"This part of the Mists seems to be reserved for the islands. Even if there was a way to get to her, by now, she's probably crossed into the Worldsea."

"Could be. But if she has, she's forgotten me. If I go there, I'll forget her too."

"Even if she's gone," Dante said. "Death can't take away the time you had together."

"Don't be wiser than your father. It's unseemly."

"Does that mean I'm right?"

"Aye, you might be. But I'm in no hurry to decide, am I?" Larsin set his broom against the side of the cabin, tilting his head. "What prompted you to come here in the first place?"

Dante laughed wryly. "Your friend Niles pretended to be you. He sent me a letter."

Something crossed the man's face, but Dante didn't know him well enough to read it. "I never wanted you to come here. I knew you had enough problems of your own. I couldn't ask you to risk your life here for me."

"Niles didn't seem to have any problem with it."

"And all it took was a letter?"

"And its deliverer." Dante rubbed his mouth. "He sent Riddi."

"So you met her!"

"In a sense. She brought me the letter, but she was netherburned. Sick with the ronone. She died. I'm sorry."

Darkness clouded Larsin's eyes. His jaw and neck tightened. He pressed his lips together, as if to prevent himself from vomiting up something vile. He snatched up the broom and smashed it against the cabin.

"I didn't want to tell you this. His voice shook; he was breathing hard. "But his actions have killed your sister, too."

"Whose actions?" Dante said. "And what do you mean, 'too'?"

"Did Niles tell you how I died?"

"Campaigning against the Tauren. You fell down a cliff."

"I didn't fall." Larsin gripped the broken broom handle tight. "I was pushed."

"By Niles?" Dante's voice was now quivering, too. "Why?"

"Because I refused to send for you. He argued with me for

weeks. But I wasn't about to put such a burden on you. Even if he'd summoned you here on the sly, he knew I would have sent you right back home. He must have decided the only way to do it was to get rid of me. And pretend to *be* me."

Dante fell silent. A cold wind cut through the shadows cast by the forest. "It was good to see you, father. You were a better man than the one I knew."

"Wait." Larsin stepped forward, grabbing Dante's forearm in a harsh grip. "You can't kill him."

Dante raised a brow. "Then why did you tell me what he'd done?"

His father gritted his teeth. "May I make one request of you?"

"Speak it."

"Make it quick."

Dante nodded. He turned his back on the cabin and walked into the woods.

He awoke in the pallet in the temple. For a moment, as the fog cleared from his aching head, he tried to tell himself it hadn't been real. That he *had* been stuck in the Pastlands, tormented by his own fears.

But this couldn't be so. After seeing his father, he'd fallen asleep, as you did to leave the Mists. And an instant later, he'd been here.

"What is it?" Blays said. "I'd say you look like you saw a ghost, but considering that was the plan, did you *not* see one?"

Dante rubbed his eyes. "I spoke to my father."

"I see. I'm glad you went, but I'm sorry it went badly."

"It was a good talk. But he told me something that was hard to hear. His death—it wasn't an accident."

Blays drew back his head. "He was beloved here. Their only hope to take down the Tauren. Why would anyone kill him?"

"Because he refused to ask me for help."

Blays' eyes went hooded. "So someone got him out of the

way. To do what he wouldn't. Do you want my blessing?"

"Would I need it?"

"He was your father. That makes you sole arbiter of this decision."

Dante stood. "We leave tomorrow morning. Be ready."

He walked alone to town, found Naran, and made plans to depart. Then he strolled into the woods. And waited.

Since the victory over the Tauren, Niles had been sleeping in a stone house on a hill overlooking the bay. At midnight, with the moon his only witness, Dante crept into the house, moved to the back room, and stood over Niles' bed.

Niles' eyes popped open. With a groan of surprise, he sat up, pawing at the side of his mattress where his sword was leaning. "Dante? Lyle's balls, you gave me a start!"

"I went into the Mists," Dante said. "And I found Larsin."

"He's still there? I would have thought he'd be off to find his wife by now."

"Were you counting on that? Whenever we went into the Mists, you made sure you were with me. Why? So I wouldn't learn the truth?"

Niles furrowed his brow. "What did he tell you? You know the dead have no respect for the living. They'll tell you anything if it suits their purposes."

"Sounds like someone else I know." Dante stepped closer. "We're past words, Niles."

The older man's face went tight with fear. He lunged for the sheathed sword. Dante rooted him to the mattress with a web of shadows. Niles slapped feebly for the weapon, but it was inches from his reach.

Niles relaxed, rolling his eyes toward Dante. "He was my friend! He meant far more to me than he did to you. But the Tauren were breathing down our neck. Growing stronger by the day. There was only one way to stand against them. And he wouldn't do it."

"So you did what was necessary."

"You're damned right I did! If the Tauren kept on, we were all dead anyway, weren't we? So what did his life matter? If he didn't have the guts to save our people, then I had to do whatever it took, didn't I?"

Dante picked up the man's sword, unsheathing it with a hiss of leather. "Do you think that absolves you?"

"I know you understand the burden of committing dark acts in the name of the light. You would have done the exact same thing. How dare you come to punish me?"

"Because," Dante said. "I'm not very nice."

Niles' jaw trembled. He shut his eyes, then opened them. "Let me stand."

Dante backed away from the mattress and released the net of shadows. Niles swung his feet off the bed, inhaled deeply, and stood.

"Put Winden in charge. The Boat-Growers respect her. So will the others."

"A fine choice."

Niles pursed his lips, eyes going stony. "I won't apologize. I did what needed to be done. I saved my people."

"I'm not saying you did wrong," Dante said. "But that won't save you."

"Will it hurt?"

He shook his head. "Larsin asked me to be quick. But I would have been anyway. After everything, a piece of me respects you."

Niles closed his eyes again, tipping back his chin. As he inhaled—perhaps to speak more, or perhaps to clear his head—Dante reached into the shadows within his heart and stilled them.

He dragged the body outside, past the bay, and dumped it in the Currents.

THE RED SEA

He slept fine. To make sure he saw Winden, he woke earlier than he would have liked. She was by the shore, overseeing a handful of shaden the divers had brought in from the bay.

Seeing him, she stood. "You're leaving today?"

"In a few hours."

"Take as many as you like." She gestured to the shells. "But they lose their power within a few weeks of death."

"Really? Then why are the Mallish so interested in them?"

"I've never even been to Mallon. But if my wild guesses are that valuable to you, I'll try."

"No need. Either they've found a way to preserve them, or they think they can." He touched her arm. "We need to talk. Alone."

She frowned, following him down the beach to a quiet patch of shade. "Is something wrong?"

He locked eyes with her. "Have you ever gone into the Mists to see Larsin?"

"The living aren't supposed to cross over. Kaval forbids it. And the dead, they're disturbed by it."

Dante found it hard to believe the living accepted such strictures, but he saw no lie in her eyes. "I found him. His death wasn't an accident. Niles killed him."

He explained what he'd learned. Winden's expression was stunned, then outraged. By the end, her face raged like the whirlpool of Arawn's Mill.

"He did it, didn't he?" she said. "Why didn't I guess this?"

"Because you wouldn't have wanted to believe it."

Shadows gathered around her hands. "Where is Niles?"

"Dead. I killed him last night."

Winden stared at him, then nodded. "Good. You may go, then. I'll tell my people what he did and why he's gone."

"You can't tell them the truth. Things are too fragile here. If it gets out that Niles murdered his best friend, it could tear Kandak apart. Drive your allies away."

"Our leader is dead. There's no hiding that!"

"You don't hide it," Dante said. "On our way out, we're going to see the Dresh. Tell your people that Niles came with us. That after we made peace with the Dresh, while crossing back, a wave knocked him off the bridge. This way, his last act was to help find forgiveness for your people."

Winden's brown eyes burned like candlefruit. "You want me to lie. To my friends."

"Your people have survived for centuries by lying. You're their leader now, Winden. You have to do whatever it takes to protect them. From their enemies, and from the truths that might destroy them."

"Tonen."

Dante nodded. "Tonen."

"I'm not sure I'm ready for this," she said. "I'm not sure I *want* it."

"No one's ever ready to lead. The only way to get there is by doing it." He wrapped his arms around her and hugged her tight. "It will be hard. Just remember how many people are relying on you. That can be scary. But it can be a source of great strength, too."

She withdrew, clear-eyed. "Do you think you'll return some day?"

"No time soon. Too much work ahead of me. But I feel like I've hardly scratched the surface of what there is to learn here." Dante walked into the sun, staring out at the twinkling sea. "Besides, I'd come back here just to feel this again."

He returned to town to gather up his few possessions, including his notebooks and a few boxed-up shaden. Blays waited by the shore, chatting with the townsfolk.

"Are you sure we have to leave?" Blays said. "I have an alternate idea: we move Narashtovik here."

"Convince the People of the Pocket to help me detach it from the coastline and float it down here, and you've got a deal."

A longboat rowed in, beaching itself. After a few hugs and farewells, they climbed aboard. The sailors pushed off. On the shore, the Kandeans broke into their song of goodbye. Dante wanted to close his eyes to remember it better, but he couldn't tear his gaze away from what they were leaving behind.

Waves crashed to either side, casting spray into his face. He walked on, barefoot for a better grip on the still-warm line of rock snaking out to Spearpoint. Blays was with him, but he was otherwise unaccompanied, with the *Sword of the South* anchored in one of the few protected coves along the Joladi Coast.

On the tiny island, the Dresh awaited him, having seen the steam. They carried arms but didn't brandish them. Their eyes were questioning. They led Dante and Blays through the woods and the orchards to the village on the aquamarine bay. Sando and Aladi sat in the shade, shelling nuts and dropping the refuse in an orderly pile.

Aladi stood first. "Are you back? Then you better have fulfilled our bargain."

"We found living seeds," Dante said. "And regrew the Star Trees."

Sando hauled himself to his feet, brushing papery remnants of nuts from his gut. "And the Tauren?"

"Spanked," Blays said. "Thoroughly. Between that and the return of the trees, the Kandeans are at the center of a new peace."

"A lasting one?"

"Is there any such thing? For now, though, I think this one's for real."

"And you claim to have a Star Tree," Aladi said. "You will bring me to it."

Dante looked over his shoulder at the trees and the strait beyond. "We could do that. Or I could grow one for you on Spearpoint."

Sando smacked his thigh. "You can do that? Right here?"

Aladi moved as if to brush something from her face. "Not so fast. We don't know that we can trust them."

"What are they going to do? Kill our already-dead tree? Grow us a patch of weeds and laugh at us?" He twirled his finger at Dante. "This man, he raised the land like Loda. If he wishes us harm, I'm sure he can do a great deal more than fool us about the Star Tree."

Aladi's mouth quirked. Despite her best efforts, it bent into a smile. She quashed this and gestured to the open ground at the edge of the village. "Show us."

Dante walked into the sunlight, dug a small hole, and deposited one of the starred fruit pits within it. He activated the inner chamber. White leaves unfurled from the earth. Sando laughed out loud, rocking up on his toes. Aladi kept her expression neutral. Dante had used much of his strength to form the bridge, but he poured what he had left into the seedling. When he stopped, the tree was waist high, its pale trunk and leaves shimmering with the colors of the rainbow.

"That," Aladi said, "is a Star Tree."

Dante lifted a leaf, revealing a small white flower. "They grow very slowly. But if something happens to this one, there will be others on the island."

They headed back toward the south end of Spearpoint Rock. There, Dante motioned to the bridge. "Would you like me to tear it down again?"

Sando and Aladi shared one of their looks.

"The island," Aladi said. "It was once our home. I think it's time we rejoin it."

Sando extended his right leg and bowed over it. "Safe sailing."

Blays gave them a little wave. "When you make the statues of us, make sure mine's taller."

Dante and Blays crossed back to the Joladi beach, found their sandals where they'd left them, and headed south to where Naran's two ships were anchored.

"What do you think?" Dante said. "Think they'll rejoin the island?"

Blays glanced behind them. "What, you're worried about them?"

"After Niles, it would be nice to think there's some hope for this place."

Blays was quiet for several moments. "Who knows if it'll last. For now, I think there's more hope here than most places."

After an hour of strenuous hiking, they reached the cove hiding the two ships. A longboat brought them aboard the *Sword of the South*. Naran examined them. Today, on top of his shiny-buttoned captain's jacket, he wore a two-cornered black hat sporting the long red tail feather of a local bird.

He nodded to the islands. "Is our business here complete?"

"Looks like," Dante said. "Should we go take care of things in Bressel?"

"With pleasure."

Naran called out to his crew—which no longer included Juleson, who'd elected to stay in Kandak with Nassea. The *Sword* made way past the rocks enclosing the cove, then heaved east, meaning to get beyond the worst of the Currents before turning north.

Naran seemed quite confident about the upcoming venture. Dante was less certain. For him, it would be about more than taking vengeance on Gladdic. Something sinister was under way in Mallon. They were stoking the old hostilities toward Arawn and all who followed him. In times past, these had led to purges. Wars. Centuries of oppression. Most of the prior scours had been aimed inward, at their own people. But they were now looking outward, to the Plagued Islands. And who knew where else.

If Gladdic's murder was connected back to Narashtovik, it would do nothing to lessen Mallon's paranoia.

"Not to interrupt your frowning session," Blays said. "But if you've got a moment, you might want to come see this."

He led Dante up the steps of the aftercastle. Behind them, the green blades of the Joladi Coast soared toward the blue of the sky, which was rivaled only by the sapphire tones of the open sea. Dante might live another hundred years and never see anything so fantastic.

Their worries in Mallon tugged at his mind. He knew he'd soon have to turn and face the responsibilities that awaited him. Yet before he knew it, the islands would recede beyond the horizon, as lost as last summer, or the Mist-like happiness of childhood.

He intended to hang onto them for as long as he had left.

EPILOGUE

Hopp of the Clan of the Broken Herons had never built a great cathedral. He'd never walked ten thousand miles in a row. He'd never tried to govern one of those noisome anthills that humans called a "city." Lacking these experiences, he couldn't swear to the truth of his feelings.

Even so, he was certain there was nothing more annoying and time-consuming than trying to find the right spot for a norren clan to settle down for the summer.

He walked through the waist-high grass, stirring it with the butt of his spear. At the moment, most of the clan was poking around a lake on the other side of the hill. Hopp was pretending to scout the surrounding hunting grounds, but mostly he couldn't stand to watch the clansmen fuss about their decision to plant their tents or keep looking. "I don't like the way the stream bends as it leaves the lake," one might say. Or, "This feels right—for next year. But it's not right for now." Most frustratingly of all, the clan might reject one spot, then spend the next two weeks wandering in circles, only to return to the rejected spot and declare that it was perfect.

Theoretically, as chieftain, he could order them to make camp in the middle of a latrine if he wished. But people weren't nails to be hammered down. Leadership was like flowing water. Sometimes, your people took courses you didn't expect. All you could do was follow the stream and see where it led you.

He walked on, poking here and there with his spear. Deer tracks dented the soil. There would be good hunting here along with fine fishing. Then again, this had been true of the last five spots they'd considered. Early summer—his favorite time, when the mornings and nights remained cool, and everything was at its greenest—was threatening to turn hot and dry. And still they had no camp.

He was frustrated by more than their indecision. He was a line-painter. Black paint on white canvas. A few dozen strokes, no more. Line art was his nulla, his life's calling. Some people, especially poets and philosophers whose nulla didn't involve physical, tangible creations, preferred to do their work on the march. They said the change of scenery inspired them. Besides, they didn't understand why it took him so long to complete a painting. With so few lines, surely it couldn't take more than a few minutes!

But with so few lines to work with, so little for the eye to home in on, each one had to be perfect. And yet—and this was the true beauty of the art—because these lines were drawn by a mortal hand, they were inevitably *im*perfect. With each imperfection deviating from the vision in his head, his plan for the next stroke was disrupted. He had to reconsider. See what sort of line would be correct for the mess he'd made of things.

And when he made *that* stroke, and it too was flawed, the process repeated.

So it took time. Gobs of it. Beyond that, the need to readjust his vision with each stroke meant that he couldn't plan out the entire work in his head like the philosophers and the poets. The only way for him to pursue his nulla was to settle in one place for days on end.

Paradoxically, their constant wandering was making him

restless. If they didn't choose their spot soon—

The butt of his spear clonked against something hard yet hollow. It didn't have the ring of wood or stone. He bent his broad back and picked up a black object the size of a human fist. It was lighter than he expected and felt almost like ceramic. It carried a faint whiff of the sea. It was spiraled like a snail, but it was many times larger than any of the freshwater varieties he'd seen crawling about in the hills.

Logic indicated it couldn't be a seashell. The nearest sea was more than two hundred miles north at the bay in Narashtovik. Seafood, like riverfood and lakefood, spoiled notoriously fast. No one would reasonably expect a seashell to last all this way. Then again, that *was* what it looked like. The brain and its logic might rule the body, but the eyes were the body's jester, able to defy the brain without fear of punishment, and expose truths it didn't want to hear.

He turned in a circle, taking in the low hills to east, north, and west. To the south, he could barely make out the blue of the Dunden Mountains separating them from the human nation of Mallon. Just as he suspected, there was no ocean in sight.

Whatever its origins, the shell was very pretty. The ratio of each layer of its spiral to those before and after appeared perfect. And the unusualness of it, wouldn't that make a good painting? A seashell lost hundreds of miles from its home? It would be a challenge to represent the fact the shell was being seen in the middle of a prairie so far removed from the ocean that was its home, but that challenge was part of the appeal. And who or what had brought it here? A condor? A traveler who'd picked it up as a souvenir, only to discard it, deciding it wasn't worth carrying all the way home?

Hefting it in his hand, he turned around and walked back toward his clan, forgetting all about their squabbles.

Raxa Dosse stretched in bed. Daylight poked through the

cracks in the shutters. That was no good. She rolled over, draped her arm over her eyes, and went back to sleep.

The next time she woke, it was dark. She would have known that by sound alone: crickets and owls weren't the only things that came out at night. Narashtovik changed, too. During the daytime, when everyone was out and a-bustling, the noise became a generic thing where no individual stood out. Like the splashing of a brook, or the steady murmur in a crowded pub.

At night, though? Most of the respectable citizens fled the streets. The honest folk still out on business went quiet. Like the mice in the fields, they didn't want to draw any attention. The not-so-honest folk, though? They were the owls. They didn't care *who* heard them. And with the murmur of daytime gone, each voice, each individual, rang out like the bells of an unholy church carillon.

She dressed, belting on her short sword and dagger, and hit the streets. She lived in an awful part of town, and despite her blades and her modest reputation, she put the eye to every man and woman she passed. After several blocks of crooked rowhouses and outdoor gambling tents, she crossed Decken Street into the Sharps. So-named because, if you stepped out of line here, "sharp" would be the common trait of the many tools you'd find yourself introduced to.

A few people nodded her way. Raxa nodded back to two of them, arriving at a six-story structure with stone walls and a roof barnacled with enough shacks and towers to host a town of its own. It looked like, and had indeed once been, the manor/fortress of a wealthy lord.

Now, it protected those who ran the night.

Gurles, who could have been mistaken for a norren if not for his bald head, barred the door. Seeing her, he nodded and stepped aside.

Raxa opened the door, greeted by a swirl of minty-smelling chander smoke. Decent crowd, mostly lowlings looking for any scrap deemed too measly for the regs. She leaned against the bar and ordered a beer and a plate of eggs and bread.

As she dug in, Blackeyed Gaits saddled the seat beside her. "Raxa. Here for work? Or did that rathole you live in finally burn down?

"It's called fiscal responsibility." She pointedly eyed his bejeweled fingers. "Something you could stand to learn."

"Why work hard if you're not going to spend it? And you haven't answered my question. Should I take that as a no?"

She stirred her eggs, which were somehow both under- and overcooked. "You know I'm not here for the food."

"Excellent. Got a grab for you. The jewel of Kade Street."

"Sonnagen House?" Raxa didn't try to restrain her eyebrows from lifting. "I'm in."

Gaits grinned, enjoying the moment. "There's a catch. You'll be working with Fedder."

She laughed, spewing crumbs. "Not if you want me on this. You know I work alone."

He shoved back from the bar. "Then I'll see if Stump wants it."

"Don't bullshit me. You know I'm the best you've got."

"At grabs? Maybe. When it comes to fostering the next generation of pups, however, you're the worst in the guild. We've been here for hundreds of years, Raxa. That's because we take an inhumanly long view of things. A mediocrity who makes the next generation stronger is more valuable than the genius who's only here for herself."

She took a long quaff and smacked the mug back down on the bar. A chip flew from the base, drawing a crooked eye from Jana lurking behind the bar.

"I'll take Fedder," she said. "But you let him know that when I speak, he hops to it."

"Why don't you tell him yourself?" Gaits gestured to the wall. A young man detached from it, smirking like he'd just grabbed the serving girl's ass. He looked the portrait of arrogance and entitlement.

Over the next few days of preparation, Fedder was proven worse than his first impression. But the job was one of the largest Raxa'd ever been in on. The Sonnagens had supposedly just cashed out two seasons of shipping receipts from the Denbank. In silver, mostly, which was too heavy to steal in bulk—but also the Torc of Dalder. The sapphires alone would be worth thousands.

The night of the grab was pleasantly cool, with a kelpy smell drifting in from the bay. She met Fedder at Torton Square.

"Ready?" she said.

He smirked. That seemed to be pretty much his sole form of expression. "Let's show them what their locks are worth, shall we?"

Initial entry was a snap; Gaits had paid off a servant to lob a line over the south wall, away from the street. They snapped on their cleats and climbed right up into a fourth-floor bedroom. The room was dark, but below them, the scrape of chairs and the laughter of guests was enough to remind even an idiot like Fedder that it was time to get serious.

The torc was in the grandiosely named Moonroost, a two-story tower atop the main house. Raxa checked the hall. Finding nothing but a lone lantern, she exited the bedroom and made her way to the stairwell. At the fifth floor landing, she peeked out. Down the carpeted hall, two lanterns illuminated the way up to the Moonroost. Guarded, of course. Two big men with bigger halberds.

She moved back into the stairwell. "Keep watch down here. I'll grab the torc."

Fedder folded his arms. "How do you intend to squeeze past the two statues?"

"Trade secret. Afterwards, I don't want to bump into any unexpected guests on the way out. So keep your eyes on the fourth floor. Got me?"

She expected resistance, but he nodded and went back downstairs. Raxa gave him half a minute, then walked forward.

Into the darkness.

The stairwell became a realm of bright shadows and ethereal, glowing outlines. Like Raxa had walked into the land of fairies and gnomes. Invisible to human eyes — though who knew about the fairies — she strolled into the well-lit hall. Neither guard looked her way. The wall was stone. She walked into the shadows within the rock, emerging in a spiral staircase that led up to a small round room.

The torc sat on a stand of black velvet. In the netherworld, its sapphires glowed like the Ghost Lights of the northern winter sky. She sacked it up, along with a double handful of less impressive but still expensive jewelry, then walked downstairs. She exited the wall into the hallway and continued to the main stairwell.

There, she smiled and returned to the mundane realm.

Fedder gasped. He was pressed tight into the corner; she'd totally missed him. "How'd you—?"

She clapped her hand to his mouth and gestured downstairs. Descending to the fourth floor, they rushed to the darkened bedroom.

"One second, you weren't there," Fedder whispered. "The next, you were. Like you'd walked out of another world."

"I don't know what you think you saw," Raxa said. "But your eyes are as bad as your ears."

"I *saw* you." He moved closer. "Tell me how you did it."

Every nerve in her body burned. *No one* knew what she could do — not Gaits, not anyone. And she'd been so sloppy she'd been outed by the punkiest of punk kids.

"There was a secret entrance," she said. "That's how I got in. And that's why it looked like I walked out of nowhere."

At last, his smirk returned. "I know what I saw. Tell me how to do it. Or I'll tell everyone what *really* makes you the best sneak in the house."

"You want to know how I do what I do?" She beckoned him nearer. "Listen close."

She grabbed his hair with one hand and cut his throat with the other. Twisting her fingers into his scalp, she pulled back; his breath burbled out the wound along with his blood. Once he was done, she dropped the body and climbed down into the dark yard behind the house.

Gaits was expecting them before dawn. Enough time to clean herself up. But not to extract Fedder's carcass. In public, the Sonnagens would *probably* claim credit for the thief's death—but they would make private inquiries after their goods. What would the black market tell them? The story there might be closer to the truth: that the thieves had taken the torc, and, for reasons unknown, left a body behind. Her story would have to match it.

She walked away from the house. Seven blocks later, she swerved down an alley. She drained half her flask, then got out her knife. She slashed the skin on her collarbone and stomach, then added several more wounds to her arms, especially the hands. As if she'd been warding someone off.

On the way back to their building, her bloody body drew so many looks she was afraid she'd overdone it. Finally, she staggered into Gurles standing watch on the front doors. He gaped, then swept her off her feet and rushed her to a room.

Gaits dashed in a minute later. "Where's the torc?"

"Glad to see your priorities are in order." She flung the bag at his feet. It landed with a heavy metallic clunk.

"The hell happened to you? Where's Fedder?"

"One answer to both questions. After I grabbed the torc, he came at me. Looking to snatch it and run off. I put him down."

Gaits' jaw dropped. "He's dead?"

"It was him or me. Guess which I was inclined to choose?"

"Do you have any idea who he was?"

"A fool too greedy to do his job?"

"He's a Dallagor! Fedder Dallagor!"

Raxa cocked her head; pain shot up her neck as her wounded shoulder shifted. "He's a scion of the tea family? Why in hell was he slumming with us?"

"The same reason all scions do: they're mad at their parents."

"Well, he should have stuck with the family business."

Gait laced his fingers into his dark hair. "They'll come for us. I should throw you to the wolves. Offer you up on a platter."

Raxa straightened, wincing at the pain. "But you're not going to. Why not?"

The Arbiter of Tasks sighed through his teeth and sat in a chair against the wall. "Oh, how it pains me to admit this. I'm sparing you because I…need you."

She wanted badly to toy with him, but didn't think it was quite the right moment. "For what?"

"We have a little sparrow in the Sealed Citadel. They've kept an extremely tight lid on recent events. But it seems like Dante Galand himself has been gone for weeks. The Council priests have no idea when he'll be back—or if he ever will."

"If he's gone, he may have left some very interesting trinkets behind."

"Which, during this time of uncertainty, might go missing without being noticed. But that's small-time thinking. Not so long ago, we had the run of this city. That ended when Cally and Dante swept out the old order. But now that *they're* gone? I smell…" He leaned forward, sniffing like a dog. "Opportunity."

Raxa laughed lowly. "You know what they say: when the cat's away, the rats will take advantage of the ensuing anarchy to grab everything they can get their clever little paws on."

He grinned at her. "Indeed, my dear. So while I clean up the dreadful mess you've left me, are you ready for your next job?"

Gladdic placed the letter back upon his desk. The messenger

stood across from him, very careful not to meet his gaze. Should he execute the wretch? He wanted to very badly.

But this was the false lure of emotion. Real justice—the justice handed down by Taim from the order of the heavens—wouldn't allow for punishing the one who'd carried the message. Killing him would only dilute focus from he who truly deserved it.

The subject *of* the letter.

Even so, wouldn't executing the man serve as a statement to the cosmos? That such news would not—*could* not—be tolerated by those who followed the holy path? He tapped his fingers on the desk. Tempting. As tempting as the shadows. However, Gladdic had just stepped in a great pile of shit. Killing the man might be mistaken for anger at his own mistakes. For evidence of his guilt.

With effort, Gladdic nodded at the messenger. "You may go."

The man turned, producing a squeaking noise—Gladdic wasn't sure if it was the sole of his boot or a fear-induced fart—and all but ran from the room. Gladdic closed his eyes. How could this have slipped past him? Children should be marked at birth with their names. Branded or scarred, perhaps. If they lived innocent lives, bearing their name on their skin would only honor them. And if they were guilty…then there would be no hiding from their crimes.

He was drifting away from the matter at hand. Whatever path he chose, he needed to do so quickly. A good liar might keep this to himself. To hide his incompetence until he'd had the chance to undo his errors.

But Gladdic wasn't a good liar. He was a great one. When you wanted to keep your darkest truth hidden, you had to be open with all others. Especially those truths that could hurt you. If you exposed mistakes so great they might cost you your station, who could ever suspect you of deceit?

He sent a letter ahead to the Eldor, then called for his carriage. It rattled through the sun-warmed streets, rocking to a stop at the Eldor's palace, which was too grand by half. Gladdic entered the cool marble building and allowed himself to be escorted upstairs by Albert Sorsen, Eldor's too-prying majordomo.

Outside the Eldor's door, Gladdic didn't favor the man with a glance. "That will be all."

Sorsen hesitated, then strode away. Gladdic knocked. The Eldor opened the door, as bald and wizened as ever.

"You're sweating like a dairymaid, Gladdic. Come inside."

Gladdic did so, closing the door behind him. "Your Righteousness." He fell to his knees. "Forgive me. I've failed you."

"Oh, streaming Celeset." The Eldor waved his gnarled hand. "Get up, would you? Whatever's happened, surely it doesn't require *prostration*."

Gladdic kept his head bowed a moment longer, hiding his contempt at the man's lack of seriousness. He stood. "I have received a letter from our spies. Do you remember the defiler we recently had in custody? The nethermancer?"

The old man tapped the side of his head. "I'm not so ancient to forget a thing like that."

"Righteousness, this man was no ordinary defiler. It was Dante Galand."

For once in his life, the Eldor was speechless, doddering about the room as if he'd lost the answers in one of the corners. "Galand? You're sure of this?"

"There is no doubt. Just as there can be no doubt that his presence here was no coincidence."

"He was wrapped up in the to-do with the smugglers, wasn't he? From the Plagued Islands? Maybe he's after the shaden for himself."

"Or maybe he's after us."

The Eldor seated himself in his striking red-lacquered throne. "Do we have any hard evidence of this? Or merely the circumstantial sort?"

"Given our position, I fear we must plan for the worst. We

know he sailed south and we must assume he'll return in time—possibly at this very port. I ask full authority to search for him."

"Granted. If you find him, though, I will be present for the questioning."

"Naturally." Gladdic lowered his eyes. "Whatever his initial reasons for coming here, we must also assume he's learned which way the breeze blows in Mallon."

"Surely he doesn't know everything. There are times I think that *I* don't!"

"You know all there is to know, Righteousness. With Galand, however, any knowledge is too much. It threatens everything. We must move forward now."

"If we do this, we risk war with Narashtovik."

"And if we don't do this, we'll damn our people to live out their lives under the specter of Arawn's thrall."

The Eldor stroked the white bristles on his chin. He nodded. For the first time that day, Gladdic allowed himself to smile.

THE RED SEA

AUTHOR'S NOTE

The Red Sea is the first book in a new trilogy. The next book, *The Silver Thief*, will be available in late 2015. If you're getting a kick out of these characters, you can read about their younger exploits in *The Cycle of Arawn* trilogy.

ABOUT THE AUTHOR

Along with *The Cycle of Arawn*, Ed is the author of the post-apocalyptic *Breakers* series. Born in the deserts of Eastern Washington, he's since lived in New York, Idaho, and most recently Los Angeles, all of which have been thoroughly destroyed in *Breakers*.

He lives with his fiancée and spends most of his time writing on the couch and overseeing the uneasy truce between two dogs and two cats.

He blogs at http://www.edwardwrobertson.com

Printed in Great Britain
by Amazon